Praise for Kelly Meding and the Dreg City novels

"A fast-paced adventure."

—Charlaine Harris, #1 *New York Times* bestselling author

"Gritty, imaginative, and a terrific read."

—Patricia Briggs, #1 *New York Times* bestselling author

"Action-packed, edgy, and thrilling. . . . You won't want to miss this one."

—Jeaniene Frost, *New York Times* bestselling author

"A phenomenal story . . . utterly addictive."

—Jackie Kessler, critically acclaimed author

"Thrilling. . . . Especially impressive are her worldbuilding skills."

—*Romantic Times*

"[An] excellent series."

—Bitten By Books

"Will keep you on the edge of your seat."

—Book Lovers Inc.

Trance is also available as an eBook

KELLY MEDING

TRANCE

POCKET BOOKS

New York   London   Toronto   Sydney   New Delhi

Pocket Books
A Division of Simon & Schuster, Inc.
1230 Avenue of the Americas
New York, NY 10020

This book is a work of fiction. Names, characters, places, and incidents either are products of the author's imagination or are used fictitiously. Any resemblance to actual events or locales or persons, living or dead, is entirely coincidental.

First Pocket Books paperback edition November 2011

POCKET and colophon are registered trademarks of Simon & Schuster, Inc.

For information about special discounts for bulk purchases, please contact Simon & Schuster Special Sales at 1-866-506-1949 or business@simonandschuster.com.

The Simon & Schuster Speakers Bureau can bring authors to your live event. For more information or to book an event contact the Simon & Schuster Speakers Bureau at 1-866-248-3049 or visit our website at www.simonspeakers.com.

Cover illustration by Don Sipley

Manufactured in the United States of America

10 9 8 7 6 5 4 3 2 1

ISBN 978-1-4516-2092-4
ISBN 978-1-4516-2094-8 (ebook)

*For all the girls who ever closed their eyes
and dreamed of being a superhero.*

Acknowledgments

This book is the culmination of more than sixteen years of work—from the first inkling of an idea to the final product in your hands. A lot of people touched this manuscript over the years, and I'll probably forget to thank someone, but here goes.

Mega-hugs to my fabulous agent, Jonathan Lyons, for believing in a trunked manuscript and helping me smack it into submission shape. More hugs and chocolate to my editor, Jennifer Heddle, for falling in love with my take on superheroes and making this book even better than I imagined.

To the amazing peeps who read this book in its various stages: there have been a lot of you, but especially to Melissa, Sassy, and Nancy. You three were troopers. A special thank-you to Jeaniene Frost for seeing something special in my query and first pages, and for offering some amazing advice to a novice.

And even though they don't know me, thank you to Marv Wolfman and George Pèrez for creating a comic book series that captured the imagination of a preteen and launched her obsession with superheroes. This book wouldn't exist without your Teen Titans.

Finally, thanks to my dad for having that copy of *The New Teen Titans* #9 in your box of comics, and for letting me swipe it.

TRANCE

One

Central Park

The bronze man's head was melting. It oozed fat splats of liquid metal and swirled down the front of his old-fashioned suit jacket to puddle at his feet. Some of it hit the bronze duck below him, adding layers of new metal that mutated it into a nightmarish goose. The molten metal cooled and hardened as it hit the sidewalk. Mayhem's heat blasts were concentrated above the statue, and metal needs a constant heat source to stay liquid. I learned that in class.

Gage had told me the statue was of a once-famous man who wrote stories for kids. I don't know for sure, but if Gage says so, it must be true. He's in charge while the adults are fighting for all of our lives, and he kept us quiet and hidden. For a while.

Until Mayhem found our hiding place.

"We have to run for it," Gage said.

I didn't want to run. We'd been running for hours, from the southernmost point of Central Park to where we were now. I don't know how many blocks, but a lot, and it was raining, too—light, chilly rain and heavy, splattering rain.

Sometimes it stopped and just blew cold wind; then Ethan would use his Tempest powers to try to redirect it so we didn't freeze.

Hours of it, and I was exhausted. We all were. Each time the Banes gained ground and pushed the last of the grown-up Rangers north, we kids ran ahead and took cover. We were there to fight if we had to, but the grown-ups didn't want us to—not until absolutely necessary. At fifteen, Gage was the oldest; I'm the youngest at ten-almost-eleven. He says we're the last line of defense for the city of New York.

We're the last line of defense for the rest of the country.

And we're just a bunch of kids.

Mayhem kept blasting.

Ethan stepped out from the shelter of the stone wall, all wiry and red-haired and cocky thirteen. He raised his hands to the sky. A blast of wind shot away from him and swirled toward Mayhem. She was a good hundred yards away, across a cement hole that had once been a lake or something, near a statue of a bronze girl on a mushroom. The statue was losing shape, turning into goo from her being so close to it.

Ethan's air blast slammed Mayhem's heat back at her. She was wearing street clothes, just jeans and a black shirt, and they were nothing like our special uniforms. No armor to protect Mayhem from her own powers or ours, so she flew backward with a piercing shriek. Her braided black hair flipped around like snakes, and she landed out of sight on the other side of the mushroom.

"Go!" Gage shouted.

Mellie ran first, as fast as she could across the cement

ground, toward the nearest clutch of unburned trees. Renee went next, a streak of blue skin and honey-blond hair, with William behind her. He carried Janel, who was unconscious from power overload; William had superstrength so he could run and carry her at the same time, while I could barely run and carry myself.

I followed the big kids, including Marco, who was still in panther form, and fifteen of us streaked across the way, rounding the edge of the cement pit, seeking our next place to hide. Just like we'd done all day. My lungs were burning, aching with smoke and cold and overuse and unshed tears. I just wanted to curl up in a ball and cry myself to sleep. I was sick of being cold. I didn't want to be afraid anymore. I didn't want to have to think about tomorrow—if we had a tomorrow.

I was only ten. Almost eleven. I wasn't ready to die.

None of us was.

Mellie sure wasn't when one of Mayhem's heat blasts caught her full in the face and melted her skin down to her bones. Mellie didn't even get to scream. I screamed plenty. So did Renee and Nate and William. Only panther-Marco paused long enough to sniff her, then loped past.

Ethan cried out, and then he wasn't running with the group anymore. I didn't stop to see what happened, but a few seconds later, Mayhem shouted again. This time, the roar of wind was louder. I hoped he tossed her into a tree or something.

We left poor Mellie on the ground and kept going, like we'd left three others behind already. My jelly legs didn't want to keep running, and one by one the older kids moved ahead of me. Toward the trees and the promise of safety somewhere else. I'd get left behind and it wouldn't matter. My powers were stupid; I couldn't help in a fight. My ability to hypnotize people and alter their thoughts worked only if I looked them in the eye. That was hard to do in the middle of a war zone. I hadn't done anything today but cry and scream and get in the way.

Not like my dad, Hinder, one of the greatest heroes in the Ranger Corps. He was fighting south of us with the last half dozen grown-up Rangers, keeping the horde of Banes (sixty-something of them, Gage had said) from overrunning us. We were kids training to be heroes. If our parents and mentors died, how did anyone expect *us* to stop them?

We could barely save ourselves from one Bane with a superheat blast. Once the line fell and the Banes got through, sixty-something of them would crush us in seconds.

No, the line couldn't fall. Not with my dad in charge. He'd save us.

A hand grabbed my arm and yanked me forward. I nearly tripped. Gage didn't let go as we ran; he was practically pulling me along. It was as close as we'd ever come—or ever would—to holding hands. I'm still a baby and he's a teenager. He's just helping me because he's in charge. He can't let me lag behind.

We found a wide path. It took us under a stone archway and we emerged onto an open lawn. If it was ever green, it was now brown and rutted and overrun here and there with clumps of dried weeds. A lot of Central Park looked like that now. After New York City's first major battle in the War, most of the city had been evacuated and a lot of the buildings destroyed. I'd seen it from the helicopter that brought us here this morning—burning, crumbling skyscrapers, gutted old theaters, debris in the empty streets. William had pointed at a tall, skinny building called the Empire or something, and said it used to be twice as tall. I didn't believe him.

Manhattan was a good place to fight, we were told. Early evacuation meant fewer civilian injuries. One of the major rules of the Ranger Corps code is protect civilians at all costs. Even the dumb ones who stand there and scream, instead of getting out of the way.

I once overheard Gage's mentor, Delphi, say that any civilian who didn't get out of the way of battling Metas was too stupid to save. It had made the other adults laugh. I didn't know why it was funny, and I couldn't ask her to explain it. I shouldn't have been listening in the first place. But Delphi was smart, so it had to be important. She'd mentored a lot of kids who didn't have anyone to teach them about their powers and how to be a Ranger. If I'd been an orphan like Gage, I'd have liked Delphi to be my mentor, too.

No one else attacked us on the lawn, but it was too open. Gage changed our direction, sideways instead of across the lawn. It felt like forever before we hit the cover of trees again. In the distance, peeking through the crisping, late summer leaves, was the turret of a big stone building.

"Head toward the castle," Gage yelled toward the front of the line. William and Renee altered their path just a little. We passed what had once been a pond of some kind, and soon we were all going up.

"Can we hide there?" I gasped. The cold and wet made my lungs burn.

"I think so."

Somewhere south of us, something exploded. It sounded like a truck got dropped from the sky and hit another one on the ground. I felt the rattle of it in my bones. Gage looked over his shoulder. I couldn't. Every ounce of my attention was on not falling over my own tired feet.

We went up a set of stone steps. The paths intersected at the top and seemed to go off in four different directions. To our left was the castle—a stone building that had so far avoided complete destruction and shone like a hopeful beacon. Thick, round stones made a sort of patio that led to the castle itself, and it had two fancy pavilions on the left and right of the steps we came up. Except for a few blown-out windows, the castle was intact. Past it, farther to the north, was something that looked like an outdoor theater surrounded by bony winter trees.

A figure emerged from the castle, and everyone ahead of us came to a clumsy, jumbled halt. Gage let me go and jogged to the front to see. I sidled closer to Renee, who stretched one blue arm out to grasp me around the shoulders. She was twelve, almost a teenager, and my best friend. I loved her Flex power that let her bend and twist into funny lengths and shapes. It was a useful power, too. When we first got here, she'd used it to yank me out of the way of Mayhem's heat blast.

"You gotta keep up, T," Renee said. Her teeth chattered and, instead of red, the cold made her cheeks look purple. "Can't lose you, too."

"I'm trying," I replied.

"Who are you?" Gage asked the stranger. His voice was still changing, going unpredictably from high-pitched to deep in timbre, so it squeaked a little when he tried to be bossy. Like now.

I peeked around William's bulk—twelve and almost six feet tall—to get a better look.

A dirty man in ragged clothes was leaning hard against the stone wall. His face was sunken and filthy, and he probably stank, if the look on Gage's face said anything. All five of Gage's senses were hypersensitive and picked up on all sorts of things. Something about the stranger, other than being homeless and in our hiding place—was bothering Gage.

"Sir, you shouldn't be here," Gage said. "It isn't safe."

"Nowhere's safe from your kind nowadays," the man said. His voice was slurred, thick, like he was both drunk and half asleep. He wouldn't look up from some interesting spot on the stone. Loose, torn clothing hung limply, covering his hands and feet, as if he'd shrunk inside them.

"There's a battle moving this way. You can't stay here."

The man shrugged.

Another explosion, similar to the first, rocked the ground. It was closer this time, louder. One of the younger boys whimpered. Panther-Marco stalked around the group to stand sentry next to Gage and hissed at the man. The two boys with the best noses knew something was wrong.

Nate's voice rang through all of our heads as his telepathic warning blared like a neon sign: *Back up and get out of—*

The stranger raised his right hand as he looked up. His

sunken eyes glowed with yellow-orange power as he fired the little revolver in his hand, creating chaos.

Her arm still around me, Renee practically dragged me toward the larger pavilion. We all fled there while three more shots were fired. I couldn't see for the flurry of moving bodies. I didn't know where Gage was. Someone was screaming about Nate.

At the back of the pavilion, more stone steps led down to a rocky surface that overlooked the dried-up pond. We crouched there, using what little cover our hiding place provided. Fear clutched me colder than the January freeze, but I still glanced up and around a stone column, heart kicking against my ribs, a bitter taste in my mouth.

Nate was dead on the ground, a hole in his chest. The homeless man looked on, his eyes glowing death, smug like a Bane. He threw back his head and laughed—it might have been scarier if he weren't so hoarse.

Nearby, under the pavilion and behind a stone wall, William was bleeding at the hip. Down on the rock floor with us, Ethan was shot in the left shoulder. Both were panting, trying to be brave and to not cry. I looked away before I started crying, too.

"We're ending this tonight!" the man shouted. "Your pathetic Rangers are falling as we speak. You'll see your parents in hell soon enough."

I shivered.

"Specter," Gage said, and I jumped at the sound of his voice right beside me.

It couldn't be Specter, the leader of the Banes. My dad said he was the one who'd rallied them together and initiated the War that had raged and ruined the country, killed hundreds on both sides, and left Metas nearly extinct. The last surviving Metas in the world had descended on Central Park to fight each other today. Dad said Specter could possess anyone who was unconscious or had a weak mind—take them over like a puppeteer, and make them do whatever he wanted.

Specter had found a man with a gun who could cut us kids down as surely as superpowers had taken five of us since the morning.

He strode out to the middle of the stone patio, gun raised but pointed nowhere. We didn't have a lot of cover, crowding low on the cold stone steps and behind two columns and two bits of waist-high stone wall. The wounded were now in the rear, the most powerful in the front. I was somewhere in the middle beside Gage, whose hands were shaking. His lips were pressed together so tight I couldn't see them. He looked like he wanted to barf all over the ground.

He was terrified.

Gage couldn't be terrified. He had to lead us, tell us what to do so we survived this.

"Gage?" I said.

He didn't look at me. He scrubbed a hand through his spiky blond hair, down over his face, then clenched it in front of his blue jumpsuit. Tugged and pulled at the material.

I tried again. Maybe my powers couldn't save us, but I could help him save us. "Gage?"

He just wasn't paying attention to me, like usual, so I grabbed his hand and gave it a solid yank. He looked at me then, his dark eyes flecked with little bits of silver that made them look like a starry night sky. As soon as I caught his gaze, I locked in and let my Trance powers do the rest.

You're a brave man, Gage. You wouldn't be our leader if you weren't brave. We need you to lead us. We need you to save us. You can do this.

Tears glistened in his eyes. I felt him fighting it, fighting the Trance, the urge to do anything I told him. Being scared was easier—I knew it and so did he. I forced a little more at him, as much as I could muster through my own terror.

Trust me.

His hands stopped shaking. He was calming down, bucking up, accepting my influence. My own fear lessened a little, but not enough. I wished I could Trance myself.

Trust me, Gage, and lead us. Save us.

The Specter-host took three more potshots. Someone screamed—I couldn't look, didn't want to know. Didn't want to see any more of my classmates hurt or dying or dead. A third explosion, horrifyingly close, sent a blast of hot air scorching across the pavilion, layered with the stink of smoke and ash. And something burning sweet.

Death was coming closer.

"Angela, I need a distraction," Gage said, breaking our lock. He moved away, toward a blond girl who could leave up to twelve copies of herself behind as she walked, like holographic bread crumbs. "Marco, raven form."

Nearby I heard the funny, wet-Velcro sound Marco made when he shifted. The large black bird hopped over to Gage and waited for orders.

"I can still help," Ethan said. He was sweating, so pale his freckles looked like pimples, his uniform front soaked with blood.

Gage whispered a plan I couldn't hear while our attacker shot at us twice more, exploding stone and cement, in no hurry to kill us all. Or he was waiting for something.

"Ready?" Gage asked. The other big kids nodded. They all turned, prepared with their plan.

An energy orb slammed into the Specter-host and spun him around—but it wasn't from any of us. He squeezed off a wild shot that shattered the stone near Gage's head, and then the dirty man fell facedown on the cobblestones. The cold rain started falling harder.

A hunched, bleeding figure shambled toward us from around the stairs. Her white hair was stained red, plastered to her skull, and she looked a hundred years old. Gage and Angela ran out to help her, and they practically carried the old woman into the pavilion. She was bleeding from a dozen wounds, her hands and knees scraped from multiple falls. I saw her face and started to cry.

"Granny Dell," I said, shouldering my way through the older kids. I dropped to my knees next to my maternal grandmother, confused and horrified. She shouldn't be here. She'd retired forty years ago, long before I was born, and had lived my entire lifetime in Europe. We'd only met once, but had chatted on the phone dozens of times. She told me stories about my mom, who I didn't remember much.

And now Granny Dell was in Central Park. I'd heard the

grown-ups say that everyone was being called to duty, but I had never imagined they meant my grandmother.

She turned weepy eyes toward me, like someone so desperately tired she wanted to burst out crying. I couldn't stop my own tears from falling, or the desperate sobs that hurt my chest.

"You kids need to go," she gasped. She was trying so hard. "They're coming. He's coming."

"We have wounded," Gage said behind me. "We can't leave them."

"Have to, son. You kids . . . you're the last. Have to live."

"We're not," I said. "Dad's still fighting. He'll save us." Her sad, sad face told me something about my dad I didn't want to know. My lungs hitched. I ignored her face. If I ignored her, it simply wasn't true.

"They'll be here soon, Teresa," Granny Dell said. "You have to run. Hide."

"Rangers don't hide." Dad taught me that. All I wanted to do was hide until the bad guys went away, but we couldn't. If we hid from the Banes now, we'd never live it down later. Unless we died after all.

Was it better to die a hero or live a coward?

I didn't know. All I knew was that I wanted to live.

Granny Dell choked up blood and stopped breathing. I kept holding her hand, afraid that if I let go, I'd run and hide just like she wanted me to, find a tree to climb or a hole to burrow into and stay there until the battle was over.

"We stand here," Gage said, rising up and addressing us like a general. Still brave, still saving us. Not giving up. "The man out there was right. It comes down to what we do tonight. We have to make our parents and mentors proud."

They were all talking at once, a buzz of voices and sounds and movements, and situating those who were too hurt to fight in the back of the pavilion, down in that rock-bottom hiding place. Forming a defensive line based on powers. Someone dashed outside to retrieve the gun. No one would use it; they just couldn't leave it lying around for a Bane to pick up. I stayed in the rear with the wounded and the dead, too cold and scared to help. I was useless.

Again.

An agony-filled shriek rose up from the trees surrounding the south side of the castle, carried on a wind that brought more of that awful roasted-sweet odor. Female scream, I thought, unable to think of the other adult Rangers who'd been left. I couldn't think of anyone except my dad, hurt, maybe . . . No. Just hurt. Or still battling his way toward us, leading his Rangers as only he could. Hinder would save us.

Renee and William stood together. I was surprised that William could be shot and still standing. He was strong. I thought he had a good power, just like Renee. But he didn't like her ability to stretch her blue body out like taffy. He said it was creepy, and she loved to torment him. Seeing them together was weird.

Marco was back in panther form. He paced the length of the pavilion, thick tail swishing, a predator. He told me once he'd rather be a big cat than a person. I didn't understand, but I was always jealous of his being a shapeshifter.

Even hurt, Ethan was waiting to help. He had one of the

strongest powers among us, and he knew it. He was being brave. Everyone was being brave, except me. Might as well only be eleven of us left, instead of twelve.

Stupid, useless Trance.

The castle's spire exploded. Fire and rock blasted outward and rained down on the cobblestones in front of the pavilion. Some of us shrieked. I know I did. A second blast took out the rest of the turret. Smoke choked me and stung my eyes. Gage was shouting orders.

The first Bane crested the stairs at the far end of the stone patio. I didn't know her. Just saw her stop, locate us, then let out an excited war whoop. Terror hit me like a blast of fire all over my body as more Banes joined her.

The heat of the fire increased to all-over agony. This wasn't fear. Something was happening. Marco screamed, a too human sound. Everything went gray, and then the agony swallowed me whole.

Two

Portland, Oregon
Fifteen years later

Having superpowers rudely restored after a fifteen-year disruption is a lot like childbirth: painful, beautiful, messy, and with lots of screaming. Unlike childbirth, superpower restoration was an event I just didn't see coming. I thought it was heartburn.

Four long hours into my ten-to-three swing shift at Whiskey Jack's (second job of the day, straight off ten hours at the House of Chicken), I sneaked a handful of leftover chili cheese fries before Freddy the busboy dumped them into the garbage. The owner (whose name is Ted, not Jack) didn't care if we filched, as long as we did it in the back room. Even for a girl working three jobs (including two glamorous days a week scrubbing toilets for a home-cleaning service), hearty food was still mostly unaffordable. Not if I wanted little luxuries like electricity and heat during Portland's cold winters.

Cold and congealed, those fries tasted divine. I followed them with a large glass of filtered water. For my empty stomach, it was too much, too fast. Hot, cramping fingers twisted my belly. I doubled over and almost knocked Freddy down.

He grabbed my arm, brushing my left breast quite deliberately. Leave it to a teenager to use an act of compassion to cop a feel. "Geez, Teresa, you okay?" he asked.

Dumb question. "No, do I look okay?" I pulled my arm away and backed up until my hip hit the sink. The back room was small and seemed to grow smaller. Dingy basins reeking of mildew and old detergent pressed in too close. Odors of grease and salty food filtered in from the nearby kitchen. I swallowed, longing for my toothbrush.

"Shouldn't have eaten those fries, huh?" he said.

I shot him a withering stare. He took the hint, grabbed his basin, and headed out to the floor to clear more tables. With an hour left on my shift, I couldn't drum up the energy to hit the floor and hustle drinks for the house. Whiskey Jack's had a reputation in Portland as a high-class-ass bar—the more you paid, the more you could touch. I needed the tips, but the idea of liquor breath and sweaty hands increased my nausea.

I couldn't afford to leave early, either. This late at night—or early in the morning, depending on your internal clock—men had no trouble giving up a ten-spot for a chance to pour their own shot into a glass nestled between a woman's breasts. Short black skirts and tight yellow tank tops were the preferred uniform at WJ's, the better to show off the waitress staff's assets. I needed an extra-padded bra to give my small chest the bounce the other servers possessed (naturally or surgically, take your pick), but the luxury investment had been worth it.

Another sharp cramp knotted my stomach. Fingers of pain danced through my lower back. For one panicked instant, I thought my appendix had burst. I would become septic and die. The perfect ending to a perfect week of hell, seasoned with a bounced rent check. Shake and serve with a side of hopelessness.

Appendicitis, while a good way to avoid my default-happy landlord and collect sick pay from my job at the House of Chicken, would be the moldy cherry on the melted sundae. Or whatever that saying is.

I bucked up, splashed water on my face, and inhaled. Held it, exhaled. Rinse, repeat. The cramps calmed somewhat, but shakiness had set into my limbs. Hands trembling and with sweat popping out on my forehead, I returned to the floor for a few more tip attempts. I had about a hundred bucks in my pocket—nowhere near enough to cover the fee for the bounced rent check.

At two in the morning, the bar was still in full swing. Dim lights barely illuminated a South Pacific–themed interior, complete with strung tiki lanterns and fake potted palm trees that doubled as ash trays. Reggae music blared over half a dozen loudspeakers. Drunken men and women lurched around the narrow dance floor. Some laughed in groups at their tables, while others milled about looking for action.

Five paces into the bar, action planted itself right in front of me in the form of a six-foot-four, slobbering giant of a man. His bloodshot eyes leered down, mouth twisted into a drunken grin. "Titty shot?" he slurred, bourbon breath puffing into my face.

The smell curled my nostrils and churned my stomach. Hell, no. This guy was not touching me. "I'm not pouring right now." I sidestepped and was in the crowd before his foggy brain caught up.

Bartender Minnie was doing her hourly show of tossing liquor bottles and pouring shots, much to the glazed amazement of the patrons. Money flowed her way. I often longed for that kind of coordination. Better cash might mean not working three different jobs and letting men ogle my boobs for cash. Too bad I could barely walk a straight line stone-cold sober, let alone juggle liquor bottles without breaking every single one (and probably cracking a few heads in the process).

Minnie put on a show for their entertainment, doing her part to amuse the max-capacity 145 lost souls who had come to Whiskey Jack's to celebrate the fifteenth anniversary of America's Other Independence Day. Some came (as they always do) as an excuse to party; others came to forget their troubles and expound (in the mystifying way that only drunk people can) upon the struggling post–Meta War years and flatlining economy.

The whole world changed fifteen years ago. The Meta War ended. All the superpowers disappeared. And my dad died; I was ten.

Happy freaking anniversary.

One of the muted televisions was running some feature on Metas, showing stock footage of long-ago battles and burning buildings. The scroll across the bottom of the screen asked: Would the world have been safer without Metas?

I was kind of glad I couldn't hear the answer to that question.

Depressed and still in some amount of pain, I wandered toward an empty table in the corner, hoping to sit down for a minute. I ignored the pile of dirty plates and glasses that Freddy still hadn't picked up, and pulled out a wooden chair. A meaty hand closed over mine and squeezed. Sasquatch, the bourbon drooler from a minute ago, leered down at me.

"Too good to pour for me, lady?" he said. His other hand produced a wad of cash and he waved it in front of me like a flag. "If you won't pour, how much for the whole night?"

I'd waitressed in dives like this for years and been called a whore before. But whoring wasn't my career of choice, and I would never cross that line. Normally I'd chalk up the solicitation to the alcohol soaking his breath, or simply blame bad manners.

Tonight I let my tangled emotions and unhappy stomach dictate action. I kicked Sasquatch in the groin. He howled and hit the floor. The ruckus caught the attention of half the bar, including Ted, who was squirreled away in his usual place in the DJ booth, and that put an end to my night at Whiskey Jack's.

And my employment there.

The heartburn remained with me during the long walk home. I stumbled into my one-room apartment, clothes and hair rank with the odors of liquor and stale cigarette smoke. After a short debate over showering—too much energy required, not enough on reserve—I sprawled out on my saggy bed and tried to ignore the pain in my stomach and throat. Antacids cost money and . . . well, I didn't have any to spare.

Milk helped sometimes. Did I have milk in the fridge? I squeezed my eyes closed and tried to picture the contents of my wheezing icebox, an original installation in the aging apartment. Two cans of soda, half a loaf of bread, a few slices of faux cheddar, maybe a Styrofoam carton of last week's filched leftovers. If I had milk in there, it was curdling into cottage cheese.

With nothing to save me, I curled onto my side and pondered the tip money in my back pocket. Five hours and only twenty extra bucks. My jackass of a boss docked me for kicking that guy in the crotch. As if firing me wasn't humiliating enough.

I wished I'd controlled my temper.

This was the fourth time in three years that I'd been fired for not reining it in. Sooner or later, I'd run out of noncareer opportunities in Portland and then I'd really be screwed. And I had to go job hunting tomorrow if I didn't want to end up on the street by the end of the week. Work and sleep—there had to be more to life than this. Oh yeah, there was. Pain.

Those invisible hands returned and twisted my intestines into knots. Scalding tears pricked the corners of my eyes. Drawing my knees up to my chest, I ground my teeth and waited for it to pass. No such luck. I tried to stand, preparing to run to the toilet and yak. Threadbare sheets had tangled around my ankles and legs. My left elbow scraped against the industrial carpet as I hit the floor.

Had to be my appendix. I was going to die after all.

The pain spread as I lay on my cold apartment floor—had I bounced another check on the heating bill? The water-stained plaster ceiling pressed down on me. No, it couldn't be my appendix. That pain stayed in the abdomen and lower back. This pain was spreading all over, from my stomach to my chest to my throat. It radiated outward from my belly button, nothing like what I'd earlier mistaken for heartburn. Gooseflesh dotted my arms. My nipples hardened. Searing heat, like swallowing a gallon of boiling water, raced through my veins and arteries, heating my extremities and curling my toes. My mouth opened to scream—no sound came out. My eyes burned; I squeezed them shut.

Had I really worked so hard and survived so much only to die alone, on the floor of my crappy apartment?

The blazing heat ended as abruptly as it began. I curled into a ball and pressed numb hands against my chest. Chills tore up and down my spine. Something was happening to me, something bad. Fear warred with an odd sense of déjà vu. I longed to cry, but no tears came. My eyes still burned. I slit one open. The chilly apartment air cooled the hot cornea, and I opened the other for similar relief.

I tested the muscles in my abdomen. Nothing twinged. Legs and arms seemed equally okay for use. I rolled onto my right side. A lock of hair fell across my face and into my mouth. I spat it out. It tasted as bad as it smelled. A flash of misplaced color caught my eye. I grabbed a handful of hair and inspected the strands. Thin streaks of purple colored half of the light brown.

Crap.

Every six weeks, I splurged on a box of cheap hair dye to keep up the pretense of boring nut brown. The purple streaks had existed since I was a toddler, a random side effect of being born the daughter of two superheroes. But the heroes were gone, and while people still did funny things to their hair, I had wanted to forget the life I'd lost when my powers were ripped away. More than anything, I'd wanted to be normal.

The last box of dye wasn't temporary, so why was the purple back? I rolled the colored hair between my lavender-hued fingertips.

What the huh?

All ten fingers had adopted a pale, violet hue, like the beginning of a bruise. Or like I'd played in permanent finger paints.

I stood on shaky legs and padded barefoot to the bathroom. A colorful towel created the only privacy barrier between bed and bath. I pushed through it so hard two of the tacks popped out of the plaster wall and clattered to the floor. Ignoring the chilly tiles, I flipped the wall switch and flinched against the yellow light that bathed the room.

As my eyes adjusted, I leaned over the cracked porcelain sink, studying my reflection. Chills wiggled down my spine. Purple streaks as thin as fingers highlighted my hair in no discernable pattern, just like before I started dyeing it. Odd, yes, but not scary. Scary was reserved for my eyes. Formerly brown irises now shone an iridescent purple that moved like oceans of light. I'd seen eyes like that once, and not in my head. I remembered an age-lined face and white hair stained with blood, an old woman as she lay dying.

I gripped the sink's edge. "No."

I ran my fingers through hair no longer familiar, convincing myself that it was not an illusion. Purple hair was at least familiar. Purple fingertips? Not so much. I rubbed my thumb and index finger together, testing the texture of the skin. Lavender sparks shot off like a party sparkler. I yelped. My heart slammed against my ribs as a strange odor filled the room, like a scraped matchbook cover.

I had to get a grip—easier said than done. I rubbed again. More sparks. On a whim, I snapped my fingers. A marble-size ball of purple light appeared. It hovered above my palm like an extension of my hand, connected by a faint warmth I couldn't explain.

"Whoa."

I didn't move. Neither did the light. After a moment of concentration, the marble grew into a walnut, and then into an apple-size orb. Holy crap. The oddest sensation of heat still connected the hovering sphere to my hand, pulled taut like a rubber band. I could control it, shrink it, expand it. Could I make it fly?

"This is bad," I said, stumbling away from the sink. I tripped over a well-worn tub mat and fell, landing flat on my ass. The orb disappeared. Sharp pain skewered my lower back, and a few choice curses tumbled out of my mouth.

I sat up, breathing hard, and tried to drum up some explanation. Anything to account for this. My powers were gone, had been for fifteen years. Just like every other Meta. No one knew why our powers went away that day in Central Park. One instant we were huddled together, preparing to kill or be killed, and the next we were all writhing in pain as some unknown force tore our abilities away from us. The world saw it as a blessing—no more superpowered freaks wreaking havoc. No more destruction. No more killing.

No one considered how it affected *us*.

Like most explosive and devastating conflicts, the spark that lit the five-year Meta War was decades in the making. For more than two hundred years, superpowered Metas had been a part of our collective history, but it wasn't until the first half of the twentieth century that the minor Meta disagreements became full-blown conflicts. Conflicts that grew bolder and bloodier over the next century. During that time, the Ranger Corps was established, and Washington bureaucrats coined the term "Banes"—a catch-all for the Metas our Ranger ancestors were tasked to capture and neutralize.

Over time, career-criminal Metas embraced the distinction and their identity as Banes. Schoolchildren were taught that Banes were bad, but the Rangers would always save us. It was a nice fairy tale.

A decade or so before the outbreak of the War—right around the time my generation was born—Specter showed up. More powerful than any other Bane, his abilities were a fierce blend of telekinesis and telepathy—once in your mind, he could control your actions until unconsciousness or death forced him out. This power to possess from a distance and turn the possessed's powers against them helped him command loyalty from the fractured groups of Banes scattered around the world without ever showing his face to the public.

For the first time in history, the Rangers were outmatched. The Banes came at us sideways, using deadly force against anyone who stood in their way, children and trainees included. Everything came to a head in Trenton, New Jersey, after four innocents and one Ranger were killed during a string of jewelry heists. Five cold-blooded murders. Six city blocks burned to the ground. Five years of bitter, violent fighting followed.

Chicago was left a smoldering husk. The Great Salt Lake became too alkaline to live near, and most of Salt Lake City remains unoccupied. Los Angeles and New York City bore the brunt of the attacks. L.A. still has half a million stubborn inhabitants, but the majority of New York's five boroughs are abandoned. The War trickled overseas a few times—Paris, Moscow, some tiny village in the Philippines. London took the worst of it, and kids over there still sing some little ditty called "London Bridge Is Burning Down."

Mostly it stayed here in the States, drawing all known Metas to its center like a crow to a cornfield. Battles devastated small towns and large cities with alarming frequency. The War finally ended on the evacuated island of Manhattan and left the surviving Metas as powerless as any other Joe (and Jane) Citizen.

As powerless as I'd lived for the last fifteen years. Powerless to remain in Los Angeles where I'd grown up, raised to be a hero. Powerless to stop the taunts of other children who saw my purple hair and hated what I no longer was. Powerless to affect the course of my own life.

Bitter fear coated the back of my tongue. Not fear of my strange appearance. No, that particular fear lived in a tiny block of ice, deep inside my gut. This was an old fear of imminent death. Fear of how painful it would be to die at the hands of an angry Bane. Fear of my own cowardice.

"No, no, no."

That part of my life was over. I tried to shut off the unbidden, unfocused slide show. Colorful faces from long ago, wearing strange uniforms of all shapes and sizes. Raging battles. Destroyed towns and leveled city blocks. Hundreds of innocents dead or dying.

No. No!

I hauled ass to my feet and pushed through the towel, managing to rip it the rest of the way down, and stalked to the opposite side of the apartment. As far from the mirror as I could get. I needed a drink. Badly. With no liquor on hand, I settled on bottled water from the refrigerator. I gave the outdated milk quart a suspicious glare.

Cool air from the interior of the fridge caressed my face. I shivered. It had been cold and raining, the devastated skyline black with smoke. Air thick with the stench of death. My father had led the final Ranger assault—a mixed unit of active and retired Rangers. Eighteen inexperienced children tried to fight. Six died. I thought I would die, too.

The overwhelming terror of that day still held my heart in its icy vise—terror I'd revisited in violent nightmares for years. Huddling with the other Ranger children, listening as the Banes blazed a path across Central Park. I remembered a handsome boy with silver eyes trying so hard to be brave for us as we prepared to make our final stand. They prepared—I'd cowered, too afraid to fight.

The last of the Banes had found our hiding place. And then the pain had started, radiating from within and spreading outward, burning through my body like fire and destroying the thing inside that made me special. Made me a Meta. All at once, for no real reason, Rangers and Banes alike were left without power—confused and exhausted and unable to remember why we were there in the first place.

The bottle of water slid from my boneless fingers. It hit the floor, bounced, and rolled toward the front door. I slammed the fridge shut and backpedaled, not stopping until my hip slammed against the counter. Distant bass from somewhere else in the building thrummed through the floor.

Had whatever mysterious force that stole our powers reversed itself? Confusion and incredulity momentarily blurred my vision and set my head spinning. Standing alone in my cold apartment, I desperately wanted to be wrong. I wanted to return to my dull, purposeless existence. I didn't want my powers back, didn't want the fear and uncertainty and responsibility of the Ranger legacy.

We didn't know why our powers left and had no chance to ask. We were just children—separated, split up, and shipped out to different corners of the country. Schools enrolled me under my first foster family's name, Kimble. A name I'd kept, only Teresa Kimble wasn't really me.

My father's surname was West. I was Teresa West— someone who'd ceased to exist fifteen years ago.

I balled my trembling hands into fists and waited for my brain to catch up and tell me I was wrong. It was an illusion, all of it—Metas didn't exist anymore. Two years of working three jobs, eating crap food and barely sleeping had finally culminated in an hysterical breakdown. Or I really had burst my appendix at work, and I was in the ICU, slowly dying from complications. I just had to play along with the delusion until death claimed me.

No problem.

Unless this really was happening, in which case I needed to accept it and move on, before I collapsed into a puddle of hysteria.

Move on to what, though? Tomorrow's House of Chicken shift? Forget it. My eyes were lavender, and I couldn't afford contacts. My fingers looked filthy. The boss would take one look and fire me on the spot. Two firings in twenty-four hours would completely suck.

I gazed at my hands. This was my future now, as it always should have been, and as right as it felt it was also very wrong. I swallowed, stomach quaking, mouth dry. Nothing about my life as a Ranger trainee reconciled with the appearance of my hands and eyes.

I could accept that I was once again a Meta (maybe). I could accept that my brain was more than a little trauma-warped (definitely). I could even accept that everything I remembered about my life before the age of ten wasn't all childish cowardice and failure (with more therapy). I just couldn't accept the extra purple or the floating orbs.

Of all the things I had ignored or forgotten, I knew this for certain: they weren't my original powers. My Trance ability had been a kind of telepathy—the power to plant suggestions and influence the minds of others. While not exactly the same, these new powers were oddly similar to Granny Dell's.

Had all the powers been released from the ether and played musical chairs with their former owners? Like me, were the other eleven kids-now-adults waking up with someone else's powers? What about the sixty-odd Banes imprisoned on Manhattan Island?

Dozens of tiny tremors shot up my spine.

The high walls and harbor patrols of the world's largest man-made prison would not keep the Banes contained once they began to manifest their powers. *If* they began to manifest. At that moment, I had no proof anyone besides myself had powered up. I also had no proof that this wasn't some sort of psychotic break. The result of too many sleepless nights, unsanitized bathwater, and bad nutrition.

My ICU/appendicitis theory was still on the table.

I squinted at my reflection in the dented surface of a toaster. Those eerie eyes winked and shimmered. If I had some warped version of Granny Dell's power, who had mine? I had to find the others (if they were still alive) and make sure I wasn't the only one turning strange colors.

Something squealed, sharp and muffled. A smoke detector in a nearby apartment, maybe. It ceased, and something new niggled at my memory. An item I'd kept ever since the War. Something I hadn't allowed any of my foster parents to take away. The squeal repeated itself, lasting only a few seconds. Definitely not a fire alarm.

Half a minute passed. *Scree!*

I stumbled across the small apartment to a warped closet

door. It screeched on its rusty hinges, and I yanked on the string of a bare bulb, drenching the small space in sickly light. *Scree!* Behind a pile of winter boots, old sneakers, and an antique wooden baseball bat, I found a dusty cardboard box. Inside the box, swaddled in an old T-shirt that had belonged to my dad, was a six-inch-square, carved jewelry box. I held it to my nose and inhaled. It still smelled like roses, even after all this time.

Scree! I almost dropped the jewelry box. The sound, so familiar now, came from inside. I lifted the lid and put it aside. Picked out the small assortment of pins and baubles I'd collected as a teenager. I pulled at the bottom of the box, and the faded satin gave way.

An old Corps Vox communicator was nestled on top of the cotton batting, shiny black and unmarred by age or war. My hand jerked. I struggled to breathe as I picked up the Vox, smaller than the palm of my hand, smooth and warm. My thumb brushed across the silver *R* and overlapping *C* engraved on the plating, and beneath it, the name *Hinder*.

Hinder. Dad's alias in the Corps.

I closed my eyes and held the Vox close. I could see his face, rugged and tired. Wide brow, thick hair, and an everpresent grin, always trying to keep us in good spirits. He told terrible jokes, and we laughed at their sheer awfulness. We read the comic strips every Sunday morning. He made pancakes shaped like the letter T. His laugh sounded like music, reverberating in my chest long after he stopped.

Grief squeezed my heart; an ache settled deep in my gut; tears stung my eyes. How could it hurt so badly to remember a man who died more than half a lifetime ago? Mom died when I was five. She was only a shadow in my mind, unformed and barely visible. But Dad . . . I'd tried so hard to box him up and push him away, so that the grief of losing him didn't kill me.

It hadn't worked too well.

I flipped open the Vox and studied the colorful buttons. Open channel. Private channel. Alert. Vibrate. It fit in my hand perfectly, fingertips lined up with small grip indents along the sides. I pressed the red "alert" button, praying it still worked and that someone received the signal.

"Identify," a computerized voice squawked out of the Vox.

Since it was Dad's Vox, I said, "Hinder."

"Invalid identification. Identify."

I grunted. We each had code names, given the day we officially became Ranger Corps trainees. My father chose mine—a name that matched my old powers.

"Trance," I said.

"Identification accepted. Message sent."

"Thanks."

I put the Vox down on an overturned crate serving as my coffee table. It stayed in plain sight as I yanked a gray sweater off its wire hanger. Corps Headquarters still existed in Los Angeles—a crumbling monument to an era of failed heroics. Someone there would know what to do next.

Was that what I wanted? To walk out of my life and its never-ending cycle of dead-end jobs, which were relatively safe? To return to a life that had almost killed me once but had also, even as a child, made me feel necessary, like I was doing more than just floating through my life?

I was no hero, but I was sick of being a waitress—of simply existing, rather than living. It was time to get dressed and figure out how to get almost a thousand miles from my little apartment in Portland, Oregon, to Southern California as quickly as possible with no car and twenty bucks in cash. My next payday was five days away, so short of bumming train fare from a Good Samaritan or using my newly acquired powers to rob a bank, I would be hitching.

My other unique challenge: concealing my newly acquired amethyst eyes from the general public. I scrounged a blue knit cap from a box of winter clothes to hide the purple hair streaks. Odd-colored hair wasn't altogether unusual; the eyes were harder. I finally settled on a pair of cracked sunglasses.

With my father's Vox—mine now, I supposed—in my jeans pocket, and extra clothes, and the last of my cheap, taste-like-cardboard protein bars in the cloth knapsack slung across my shoulder, I set out, wondering if there was anything more pathetic than a broke superhero.

Three

Cipher

I don't remember dozing, just jerking awake with a cramp in my neck and no idea where I was. The faint odors of gasoline, deep fryer grease, and stale cigarette smoke assaulted my nostrils. The tractor trailer I'd hitched on was turning into a truck stop off I-99. It was busy enough, with dozens of rigs and trucks and traveling families coming and going at regular intervals. A huge fueling plaza was connected to a convenience store and greasy spoon diner. Two hundred yards away, across a service road, was a low-rent motel. It was after 6:00 p.m., dark again, and the place was jumping with activity.

"We're in Bakersfield," Cliff said.

I jerked my head toward him, self-consciously brushing a hand over my chin for a quick drool check. Sleeping upright in cars meant my mouth falling open, but I found no evidence of my slumber and sat up a little straighter. Some of the immediate panic died away, but not all. I'd fallen asleep—let my guard down while locked in a moving semi with a complete stranger. Stupid.

Neon lights from the diner sign glinted off Cliff's bald head. His plaid flannel shirt was untucked, covering his lap and substantial gut. He navigated his rig through the lot behind the diner. It looked like a boneyard for trucks—I had never seen so many in one place. He found a space and turned off the ignition. His hands clenched the steering wheel. I held tight to my knapsack, which hadn't left my side since we began our trip in the early-dawn hours. The rig's engine hissed as it cooled.

The way he shifted in his seat made the skin on my forearms crawl. Maybe accepting the hitch had been a bad idea. I dreaded what Cliff might demand as compensation for this trip. We'd barely spoken when he picked me up. Enough words to communicate that our destinations coincided and he was willing to take on a passenger.

And that he didn't want my money.

My bladder throbbed. "How long was I asleep?"

"About four hours. You up for a stretch and some dinner?"

"Definitely a stretch, but I really should be getting on my way." And as far away from his leering eyes as possible. "I wish you'd take my money."

"Nah, thanks, though. Didn't chafe my ass any, since we're going the same way. Where're you headed to from here?"

"South. We're only about two hours from L.A. I'll get there somehow. Thanks for the lift."

Meaty fists tightened around the wheel, and he still didn't look at me. I eyed him, clenching my own hands, half expecting some sort of attack; a snarled demand for physical reparations. Instead, he climbed out. He walked around to my side, opened the door, and then offered me his hand.

I smiled warmly, feeling a bit like an ass, and accepted his offer. I bounced to the ground and slung my knapsack over my shoulder.

"Sure I can't buy you dinner?" he asked.

One more hash mark on the scorecard of things I would owe. No, thanks. "Thank you, again, for the ride, Cliff. I can manage it from here. Take care."

His left eye twitched. He nodded. "Yeah." With that, he pivoted and strode toward the diner. Okay, waddled more than strode.

My stomach grumbled, reminding me that I hadn't eaten for hours. I eyed the convenience store. Food in there was overpriced, and I might need my cash for the rest of the trip south. The cold fist of hunger tightened around my belly. Dinner with Cliff, even if he gave me the squiggles, was sounding better and better.

Food later. Bathroom first, and then back on the road.

I chose the convenience store's bathroom, since I needed a key to get in. I wanted the privacy, if only for a few minutes. On my way to the rear of the store, key in hand, I passed a large display rack of newspapers. Half a dozen different headlines screamed information at me. A man was placing fresh copies of the *Valley Gazette* on a smallish rack near the bottom.

"Fairview Hospital Fire, Two Dead, Accident or Arson?" Oddly professional headline from what looked like a low-budget gossip rag, if the "Aliens Impregnated Me" story below it was any indication.

After washing my hands, I took a moment to let my hair down. A few more purple streaks had sprouted along my part, working their way from root to tip. It might have been a nice look if my damned eyes hadn't gone all amethyst on me. Unusually colored contact lenses had been banned decades ago, when civilians started going around pretending to be Metas, and several got themselves killed. Even after the War, the ban wasn't lifted. No one wanted to be a Meta. Few wanted to remember we'd ever existed.

I leaned closer and inspected my hairline. The lightest purple haze had settled over the skin at the top of my forehead, like the start of a bruise.

"Now I'm really going to scare the locals."

Roughly half of the old Rangers had been able to blend into a crowd. I'd managed to pass, even with faint lavender streaks, and to use my Trance power without being caught. Now I looked like a reject from a last-century bubblegum band.

A shadow flickered behind me, reflected in the mirror. I froze. How the hell had someone gotten in? A woman's face watched me, out of focus. Underwater. Eyes that were there one instant, and hollow the next. A coalescing swirl of color and nothingness. Impossible.

I spun around. A single toilet and handicap railing faced me. I was very much alone. Chalking it up to lack of sleep and fried nerves, I stuffed my hair back into the cap and left.

Back outside in the cool night air, I started to relax. Hunger was making me see things in the mirror. I probably should have splurged on overpriced snack cakes, just to stave off my admission to the funny farm.

I navigated my way through the maze of the parking lot, past dozens of tractor trailers in long rows of angled spaces that stank of rubber and oil. Their drivers were either eating or sleeping. Furniture deliveries, grocery trucks, and unmarked trailers of all sorts, with license plates from across the country.

Something shuffled behind me; I froze. I glanced over my shoulder—only shadows cast by the trucks and moonlight. Their presence was oppressive, ominous. The rumble of traffic seemed far away, the din of the fuel plaza even farther. I doubled back, determined to get out of the truck maze and into the open.

As I passed a silver cab, something spun me around. The cloth knapsack fell off my shoulder, hit my ankle, and tripped me. I hit the grill with my left shoulder, cracked the back of my head, and saw stars. The sunglasses clattered to the ground. A meaty hand closed around my throat and squeezed, while a second grabbed my right wrist, twisted it, and pinned it against the cab by my head.

Idiot!

Panic hit me in the face like ice water. I raised my knee, hoping to find a soft target, and hit nothing. Hot air wafted over my face, reeking of stale smoke.

"Guess I wanted my twenty bucks' worth after all," Cliff said, coating my sense of smell with his noxious breath.

My stomach quailed. I tried to scream. His hand constricted my throat, and he pushed his gut against my stomach. He had at least six inches on me, plus seventy pounds of flab in all the wrong places. I put my left hand on his shoulder and tried to push—like shoving against a granite pillar. I needed a weapon, something to get him off before he contaminated me with his stink. And worse.

A car rumbled past on the opposite side of the lot, its headlights briefly illuminating our row, giving me a glimpse of my fingertips. Their purplish tinge. The power orbs. I didn't need a weapon. Hell, I *was* a weapon—untested, but had there ever been a better time?

I grinned, channeling my fear into my hands. The skin warmed.

"What's so funny?" Cliff asked, squeezing my throat just a little harder.

My new eyes met his soggy gaze. He blinked. His brow furrowed. Ignoring my seizing lungs, I raised my left hand and snapped my fingers. Instantly a lavender orb of energy appeared and hovered above my palm. He gaped at it, the pale light casting a bizarre pallor on his jowls. His grip loosened, and I sucked in air.

"Let me go," I said, "and I won't shove this orb up your ample ass." I found hitherto undiscovered confidence in the oxygen and my newfound powers. Okay, maybe they weren't actually *my* powers, but they were proving seriously useful.

"What the hell are you?" he asked, tightening his grip again. The lack of constant air was making me light-headed, and I struggled to keep the orb bright enough to scare him.

"I'm annoyed." He wanted to do this the hard way, fine. "And you're in pain."

His eyes widened. I slammed the orb into his left shoulder with a solid crack. His entire left side snapped backward as he bellowed—surprise or pain, I didn't care which—and his hold loosened. I shoved. He hit the filthy pavement with a splat and rolled onto his left side, groaning.

Inhaling greedily, I touched my sore throat, disgusted by the slick substance I found. I wiped my hand on my jeans, then snapped my fingers. A second orb flared to life, roughly the size of a chicken's egg. Paler and translucent, this one wouldn't hurt as much; the larger the orb, it seemed, the less solid its form.

Probably. Granny Dell's orbs had been nothing quite so controlled—one of the reasons, according to Dad, that she'd retired so young. Further testing of my orbs was required, and the perfect subject was squirming at my feet.

I pushed Cliff's shoulder with the toe of my sneaker, and he rolled onto his back. He stared up at me with glassy eyes. His shirt wasn't torn and the area of impact wasn't bleeding, but I bet he'd have one hell of a bruise. I loomed over him with the orb and poised my hand dramatically over his crotch.

"Something tells me I'm not the first girl you've demanded your twenty bucks' worth from," I said, indignation boiling over.

My entire life I'd felt helpless to stop the violence around me. Compared to the more powerful Rangers and trainees, Trancing someone seemed weak and stupid. My cowardice in Central Park had haunted me through my adolescence and four different foster homes while I ignored the school bullies I should have stood up to and absorbed the taunts of my foster siblings, who knew I was different but weren't sure why.

I came to understand that I couldn't count on anyone but myself, so I kept my head down and lived my life, the rest of the world be damned. I tried to block out the violence running rampant in the decaying cities and in the hearts of people I passed in the street every day. For years I'd felt weak and naked and unreliable, and now I stood with the power to take some of that control back. To make my life mean something.

Very cool.

And really friggin' scary.

"Please," he muttered.

"Please what?" I asked. "Please don't burn my balls off? Would 'please' have stopped you from raping me?"

He didn't respond, which was answer enough. I bent at the waist. Several strands of my hair fell loose from the disheveled cap and curled purple around my face. In the pale parking lot lights, I must have looked terrifying, because he started to whimper like a puppy whose tail I'd just ground into the pavement.

"How about we make a deal?" I said. "You get to keep your dick, and in exchange, you tell your friends about this. Let them think about me the next time they pick up a hitchhiker with the expectations of getting a blow job in exchange for miles."

He nodded, still whimpering, his Adam's apple bobbing up and down. "Who are you?"

"Trance?"

The new voice broke my concentration. The orb disappeared. I snapped my head toward the sound, intent on giving the arrival a taste of my annoyance. The barb died on my lips, as did all thoughts of the man at my feet. I gazed at a pair of black and silver eyes that shimmered and danced, swimming in brilliance, like a starry night sky.

A man about my age stood on the sidewalk, his lean, athletic body dressed snugly in black jeans, a black sweater, and a leather bomber jacket. He had a firm jawline, tousled brown-blond hair, and dark eyebrows that creased in a sharp V as he stared at me as if a third arm were growing out of my forehead. His face had changed, narrowed and aged, but those beautiful eyes were unmistakable. Eyes I hadn't seen in a lifetime.

"Gage?" I asked.

"Call me Cipher. Remember?"

I did remember. Vividly. Then fifteen years old, Gage "Cipher" McAllister had been the senior trainee. The last time I'd seen him had been at a hospital in Princeton, New Jersey, two days after we lost our powers. The day MHC (Meta-Human Control) separated us kids and divvied us up to foster homes ill-equipped to handle us. We'd passed each other in the corridor. His dark brown eyes had looked so empty, the silver barely there. Haunted. Dead.

He stood in front of me again, those engaging flecks sharp and bright; the last person I'd seen then, and the first I was seeing now. I was surprised as hell by his random appearance at a highway truck stop. At the same time, I felt an odd sense of rightness in having him there.

"What are you doing here?" I asked.

"Interrupting something, apparently. Everything under control?"

I spared an eyebrow quirk for Cliff, who winced and closed his eyes. "Yep." I gave Cliff a sharp nudge. "Hey, buddy, remember what we talked about?"

He nodded. Each bobble shrank and expanded the doughy flesh beneath his first chin.

"Good." I stepped back and waved a hand at the open parking lot to my left. "Now get the hell out of here."

Cliff wasted no time scrambling to his knees and then his feet. Something greenish-brown stained the back of his shirt and trousers, and I didn't want to imagine what nasty things had pooled together to create that special color. He lumbered down the row of trailers, stumbling a few times in his haste, hurling curses each time he stepped on his own foot. His ample backside made quite a nice target. I rubbed my thumb and forefinger together, creating lavender sparks, and debated a parting shot.

Gage's hand gripped my forearm, warm and firm and unmistakably telling me not even to think about it. The sparks diminished. I yanked out of his grip and took a step back, scowling.

"How are you, Teresa?" he asked.

"I've had better days."

"You look different."

I quirked an eyebrow. "Different good or different bad?"

"Just different." He reached out and flicked at a lock of purple hair. "I remember this—not the eyes or those powers. That wasn't you."

"No, it wasn't."

My fingers trembled as the adrenaline surge from Cliff's attack began to wear off. Thank God for my new powers. Having Gage there made me feel strangely safe when I should have been more cautious; I didn't know this adult. I yanked off the cap and let the rest of my hair tumble down around my shoulders. "So can I assume your powers are back, too?"

"They came back last night." A flash of pain passed across his face, leaving its shadow behind. Deeper shadows lurked beneath his eyes, hinting at hidden agony he couldn't quite put into words. "Not an experience I want to repeat. Ever."

"I hear that. And I think whatever reactivated us had a few flaws. I seem to have gotten my grandmother's powers back this morning, or some screwed-up version of them." I snapped and an orb flared to life. I tossed it at an empty glass bottle; it exploded in a shower of shards.

"Wow," Gage said.

"I'm still getting the hang of it."

He glanced around at the shifting shadows and rows of quiet semis. "We should get out of here."

"Definitely." I slung the knapsack over my shoulder with the grease spot facing outward and followed him through the parking lot. "How did you find me, anyway?"

He sucked his lower lip into his mouth, a very boyish gesture that betrayed his discomfort. He fished into the back pocket of his jeans and pulled out a Vox. "I picked up your signal briefly outside of Salem. I found it again ten minutes ago when, I'm assuming, you arrived here at the truck stop."

I nodded, affirming his assumption. There were only so many direct routes from Oregon to L.A., so running into each other wasn't entirely implausible. "My dad's Vox was with my stuff. I'm glad it still works."

"Me too." His mouth twitched into a pained frown. "Controlling my powers again is a bitch. It's hard trying to filter everything like I used to. Putting all of the information in its own place."

"I bet." Relearning control of his hypersenses had to be a pain (no pun intended). My stomach grumbled, reminding me again of its empty state. The adrenaline was gone and a gentle ache had begun at the base of my skull. "You know, I wish you'd found me before we left Salem. I think the trip would have been a lot more pleasant."

Gage's eyebrows knotted and his eyes narrowed. "Did he hurt you?"

"No, just unnerved me a bit."

He didn't seem convinced. "Are you hungry?"

"Famished," I said before I could stop myself. The last thing I needed was to explain why the diner was out of my price range. "Where's your car?"

"In front of the motel."

"Staying the night?"

"I planned to, yes, and then get a fresh start in the morning."

Not a terrible idea. I felt disgusting and was desperate for a hot shower. "I don't suppose they have any more rooms available?" I asked, even though I couldn't afford one. No sense in saying so and advertising my poverty to Gage. For all I knew he was a successful investor.

"The desk clerk said I got the last one, but there's plenty of space to share," he replied.

Share? Spend the night locked in a room with a strange man. The idea raised my hackles, but knowing it was Gage— a former Ranger who understood what I was going through, to an extent—kept me from falling into full-on panic. And it beat sleeping in an alley or under a car.

I flashed him a smile, using it to hide my apprehension. "Should we flip a coin to see who gets the floor?"

He shook his head. "I'll take the floor."

"It's your room, Gage, I was kidding." I rolled my eyes at his mile-wide gentlemanly streak. "It's not like I think you'll attack me in my sleep, and as long as you're not a warrants officer, we'll get along fine."

Gage stared, and I could have bitten off my own tongue. What was wrong with me? I don't let things like that just slip out.

"Warrants officer?" he repeated. "Were you in jail?"

I tried to shrug it off. Four years ago, an accessory to burglary charge had landed me in the Coffee Creek Correctional Facility, where I spent the worst twelve months of my life. Which had, naturally, led to lack of good employment opportunities and the current state of my craptastic life. Not that I was doing so hot before I agreed to drive the van for a guy I thought I loved in exchange for 20 percent of the fenced merchandise. The money was supposed to buy us tickets to Arizona and a fresh start.

Now I couldn't technically leave the state of Oregon for two more years. Not that it had stopped me last night. "Let's just say I had a rebellious, misspent youth and not dive into details."

"Fair enough. You know, we got our powers back, so there's a chance the Banes did, too. I think the state of Oregon can forgive your debt if we're being called back into service."

Called into service. Put like that, it sounded almost noble. Would the American public, still recovering from the previous decade's atrocities and the loss of their largest cities, readily embrace a new generation of Rangers? Or would they sooner burn us all at the stake?

"You know, you're really starting to look the part," he said as he led the way toward the motel. "The purple becomes you."

"I'm glad." I tossed a lock of hair over my shoulder, relaxing under the spell of the friendly banter. "I'd hate to be stuck with a color that looked awful. Can you see me with green hair? Or orange, even? I'd look like a carrot."

"But a cute carrot."

I grinned. At the tender age of ten, such a simple compliment from Gage would have sent my girlish pulse racing. I noticed our direction and asked, "Hey, aren't we eating?"

"The motel room has take-out menus. It might be better to eat in until we know for sure what's going on. Room's the third one over," Gage said, pointing.

I followed his lead, a few paces behind. The door next to ours opened abruptly and a man in torn jeans and a stained flannel shirt stepped out, right into my path. I backpedaled and started to fall. The stranger caught me by the arm. Before my instinct to groin-kick him took over, a greasy blonde stepped out next to him. Her hair was unkempt, her clothes frayed, and she had a big black duffel bag slung over one shoulder.

"Sorry about that," the man said. "Didn't see you comin'."

"S'okay," I said and ducked my head, hoping to hide my face and eyes behind a curtain of hair. Should have been faster about that.

The man glanced over his shoulder and nodded at Gage, who offered only a steely, suspicious gaze. His attention jumped to me. I winked at Gage, my head still angled away from the pair, and he relaxed just a fraction.

"Cool contacts," the woman said. "Very risqué."

Definitely not fast enough. "Thanks." I ducked around the man and followed Gage into his room.

He locked the door and slid the bolt. "You okay?"

"I'm fine, bare minimum rating on the scare-o-meter." The question surprised me. It was nice having someone around who cared, even if the question was probably more knee-jerk politeness than genuine concern.

I turned the motel room's heat up to a balmy 75 degrees and dropped my small knapsack on a cheaply upholstered chair, which matched the striped bedspread. Two abstract prints hung opposite each other on plain ivory walls. Ugly, but the quality was a step up from my personal squalor.

Gage's expensive-looking suitcase sat in the middle of the king-size bed, leering at me. I eyed it, not bothering to hide my jealousy. He probably had three sets of clothes, all neatly folded, a leather shaving kit, and clean underwear.

Damn.

"What?" Gage asked.

I snapped my mouth shut, unaware I'd made a noise. Or maybe he heard the spike in my heart rate. Gage's powers had fascinated me as a child. Instead of supersight or superhearing, all five of Gage's senses were enhanced to an extraordinary degree. He could increase and decrease the amount of information they collected and received. Eyesight and hearing had been the strongest, with smell in the middle, and taste and touch trailing behind. That could all be different now, but I imagined I was close enough for him to hear my heartbeat if he tried.

"Just admiring your suitcase," I replied.

"There's a shopping center a few miles away—"

"No." He had just flipped a bad switch. Buying me dinner was one thing. I would not be beholden to him for little luxuries that I could do without. I'd managed on my own since I was sixteen; I didn't need to be taken care of by Gage.

"If you need something, we can get it, Teresa, and if it's about the money—"

"It *is* about the money, Gage." I spun on my heel, hair flying, and planted both hands on my hips. "I don't do charity. I took a handout from Cliff and look what it almost got me."

He closed the space between us in three long strides. Muscles in my arms and back coiled as I braced for attack, and I found myself eye level with his neck. I swallowed. Gage wasn't Cliff. He was on my side.

"Look at me," he said, his voice soft and gentle. Warm breath tickled the top of my head.

I looked down instead, but his hand cupped my chin; and I allowed him to tilt my head up. His flecked eyes bore down on me, mesmerizing and kind. A gentle look—one I'd not received from a man in too many years. It made my stomach flip in a pleasant way.

"I'm sorry if I insulted you." His breath smelled like apples. "That wasn't my intention. The world rocked sideways last night, and I'm still getting back on my feet."

"I'm grateful you want to help, Gage, but trusting people always comes with a price." I'd learned that lesson the hard way—multiple times.

"Not always, Teresa. I'm not going to buy you dinner and then demand sex." He sucked in his lower lip, adopting that scrunched, thoughtful look I'd seen twice in the last fifteen minutes. For a guy with learned control over his five enhanced senses, his face was pretty easy to read. "We may have been kids together a lifetime ago, but in so many ways we just met. I'm not expecting you to hand me your trust immediately, just hoping you'll give me a chance to earn it."

He was right. I didn't know the adult standing in front of me, or what he was capable of doing (or lying about). History showed that my judgment sucked when it came to trusting men—especially when my last boyfriend abused that trust so badly. I knew better.

Yet for some reason, on an instinctual level built upon Meta kinship and the girlish crush of the child I'd once been, I knew I *could* trust him. Eventually.

Enough to let him buy me dinner.

We phoned in a pizza and made polite conversation until it arrived. I attempted to pick his brain one question at a time over pepperoni and extra cheese, but hit wall after metaphorical wall when my questions delved deeper than surface stuff. I found out he'd been sent to St. Louis after the War, worked as a finishing carpenter in his early twenties, and then moved to Oregon. He'd lived twenty miles away from me for the last three years.

He wouldn't talk about what brought him to Oregon or engage in reverse questioning. I didn't enjoy talking about my meager existence in the service industry or the hell I'd made of my life, but I would have liked some personal interest on his part.

"Foster homes and therapy seem to be the norm for us," I said, once again leading the topic. "I wonder if the others had the same problems adjusting to life-after-theft."

"After what?"

"After our powers were stolen and our lives as we knew them shattered to bits. You know, I had the same damned nightmares for three years?" My stomach twisted at the recollection, the pizza no longer sitting well.

Gage's left hand curled around the edge of the table. "Nightmares about that last day in the park?"

A tremor wracked my spine. I have never felt terror again in my life like the terror I experienced that day. Encompassing, mortifying, and ugly, it was fear of certain death in the most gruesome manner imaginable.

"Yes," I said when I found my voice. "A variation of it, anyway. Sometimes I'd dream about my dad leading the Banes toward us kids, shouting orders to capture first and kill later. It would be him coming up the steps first." Things got fuzzy after that charge, because that's when the gut-twisting, brain-numbing power loss began.

Gage's right hand reached across the plastic table and squeezed my left. I tucked my fingers around his and held tight, focusing on his warmth. The nightmare had not returned in more than a decade, but the emotions behind it still ran deep and threatened to return in a wave of hot tears. Too bad memories didn't come with an emotional mute button.

"Hinder was a good man," Gage said. "I remember how bravely he fought, even before the War, and how proudly he led his Corps Unit."

I rubbed my free hand across my forehead, as if the motion could erase the dream's images from my conscious mind. "One of my shrinks used to say that the dream was my subconscious mind's way of dealing with my own survivor's guilt."

"Sounds reasonable."

"Yeah, well, another shrink said I had abandonment issues, so I don't trust their analyses very much." Even if the abandonment issue seemed pretty spot-on at times—but I wasn't keen to delve into that particular neurosis tonight. "Do you remember your parents?" As soon as I asked it, I remembered the answer. Stupid.

He released my hand. "No, we were orphans when the Corps adopted us. My mentor, Delphi, raised me and Jasper."

Jasper McAllister had possessed superspeed and enhanced reflexes, and had joined an active Corps Unit eighteen months into the War. The entire unit was killed a month later, trying to prevent a Chicago apartment complex from collapsing. He was sixteen.

Gage had been barely thirteen when his big brother, Jasper, died, and from the brackets of sorrow around his eyes, the pain was just as fresh now as it had been then. Picking at a pepperoni, he said, "It was the loneliest way for a kid to grow up."

I held back a question and gave him a chance to continue the thought without prompting. I was afraid of shutting him up if I pushed.

"Maybe it wouldn't have been so bad if Jasper had lived," he continued. "I could have had someone to talk to, someone who understood what it was like to hear people trash-talk the Rangers, curse Metas in general, and blame us for all the problems of the world. Like those problems hadn't existed long before we did."

I understood, probably better than he realized. I'd spent years pretending to hate Metas as much as my classmates, laughing at their cruel jokes, and convincing myself I'd never been different. Never been the daughter of Rangers, never been trained to save lives, never raised for a greater purpose.

"I used to wish I could just forget it all completely and start fresh. Put all that pain behind me and never look back." Gage sighed heavily. "Wishes and horses and all that."

I didn't get the reference. I did understand the sentiment. We'd never be free from our pasts, whether personal or Corps-related. There was no way to gauge how the world would react to our empowerment. No way to know if we'd be welcomed or despised, or both.

And I truly didn't know which I'd prefer.

Four

Specter

The digital clock-radio ticked off another minute, and the bathroom door still hadn't opened. Thirty minutes was a long shower for a guy—even though I'd taken nearly an hour. Hotels charged extra for water consumption that exceeded the regulated clean water limit, same as apartments and rentals. Between the two of us, we had racked up a pretty hefty fee. I was planning to pay him back for part of the motel (how exactly I'd get the money was still open to debate), so what was another fifty bucks in exchange for a shower that actually ran hot for longer than five minutes?

I unscrewed the cap on a bottle of water, swallowed a couple mouthfuls, and put the open bottle down on the small side table. Having Gage on the other side of that door, in some state of un- or half-dress, left me on edge. I'd believed him earlier, when he said he'd never demand sex in return for his kindness—old apprehensions just die hard, I suppose.

Out of boredom and a need to redirect my thoughts, I snapped my fingers and a small sphere popped into existence. It hovered, perfectly aligned with the tip of my index finger, waiting to go where I sent it. Trouble was, any likely target in the room would just get billed to Gage.

The sphere fizzled out and disappeared.

Practice makes perfect, Teresa. A woman's voice, sweet and lilting, danced through my mind. *Practice makes perfect.*

"Mom," I whispered. I could recall the silliest details about my father—the mole on his left cheek; the way he wheezed when he laughed too hard; he couldn't roll his tongue or whistle. So little remained of my mom.

Right before the official start of the War, when I was just five, she was shot by a panicked citizen as she tried to stop a bank robbery in progress—a citizen who probably thought she was a bad guy because she had green skin. It wasn't the first and wouldn't be the last time the Rangers were turned on by the people we'd sworn to protect.

My gaze flickered to the bathroom door, and a single butterfly fluttered through my stomach. My various foster mothers had never invested themselves in my personal life, and there were so many times in my adolescence when I'd wished for my mom, yearned for her advice and a comforting hand to wipe away the tears. Someone to warn me about the danger of attaching myself to any adult male who showed me kindness, because I missed my father so badly—missed that connection and closeness. Someone to soothe me when I was sixteen and lost my virginity to a thirty-year-old man who told me he loved me and then never spoke to me again. Someone to explain why I trusted Gage so easily when every survival instinct told me not to.

The water finally shut off. A few minutes later, Gage

emerged in a cloud of steam, clad only in a pair of blue boxers, scrubbing a rumpled towel over his hair and neck. My attention dropped to his toned abs, their perfection marred by a thin scar the width of a pencil and the length of my hand. A second, similar scar peeked from around his back on the left side, just under his ribs. He retrieved a T-shirt from his suitcase and slipped it on.

"Squeaky clean?" I asked, looking away.

"Hope so." He padded around to the side of the bed nearest the wall, since I'd made myself at home by the door. "Anything good on television?"

"There hasn't been anything good in ten years."

He chuckled and sat down, his weight sinking the mattress. I sat up a little straighter, stomach knotting. I closed my eyes, annoyed at myself for being so paranoid. He didn't seem to notice.

"This is kind of funny, isn't it?"

I gave him a curious look. "You want to narrow that down?"

"We've been back in each other's lives for three hours, and we're already in bed together." His teasing smile coaxed a grin of my own, and I couldn't help wondering if he'd known about my childhood crush.

I nearly fell out of bed at a sudden, thunderous pounding of fists against the motel door and a female shriek for help. I lurched to my feet and stumbled toward the door to the beat of the erratic knocking, adrenaline warming my hands and urging me to use my newfound power to help this terrified person. I peered through the peephole and saw the blond woman from next door, her hair askew and matted red. Blood streamed down the side of her face. "Oh, God." I wrapped my hand around the knob and twisted.

"Trance, don't!" Gage said.

I turned my head to ask why not, as the center of the door exploded. The blast tossed me to the floor, peppering my neck and hair with shards of wood and glass. I rolled to the side, instinct propelling me out of the line of fire, and I came up in a crouch next to the table.

The rest of the door blasted in with the second shotgun report. I screamed, startled by the sheer volume of sound it created, and brought both hands up to my sides, creating twin orbs, each the size of a grapefruit. A quick glance to my right found Gage on his feet by the corner of the bed.

The blonde entered, her eyes radiating a garish, sickly shade of yellow. She eyed me, then Gage as she reloaded the shotgun. The odor of burned wood filled the room. Fresh blood continued to run down the side of her face, and with chilling certainty, I understood. I had seen this before. In training videos. That day in Central Park. In my nightmares.

The possessed woman snapped the barrel back into place.

"Gage, duck!" I shouted.

He dove behind the bed just as she fired. The shot struck the wall, blasting through the thin plaster to create a hole two feet wide.

I threw the twin orbs at the woman. She moved faster than she should have been able to. One missed and blasted a hole through the wall, straight into her adjoining room. The second clipped her shoulder and spun her around. The gun belched an erratic shot that took out the room's front window in a shower of glass and wood.

"Trance?" Gage said.

"I'm fine, stay down!"

I called up two more orbs, smaller this time, and released them both straight at the convulsing woman's midsection. She screamed and the yellow light faded from her eyes. Her body jerked once, twice, and then lay still. I stood on shaky feet, ignoring the screaming cuts on my face and arms.

"Tell me that wasn't who I thought it was," Gage said.

I wished I could. "Specter." Even saying the name chilled me, like calling on the Bogeyman.

Gage made a choking sound. "But how?"

"I don't know."

I nudged the dead woman's hand with my bare toes. The third finger had two rings on it, one a very large (and probably fake) diamond. My first thought was to wonder how much a pawnbroker would give me for that ring. My second—and much more pressing—concern was about the man who had probably given the rings to her.

"Where's the other guy?" I asked.

A looming shadow filled the door, still dressed in the same jeans and flannel. I looked up, right into a pair of yellow eyes and a sawed-off shotgun. No time to duck, nowhere to go.

"Say hi to your father for me," he sneered, his voice a queer blend of the man's and someone else's. Monstrous and terrifying.

Enraged, I clapped my hands together with no real idea what would happen, and he fired immediately after. The buckshot struck a haze of violet energy and ricocheted, like a thousand Ping-Pong balls. Blood and gore splattered the open doorway and walls.

I had little time to be nauseated by the sight. The kinetic energy of the shotgun blast reacted to the force field I'd instinctively created. The feedback struck me like a speeding truck and tossed me backward onto my ass. The gunman wailed and gurgled in someone else's voice. The voice of a man not quite human, full of anger and pain and frustration, filled my ears. I lay on my back, too stunned to care if he was dead. My nerves burned. I couldn't feel my feet.

Gage's face loomed over mine. "Trance? Jesus, are you all right?"

My head throbbed. My tongue felt thick and dried out. I swallowed and tasted blood. I'd bitten into my lower lip. Every single joint in my arms and legs ached.

"Him?" I hissed through the pain settling into my bones.

"He's dead. If Specter was possessing them, he's gone now. We need to get out of here."

"Hurts."

"I know. Damn it, the entire motel must have heard us. I'm going to sit you up, and then get our stuff together, okay?"

I nodded. Stopped smiling when my lip twinged. He looped an arm around my shoulders and hauled me up into a sitting position. The room spun in loopy circles; I tilted sideways. Gage caught me and helped me lean back against the foot of the bed.

"It's already starting," I said.

"What is?"

I caught his gaze and held it, feeling a little drunk. And not the good kind of drunk. "Banes trying to kill us. They have their powers, too. Why isn't he in jail?"

Something flickered across his face, an expression mixed with equal parts fear and fury. He cupped my face in his hands and leaned close. "Just hold on, Teresa."

"'Kay." The power feedback I'd experienced had fried my nerves and worn me out. I tried to stay awake while Gage darted around the room, tossing our things into his suitcase. I stared at the print on the wall. The pastel paints began to melt and run, turning the watercolor landscape into puddles and swirls.

Gage was speaking. He needed to stop mumbling. My head felt swaddled in cotton. Everything was out of focus. Strong arms wrapped around my shoulders and looped beneath my knees. I rose up into the air. Floated. So over this pain thing. Had to stay awake. Concussed people couldn't sleep. Power-fried people really couldn't sleep.

"Stay with me, Teresa, I've got you," he whispered as we continued to float along. Far from the odors of smoke and blood and motel deodorizer.

Five

William Hill

Disinfectant—the worst possible smell to wake up to—greeted me when the fog finally lifted. It took some effort to peel my eyelids apart. They felt weighted down, glued together. I licked my dry lips and tasted something sticky over the cut. A stark, white ceiling loomed above me, and the gentle bleep of a monitor kept me company. Had Gage taken me to a hospital?

I tilted my head and something on my neck pulled. My fingers explored upward and found a taped bandage. A monitor was attached to a cord, which led to a plastic tube clamped down on my index finger.

Except for a dark green door and matching plastic chair, the room was empty. No windows, no other furniture. Probably more dials and gizmos above my head. I had no energy to twist around and look. My stomach growled, reminding me that I was alone and didn't know how much time had passed.

I needed to get someone's attention.

I felt around for some sort of call button or remote control and came up dry. Fine, I'd do it the hard way. With a snap of my fingers and flick of my wrist, a walnut-size lavender orb zinged across the room and cracked against the center of the green door. Just like a loud knock. I was getting the hang of this. Less than ten seconds passed before the door opened. I tensed, no idea who to expect.

Gage entered first, dressed in black slacks and a green shirt. He faltered just inside, his face brightening into a relieved grin. Dark smudges colored the skin beneath his eyes, betraying lack of rest. Bits of silver had sparked in his hair— something new since this morning. Or yesterday, whenever. Just seeing him there eased some of my tension.

A second man entered behind Gage, wearing a form-fitting gray jumpsuit that contrasted sharply with his ebony skin. Thick muscles rippled beneath the suit. Even his jaw looked strong, able to crack nuts with the slightest pressure. As strong as the rest of him. His name fell easily from my lips. "William," I said.

"Hey, princess," William Hill replied. A shy smile stole across his face. Alias Caliber, as a kid William had been the most easily spooked strongman I'd ever met. He used to shriek when Renee slithered her superflexible feet under the bathroom door. Renee . . . I hadn't thought of my childhood best friend in years. Was she still alive? On her way here, wherever here was?

William stood across from me like the stone statue of a Greek god. He had been twelve when I saw him last, nearly as tall at that young age, but leaner and less muscular. Even without his superstrength, he had been keeping in shape, and looked like he could pick me up and snap me in half without breaking a sweat.

"Where are we?" I directed the question at Gage.

It was William who answered: "Corps Headquarters in Century City. Between your state and thinking Specter was after you, Gage was out of his head when he got here yesterday."

"Yesterday?"

"Yep. You've been asleep for almost thirty hours."

Thirty hours. It was Saturday already. Crap.

"How do you feel?" Gage asked. He moved to the right side of the bed, carefully scrutinizing my face.

"I feel like I've been asleep for a day and a half," I replied. "Was it the feedback from Specter?"

"We think so," William said. "Dr. Seward is still running some tests, but it looks like you overloaded your system. The good news is you saved your own life, and Gage's too. A shotgun blast at that range should have cut you in half."

That conjured up a pleasant image. I barely recalled the blast. Mostly I remembered the pain. And the look on the possessed man's face when he said to say hello to my dad. Vengeful and mocking. Odd. Specter hadn't killed my father. I was told my father died at the hands of a man named Scar, minutes before the power loss hit.

I asked, "Who is Dr. Seward?"

"He's on the MHC's payroll."

Figures. MetaHuman Control was a self-contained subdivision of the Bureau of Alcohol, Tobacco, Firearms and Explosives, or ATF, specializing in (according to them) monitoring the most dangerous "firearms" in the world. Currently defunct, MHC had been organized more than a century ago, in the 1960s, and had bankrolled the Rangers for decades, providing us with the finances to police the Banes, information on their whereabouts, and a pretty nifty HQ. Throughout the Meta War, they stood by the Rangers. After the War and the loss of our powers, they hid us to protect us from an angry public. Or so they said.

William continued. "After what happened on Wednesday night, ATF called in some of the people who used to work for MHC. The ones not retired or transferred out of ATF, anyway, which is only a handful. They're also working on locating the rest of the us."

Us. The others were alive. Or suspected to be alive. So far, we had three out of the twelve of us who'd survived the massacre in Central Park. My mind swirled with the new information, trying to store the important bits away for later scrutiny. I was too hungry to concentrate right now. And I still didn't recognize the name Seward.

"I don't suppose this Dr. Seward has a theory on why I've got different powers?" I asked.

"I'm sure he has a theory," William said. "He won't say anything until he's certain, and in this business—"

"It's hard to be certain of anything." Great, I got the dubious honor of being the group oddball. "Is anyone else here?"

"Renee Duvall and Marco Mendoza have found their way," William said. "We're having trouble finding the other seven."

Okay, five out of twelve. And Renee was one of them. I

couldn't help a small smile and a pang of curiosity about my old friend. How had she managed for fifteen years? Blue skin is a lot harder to hide than purple hair.

"How about a theory on why we all reactivated in the first place? Does Dr. Seward have one?" I didn't have one of my own, so I wanted to hear what the eggheads thought. They were paid to analyze, not me. I wasn't being paid at all, and after missing three days of work, I was certainly fired from my two remaining jobs.

William and Gage looked at each other. I couldn't read their expressions, just that they'd had this conversation before. "No one is sure," William said. "Right now it's all theory, since we don't know why we lost our powers in the first place."

"Lost implies that they were misplaced, or that we were somehow active in their removal, which we weren't. They were taken, not lost."

William nodded, but didn't reply. An awkward silence fell over the room, interrupted only by the bleep of the pulse monitor.

"Are you hungry?" Gage asked.

"Famished. How's the room service around here?"

"It's decent," William said. "I'll go see what I can scare up for you. Just try not to get out of bed until Dr. Seward comes to see you. Okay?"

I snapped off a mock salute. He departed, pulling the door shut behind him. Gage perched on the edge of the bed near my knees. "Thank you, Teresa."

"For what?"

"For saving my life." The bald emotion in his voice startled me.

"Well, I couldn't let you die," I said, falling back on humor and pretending to pout. "I owe you money."

He blinked, then smiled. "Shouldn't it be the other way around?"

"You owe me money?"

"No."

"Would you like to owe me money?"

"You're impossible."

I stuck my tongue out at him. He tried to be serious. The corners of his mouth twitched. I dissolved into giggles, laughing until my stomach hurt and the last wisps of fear had evaporated. Gage remained by me, his smile never quite reaching his haunted eyes.

We had survived our first battle in this strange new war, our first brush with death. I just hoped I didn't get the giggles every time, because we would face many more before the fight was over, and I didn't want people to think I was insane.

Dr. Angus Seward stopped by my room in the middle of a boring dinner of broiled chicken breast, rosemary pasta, and steamed snap peas, all courtesy of William. Food staples had been brought in, but the still-assembling kitchen staff hadn't quite organized themselves. Blah or not, it was better food than I'd had in months. The carb-heavy meal filled me up quickly, and I started feeling human again. So to speak.

Gage stayed nearby and acknowledged Dr. Seward with

a nod. The older man was tall and lean, and sported a shock of more-white-than-black hair and a neatly trimmed peppered beard. A white lab coat and tan slacks completed the ensemble. He looked like a dirty icicle on two legs.

"You have quite a strong constitution, Trance," Dr. Seward said. He held a chart against his chest. "Cipher said the combined blast blackened the motel room walls."

News to me. And the use of our code names was distracting. MHC had its own rules of conduct when engaging Rangers. Code names were used exclusively during official business (which was technically all the time). Something about keeping private and professional lives separate.

"So am I free to get out of bed yet?" I speared another bite of chicken and twirled the fork between my fingers.

"As soon as you feel able, yes. All of your blood work is within acceptable limits, and if your appetite is any indication, you are well on your way to recovering from the power spike."

"What does acceptable limits mean?" Gage asked.

"It means she never attended a regular physician as a teenager or adult, so all of our medical records for Trance end when she was ten years old. Her powers were completely different then. Her body and metabolism have also changed in fifteen years, so, like the rest of you, we are relearning your standard functions. With Trance, we're practically starting over. After a few more days of observation, my conclusion will be a bit more . . . ah, conclusive."

A scientist that sounded like a human being; I could learn to like this guy. "So what you're saying is that I'm free to go, while you keep trying to reach your conclusive conclusions about my condition?"

Dr. Seward tilted his head. "Precisely."

"Fabulous. What about Specter?"

"As far as our records show, his physical body is still in Manhattan Island Prison. However, his astral powers, which he has obviously regained, allow him to move freely, unlike many of his compatriots. We're doing what we can to protect you."

"Which is what? All Specter needs is a weak or semiconscious mind to channel his will, right? That's why he was able to attack us so easily at that motel. How do we keep him out of the HQ?"

"You've been safe here since you arrived, because experience tells us that Specter requires time to recharge after every possession. It's been thirty-six hours since your interaction, so our window is closing fast."

"He could attack us here at any time?" Gage asked.

Seward nodded. "Which is one of the reasons we are keeping the staff to minimum numbers. The fewer people running around HQ, the fewer chances Specter has to use someone against you."

"He first showed up almost thirty years ago. In all that time, the MHC hasn't developed protection?"

"Unfortunately, no. Powers of mind control and telepathy are difficult to fight, because they aren't physically manifested. Trance's original power worked through eye contact, so it had a physical limitation. Specter doesn't even require proximity, much less contact. Technology still hasn't provided us with the ability to censor someone as powerful as Specter. During the War, our only real HQ protection was Static."

"Who?" I asked. The name didn't ring a bell.

"Static was a telepath capable of creating psyonic shields. They prevented external telepathic interference, but only to a certain radius and only when she was consciously creating them."

"Did Static die in New York?"

"No." A shadow of grief stole across Seward's face. "She had a massive stroke three days before the end."

Fabulous. "So what if Specter takes one of us? God, what if he manages to take over me? I could kill everyone." Fear sent shivers down my spine.

"You're very strong, Trance. Specter always had some degree of difficulty taking over powerful Metas. Their minds are stronger, less likely to give in to a foreign invader, which is why he generally stuck to willing Banes and innocent bystanders. I can't guarantee that Specter won't try to possess you. I am, however, confident that he'll fail."

I didn't know if I wanted to bank on Seward's confidence, despite his sincerity. Especially if I fried myself again and ended up susceptible to takeover. "You said Specter is still in prison. Have the island guards brought him in for questioning?"

"They sent a squad onto the island to collect him, yes. We should have something from them within the hour."

"Good." I pushed my lunch tray to the end of the bed and tossed the blanket aside. "Call me when you know something."

Gage walked to the other side of the bed to offer his hand. I looped my arm through his and stood up. My knees buckled as a wave of dizziness smacked me around the head. His strong arm slid around my waist and held me upright.

"Take it easy, Trance," Dr. Seward said. "You're relearning your body just like we are."

"Yeah, then make a note," I said. "I'm an impatient patient and a very grumpy sick person. And curious. Is this cafeteria open all the time?"

"Once we're at full staff again, the cafeteria will be open twenty-four hours. Before things began to deteriorate, we had more than one hundred eighty full-time Rangers living here. Until then, though, we'll arrange what we can."

Deteriorate was an interesting word choice for what happened to our mentors and families. I would have chosen massacred, or even serial-killed. Deteriorate made it sound like they all aged and went feeble-minded.

"All of your things are in your room," Gage said. "I'll take you up, if that's okay with Dr. Seward."

Dr. Seward nodded and stepped to the side. Gage led me out, and I leaned against him, the dizziness finally starting to go away.

Six

Flex and Onyx

Ranger Corps Headquarters was larger than I remembered. Built on several acres of land that had once belonged to a movie studio, the HQ was actually three enormous buildings. We passed through the Medical Center, which housed dozens of labs, emergency medical services, hospital facilities that once rivaled the most advanced in the country, and a basement that stored two hundred years of Ranger history.

Between the Medical Center and the Housing Unit stood the Base. Partially enclosed, the Base was both a dream and a nightmare. The world's strangest gymnasium—designed to accommodate Rangers with powers that spanned from simple telepathy to shapeshifting to elemental transmutation—came complete with a pool, a track, exercise equipment, a firing range, and an open court for practice of just about any kind. It once bustled with activity, full of eager faces and toned muscles. Now everything seemed empty, displaced. On hold.

And why not? The entire facility had been shut down after the War. No Rangers meant no need for an active HQ.

I leaned on Gage the entire walk to the Housing Unit, enjoying the novelty of his protectiveness, and of being physically close to someone who wasn't trying to cop a feel. He'd saved my life by getting me here, earning my trust in a big way. He was also the best friend I had at the moment.

The main lobby looked like a shabby hotel with a bank of windows in need of washing, lush red carpet in need of vacuuming, and dark wood walls that tried to be homey and just felt fake. Not everything on the lot was in perfect order yet. The first floor hosted the cafeteria, and even though I'd just eaten, the scent of cooking food made my mouth water. There was also a social lounge, a recreational lounge, a film room, and an art studio. I recalled the oily scent of the paints I had used on a daily basis, nurturing an art talent that evaporated along with my old Trance powers. I hadn't painted a stroke since the War ended.

The top eight stories housed everything from single-bunk dormitory style rooms to full-fledged family apartments. I had lived in one of the latter with my parents, all the way on the top floor. My room had a lovely view of the ocean, always dark blue in the distance. I never went back to clean it out afterward.

"They set us up on the second floor," Gage said. "Those are the single rooms. The other floors haven't been cleaned yet. There's still a lot of work to do."

"I can imagine," I said.

He let me go once we stepped into the chilly wood-paneled elevator. My waist felt cold everywhere his arm had been, and I tucked my hands under my armpits. I'd have to ask someone about the heat in this place. Anyone who thinks it's always sunny and eighty degrees in Los Angeles needs a swift kick in the head. Although the January chill was down-right balmy compared to a Portland winter.

The short ride up ended with a sharp jolt. The second floor corridor reeked of disinfectant, furniture polish, and glass cleaner. The burgundy carpet looked swept and the walls freshly scrubbed. Loud music blasted from a room down the hall. Gage steered me in the opposite direction. He stopped in front of room 28 and handed me an index card.

"Your room and the lock code," he said.

I read the numbers on the card, punched them into the pad by the knob, and pulled. The door clicked and swung open. The interior of the room was large, twice the size of our motel room, with the same freshly scrubbed odor as the hallway. The walls were painted pale yellow (or had yellowed with age, I couldn't tell) and were blessedly free of any garish artwork.

I had a full-size bed, neatly made with clean sheets and a navy blue coverlet. A long dresser and matching mirror took up one wall, a freestanding armoire a second, and against the third stood a writing desk and chair. My knapsack rested on the dresser next to a stack of folded clothing. I stood in the middle of the room, looking for another door.

"Don't tell me," I said when I didn't find it.

"The bathrooms and showers are in the middle of the hall by the elevators," Gage said. "Communal. It was the first sec-tion they were able to clean and renovate fast enough to ac-commodate us. I'm across the hall in twenty-seven."

"Teresa!"

A blue and black blur rushed past Gage, and long, thin arms looped around my shoulders and squeezed.

"Oh my word," a breathy, female voice screeched in my ear. "It's so good to see you, Teresa, you look amazing, how're you doing, sweetie?"

"Uh, you too," was all I could manage. I gently patted the woman's back, hoping her death-grip of a hug didn't smother me.

"Easy there, Renee," Gage said, saving me from asphyxiation. "She's had a hard day."

"Oh, right, sorry, so sorry."

Renee "Flex" Duvall let go and stepped back, and I got my first real look at the woman she had grown into. Every bare inch of her skin had a smoky blue hue; even the whites of her eyes were the palest shade of blue around the cobalt irises. Only her lips retained some mundane color; they stood out like cherries. Both colorations contrasted sharply with her butt-length, straw-colored hair. She wore a form-fitting black body suit, textured like snakeskin, with a deep V cut down the back, showing off more shimmering blue skin. We had been good friends once, a lifetime ago—stuck together like peanut butter and jelly, my dad used to say.

"Wow," Renee said, her head bobbing up and down as she looked me over. "I mean, Gage said that you'd changed, but wow. You look different, but different in a good way, of course."

"You look the same," I said. "Taller, and your hair's longer."

"Yeah, and look!" She ran her hands over her breasts,

neatly protected in black leather cups, and a bit too large for her small frame. "I got them three years ago, aren't they great? For a minute, I thought they'd go back to normal size when my powers returned, but I got to keep my boob job!"

I had absolutely nothing to say.

Gage saved me with "Renee was a dancer in Las Vegas."

"Yeah," she said. "Goodness, but I love dancing. I got into an act with a brilliant manager who had the other girls dress up in blue body paint, so something good came out of being blue back then. I thought about trying out a new act now that I've got my powers back, but then William called me, completely out of the blue—no pun—and said we should gather here, so here I came. Have you seen William yet? Doesn't he look great?"

Wow, had that been one breath? "Yeah, he, um, really fills out his uniform," I said.

"Yes, he does. Oh, you guys need to pick out uniforms, too! They have all of them downstairs, and not first floor downstairs, the basement downstairs. We raided yesterday, but there are still tons left." She ran her hands up and down her arms, scraping her cobalt fingernails over the material. "Dr. Seward said this one would stretch pretty well, so it's a good match for my powers, and I love the texture, don't you?"

I would never understand how so many words came out of one mouth so quickly. Renee Duvall had the excitability levels of a cocker spaniel puppy and giggled like she had inhaled a helium balloon. If our current situation bothered her at all, she showed no sign—only pure joy at life itself and an eagerness to interact.

She had not changed a bit since we were children.

Except for the boob job.

Renee left us in front of the elevator and bounced back down the hall to her room, yelling over her shoulder about forgetting something. I wasn't thrilled with the idea of wearing a uniform. As children and trainees, we'd worn primary-colored jumpsuits—something I'd learned quickly to despise. Uniforms came after official Corps membership and were often assigned based on powers and mobility needs. Rangers were meant to stand out from the crowd. For the time being, I'd rather run around in my jeans and T-shirt.

As Hinder, my dad's uniform had been straightforward and simple, just like him: a black body suit with a graffiti *H* emblazoned across the chest in green. The collar of the suit had covered his neck, stopping at his shorn hairline. He wore a small eye mask for effect, he said, more than for protecting his identity. His identity *was* Hinder.

"So we just what?" I asked. "Put something together?"

"Sounds like it," Gage said. "Any thoughts?"

"As long as it's not purple. Might be overkill."

He chuckled. "We could put you in orange and make you look like a carrot."

"A cute carrot," I amended.

"Very cute."

Something rubbed against my ankle, which gave me an excuse to look down before I blushed. A black house cat sat by my foot and gazed up at me with big green eyes. For an

instant, I expected it to leap for my throat, hissing and clawing—which was stupid. Specter couldn't inhabit animals,
only human beings. The cat meowed and licked its lips.

"Hey, Renee?" I shouted as I bent to pick up the slim
beast. It didn't struggle, just sniffed my mouth.

"Yeah?" Her head appeared in the hallway, stretched from
the neck in comical proportions.

"Do we have a cat?"

Renee looked at the animal in my arms, then at me, and
laughed. Her head disappeared, the laughter going with it.

"What?" I looked down at the cat, perplexed. It tilted its
head, licked my nose, then leapt to the floor.

It began to grow, every part of its body increasing in size.
The black hair disappeared, as though erased by a magical
pencil, revealing smooth, color-mottled skin. The legs lengthened while the front arms shortened. Toes separated and
grew, and its face flattened out. The entire transformation
took less than five seconds and sounded like fingers rubbing
across sandpaper.

"I should have known it was you," I said.

Marco "Onyx" Mendoza grinned at me with perfectly
straight teeth, glaring white against his black and brown skin.
At first glance, he appeared to be covered with bruises. Closer
inspection showed that the coloration matched the fine hairs
on his arms and chest, mottling the bronze skin inherited by
his mixed Colombian-Japanese heritage. His jet-black hair
was combed back neatly, and his eyes—iris and sclera—radiated green, something between emerald and lime. Except for
a pair of black briefs, he was also completely naked.

"*Dios*, William was right," Marco said. "You are a looker."

I rolled my eyes. "You licked my nose."

"You picked me up." His accent had faded a bit over the years as his English improved. He'd come to the Corps in the most unusual way imaginable—rescued from game smugglers in Brazil who were trying to sell him to rare animal collectors in New Jersey. Regular police had made the bust and called in the Rangers when they realized one of the panther cubs wasn't quite what it seemed. He'd initially been kept separate from the other children, because he was feral—no matter his form—and could barely communicate. He had just started coming out of his shell by War's end.

The man in front of me now seemed completely in control of his limited shapeshifting abilities. I was still the only Ranger with the wrong powers.

"Don't tell me you're going out in public in that thing," Gage said.

"I was testing the material," Marco said. "Dr. Seward says it is a prototype developed years ago. It is supposed to shift with my body and become part of the change. I will not ruin or lose clothing each time. A good idea, no?"

"Sounds great," I said.

"Come on, you two," Renee said. The top half of her body appeared in the hall. An instant later, the rest of it walked around the corner, her torso slowly shrinking back into itself. It looked like a taffy pull in reverse; it was simultaneously fascinating and disgusting. "We can all play catch up at dinner, but we aren't a proper Corps Unit until all are fitted for their uniforms."

I rolled my eyes. Given the situation, her fixation on our clothes seemed misplaced. I didn't care if we all went out in pink spandex and bike helmets, as long as we neutralized Specter before he attacked us again.

"They're making us a unit?" Gage asked.

"First ones here, first ones assigned," she said.

"Do you think they'll find the other seven?" I asked.

"We must hope so," Marco said. "Right now the odds are twenty to one. If our side starts hiding, *temeroso*—afraid of what happened before—"

"It won't," I said. "It's already different this time. Can't you feel that it's different?"

They all looked at each other and shook their heads no like a trio of bobbly clown dolls.

"I don't feel it, but I hope you're right, T," Renee said.

High-pitched squealing cut through the room and set my teeth on edge. Then a computerized voice rumbled over a hidden loudspeaker, "All Rangers, report to Conference Room A. All Rangers, report to Conference Room A."

"That's us," Renee said, grinning broadly.

Our first official meeting. Good. I had too many Specter-related questions and I was itching to get some answers.

Seven

Angus Seward

Marco knew where to find the conference room. William and Dr. Seward were already seated at a long oval table when we arrived. Computer screens were spaced at intervals along the four walls. One of them displayed an aerial shot of Manhattan Island. The high walls of the prison outlined the shape of the island like chalk, dotted every half a mile or so with the square roof of a guard tower. The long gray patch of Central Park drew my attention.

After so many years, seeing it again—even from the distance of a satellite shot—brought back all of the fear I'd tried to forget. Fear of death. Fear of Specter and the day a few dozen surviving adults and eighteen adolescents made our last stand.

MHC came in after we lost our powers and cleaned it up. The devastated island was turned into a prison, and every single surviving Bane was tagged and accounted for, including Specter. For fifteen years they had lived there, fed by drop shipments, and ignored by the public. An island prison in the center of a ruined, largely abandoned city.

Gage touched my shoulder; I'd been staring too long. I turned around, seeking out Dr. Seward. "I don't suppose you've got anything new on me?" I asked.

"On your physiology, no," Dr. Seward replied. "But we may have something new on Specter."

He had my attention. I slid into a chair next to Gage, across the table from Seward.

William stood up, taking point on the conversation, and said, "So far, all preliminary reports show that the Banes imprisoned on Manhattan Island are accounted for. Each one was tagged with a tracking collar, which allows them to move freely on the island, without being able to leave it. No Bane has gone on or off the island in fifteen years."

"That's old news." I leaned forward on my elbows, intently focused on the strongman. "What's the punch line?"

"We had the warden authorize a sight check on all prisoners, to confirm that every tracker matched up to someone. When they found Specter's tracker, someone else was attached to it."

I shivered.

"Who?" Gage asked.

"We don't know yet, but we think a civilian," Dr. Seward said. "The FBI has him now. He was chained up in a room, gibbering nonsense, so it's likely he's been kept that way for a long time."

"How is that possible?" Marco asked. "The prison warden must know when a collar is removed from a body. They would have known if Specter removed it and placed it on someone else."

"We asked the warden that very thing. Their records show no break in contact from the minute it was attached fifteen years ago to now."

"He was never captured," I said. My stomach knotted. "This whole time they've had the wrong man secured on the island. Specter has been out there, moving freely, all these years."

"Freely, but powerless," William said.

"Any idiot with five fingers can fire a gun. He didn't need his powers to be able to hurt us."

"No, but he needed to find you first," Dr. Seward said. His calm exterior was insanely irritating.

"Not all of us blended into the crowd," I shot back, glancing at Renee and Marco.

"We did our best to hide you children back then, and that may have saved your lives."

We? Seward was involved in the . . . what? Conspiracy? That didn't seem quite fair, but it was the only word I could connect to what had been done to us. We were just children, ripped away from everything we knew. Torn from our roots and replanted elsewhere, without the resources to thrive.

Renee snorted and said, "That's one way to spin an averted disaster, Doc. How about the guy who collared Specter? You talk to him?"

Dr. Seward nodded. "He was our first step once we discovered the deception, but that guard, Lorne Andrews, was killed during an apparent mugging eleven years ago. No one else we've questioned remembers seeing Specter that day, and all of the security footage has been compromised."

"Meaning what?" I asked.

"It means that anything pertaining to Specter was erased," William replied. He glared at Seward. "Right?"

"Correct," Dr. Seward said.

"So is Specter responsible for all of this?" I asked. The puzzle pieces kept growing more and more numerous, and it seemed unlikely they would ever fit together and make sense.

"He is the most likely suspect. The Banes were kept together after the end of the War. Fifteen years is a long time to plot revenge. We just have no idea how he reactivated everyone."

"If he did it at all."

"So what's his plan?" Renee asked. "Break the other Banes out, get them off the island, and start the fight all over again?"

"That was our initial hypothesis, yes," Dr. Seward said. "After all, you twelve are the oldest living Rangers we know of, and it will take time to find and train any new Metas. If the Banes manage to escape and eliminate you, they'll be unstoppable."

"Just like the first time," I said. "Why did your hypothesis change?"

Dr. Seward pointed to the map behind him and the colorful lines and dots that indicated security measures I couldn't hope to understand. "His best opportunity would have been Thursday, the day of the activation, before we could get you organized here and figure out what happened. But it's two days later, we have tripled the watch around the island, and there aren't enough Banes in any one part of it to successfully revolt. Not even with Specter on the outside."

His logic worked, even for me, but it wouldn't always be

five against one (or twelve, if we managed to locate the seven of us still MIA). The other Banes would escape; new Metas would—I assumed—discover their powers and be free to wander. Sides would be chosen just like before. And this new Ranger team had inexperience to spare.

I was teetering on information overload, and had no idea how the others were faring. The tension in the room became a living thing, as tangible as our own bodies. Gaining these powers had seemed like a miraculous turning point in my life—a chance to finally have a purpose greater than struggling to pay my rent each month. Powers that could have saved lives. Now that miracle felt like a death sentence.

"So the plan, as I see it," I said, "is to stay out of Specter's way until our missing seven are brought in, to keep an eye on Manhattan Island, and to train any newly activated Metas as they're found to keep them on our side. Does that sound about right?"

"Yes, that's right," Seward said. He hesitated, but didn't add anything to his statement.

"Dr. Seward?" Gage said. "Your heart rate just spiked, in case you forgot I can hear that. What aren't you telling us?"

Dr. Seward dropped his gaze to the table. The good doctor was hiding something, and it didn't take Gage's honed senses to know it. We heard it in what he didn't say, and how he avoided eye contact with us. I stood up, drawing confidence from the stance, and braced my palms flat on top of the table.

"What aren't you telling us, Dr. Seward?" I asked. "Why haven't you found the other seven?"

"We know where three of them are," he told the table.

A frozen fist seized my insides and squeezed.

"That's good, right?" Renee asked. She seemed genuinely confused and unaffected by Seward's words.

"No, Flex, it's not good," Dr. Seward said. "Their bodies are being flown in by private helicopter. They'll arrive by evening."

Her cobalt eyes widened, and I looked away. I could see in her what I felt in myself. Loss without actually losing is an odd sensation to describe. Even though I hadn't seen the other seven in half a lifetime, knowledge of three of their deaths seared through my heart and left hollow pain behind.

Gage's hand covered mine. I dropped back into my chair.

"I'm sorry," Dr. Seward said. "I didn't want to say anything until we were certain."

"That they were really dead?" William asked.

"No, until we were certain Specter killed them. Because of the nature of Specter's powers, we can't be sure yet. He possesses and uses his victims to commit the crimes, so they aren't always distinguishable from standard murders. So far, Trance and Cipher are the only two who can honestly say they faced off with Specter. None of the other deaths had witnesses."

I wanted to ask their names and how they'd died, but couldn't bring myself to do it and not feel morbid. No one else asked, and I was glad. We would find out soon enough which of our childhood friends were dead.

"Maybe if we'd been allowed to grow up near each other," Gage said calmly, "they wouldn't have had to die alone."

"Possibly," Dr. Seward said. "You children faced a horrible trauma that day, watching your parents and mentors and classmates die. I wish I could tell you why and how your powers were taken away, or why and how they were given back. At the time, we thought keeping you together would be more painful than separating you. We thought it would save you the pain of growing up with constant reminders of the heartache of all that you'd lost."

I quirked an eyebrow. "I think I speak for everyone when I say that we still grew up with the heartache. You have no idea how many therapists I kept in business over the years."

"Regardless, MHC thought it was doing the right thing by separating you."

"What's that saying?" Gage asked. "The road to hell is lined with good intentions?"

Amen.

Dr. Seward grunted, but didn't otherwise reply.

"It's been two days since we got our powers back," Renee said. "Do people know about it yet? I mean, I guess they would, but how much do they know?"

"ATF has spread the word to other government law enforcement agencies," Dr. Seward said. "It's being shared with state and local authorities, as well, so that they can be prepared when we go public with your return. They want to control the flow of information as much as possible. The last thing this country needs is widespread panic."

"You think?"

"Yes, I do. But that shouldn't be your focus right now. There'll be time to deal with the media once your peers are safe."

"So the plan changes," I said. "We find the other four

before Specter does, and we get them here safely. Everything else takes a back seat to that goal."

"Trance—"

I cut Seward's protest off with a snap of my fingers and the amethyst flare of an orb. "You were saying?"

He looked away. I felt no satisfaction in my small victory. We were all on the same side. We couldn't waste time and energy fighting one another.

"So how do we find them?" Renee asked.

All Ranger eyes landed on me. I sat there dumbly for ten seconds before I realized they wanted an answer. I wasn't a cop; I had no idea how to go about finding missing people. Besides, Gage had been our leader once.

"We find their last known whereabouts and go from there," Gage said into the silence. "The only way to do this quickly is to split up."

Renee blanched. "Alone?"

"No, not alone," I said. "We go two and three. It's not ideal, but we're an odd five."

"Four," Dr. Seward said. "I don't want Trance out in the field until we know more about her powers."

I bristled. "If you want me to stay here, you'll have to shackle me. I am now the most powerful person in this room. I am not being left behind."

He seemed poised to argue, then deflated like a leaking balloon. If I'd inherited anything from my father, it was his stubborn nature, and Seward knew it. "Fine," he said.

"Good." I turned back to the others. "So who picks the teams?"

Eight

Tempest

I had earned the unofficial position of team leader—by standing up to Dr. Seward, or out of respect for my dad's former position as a unit leader, or quite possibly because I could blast a hole in the wall as easy as blinking, take your pick—so they let me divide us into teams. I wasn't sure I wanted the job. It meant being responsible for the lives of four people who weren't me. More when we found the others.

I convinced myself I had divvied us up based on our powers, but that wasn't true. Gage and I had started this journey together, and I owed him for the motel. Experience in something (not likely carpentry, and I couldn't imagine him as a police officer) gave him investigative instincts that I sorely lacked. Granted, what I lacked in experience I could make up for with bravado, but no amount of blustering would protect us when the chips were down. So I picked us as the duo.

The others agreed to be the trio, and we reassembled ten minutes later on the roof of the Base. Flex and Caliber had their personal Voxes. Their cases snapped nicely to the belts of their uniforms. Onyx couldn't keep one, because each time he shifted he lost anything except those special bikini briefs. Mine clipped nicely on my jeans.

Standing there on the roof, a united team for the first time, we just looked at each other. Gage and I were out of uniform, but we still fit. Our oddball quintet of two shape-shifters, a strongman, a power blaster, and a man with five enhanced senses fit together in a way that regular people could never understand. We'd been raised to do this. No matter where our lives had taken us these last fifteen years, this was where we were meant to end up.

"You sure you're up to this, T?" Flex asked.

"Definitely," I said. "We need to bring the others home."

"Let's make sure we bring ourselves home, too," Caliber said.

We just found each other seemed to dangle at the end of his comment. And I wholeheartedly agreed. "Good luck," I said.

Flex grinned. "Back at you."

Gage and I climbed into a private helicopter, piloted by a serious-looking fellow in military fatigues. He didn't introduce himself, so I designated our pilot Flyboy. Our first assignment was Angela "Trickster" Bourne, last known address in Kingman, Arizona. She did visual retail merchandising for some home furnishing company, and her work took her all over the state. She had been on the road the night of the re-activation, somewhere between Flagstaff and Kingman, and no one had seen her since.

That stretch of desert seemed like the best place to start.

All those lonely miles offered a lot of opportunities for Angela to have been ambushed.

Our helicopter might have been state of the art, but it was still damned noisy, so Gage and I spent the trip in silence. I practiced making orbs until Flyboy warned me about setting off the copter's internal fire sensors. Under threat of a dousing, I quit and spent the remainder of the thirty-minute flight trying to remember what Angela looked like. Pale complexion, curly blond hair, green eyes. She could create illusions of her own image, copying herself up to a dozen times. She had stood up and faced the final Bane attack, creating twelve more targets for the adults bearing down on us. For one brief moment, I hadn't been sure which was the real Angela. Then our powers disappeared and took her illusions with them.

Ten minutes across the Arizona border, we flew low over rocky terrain, marred by the occasional dry gulch and freestanding mountain. The Grand Canyon was somewhere north of us, the city of Flagstaff south, and miles of open countryside in between. Flyboy made a turn toward I-40.

I was the first to spot the tornado. It danced across the desert, at least six stories tall, zigging and zagging like a drunken top beneath a bright, cloudless sky.

"There." I pointed.

Gage leaned across my lap to look out the side window. "Five gets you twenty that's Ethan, but what the hell is he doing?"

"He's got to be inside the funnel."

"I don't think so."

The funnel proved Gage right by ejecting the twisted

hulk of a pulverized pickup truck. It flew through the air like a wad of tissue paper, careened past us, and missed the helicopter by thirty feet, before landing by the side of a dirt road. It hit on its side—at least, I think so, because it was hard to discern its exact shape—and lay in a smoldering, dusty heap.

"Coming around," Flyboy said.

The copter swerved sideways, tossing me across Gage's lap. He caught my shoulders to steady me, and I looked up to see him smiling down at me. Embarrassed, I reached for the handlebar by the door and hauled myself upright. The funnel cloud was gone, the dirt and debris in its core settling back to the earth with a few scattered car parts.

Flyboy landed across the road from the wreck. I tossed my headset onto the seat and scrambled out of the copter. The chilly, swirling air surprised me. We must have been pretty far north, where the desert actually got cold in January.

Gage and I walked toward the wreck, wary of our unfamiliar surroundings. A few hills rose up a quarter mile away. Tall scrub trees dotted the landscape, providing some cover, and a thick shadow cut across the ground ten yards past the wreck. A dry gulch, if I correctly remembered the aerial view of the terrain. Good place for an air manipulator to hide.

An orb sparked from the tips of my fingers as I approached the car, more as a precaution than from any real sense of danger. As the old Trance, with my mostly inactive powers, I never would have been so bold. I probably wouldn't have left the safety of the copter. This unexpected gift emboldened me beyond simple caution. I found myself craving a confrontation, hoping for a chance to zap someone with an orb.

The realization stopped me short, and Gage slammed into my back.

"Trance? You okay?"

I blinked, clearing the thoughts away. This was no time for a self-assessment. I'd ponder the meaning behind my newfound bloodlust once we had the rest of the Rangers safely back at HQ—not in the middle of the desert, vulnerable to attack from all sides.

"I'm fine, sorry," I said. "Can you smell anyone?"

He didn't have a chance to try. Cold, gritty wind hit us like a giant hand and slapped me backward. I expected to go toppling, but Gage kept us upright against the sudden gale. Squinting through the sand, I released my orb in the general direction of the earth fracture. It hit on the edge and splattered dirt and rock into the air. Bad idea, because the intensity of the wind increased.

"Cut it out!" I shouted into the tempest and received a mouthful of dirt. I coughed, spat. It became increasingly difficult to take a good breath.

Gage shifted to my side, still hovering protectively, and cupped his hands around his mouth. "Ethan! Turn it off, windbag!"

The gale ceased. Spinning grit stopped in midair like the freeze frame of a film, and then fell to the ground in a puff. I spat out a wad of mud, disgusted by the bitter taste. Grateful for fresh air.

"There," Gage said, pointing.

A head of flaming red hair appeared over the lip of the gulch, rising slowly until a face was revealed, followed by a neck and shoulders. He stared. We didn't move, and neither did he.

"Okay," I said to Gage, "I could never win stare-downs without cheating. Should we go over there?"

"He's terrified. I can hear his rapid heartbeat and smell his perspiration. I can smell blood, too. He might be hurt."

I took an instinctual step forward, concerned about possible injury now that Gage brought it to my attention. "Ethan? It's Teresa. Do you remember me?"

He turned his head a few degrees, back and forth, as if looking from me to Gage and back again. His head dipped back out of sight. I almost screamed with frustration. Ethan reappeared a few yards further left, carrying someone in his arms. Her head and legs hung limply, arms tucked against her body. Even from a distance, I saw the blood covering her clothes, staining the front of his shirt.

I started running, my boots crunching over rock and sand. I reached them first. Ethan "Tempest" Swift had a round face, thin lips and hazel eyes, and a smattering of freckles along the ridge of his nose. Save the pain bracketing his eyes, he appeared uninjured. Not like the last time we'd seen each other, when he'd been shot in the shoulder and was still desperately trying to help. Not hiding from the Bogeyman.

He held Angela in his arms, and I knew without checking her pulse that she was dead. Blood had seeped from a variety of deep gashes on her face and chest. My heart constricted, squeezed by a steel band of grief. Looking at her adult face, I barely recalled the preteen she had been, and yet her death hurt like we'd been friends for years. I had lost a part of me; we all lost a part of each other every time one of us died.

"Hey, Teresa," Ethan said. "Gage." His voice carried the fatigue of an elderly man and more pain than any human being should be forced to carry.

"What happened?" Gage asked.

"Angela and I ran into each other in Flagstaff and decided to travel together. Twenty minutes ago someone ran us off the road. She wasn't wearing her seat belt and was pretty banged up when we crashed. The other driver got out of the car and his eyes—"

Specter.

"—were bright yellow. He fired a shotgun at us a few times. I threw him back with some wind and got Angela out of the car. He tried to run us down again. Clipped me, but he got her hard. I picked her up and hid her in that ditch, but by the time I got us there . . ." His voice cracked. "Then I called up the biggest damned cyclone I could manage."

I looked over my shoulder at the ball of metal that had once been a truck. "The driver is still inside?"

"Yeah." He shifted the weight of Angela's body, which couldn't have been much. She was a tiny woman, maybe five feet tall and small-boned, but Ethan was a thin guy and the muscles in his arms vibrated from the strain.

Gage eased her body out of Ethan's arms, releasing him from the burden. Ethan's shoulders slumped. I slipped my arm around his waist, offering silent support while we walked back to the waiting copter. There was little use in inspecting the hunk of metal. Specter's latest host was hamburger.

"I remember the hair, but what's with the eyes?" Ethan asked.

"I got back the wrong powers," I said. "Something like what my grandmother had."

He stumbled. "Really? Anyone else get them back wrong?"

"Not so far. In addition to my sparkling amethyst eyes, I can blast things with purple energy orbs. It would be more fun if it didn't make me so damned hungry."

The copter blades kicked up dust, and I coughed, desperate for a drink of water after taking in that mouthful of sand.

Ethan raised his right hand. The wind whirled in a different direction at first and then formed into one solid, swirling motion. In seconds, he created a tunnel of clean air, its walls made of shifting layers of desert sand. It led right up to the side of the copter, and it made the rest of our legwork easier.

Once we were strapped back in, and Angela was laid at our feet, I rifled through the supply compartment above my head. I felt around and retrieved two bottles of water and tossed one to Ethan. I gulped from mine, swishing it around to clear out the grit. Only when I was ready to spit did I realize we'd already taken off. I looked around the small interior. Nothing.

Everyone eats a peck of dirt in their lifetime (or so I'd heard once), so I swallowed. And then guzzled more water. My stomach churned from drinking so much on an empty stomach. The filling lunch of chicken and pasta seemed like days ago.

Ethan passed his bottle over to Gage, and then asked, "Who else is with you guys?"

As we told him about Specter and the three dead Rangers, he sank deeper into his seat and crossed his arms over his chest.

<Trance? Onyx.>

My hand jerked, spilling a bit of water on my T-shirt. I sat, still as stone, unsure where the voice came from.

<Trance, are you there? Onyx here.>

Gage nudged me with his elbow, and I understood. I retrieved my Vox and pressed the silver button. "Onyx, it's Trance, go ahead."

<Scythe is dead. His apartment burned down last night. We are heading to our last location now. What is your status?>

I bit my tongue hard. Every death hurt like a physical blow, in a way that I couldn't explain. The men seemed sad, but not quite as affected by the news.

"Trickster is dead, too," I replied. "We have Tempest. He's a little tired, but uninjured. We're heading back to HQ."

<*Entendido*, Trance. I will contact you when we have located Frost. Onyx out.>

I slipped the Vox back into my belt with shaking fingers. Half of us dead in two days; it didn't seem possible.

Gage's hand curled around mine and squeezed tight. "Your heartbeat just spiked," he said softly. "You okay?"

"No, not really."

I leaned my head against his shoulder, mourning the deaths of my old schoolmates. Each one tore at my heart, and I wanted it to stop. If it hurt so badly to lose five people I hadn't seen since I was ten, how would it feel to lose one I had back in my life? To lose Renee or Marco or Ethan or William? To lose Gage?

We had to find Specter and quickly. I couldn't lose them, not when I felt needed for the first time in my adult life. Needed and part of something. Able to make a positive difference.

Even if it was only temporary.

Nine

Meltdown

Full physicals from Dr. Seward seemed to be the standard greeting for new Rangers. He was waiting for us on the roof of the Base when we landed, and his team whisked Angela's body and Ethan off to the Medical Center. During the flight, my state of nausea doubled. It had stayed in check while we were airborne, but as soon as my feet touched solid ground, my stomach twisted. I chewed on the inside of my cheek and concentrated on that pain as I followed Gage off the roof. I wanted to lie down and curl into a ball until the queasiness went away.

"I'm sure Dr. Seward will want a full report as soon as he's done poking and prodding Ethan," he said once we were in the elevator.

"No doubt," I said between clenched teeth. I leaned against the wall, concerned by the sudden lavender haze that tinged the corners of my vision. Just like when I overloaded fighting Specter. Not good.

"Teresa, are you okay?" He was staring at me.

I pasted on a fake smile. "Just a little overwhelmed. Long day, and a lot of bad news."

"I hear that."

Yeah, I bet he did.

The elevator stopped on ground level, and we stepped out into the lobby.

"Do you want me to walk you back to your room?" he asked.

The offer was endearing, but no. If I just lay down for a while, I was certain I'd feel better. It was a powers hiccup, nothing serious. Mostly I wanted to get back to my room without vomiting. That weakness was reserved for me and no one else.

"Actually, I'm kind of hungry," I said, and hated that I was lying to him. "Tell you what, why don't you run ahead and make sure the kitchen is cooking something? I'm going to stop by the ladies' room. There has to be one down here."

He smiled. "Are you ever not hungry?"

Right now, very much not hungry. If he scanned carefully for my heart rate, he'd know I was lying. I grinned back. "Call it a job hazard. Now go, I'll catch up."

"I'll save you a seat."

I waited until he passed through the outer doors, leaving me alone, and I then collapsed to my knees, arms tight around my middle. Chills and shivers sent goose flesh crawling across my neck and back. A strong shudder tore along my spine and sent cramps into my midsection. The lavender haze turned the green rug a strange shade of brown. I closed my eyes.

"Help me," I whispered.

If I couldn't get a handle on this, Dr. Seward would strap me back into a hospital bed, and I didn't want that. I didn't want to be an experiment, tested and examined until they found their elusive answers to my problem. Crippling cramps and purple vision were pretty damned big problems, and meant days—if not weeks—of testing. I didn't have that kind of time, not with five dead Rangers and a homicidal Bane on the loose.

I forced my eyes open; the world had gone purple, like someone had taped a sheet of colored plastic over my vision. Another cramp seized my guts, and I swallowed hard. On my left, a small sign indicated locker rooms down the hall. I took a deep breath, launched out of my kneeling position, and bolted. I overshot the bathroom door and almost crashed into a wall as I turned around.

Ignoring the fact that it was the men's room, I shoved the door open, ran into the nearest stall, and vomited into the toilet. It didn't take long to empty what little was in my stomach. Mostly water and grit particles (probably that sand I had swallowed), all colored purple like the rest of my world.

The pressure in my abdomen decreased without going away completely. I spat again, trying to rid my mouth of the sour taste of bile, and pushed the manual button to flush. I pulled up on shaky legs to the tune of water swirling and stumbled over to one of the sinks. After a few mouthfuls of tap water to clean out that horrid taste, I hazarded a look at myself in the mirror.

My pupils were dilated, but I couldn't judge any other changes with my eyes acting so strangely. Now I knew how Renee felt when she looked in the mirror and saw blue skin and wished it had been ivory.

"It figures," I said to my reflection. "Not only did you possibly inherit your grandmother's powers, but now it looks like you're allergic to them. Bravo."

The cramping subsided enough to convince me that I wouldn't internally combust during dinner. I washed my hands, checked my hair for any residual barf, and left the safety of the men's room, praying for the strength to get through the day.

Eating food that looked the wrong color—on top of having an upset stomach—made dinner an exercise in durability and stamina. The two-person kitchen staff surprised me with a selection of roast beef, parslied potatoes, and steamed carrots, and I surprised Gage by taking only a small helping. I made a joke about watching my figure and being hungry again in an hour. He didn't push, and I appreciated that.

He did, however, watch me like a hawk as we ate. I tried to ignore the concerned glances and keep up idle banter. We hadn't heard from the other group in almost two hours, and that elephant stalked the room and dulled conversation.

The cafeteria sparkled in a way that the rest of the building did not. Tiled floors were freshly mopped, each homey wooden table wiped down and waxed. The chairs were wood, with upholstered seats (the exact color I'd have to figure out later), and quite comfortable. We were the only people in a room large enough to hold two hundred.

Gage pushed half-eaten roast beef around his plate and asked, "Is this how you usually spend your Saturday evenings?"

"Absolutely not," I replied. "I used to slave away at three different menial, dead-end jobs to pay my rent and buy food, because most good employers have a problem hiring convicted felons, so I blew off my steam any night I had a few free hours. I'd find a nice, dirty dive bar within walking distance of my place, hustle drinks from losers I wouldn't let touch me with a three-meter pole, dance away my frustrations, and then go home and sleep it off."

"That sounds exhausting."

"It is, especially in heels."

His left eye twitched with . . . what? Annoyance? I almost added to my statement, wanting to assure him that I hadn't slept with any of my dancing partners, only I had no need to defend my (lack of) sex life.

"So what about you?" I asked. "How do you normally spend your Saturday nights?"

"Saturday was movie night," he said after a moment's hesitation. "Since the only open cinema was in the city, it was a once-a-week trek. Sometimes I'd go with a buddy from work, sometimes I'd have a date. Usually I went alone. Didn't matter much what was playing or who was in it."

He mentioned work again. I didn't have the energy to pursue the opening, especially if he pulled his standard deflection. "I can't imagine you had a lot of film options, with there only being four movie studios left in Vancouver."

A few years before the War even began, serious inflation and a failing economy had already forced the consolidation of several major studios. One year into the fighting, a showdown between a fire-starter Bane named Blaze and a water-manipulator named Ariel led to the devastation of everything south of I-10, all the way to Anaheim. The remains of a theme park that had been shut down a decade ago were featured heavily on the newscasts that week.

Smaller battles in Burbank and Van Nuys added to the ruination of a once-sprawling metropolis. Residents fled as neighborhoods were shut down and evacuated. It was the first major city to fall during the five-year conflict.

In a last-ditch effort to save themselves, the final three studios relocated to Canada. The money went with it, leaving the rest of Hollywood a virtual ghost town. With its main sources of income gone, L.A. struggled hardest to recover during the postwar years. The folks left behind had rebuilt small communities of services, businesses, unremarkable restaurants, and bars. It would never be what it was during the Corps' heyday.

"People want interactive entertainment," Gage said, "not moving pictures in two dimensions. It's a shame, really, because some of the films from a hundred years ago are really quite good."

"I admit, I am not a fan," I replied. "You'll have to introduce me some time."

"I'd like that."

The purple potatoes on my plate looked less and less appetizing the longer I stared at them. Movement caught my eye, just over Gage's right shoulder. Someone was standing near the far wall, by the door. Even from a distance of twenty feet, the woman's eyes flashed brightly, the only part of her that wasn't dulled, almost opaque. That was silly, though—people weren't see-through.

"Teresa? What are you staring at?"

"The woman over there."

He turned around. I blinked and she was gone, like she'd never existed. That was impossible. I would have seen her leave, or heard her shoes squeaking on the tile floor. Gage didn't say anything, just faced forward and folded his hands on top of the table. I waited for him to speak and realized too late he was clocking me; listening, smelling, observing everything he could.

"You're not okay, are you?" he asked.

"I'm just a little off. It's been a stressful day, Gage. I think I need to lie down for a while."

"Maybe Dr. Seward—"

"Forget it."

I stood up and the ground dipped. I gripped the table and stayed upright somehow. The tabletop was vibrating. I backed up, hit my chair, and plunked back down into the seat. A pair of handprints marred the table's wood surface, burned right into the grain, dark enough to appear black even through the purple glaze.

"Teresa—"

"Don't!"

I only meant to hold up my hand as a "stop right there" gesture, and then something entirely unexpected happened—a haze of purple energy, like a wad of cotton candy, surged from my palm and hit Gage directly in the chest. He fell backward, bounced off a nearby chair, and landed on the ground in a groaning heap.

Oh, God. "No . . ."

The deep-seated nausea returned, twisting my stomach in its iron grip. The purple hue over my vision deepened to a shade one step up from black. I ran to the door, propelled by panic. I thought I'd explode if I couldn't release the energy churning inside me.

Sight dwindling into nonexistence, I continued on by instinct until I slammed against a glass door. It shattered. I felt no glass cutting me, no bursts of pain. My boots crunched across the littered shards until chilly air brushed my face. The sun must have set; I couldn't feel its gentle warmth.

I tilted my head toward the sky, eyes wide and unseeing, and let go. The explosion of energy surged upward with the dizzying force of a water hydrant bursting open. Up to the sky it went, and I felt it more than saw it. Felt it until I had nothing left, and the blackness rocked me to unconsciousness.

Ten

Medical Ward

The strong, medicinal odor of antiseptic placed me back in the Medical Center before I fully registered waking up. My body was too heavy, as though held down under a thick, oppressive blanket. I was also warm—so warm I wanted to stay asleep. Cocooned in velvet, rocked by indifference, avoiding all purple.

Gage.

"Gage!" I shouted the word louder than I thought possible, torn from my dry throat by panic and fear. My eyelids peeled apart, letting in glaring light. Yellowish, fluorescent light.

Warm hands pressed against my arm, and then, "I'm right here, Teresa, I'm fine."

A shadow distorted my vision, and it took some effort to pull him into focus. Then he was there, tired and concerned, but unhurt. The silver in his eyes sparkled as he took me in.

"I'm sorry," I said, groping blindly for his hands. They were warm, strong, comforting. I had almost killed him and the idea of it made my insides freeze.

"It's okay." He pulled me close, and I snaked my arms around his waist and pressed my face into his shoulder. He held me, his heart thumping wildly against mine.

"It's not okay." My words sounded muffled, ineffective against the fabric of his cotton shirt. "I couldn't control it, Gage. I didn't know what I was doing. I should have said something."

"I'm not hurt; it's fine."

His voice rumbled in his chest, a sound as soothing as the gentle way he stroked my hair with his hand. My stomach fluttered. The cramps were gone, replaced by hunger. That final dispersal of power had released whatever force was building up, turning my insides to mush. I felt tired, but better, and was reluctant to let go of him.

After a few minutes, he helped me lie back against the pillow, and then raised the bed into a sitting position. Same room as before, complete with a small dent where I'd hit the door this morning. Yesterday?

"How long this time?" I asked.

"Just a few hours." Gage perched on the side of the bed. "It's a little after midnight."

"Are the others back yet?"

"An hour ago." The change in tone alarmed me.

"Frost?"

He picked at a piece of nonexistent lint on the bed sheet. "It looks like she got into it with Specter. She was hurt pretty badly when they found her, had lost a lot of blood. Dr. Seward is with her down the hall. He'll be along soon."

"Is she going to die?"

"I don't know."

Grief came like a gut punch, as strong as before. Five dead, one critical. Only six alive and ready to fight. Five if Dr. Seward strapped me down to the bed and ran his damnable tests. Sedatives were the only things that would keep me out of this, and only in strong doses. I had the power to stop Specter, I knew I did. I just had to learn to control it.

"So I guess I'm stuck here overnight, huh?" The idea depressed me.

"At least. Dr. Seward wants to keep an eye on you for a while, make sure you don't go nova again. You know, you turned the clouds purple for about thirty seconds."

"I'm lucky I didn't bring down an airplane. At first I thought having new powers meant that I was chosen for something special. Now I wonder if it was just some sort of cosmic mistake."

The door swung open. Dr. Seward and William entered in a mirror image of yesterday, with grimmer expressions. William moved stiffly, as if afraid of getting too close.

Great, now I was scaring my teammates. "So what's the diagnosis, Doc?" I asked, uninterested in contrived greetings. "Am I dying?"

I meant it as a joke, but Dr. Seward didn't smile. He just looked at me. I've heard the expression "blood ran cold," just never understood it until it happened. Every extremity went numb, from my face to my toes. I think I forgot to breathe for a few seconds, and then Gage's hand tightened around mine. I sucked in a ragged breath through clenched teeth.

"I believe you may be, Trance," Seward finally said. His

voice had that cool, doctor-mode thing going on, but his face was a study in frustration—like he couldn't quite believe he'd come up with such a diagnosis. I couldn't quite believe it, either.

"What do you mean?" Gage asked.

"Please understand, this is still very new to us. We've never experienced a powerless Ranger receiving different powers before, so no one knew what to expect." He scratched his unshaven chin, radiating frustration. "Traditionally a Ranger's body adapts to its power, especially when the power develops before adolescence. Your body was attuned to your original Trance powers. You weren't built to channel this much energy. It's like forcing one hundred megahertz of energy through a cable capable of carrying a quarter of that."

"I *am* allergic." The words escaped before I could stop them. It had seemed crazy the first time the thought occurred to me—not so crazy now. This was stupid. I couldn't stop Specter if I was dead from power overload. "You're wrong, you have to be. We just need to figure how to get that extra current through, is all."

"You are not a lamp in need of rewiring, Trance, you're a human being."

"I'm MetaHuman. My body will adapt."

"Maybe." Seward stepped closer, as stern as a prison warden. "Every time you use your powers, you run the risk of stroke, heart attack, an aneurysm, and any number of things that are equally fatal."

"Yeah, and Specter could jump into you next time you

take a nap and then take me out with a syringe and an air bubble," I retorted. "I get it, okay? Don't you dare try to make me feel sorry for myself. Just give me whatever drugs you can, and let me do my job. Which hasn't changed, by the way. We still have an island prison to watch and a homicidal Bane to neutralize."

"We're on that," William said. He still looked like I had just killed his cat, but his voice retained every bit of its formidable tone. "Flex and I are heading to New York for first patrol at 0600 hours. We'll rotate every thirty-six hours. The four that are still here can work on locating Specter."

I turned his words over in my mind. It was a good plan. "Okay."

William nodded and left, as if his only reason for being there was getting my approval. They should learn to take orders from someone else in case their faith turned out to be misplaced. I didn't want to lead, any more than I wanted to die.

No, I couldn't think that way. This was a minor setback. I'd figure out how to channel the energy, even if I had to blast it to the sky every three days.

"We'll get you started on metabolic supplements," Dr. Seward said. "For now, get some rest. At least until morning. And I do mean rest."

"I'll rest, I promise," I said.

With another pointed look, Dr. Seward left and pulled the door behind him. I stared at it, unsure why he'd done that.

"I promise to be a perfect gentleman," Gage said, "if you let me stay with you tonight."

I arched both eyebrows; I'd have been less surprised if he'd asked to shave my head bald and paint it with green polka dots.

He chuckled. "I didn't mean it like that, Teresa. We don't know when or where Specter will attack again. You've just been through a trauma, and I'd feel better staying close than being halfway across the complex."

I wanted him to stay; I was also scared for him to do so. Not that I'd ever admit to the fear—a fear that had nothing to do with thinking he'd hurt me, not like in the motel—so I put on some false bravado. Teasing him was easier than trying to understand why I trusted him so easily when I'd made an art out of keeping men at arm's length. "Perfect gentleman, huh? That's very selfless, Gage. You aren't even going to try to steal a kiss? Something to remember me by, just in case Seward is right about my life expectancy?"

"That's not funny."

"It wasn't really a joke." Our lives were full of so many uncertain variables. Always at the top of that list was death, as we both knew well. I hated entertaining the idea that Seward might be right, but could I afford to ignore the possibility? "Look, I'm sorry—"

His head dipped, and his lips found mine, silencing the halfhearted apology. The kiss was tender, almost platonic, and it sent a shock of excitement through my system that settled deep in my belly, leaving me breathless. And frightened. I hadn't expected him to actually kiss me.

It was brief, but wonderful.

Lips still tingling, I lowered the bed to a better angle for sleeping. "Don't tell me you're going to spend the night in that chair," I said, pointing.

He eyeballed the hard, plastic piece of furniture in question. "Well, it seemed a better alternative to the floor."

I shifted over until half of the smallish bed was empty; he stood still, hesitating.

"You said you'd be a perfect gentleman."

"This wasn't quite what I had in mind."

"I know. And don't take this wrong, but get your ass in my bed. I'm exhausted and want to sleep."

He considered me a moment, his expression a mix of amused and wary—as if he thought I'd shock him with an orb if he got frisky. Not that I had any fear of that happening. Not with Gage. He shed his belt and sneakers, then slid under the thin blanket with me, still clad in jeans and shirt. I turned away to give him more room in the small bed, and I was careful to not tense when his elbow brushed the small of my back.

My inner ten-year-old smiled at his nearness, while my external grown-up slowly relaxed. I closed my eyes and drifted, lingering close to wakefulness, soothed by the sound of Gage's steady breathing.

Eleven

Medical Ward II

T he monitor above the bed casts the only light in the room. A gentle blue glow outlines the shape of the door and the woman in bed. Her head is shaved bald and dotted with wired electrodes. A tube down her throat leads to a machine that breathes for her. The pulse monitor beeps slow, steady. Her skin is smooth, ageless.

I should know her, but I don't.

Her face unfocuses, sharpens, unfocuses. She opens her eyes. Pale light glints off lovely luminescence. I know those eyes.

Who are you? *I ask.*

Her eyes flicker sideways, at a second bed. Another shape on it, impossible to see. She looks at me again. Her words come, though her lips don't move. Stay the course. *Her voice is ethereal and lingers like a mist.*

I fall into her eyes, into an abyss of color and light and sound and warmth as inspiring as it is terrifying. Voices speak all around me, unified and alone, one and many. Sanity and madness exist together, and I burn.

A pleasant warmth all along my back greeted me as I woke, and I was grateful for it. Grateful to Gage for being there last night, and even more grateful that he was still there in the morning. I held onto the moment of pure contentment as long as possible, unsure I'd get it again.

Until my very full bladder forced me out of bed.

The dream stayed vividly on my mind during breakfast. I didn't mention it to Gage. Getting the wrong powers was no accident, I felt certain of that now. Had this woman I dreamed of taken them away? Been responsible for giving them back?

No one truly knew how the first MetaHumans received their powers. Reports of people with superhuman powers existed as far back as the American Civil War. The Pinkertons employed Metas, and some historians have argued that Billy the Kid and Harry Houdini were Metas. As our numbers grew in the early part of the twentieth century, so did our notoriety.

It wasn't until our people were formally asked for help during the First World War that the divisions between us took hold, and it planted the seeds of what would become the schism between MHC's Ranger Corps and the more nebulous "bad guy" Banes. And, while we could narrow down the start of the Rangers and Banes, we still didn't know where Metas came from to begin with; no one seemed to know the source of it all. God. Radiation. Space aliens. Evolution. The words held no real meaning; they didn't rationalize what we were, or why we existed. We did, we didn't, we did again.

Dr. Seward came in as we finished eating breakfast. I half expected to see William at his side, as he'd been every other time. Then I remembered that he was in New York with Renee. "Sleep well, Trance?"

"Pretty well, yeah." Except for the strange dream.

"All of your vitals have returned to normal levels, so you're free to return to your room. I would like you to come back after lunch for some tests."

"What kind of tests?"

"I want to see how your body reacts to the use of your powers and study its absorption rate. Your electrolyte levels were dangerously low yesterday, which is one of the reasons you felt so sick. If we can figure out a way to supplement your system with nutrients, it won't be as dangerous for you to use your powers when you need to."

"So we *are* rewiring the lamp." Maybe I wasn't dying after all. That would be great.

He nodded. "Over time, your body may adapt, but it also may not. This isn't a cure, just a trial run. You still need to limit your power usage today, until we run our tests."

"I will try, I swear."

"I'll keep an eye on her," Gage said.

I did not need a babysitter. "How's Frost?"

"Still in a coma," Dr. Seward replied. "There's little we can do for her now, except wait and hope."

"Can I see her?"

"Of course."

————————

Janel "Frost" Murphy looked like a ghost against the stark white bedsheets. Her silver hair framed her narrow face in a limp curtain. Deep purple bruises shadowed the skin below her eyes, the only noticeable color on her face. Bandages covered her throat and arms, leaving just a few patches of translucent skin visible.

I shivered and could see my breath in the room. Janel liked cold; the temperature must have been to keep her comfortable. I wanted to hold her hand, but was afraid. Her cold skin would only get me thinking she was dead, and I didn't want to think that way. We needed her.

I remembered the tall, timid twelve-year-old she'd been those last few weeks before being sent to New York. She'd mastered her power over ice by the age of nine, but she resisted using it. She'd given Mellie severe frostbite the year before, when she first heard that her father had been killed in battle. No one blamed her for the accident, but Janel blamed herself. She tried to withdraw from the rest of us. Renee refused to let her. She and I smothered Janel with friendship and understanding, and after a few months, Janel started smiling again. She taught me how to French-braid my hair. And she fought so bravely that day in Central Park.

"We should have protected her," I said.

"We had no way of knowing," Gage replied, standing by my left shoulder. "They got there as fast as they could. She survived this long, Teresa. She'll make it through."

"There has to be a way to stop Specter, to keep him from doing this again."

"And we'll find it. You know that."

"I don't know that." Had that really just come out of my mouth? "I really, truly wish I did, Gage, but I don't. This is the most bizarre situation we've ever been in. We can't track Specter. We can't fight him because he always attacks in someone else's body. So far he's forced us to kill everyone he's possessed. And the minute defenses around Manhattan Island break down, we're royally screwed."

"I know all that, Teresa. It doesn't mean we can't win." Gage tugged my hand and tilted my chin until I looked up at him. "I need you to believe we can win. That you're going to live a long, happy life, and that we'll *win*."

My stomach quaked. I wanted so much to live a long life, to grow old and crotchety and eccentric. For Gage and Renee and Marco and the others to look back on this moment forty years from now and laugh at our worries. The lovely dream lingered in the shadows of my mind, with distant knowledge that I had some unfulfilled path yet to walk. A path Gage could not follow me down.

"I believe that you believe it," I said. "Can that be enough for now?"

"It'll have to be, I guess."

He didn't like my answer—I saw it in the downturn of his mouth and slant of his eyebrows. Why couldn't I just lie and pretend I believed it? For Gage's sake. He didn't look at me like a prize to be won or body to be conquered. He'd given me friendship and loyalty from the start, and I hated hurting him. He'd had enough hurt in his life without me compounding it—we both had—but I couldn't bring myself to lie. Lying felt like a worse sin than not believing.

"So what do we do now?" I asked.

"That's supposed to be my question, boss," Gage said.

Surprised, I looked up—at the twinkle in his eyes and the broad smile. He was looking at me to lead, even though I couldn't see our path any more clearly than he could. I was chosen—not only by my fellow Rangers, but by something bigger than any of us.

Lucky me.

"Do we have satellite coverage in this place?" I asked.

"In the conference room, I think."

"Good. I want to know what's happening in New York."

"Then, let's go find out."

Twelve

MetaHuman Control

A strange man and woman sat inside the conference room. I tensed, immediately checking their eyes for signs of yellow light. They didn't appear bothered by our arrival; in fact, they seemed to be expecting us.

The woman was older, in her late fifties, with immaculate silver-blond hair that seemed shellacked into place. She wore a plain blue business suit and skirt, and she had a black briefcase on the table in front of her. Her companion, a weasel of a man in an expensive black suit and an unfortunate comb-over, stood up as we entered. He had to be six inches shorter than me (and I'm not very tall) with an air of authority that demanded immediate attention. They made me wish Gage and I were in something other than blue jeans.

"Good morning, Trance," the man said. "Good morning, Cipher. It's good to meet both of you."

I remained partially in front of Gage and didn't move from the door's entrance. "I'd say it's good to meet you, too, only I don't know who you are."

"Direct and suspicious, I like that," the woman said. She had an accent, something of a New England snarl.

"Glad you approve."

Gage's hand squeezed my elbow, and I reined in the sarcasm. These folks had been given permission to come onto the property, so they were potential allies. I just had a thing about unannounced guests who smelled like federal agents.

The gentleman said, "My name is Agent Alexander Grayson. This is my partner, Agent Rita McNally."

Ding, ding, ding! "Let me guess," I said. "MetaHuman Control?"

"Unofficially," McNally said. "The MHC hung up its spurs when the War ended, but we are still ATF, and we're here to help."

"Help? I thought all you people did was monitor us and tell us how we could be doing things better. You don't get your hands dirty."

Grayson puckered his eyebrows. Any patience that previously existed was gone. "The Ranger Corps and the ATF have always worked together to provide assistance and to further cooperation between your people and the American public. Now that everyone's powers have returned, it seems pertinent to reestablish our working relationship as quickly as possible."

Gage gently pushed me into the room a few more inches. He continued to observe them silently, hopefully checking their vitals for telltale signs.

"You should both be talking to Dr. Seward if you want to get daily progress reports," I said. "I'm not a bureaucrat, nor am I a politician. I'm a Ranger, and I need to be in here doing my job, not a meet-and-greet."

"You're wrong, if you don't think you're a politician," McNally said. "The Ranger Corps presented an image to the American public, one of service and good deeds. That image was tarnished during the War, and if you wish to continue to operate with the support of the government, you'll need to do a little PR work."

"PR?"

"Public relations. Sing a song, do a dance, remind people you're the good guys."

I bristled at her tone. "Sing a song? Our predecessors destroyed New York City, Chicago, Salt Lake City, St. Louis, and Memphis. L.A, too, in case you didn't notice on the flight over the city. Not to mention polluting the Mississippi River, alkalizing the Great Salt Lake, and turning Lake Erie into a cesspool. I don't think a song and dance is going to appease anyone.

"In fact, maybe I was only ten years old, but I recall some Senate hearings where you people starting calling for the Rangers to be disbanded and all members—what was the word? Neutralized?"

The painful memories flooded forth, as if a gate had been opened to the past. The anger and resentment returned, as did the late-night arguments between my father and other adult Rangers. My father had wanted to fight, to stand up to the politicians who saw us as a blight, as no better than the Banes they so desperately tried to stop. The very Banes whom they had, in some ways, helped create. Others wanted us to quit protecting the innocents who called for our extinction.

"It was a different time, Trance," Grayson said.

"Really?" I thought of Cliff; his fear in the truck stop parking lot had been the same. Fear never really changed.

"Yes, and in case you aren't aware, the world is already taking notice of the increased activity here and around Manhattan. A lot of people saw that stunt you pulled yesterday with turning the sky purple—"

"Stunt?" Gage said, making that single word sound like the worst profanity in the universe. "She almost died yesterday, you arrogant bastard."

Grayson's eyes narrowed. "Irregardless—"

"That's not a word," Gage said.

The older man grunted and turned his frustrated glare onto his companion.

McNally folded her hands on the top of the table, the perfect picture of calm. "Look, the point is that we are not your enemies, but we are also not your friends. My duty is to protect this country and its citizens, and to ensure their continued safety. Powered Banes present a threat to that safety. Rangers running around without guidance or thought to consequences present a threat to that safety."

"No thought to consequences," I repeated, voice a little too high. My hands clenched, fingernails digging into my palms. "You people are truly arrogant, aren't you? Do you know how many of our parents and friends and siblings died trying to defend your precious citizens? *All* of them." My voice broke, and I swallowed hard. Saying it so bluntly ripped the scab off an unhealed wound. "They sacrificed themselves for you, and for the fifty billion other people on this planet. Remind the public of that. It's not like they could go swimming in Lake Erie before."

"And that's what you'll say when *you* people pollute another body of water?" Grayson asked. "It was for the greater good, go swim someplace else?"

"What do you expect from us? To get written permission before defending a town or bus or city block?"

"No, just to think about the consequences before you act."

"Such as people dying?"

"Such as cause and effect, Trance. It's taken this country a long time to recover from the destruction of the War, and many are still suffering. Millions remain homeless and unemployed, and violent crime is up in all urban areas."

"Crime overall is up from last year by point six percent," Gage said.

Grayson fell silent, seemingly stunned. I wanted to hug Gage for saving me there, because my utter fury at Grayson had stolen away any chance of a proper response.

"Unemployment was actually lower last year than in the previous six years," Gage continued. "But then you idiots in the government increased the minimum wage again, and suddenly more small businesses can't afford to pay employees. Now they get handouts, instead of your support, and you can't blame that on us. So don't try it."

McNally leaned forward, her attention fixed on Gage. "What about violent crime rates, Cipher?"

"They spiked after the end of the War. The Rangers were gone. The police and military were in turmoil. MHC had their heads up their asses congratulating themselves on stopping the MetaHuman problem, even though they didn't do shit."

Grayson flinched. Gage's attention snapped toward the balding man a moment, then turned back to McNally. His nostrils flared. He was concentrating on more than just the conversation.

"Cipher, how do you know all of this?" McNally asked.

Exactly what I wanted to know. His understanding of current events far exceeded mine, and while I appreciated his knowledge insofar as it shut Grayson up, it made me feel a little stupid. I didn't know enough to hold my own against a pair of federal agents—maybe I wasn't the one who should be leading this unit.

Gage made a rude noise. "I can read, Agent McNally. I was fifteen when we lost our powers. I watched the news and read the feeds and kept track of Congress. I may be a freak, but I'm not an idiot."

Grayson shook his head. "I don't think—"

"Stop it, Alexander," McNally said. "Perhaps we were too quick to judge you, and I apologize."

I bit my lip to keep silent. *No kidding* danced on the tip of my tongue.

She continued: "Please understand, there is no way to gauge how the public will react to your presence. Every poll taken just this year about the results of the War has the vast majority of responders in favor of the loss of Meta powers, and that is not encouraging. We need you to work with us."

Rita McNally was a straight-talker, and I liked that. I sort of liked her. She seemed to be taking the time to consider our point of view, and she seemed genuinely interested in helping us, rather than tossing around blame like Alexander Grayson. MHC had been Ranger allies for decades prior to the War. Hopefully we could keep that relationship open. Funding was nice.

"We understand that," I said, trying to keep my frustration out of my tone. "But we're not here to parade around and assure people that we're the heroes. We don't have the luxury or the time. There is one Bane on the loose right now, and he's already killed five of us and critically wounded a sixth. Our energy lies there, and in making sure no one else gets off Manhattan Island."

"Manhattan Island is quite secure," Grayson said.

"You'll excuse me if I don't take your word for it. Is there anything else we can do for you folks today?"

McNally stood up and unlocked her briefcase. "I will be holding a press conference this evening, outside of the headquarters gate, and announcing that the Rangers have been called once again to protect us. I'll do my best to avoid directly commenting on the deaths of your friends, or on the situation in New York, but I need you to be prepared for the backlash the next time you go out in public."

"Are our faces going to be plastered all over the media?"

"If necessary, yes. Costumes and code names only, of course. I will also be making a plea for any Metas in hiding to come forward and identify themselves. Once citizens learn just how outnumbered you are, they may start to panic. We need to increase your numbers."

"No kidding."

I needed to ask Dr. Seward about his progress in locating new Metas, those whose powers hadn't been identified before the end of the War and who were too young to have chosen a side. Or been located and adopted into one or the other, like Gage and Marco. Certainly whatever magic created us in the first place wouldn't give back our powers and then leave us so outnumbered. I hoped.

McNally produced a small business card and placed it on the conference table. "This is my direct contact information, Trance," she said. "Call me if you have questions or need any advice. I was part of MHC for twelve years."

"Thank you," I said. Something else occurred to me, although I hated bringing it up. "Listen, when Specter attacked us in Bakersfield he . . . um, there were two people—"

"The bodies have been taken care of."

"Oh. Thanks?"

She nodded.

Grayson stood and left the room without a word. McNally snapped her briefcase closed, picked it up, and strolled toward us. She passed Gage, and then paused next to me.

"You remind me of your father," she whispered. "Hinder was a good man. He would have been proud of you." To Gage, she added, "So was your brother."

I gaped at her back as she left the room.

"That was certainly strange," Gage said.

"Strange, but enlightening."

"Grayson was hiding something, I'm just not sure what. I could smell his fear, Teresa. He's afraid of us."

"So is most of the planet." I debated my next words, unable to take them back once they were said, and realized I meant them. "I think I trust Agent McNally, Gage. She seems to genuinely want to help us."

"I agree she wants to help."

"But?"

He shook his head. "I'm not sure. She was so careful with her reactions, so controlled."

"Like she'd practiced her answers in anticipation of meeting you?"

"Maybe."

Huh. It didn't mean she was lying, but it did give me pause. Made me think. I picked up the woman's business card. Home and cellular numbers, plus her extension at the ATF satellite office building in Burbank. I slipped the card into my back pocket. It felt odd to want to give my trust so easily to a woman I'd known less than fifteen minutes. Just as I'd given it to Gage, Renee, Dr. Seward, and my other fellow Rangers.

Should I give it or withhold it?

We were back at home in a place where we'd grown up and been trained for what we were doing now. I didn't know what my teammates' lives had been like for the last decade; they didn't know about mine. Would they still look at me like a leader if they knew I was a felon? Did it matter? I wasn't her anymore. We weren't who the MHC had made us when they sent us away. We were Rangers, and we couldn't do this if we didn't let ourselves trust each other.

I had to let myself trust them. Not so much the agents. Not until they earned it.

"Still want to know what's happening in New York?" Gage asked.

I nodded. "More than ever."

Thirteen

Interlude

Renee's blue face filled the monitor, obscuring my view of the room behind her. She blinked, frowned, and then stepped back to reveal the Manhattan Island Penitentiary's main control room. Serious-looking armed guards walked to and fro. Some carried files or paperwork, others nothing but an angry expression.

"Hey, T, you look a lot better," Renee said.

"Thanks." I stood in front of the monitor on our end, Gage by my side. It had taken the MIP guards almost thirty minutes to locate one of our people. Renee and William had been inspecting Bane activity in the north, among the remains of Harlem, when we called. Gage teased me incessantly about my lack of patience until someone finally rustled up Renee.

"Not a lot to report here," she said. "So far, the Banes aren't making much effort to escape the island. They're mostly keeping to themselves. Only a few have actively engaged their powers, but not against us or each other. One guy transmuted dirty water into sparkling clean water."

"That seems odd, doesn't it?" Gage asked.

"Pretty odd, yeah, but I'm not knocking a good thing. Disinterested Banes are ones we don't have to fight. They just seem . . . I don't know, out of sorts."

"What do you mean?"

"Kind of dazed, I guess. Like they got their powers back, only they don't remember what they're supposed to do with them. You think it's some sort of radical rehabilitation program that actually worked?"

"Dunno," I said. "Have you tried talking to the warden about it?"

"Repeatedly, but he doesn't have time for me or Caliber. I don't think he realizes that we're not the same as those guys he's been babysitting for a decade and a half. He sees blue skin and big muscles and thinks the worst of us."

"I know the feeling." Grayson had been no different in his judgment. At the moment, I didn't care why the Banes were so apathetic about their powers, as long as it kept them from all-out rebellion. Once we had Specter under control, maybe life wouldn't be as hard as I imagined.

"Just be careful out there, Flex," Gage said. "An ATF agent is doing a press conference today in Los Angeles, announcing our return. Once people know who we are, our anonymity is out the window."

Flex giggled. "He says to the girl with blue skin. Take a look at your team, Cipher. Most of us don't fit in at a family picnic. Although I can see Trance's look becoming a popular fashion statement."

"I hope not," I said.

"Purple contact lenses will be all the rage."

"Shut up, Flex."

"Remember, Flex," Gage said, "you're our eyes and ears out there. If you see anything suspicious, let us know immediately. We both got funny vibes from one of the agents they sent to watchdog us, and I don't think everyone is on our side. You and Caliber need to watch each other's backs."

"We will," Renee said. "In fact, I'll be watching his back very seriously. Remember in school he used to hate my powers, and I'd tease him with them? You know what he told me? He had a crush on me the whole time. What do you think, T? Do you see sex in our future?"

Gage grunted.

I coughed. "I'd rather not let my mind go there, if you don't mind."

She giggled again, and then sobered. "You do the same, okay? Watch each other's backs, I mean. And maybe go have sex or something, you both look tense."

She cut the call short before I could muster a reply. I settled for staring at the blank monitor. Gage blew hard through his nose, lips twisted in a strange grimace.

"What?" I asked.

"Renee Duvall and her casual conversations. She's unbelievable," he said, an odd layer of annoyance in his voice.

"She keeps you on your toes."

"Something tells me Agent McNally will, too."

"I won't be her poster girl for Ranger support, Gage. A few photos with schoolchildren and old folks smiling won't erase decades of violence."

"No, it won't, and there's no reason to expect it to. We have to earn back that trust and not from politicking."

"So what, then? We keep a bus full of kids from toppling off a bridge into the river? Pull orphans from a burning building? Stop a mudslide in Malibu?"

He turned until he stood toe to toe with me and tried to act stern. Humor still peeked through. "Okay, you do realize that the unspoken rules of superheroing states that one of those events will magically occur within our immediate vicinity?"

"Well, good," I said, flashing him a bright smile. This close I could smell a hint of shaving cream and something else. Something decidedly male and uniquely Gage. "We can get that step in our careers over and done with, and move on to more important matters."

"Such as?"

"Picking out uniforms?"

"I'd rather wear my jeans."

"I don't know." I quirked an eyebrow and gave him a once-over. "I think you'd look good in something skintight and leather."

I expected him to laugh; I didn't anticipate his completely blank stare. Crap. "Sorry, that wasn't—"

Gage interrupted my retraction by cupping my chin with his free hand and lowering his head. My heart threatened to beat right out of my chest. He brushed his lips across my mouth so gently I thought he missed. Just the lightest of strokes that set my nerves on fire.

Indecision forced me to pause. Knowledge of a turning

point. He wouldn't talk about Oregon, but he'd offer tentative kisses. Our conversations skirted deeper pain, while remaining surface and casual. If words couldn't bring us together, maybe something else could.

Not knowing how many more "laters" I had, I captured his lips in a crushing kiss. Arms circled my waist, hands tangled in my hair. His mouth, his tongue, his intense heat and flavor and scent—all surrounded me and forced a soft moan from my throat.

He broke the kiss, but didn't pull away. Every inch of his body seemed to vibrate. His intense, silver-flecked eyes drilled into me, trying to see past the lavender exterior. The intensity of it was overwhelming. "You frighten me, Teresa."

Confusion overpowered my tumultuous emotions and I tensed, stifled by his tight embrace.

He must have read something in my expression. "I just meant I've never felt like this after knowing someone for only a couple of days. Like I've . . . I don't know."

I thought I did. "Like you've found something you didn't know you wanted in the first place? Or is that kind of corny?"

"Yeah."

"Yeah, it's corny?"

"No." He traced the side of his thumb down my cheek. "The other part."

"And you're afraid of messing up and losing it, like you've lost everything else?"

His face hardened, the once-open emotions shuttering. Shutting down.

Concerned, I splayed my fingers against his chest. Felt his

heart beating there. "Sorry, I was just remembering something a shrink said to me during one of our multiple sessions dedicated to my inability to commit to a relationship." A topic I felt awkward broaching with Gage or anyone else—one that would probably have to be broached before we went any further with . . . whatever it was we were doing.

"Gage, what is it about me that frightens you? I'd really like to know." When he didn't respond, I gave him a hint. "Is it what Dr. Seward said about my potentially dying?"

"No, that's not it." His body thrummed with tension. "The potentiality of your death does frighten me, Teresa. It terrifies me. But your powers are stronger than anyone else's here, maybe stronger than anyone else active, and they're not yours. You have them for a reason that no one knows or is sharing, and it scares me to death."

"I'm not going to explode, Gage." I thought of yesterday's episode and cringed. "At least, I hope not."

He rested his forehead against mine. Our height difference made looking up awkward, so I closed my eyes. His breath was sweet, warm, and his mouth so close. The butterflies in my stomach stirred.

"Please talk to me, Gage. About anything."

"Teresa, I—"

Whatever statement he meant to make was cut off by an obnoxious blaring noise, filtered into the room through a loudspeaker in the ceiling. We pulled apart.

"What is that?" I asked.

The computer monitor opposite us blinked to life. Live news coverage filled the screen. Half of a large complex was flattened, the street littered with dust and rubble and debris. The scroll at the bottom read "Inglewood Demolition Goes Wrong, Workers Trapped."

Just a few miles from our headquarters.

"Should we let the fire department handle it?" Gage asked.

I sensed a challenge in his words. The building had done more than simply collapse. If the news reporter was correct, it had also trapped half a dozen workers beneath the rubble. It could take the fire department hours, if not days, to safely reach them. Using our powers together, we could get there faster.

"I suppose there's no better time to introduce ourselves to the world," I said. "Let's call Onyx and Tempest. We've got our first team mission."

Fourteen

Demolition

For all of my bluster about a team mission, the scene presented enough unique challenges to tempt me into giving up before we began. The building was an abandoned apartment complex, standing on half of a city block in the shit hole that was Inglewood. Most of the neighborhood had been abandoned six years ago after a petroleum fire razed twelve square blocks to the ground. That section stood cut off by police barricades and cement K-rails. The skeletal remains of LAX were only a few miles west.

Our site stood within view of the empty blocks, themselves still littered with rubble long ago picked clean by thieves. Fire trucks, police cars, and emergency vehicles crowded the street, making it impossible for our copter to land. We competed for sky space with several news crews, one of which finally took notice of us when I pushed open the door and poked my purple-streaked head out.

Gage grabbed my wrist to anchor me in the copter, but I had no intention of falling.

"Hey, Tempest!" I had to shout over the roar of the copter

blades. Tempest sidled up next to me. "Think you can get us down there?"

He peered over the edge of the copter floor. "As long as you don't mind a slight free fall."

"Do not worry for me," Onyx said.

Over my shoulder, Onyx peeled out of his coveralls until he sat there in only those special briefs. He closed his eyes. His skin darkened as his body shrank. Feathers sprouted. His nose lengthened, and his arms disappeared into his body. Still fascinated by his shapeshifting, I watched until he had transformed completely. The raven blinked glowing green eyes at me, and then flew out the door.

"Show-off," Gage said.

Tempest grabbed my right hand with his left, and Gage's left hand with his right. Before I could ask what we should do, Tempest leapt from the copter and pulled me and Gage out with him.

Terror seized me as we free-fell toward the city street, less than three hundred feet below. I squeezed Tempest's hand, too frightened to scream. A rush of wind circled us, roaring in my ears, and our descent slowed. Grime and dirt swirled into a funnel cloud, and we floated through the center, toward the ground.

We must have made quite a sight.

I didn't let go of Tempest's hand until my feet hit pavement. The cyclone ended immediately, and the roar was replaced with shouting voices. Rescue workers backed away, creating a circle around us. Onyx swooped down and landed, remaining in raven form.

"Warn a girl next time," I said.

Tempest winked.

"Who's in charge?" I asked the nearest fireman.

He pointed toward a cluster of fire engines. "Captain Hooper. What are you?"

"The answer to your prayers," I quipped, and then looked down at Marco. "Onyx, do a flyover and get the lay of the land."

The raven nodded and took to the sky in a ruffle of feathers and air. I envied him the freedom to fly like that.

"You're Rangers, aren't you?" a female voice asked.

I turned and located the woman near an ambulance. She wore an EMT uniform badly in need of an iron. Silver glistened in her black hair, and unlike the younger men and women around her, she didn't seem at all surprised by our arrival at the scene.

"Yes, we are," I said.

"I knew you'd come back. Always knew someday."

Before I could ponder if she meant me specifically, or the Rangers as a group, Gage grabbed my arm and whisked me toward the makeshift command center. I tried to remember the woman's face, so I could seek her out later if need be, and followed the boys.

Captain Hooper was easy to find. He stood hunched over the trunk of a police car, studying several sets of building blueprints, flanked on both sides by firemen and uniformed cops. He looked up as we approached, his mouth flopping open, utter shock settling into his aged features. White hair peeked out from beneath his cap, but that didn't diminish the air of authority in his broad shoulders and square jaw.

He recovered quickly and suspicion replaced surprise. "What are you people doing here?"

"Lending a hand, if you think we're needed, sir." I pulled the civility out of my ass, even though the "you people" put my defenses up. Pissing off a police captain wouldn't do much to ingratiate us with the populace.

Hooper's attention shifted over my shoulder to Tempest and Gage. "You all have powers that can be useful in this situation?"

"Of course. We aren't here to waste anyone's time. I'm Trance, this is Tempest and Cipher. And please, Captain, tell your people not to shoot at a crow flying about, he's with us."

"We're police, not game hunters."

"Just so we understand each other. Where are the workers trapped, Captain? We need to know their locations and if any of the explosives still haven't been detonated."

"One pack hasn't." A young man wearing an orange hard hat shouldered his way forward. The name embroidered on his shirt said Anderson. "The northeast corner of the building only collapsed partway. That's where my guys were placing the last pack when everything hit the fan."

"How many men are down there?" Gage asked.

"Five still. Two got out on their own. Said they could hear the others screaming for help as they left, but their escape route fell in. We can't get to them."

I glanced at blueprints that read like gibberish. "Show me."

Anderson and Hooper led us to the edge of the rubble; they'd had the foresight to set up their base near the trapped men. Eight stories of apartment building lay on top of them. Four stories of the northeast wall survived, a totem to the destruction. Anderson pointed to a spot of freshly disturbed bricks.

"That's where they got out," he said.

I squeezed Gage's elbow. Walking as close as he dared to the rubble, he squatted down, closed his eyes, and concentrated.

"What's he doing?" Hooper asked.

"Checking to see if the workers are still alive," I replied.

Onyx landed next to Tempest and transformed back into his human shape. It was like watching a video recording backward, as he undid what he'd done earlier. He didn't seem to mind being clad in just those black briefs. The man had the body of an underwear model, all tapered hips and chiseled abs—even if his mottled skin made him look like an advertisement for camouflage paint.

"See anything useful?" I asked.

"There may be a way in through the rubble, twenty feet to the center," Onyx said. "It is a rough walk. I ventured inside, and some of the support beams created a tunnel into the first level."

"Good, thanks."

Gage stood up and walked back, his mouth pinched. "I only heard four heartbeats. Could smell a lot of blood, and something else." He looked at Hooper. "Is all of the gas and electricity to this block shut off?"

"Yes," Hooper said.

"It wasn't on before," Anderson added. "My guys went in with flashlights and lanterns. Property hasn't had good electrical service for two years, since the owner went bankrupt. Why do you think we're tearing it down?"

"Onyx found a way in," I said to Gage. "I need you with us for orientation. Tempest, can you stay out here and be my eyes and ears?"

Tempest frowned. He seemed poised to argue, but didn't. As much as I wanted to keep us together, his powers wouldn't be very useful in an enclosed space.

"I'll see about keeping a good airflow down to the workers," he said.

"Thanks."

Onyx transformed again, this time into the small black cat he'd been when we first met. With admonitions from Hooper and Anderson to be careful and "don't make it worse," Gage and I followed Onyx into the destruction.

He cut a swift trail over peaks and valleys of brick, plaster, metal beams, and wood planks. I noticed the smell that bothered Gage earlier; probably residue from the sequential explosions. The cacophony of the rescue teams melted into the background as we picked our way across, my mind focused entirely on the task at hand.

Minutes later, cat-Onyx disappeared around a twisted metal staircase. I turned the same corner and found an opening the size of a doggy door.

"This is your hole?" I asked, not sure if Onyx was in range of my voice.

I peered inside and saw nothing. The cat appeared; I jumped. He blinked twice, as if asking "what are you waiting for?" then ducked back inside.

"It sounds like it opens up a bit," Gage said.

Trusting him on that, I inhaled deeply, sat down, and slid into darkness.

Fifteen

Demolition II

My feet hit something solid. I stood up just inside the darkness. Light poured down from the hole above, and I stepped forward to allow Gage room. My eyes adjusted slowly to my surroundings. We were in a stairwell, still mostly intact. I recognized a *4* painted on the wall nearby. We had a bit of traveling to do.

Gage slid down and landed gracefully. Onyx appeared further down the makeshift corridor, his feline eyes glinting in the dim light. He blinked once, turned, and disappeared. I followed a few steps, paused, then groaned.

"What?" Gage asked.

"Flashlight."

"Shit."

No time to go back and fetch one. I raised my left hand, palm up, and concentrated. The heat formed into a tight orb the size of a walnut. I focused on the heat, rather than the size, and as the temperature increased, the light grew brighter. It glowed like a 40-watt bulb, and I held the temp steady.

"You okay, Trance?"

"No problem."

With our makeshift light source, I followed Onyx's trail. The stairwell remained mostly intact, its metal staircase bent and broken in a few places, but passable. We skirted stone and brick and plaster debris as we descended. Onyx stayed just within the glow of my orb, rarely venturing too far forward. Several times the air grew thin and I caught the distinct odor of gas, then it was dispersed by a gentle breeze. I smiled, thinking of Tempest on the outside, helping us as best he could.

"Cipher," I said, as we neared the bottom of the stairwell, "can you hear them?"

"Still four heartbeats."

Our voices reverberated in the enclosed space. Something shifted above us, showering our path with dust and bits of stone. I froze, felt Gage's hand on my shoulder, but that did nothing to calm my pounding heart. Several awful seconds passed before the wreckage settled.

"We should move faster," I whispered.

At the bottom of the stairwell, the emergency door lay twisted half open. As entrances went, it was narrow and hard to maneuver. Onyx leapt through with ease. I bent and inserted one leg. Unable to manage without both hands, our light source disappeared, blanketing the narrow space in utter blackness.

I crawled through the hole and stepped back. An indignant cat screech shattered the silence.

"Sorry," I said.

Onyx hissed.

"A little help here," Gage said.

I re-created the light orb with less thought than the first time, and it glowed brighter. I smiled, pleased with my work. Not too bad, and no side effects so far. Gage slid into the room. We stood in a crushed hallway that seemed to extend forward a good forty feet. Three support beams had fallen across the path, and we ducked below them. The walls of the corridor remained mostly intact. The ceiling was a mess of exposed cables and beams, broken sheetrock and twisted metal fixtures. Some sections hung within two feet of the floor, forcing Gage and me to crawl. Each time, I had to drop the orb, and each rekindle proved faster and brighter.

My Vox beeped. <Trance, this is Tempest. You there?>

I pulled it from my belt holster. "Tempest, this is Trance, we're here."

<How close are you guys?>

"Pretty close. We've backtracked at least thirty feet to your position, near the northeast corner of the building."

<Be advised, some of the wreckage is settling on the other side of the block. I don't know how stable your end is, so you might want to speed things up.>

"We'll do our best. Out."

I put the Vox away. I didn't need to be told to hurry; I felt the building settling.

The end of the corridor presented us with another challenge: water. Part of the floor had given away and filled in with tepid water, likely from busted pipes that hadn't properly drained. The nauseating odors of mildew and slime tingled my nostrils. Gage looked positively green, even under lavender light. Past four feet of water, a half-broken door hung askew. More water disappeared into the room beyond, and I heard a distant trickle as it ran out of sight.

Onyx sniffed the edge of the pool, stepped back, then transformed from the cat into the raven. He took off over the water and ducked into the room.

"They're in there," Gage said. "I can hear them."

"Hello?" The stranger's voice echoed from beyond and vibrated the unstable walls. Dust floated down, and deep within the structure, something groaned. The man shouted again, louder this time, and metal screamed.

I spun around, raising my hand to shine light back down our path. Ten feet behind us, the ceiling collapsed, cutting off our escape route and sending a cloud of dirt and debris into the air. The walls beside us cracked and fractured.

"Go," Gage said, shoving me forward.

I stumbled into the calf-deep water and slogged toward the broken door. About halfway there, I tripped over something beneath the water and lost the light. Gage grabbed my arm before I fell. We surged forward blindly, enveloped by darkness and the horrific squeal of collapsing metal and brick. Dust filled the air. I sneezed, splashing through the water until I hit something solid. I stopped, coughed, and waited. Gage still gripped my arm.

The noise stopped. My Vox beeped, but I ignored it in favor of creating a little light. The lavender glow illuminated the interior of an apartment kitchen. Its floor was awash in filthy water; half of the ceiling lay in the center. Raven-Onyx was perched on the middle of the debris pile.

Four men of varying ages sat huddled in the far corner. Wet and wide-eyed, the quartet stared at us. Two wore hard hats and a third was holding his left arm tight to his chest. All of them were bleeding from gashes on their faces, necks and hands. A fifth man lay facedown in the water opposite the survivors.

My Vox beeped again.

Gage plucked it from my holster. "It's Cipher," he said. "Go ahead, Tempest."

<We just saw the collapse,> Tempest replied, the concern in his voice unmistakable. <Are you all okay?>

"We're fine. We found the workers. Four of them are alive, but we can't go out the way we came in. We need an alternative."

<I'll see what we can do from this end. What's the condition of the workers?>

"Pete's dead," one of the men offered. He was the oldest of the four and looked like the man in charge. "George there's got a broken shoulder, but we're mostly okay."

<I heard that. I'll get back to you. Out.>

The older man snorted. "Sounds like you kids got yourself trapped down here with us."

"We've got a few tricks left," I said. "What's your name, sir?"

"Ben Hodges. Who are you, Missy?"

"Trance, Ranger Corps." I felt a bit of pride at the statement. "My associates, Cipher and Onyx."

Ben eyed the raven. "Trained bird?"

"Shapeshifter."

"And what do you do, make light?"

"Among other things. Can you four walk?"

"If we need to, yes."

I increased the light a bit more and stepped away from the wall. A second door was sealed shut by debris. The door we'd come in provided no way back out. Short of tunneling like moles, I saw no reliable escape route.

"Cipher?" I said. "How far are we from the street?"

Gage closed his eyes. An eerie silence befell the room, broken occasionally by the hiss of lapping water. Ben, George, and the other two workers remained oddly quiet—probably terrified of having three Rangers within spitting distance when Rangers hadn't existed for fifteen years.

"Is there another room past this wall?" Gage asked, pointing blindly.

"Yeah," Ben said. "Living room, bedroom, then the exterior wall."

He opened his eyes. "So about twenty feet between us and the outdoors?"

"Twenty feet of rubble."

I sloshed back to Gage's side. In the strange light, his eyes glittered, and I recognized the look.

"What are you thinking?" I asked.

He drew me closer and lowered his voice to say, "Do you remember back at the motel, when you put up that force field?"

"Vaguely." The protection against Specter had been instinctive, not something I remembered doing consciously, and I had not tried to repeat the experience. "I can't shield us and blast our way out, though."

"Not quite what I had in mind. If you had to re-create the shield, do you think you could do it?"

I wanted to reassure him that it was a piece of cake. Instead: "I don't know. I'd have to drop the light orb to make a shield, and I can't guarantee it would protect us all. Especially when I don't know what I'm protecting us against."

"Give me a second, and I'll let you know." Gage produced his own Vox and held it up. "Tempest, Cipher here."

<Cipher, this is Tempest. Go ahead.>

"I have a wild idea on how to get us out of here, but I need to know something first."

<What's that?>

Gage looked at me and held my gaze even as he asked Tempest, "How good's your aim?"

Perched on top of the rubble pile, I braced my feet on either side of the uncomfortable mess, resting elbows on knees. With my attention elsewhere, the light orb glowed a bit dimmer. Gage helped the last worker—a young guy named Larry, who sported a deep laceration on his face—sidle up to the base of the mound. Onyx had shifted back into a cat and sat next to me, choosing to stay for this instead of finding an alternate escape route.

Larry grabbed onto the rubble with both hands. Gage climbed around him and sat halfway up the pile, on my right, and retrieved his Vox.

My cue. I let the light orb die out completely, plunging our small band into darkness. The only sound was our collective breathing, mine a bit louder than the rest.

"Tempest, this is Cipher." Gage's voice was almost too loud in the dark. "You ready on your end?"

<I think so.> High-pitched wailing crackled over Tempest's end of the Vox. He'd already started gathering the wind. <Gotta put the Vox down. I'll count to thirty, and then I'm plowing through.>

"Understood, count now."

Cue number two. I closed my eyes and drew into myself, into the lavender light that I was learning to manipulate, into the heat that I produced, and into the source of whatever had given me these powers. The glow began in my mind, a hazy orb the size of a basketball. It expanded and thinned out, like a balloon blown too large.

I recalled the fear I'd felt during my fight with Specter, the need to protect myself and Gage. It blew the expanding bubble outward, stretched it into an opaque mist that covered the rubble pile like a net. I held it steady on the outer edges of the pile, confident that everyone was inside. Now I needed to hold it while Tempest did his part.

Compressed cyclonic air as a makeshift drill was ingenious, if Tempest could pull it off. His voice carried more confidence than I felt, but we had few options. It could take days for a rescue team to dig us out, and the guy with the broken shoulder was going into shock.

Something shrieked and groaned. The ground beneath me vibrated. I held tight to that vision of the bubble. The thin power barrier protected us from falling wreckage. The shriek grew closer. One of the workers began to cry. I ignored him, focused on the air shrieking its way through steel, cement, and mortar toward seven trapped people.

The noise invaded my mind. Ripped through my ears. I wanted to clamp my hands over them, to block out the sound. I couldn't. Moving might kill us all. Flying debris peppered the shield. I felt each strike like a pinprick on my skin. The room trembled.

Then sound and motion ceased. I did not drop the shield. The hole was drilled, but I didn't know if it would hold. Warmth dripped from my nose and trickled across my upper lip.

<Cipher, this is Tempest.>

"Tempest, Cipher. We're here, and we're okay. Is the tunnel stable?"

<Seems to be so far. I'm coming in with two firemen, so we should see you in just a minute. Out.>

A hand squeezed my elbow. "Trance, you can drop the shield," Gage said.

The confidence in his voice told me all I needed to know. I opened my eyes and the bubble burst. Dim light filtered in through a cylindrical hole in the far wall, roughly four feet in diameter. The interior appeared shorn smooth, and it was holding.

Gage appeared in front of me and grabbed both of my hands. "Are you okay?"

"I think so." Blood tickled on my lip. "We really did it, didn't we?"

"Yeah, we really did."

"Does that make us heroes now? Real heroes?"

"Don't know about anyone else," Ben said, reaching up to tap my leg, "but you're all heroes to me. That was the scariest shit I've ever seen, but it worked. Thank you."

I grinned, my heart swelling with pride. "You're welcome."

A shadow moved in the mouth of the tunnel. Tempest leapt into the room and landed in the murky water with a splash and an annoyed groan. The cavalry was here; time to get our charges to safety.

Sixteen

Dahlia Perkins

Fresh air had never smelled so good as when we emerged from the rubble. The rotten odor of the old water clung to my wet jeans and had settled in my nostrils. I wanted at least two showers when we returned to the HQ. The scene presenting itself on the Inglewood street indicated that those showers would be a long time coming.

A throng of reporters, photographers, and other camera wielders, shouting rapid-fire questions that devolved into a muddle of sound, stood behind a police barricade that threatened to break if one more person pushed against it.

EMTs surrounded the injured workers and whisked them off to waiting ambulances. I led my team to one of the fire trucks, away from the screaming crowd. A uniformed officer handed over Onyx's discarded jumpsuit, and we created a human barrier, allowing Marco to shift back into human form and slip into his clothes.

Captain Hooper approached, his previous apprehension replaced by astonishment. "You kids were amazing. I remember back when your, ah, predecessors were doing the job. They'd be mighty proud of you."

"Thank you, Captain," Gage said. "We hadn't exactly planned this to be our coming-out party."

"Far from it, actually," I said. We couldn't avoid the press conference now. Our pictures would be on all of the news stations within the hour. Footage was probably playing live.

A policewoman walked over with a cellular in her hand and held it up to Hooper. "Urgent phone call for you, sir."

Hooper took the phone. I ignored the conversation and studied the teeming crowd until he said "McNally." My attention shifted back, but he was already hanging up.

"I didn't realize you folks had a publicity agent," Hooper said.

"A what?" I asked.

"Agent McNally is on her way over to present you folks to the press. She asked that you wait until she arrives before speaking to anyone."

"Did she?"

"Trance," Gage said, a single word that came out like a warning.

I turned away from Hooper, toward my team. They watched me, and I realized that they would obey whatever I commanded next. Today's tragedy had somehow cemented my role as team leader and earned a large amount of undeserved respect. I was a child holding up a sheriff's badge, and no one else seemed to see it was just a toy.

"What do you guys think?" I asked, mustering up some

bravado. "Ready to meet the press? No specifics, just a friendly chat until McNally arrives."

"I'm game," Tempest said.

Onyx shook his head. "I am not a public speaker, *Catalepsia*."

Off what must have been a priceless look of confusion from me, Gage said, "It's Spanish for 'Trance.' And for the record, neither am I."

"Then, let Tempest and me do the talking," I said.

The dissenters shared a glance, but delivered no further protests. I breezed past Hooper with Tempest on my right and the others behind. The shouted questions grew louder and more numerous when the press realized we were heading in their direction. I heard our code names—apparently someone had leaked those already.

I stopped an arm's length from the barricade and planted my hands on my hips, trying to look authoritative in my dusty, smelly street clothes. I must have pulled it off. They started shushing each other, and the din lowered to a murmur. A burst of purple caught my interest, like a lavender camera flash. I searched the crowd, unable to distinguish the source. Instead, I found a face that stood out from the others: a nervous girl with thick waves of honey-blond hair and saucer-wide blue eyes. Something about her drew my undivided attention.

She realized I was staring, and those nervous eyes nearly popped out.

"You," I said, pointing at the blonde.

Every head in hearing range turned toward my chosen

victim. Her entire body trembled. She clutched her digital recorder. "Uh, Dahlia Perkins, the *Valley Gazette*," she said. "Wow, you guys."

Tempest snickered. I jabbed my elbow into his ribs.

"You get the first question, Miss Perkins," I said.

Terror telegraphed across her expressive face like a movie marquee. Several moments of near-silence and jealous glares from colleagues passed before Dahlia finally spoke up. "I grew up listening to my mom tell stories about the Ranger Corps," she said, with an authority in her voice that was not present on her face. "Are you really back? Are you those Rangers so many looked up to?"

"No," I said without hesitation, and could imagine the odd looks coming from my team. "The Rangers you remember, the heroes who fought in the War, died a long time ago. They were our parents and siblings, and they were our mentors. They were living legends that history will never forget." Dramatic pause. "We're a new generation of Rangers, and we're here now to create our own legend."

Okay, dramatic much?

They ate it up. The statement created a new flurry of questions from the gaggle of reporters. Dahlia shrank into the melee, finished with her moment in the spotlight. I made a slashing gesture across my throat, and the din quieted to a dull roar.

"Anything else, Miss Perkins?" I asked.

She flushed. "Are you the entire Corps, or are there others?"

"A few of our members are tending to tasks elsewhere,

and our numbers continue to increase as more Rangers find their way to our headquarters here in Los Angeles." Okay, so that was an outright lie. No sense in admitting we were six strong and not likely to get stronger in the immediate future. "New and reactivated Metas are, of course, encouraged to seek us out."

"And what of the arrested Banes? Are they active as well?" Dahlia said the name as if uttering a black curse.

"From what we know, yes, many are active." A hushed murmur spread across the crowd. "However, the government built a sturdy and powerful prison on Manhattan Island, and we are confident it will continue to hold."

"And if it doesn't?"

"That's why we're here," Tempest said. He stepped forward, shoulder to shoulder with me. A gentle breeze surrounded us both and ruffled my hair, a well-timed special effect I'd applaud him for later.

"So you're active now because they got their powers back first?" a new voice shouted. The man stood a few yards from Dahlia, hair hidden under a hat and eyes obscured by sunglasses. With our full attention, he finished his query with, "Or is it vice versa?"

I narrowed my eyes in his general direction, but felt no compunction to answer his question. He'd spoken out of turn. "And you are?"

"Alan Bates, Channel Four," he said.

To Dahlia I said, "Miss Perkins, you can thank Mr. Bates for ending this interview. Good luck with your story."

A melody of angry shouts and pointed questions followed me as I walked away from the press. Gage kept pace by my side, fighting away laughter.

"You played them pretty well, I think," Tempest said. "I have a feeling Alan Bates will become the least-liked person at Channel Four after this."

"His question was out of line," I said. "I'm just glad I didn't have to answer it and sound like an idiot, since we don't have a clue."

"We should call the copter back in," Onyx said.

"Tired of the spotlight already?" Tempest asked.

"I am not in this for the attention, Ethan."

"And I am?"

"Are you?"

"Cameras, boys," I hissed. "Smile now, argue later."

They canned it. Only Tempest pasted on a pleasant grin. Something was eating Onyx, but this wasn't the time or place to sort it out.

I snatched my Vox. "Bird One, this is Trance."

<Go ahead, Trance,> our pilot said.

"Where can you pick us up?"

<I landed half a block over, east of your position.>

"We'll be there in a—"

The ground trembled. A distant explosion belched smoke and fire into the southern sky—too far to see the source or feel the concussion, but close enough to know it wasn't a small detonation.

"We should check that out," Gage said. "See if we can—"

Three identical pulses tore from our Voxes, a sound so plaintive it gave me chills. I recognized it from my childhood, on the rare occasion my parents were home and not on call, a tone sent out to every active Ranger Vox that meant one thing: security breach at HQ.

"Onyx, you can get back faster than we can," I said.

Without reply, he stripped, transformed back into raven form, then took to the sky. Tempest snatched up his discarded jumpsuit. Our transportation waited half a block away; we ran. The copter seemed to take hours to arrive at HQ, where a devastating sight greeted us.

Thick smoke spiraled up from the remains of the Medical Center's top story. The entire floor was reduced to rubble, fire, and black haze, forcing our helicopter to hover nearby. I gaped, the destruction freezing my mind and instincts. I couldn't bark orders or decide on a course of action. We'd been attacked in the one place we'd assumed was safe.

A warm hand squeezed my wrist; Gage's eyes met mine. The expectation on his face shattered my hesitation. "We need to get down there," I said.

Tempest lowered us to the ground using his wind tunnel method, complete with the nauseating sensation of a six-story free fall. Two nurses burst through the front doors and raced past us, babbling about a sudden explosion and fire alarms.

Onyx was nowhere to be seen. We charged inside, and it occurred to me that while I'd exited the Medical Center several times, this was the first time I was walking in on my own two feet. The odd knowledge carried me toward the emergency stairs, fear and worry squelching beneath my anger. Someone had attacked our home; they would pay.

The first three floors of the building housed labs and research facilities. It might seem strange to not have the Emergency Unit on the first floor like a regular hospital, but Ranger teams often came and went via copter, so the closer to the roof the better, which put the EU on the fourth floor, where I'd spent my time. Five was offices and long-term care rooms; sixth floor, more offices and labs. Dr. Seward's office was on the fifth floor, and so was Frost's room.

Gage grabbed my hand, and I pulled him along. He didn't need support, just guidance as he listened while racing blindly up the stairs.

"I hear voices," he said, a little out of breath. "Seward is still up there, and someone else, a woman I don't . . ."

At the fifth floor landing we stopped, blocked from proceeding any higher by a pile of debris. I pushed against the door. It was stuck. And very, very cold.

"The hell?" I said.

"It's Janel." Gage's voice had an unexpected hitch. "Specter has Frost under his control."

Seventeen

Frost

"A re you sure, Gage?" I asked, for them as much as myself. I didn't doubt his certainty. We were facing one of our own, possessed by our enemy. Everyone had to understand the score.

"Yes. She's saying something to Dr. Seward about"—Gage's eyes widened—"Christ, she's got Marco."

With a trembling hand, I formed a softball-size orb and hurled it at the frozen door, where it shattered into slivers of metal and ice with a pop like a balloon bursting. Tempest charged through the door first, and I followed with an orb in each hand. A piercing scream greeted us, echoing down the corridor from someplace out of sight.

The floor and walls were coated with an inch of ice. Tempest slipped, flailed his arms, and fell flat on his back. I reached for him and lost my own balance. I hit the slippery ground on my hands and knees, scraping my palms raw. The scream came again, fueling both my determination and fury.

"It's Marco," Gage said. He remained upright, carefully balanced on the treacherous floor.

I rose to my knees, re-created the orbs, and lobbed them across the surface of the ice like mini bowling balls. They melted a swath down the middle and created a narrow running track.

Gage hooked his arms around my waist and pulled me up. Tempest stood on his own steam, a little wobbly from his wipeout, and took point down the path. At the end of the icy corridor, we hit another dead end: a wall of ice. It covered the next corridor like a waxed paper seal—translucent enough to see through, but too thick to simply hit and shatter.

Beyond it, Dr. Seward sagged against the wall, hugging his left arm to his chest. Blood poured from his nose and over his chin. In the center of the hallway, Frost loomed over Marco's prostrate form. As we stood there, a miniature snowstorm engulfed them both. Ice adhered to Marco's exposed skin. Frost's eyes glowed an unearthly yellow-orange, and her frail, battered body swayed on the verge of collapse.

"You might want to duck," I said.

One orb from each hand and as much power as I could muster went sailing toward the ice wall. It shattered with a soft boom, sending ice and snow flying. Tiny bits pricked my face and neck. Frigid wind whipped around us as Frost redirected her blizzard.

Tempest countered with his own windstorm and the battling elementals sent out enough counter-feedback to knock each other for a loop. Tempest flew backward and hit the wall, sending splinters up and down the icy coating. Frost sailed sideways, right through an open doorway.

I slid a few times before giving up, and just let myself glide up next to Marco. Beyond the snow covering his mostly naked body, I couldn't see any specific injuries, and that worried me. Especially with those earlier screams. But he was breathing and that's what mattered.

Gage slipped past me—very literally—and grabbed the doorframe for support. He peered inside and was suddenly skidding backward, hit square in the chest with a block of ice the size of a basketball. He didn't even scream—just hit the floor and lay still.

"Cipher!" I screamed.

"She's fighting him," Seward said, his voice high-pitched, unsteady. "She's trying so hard not to hurt us, but she's too weak."

Frost was in a losing battle with Specter. She'd been half dead when Renee and William brought her here; she didn't have the strength to resist Specter for long.

"You have to kill her," Seward said.

"I can't do that." Just the idea of it horrified me.

"You have to. He won't give her up. When the host dies, Specter is weakened and has to return to his own body. You have to kill her to drive him out."

My stomach churned. Bile scorched the back of my throat. "I can't; she's one of us."

"She'll kill you, Trance."

As though to prove his point, a scattering of icicle shrapnel flew out of the open doorway. Deadly, sharp icicles. They peppered the far wall just above my head, cracking the coating of ice already in place.

I backed up, slowly drawing up to my feet. Frost appeared in the doorway, her eyes alight with Specter's unholy power. Blood dribbled from her nose, down her lips and chin, staining the collar of her hospital gown. Dark smudges discolored the flesh beneath her eyes, and her sallow skin seemed stretched too thin. She was already dying from Specter's mental intrusion; my attack would make little difference.

To her.

I recalled the wounded girl William had carried across Central Park, the way she'd blasted Mayhem with icicles and saved us for a little while. This was how I thanked her. "I'm so sorry, Janel," I said.

Something mournful sparked in her eyes as the briefest glimpse of the girl I remembered peeked through. But Specter was too strong. Her eyes spat a barrage of hailstones. I erected a force shield easily, with less effort than before, and they pinged off. Frost's face twisted in fury, a terrifying combination of Specter's and her own, and she shot more icicles. Same thing. Warm power tingled through my fingertips, the only sense I had of its potency. Too many of those, and I wouldn't be able to maintain the shield.

A shield that protected myself, Marco, and Seward. Gage lay outside of my perimeter. Frost noticed this the moment I did and shifted her attention to him. The instinct to protect flared to deadly life. I dropped the shield and threw the largest orb I could muster directly at her head. It exploded against her temple and threw her weak body backward, knocking Specter's final ice blast off-target and freezing the far wall instead.

She hit the floor with a dull crack and lay still. I didn't move. The sound of my own ragged breathing was met by the distinct plink-plunk of melting ice. In moments the corridor was awash in cold water. Frost's spell was over, the effect of her powers extinguished with her precious life. A life I'd taken.

I sat for a moment in the middle of the puddle, trembling, forcing my bubble of grief to keep moving, to go away until later. I could not lose it here. Not in front of the others.

"Trance?" Dr. Seward squatted in front of me, still holding his left arm. Pain and exhaustion radiated from his scrunched brow and pursed lips. Sweat beaded on his forehead. "Come on, my dear, we need to help your teammates."

"Six," I said.

He frowned. "What?"

"Six dead, six of us left."

Had Specter planned the explosion at the construction site, effectively removing us from the HQ so he could coordinate his attack? It was very possible. The events were too perfect to be coincidental. He came in while no one was guarding the store and struck at our heart, finishing what he'd started with Janel. Half of our numbers wiped out. Murdered.

"Come on, Trance, we'll think about it later."

Dr. Seward reached out with his good hand and wiped an errant tear from my cheek. I hadn't realized I'd begun to cry and that shamed me into action. The gentle gesture changed my opinion of him. I decided then, surrounded by wounded friends and melting ice, that I trusted Angus Seward.

"Help Onyx," I said.

I crawled across the floor to Gage's body. His pulse hummed steadily beneath my fingers. I pressed gently against his chest. Nothing gave, no bones shifted. He was just knocked silly. Relief squeezed my heart and constricted my throat and colored the world a pale shade of lavender.

I blinked; the shaded vision was back. Not the best time for my powers to start going nutty again. No one's immediate health concerned me more than Gage's, Ethan's and Marco's. Specter had driven me to kill for a second time. I was determined there would not be a third.

"Trance?" Tempest limped toward me, favoring his right leg. The reddish-purple beginnings of a bruise colored the right side of his jaw. He stopped a few feet from Seward and Onyx. "What about the sixth floor? There's still a fire up there."

My hand tightened around Gage's wrist. My irrational need to stay by his side and protect him battled my duty to this facility. If we didn't get the fire under control, it could consume everything we were trying to rebuild.

"Go," Dr. Seward said. "I'll get help up here now that the threat is neutralized."

This clinical description of Frost's death rankled, but I channeled my annoyance into action and stood up, icy water dripping off my soaked jeans. The ceiling above snapped and groaned. I looked up, seeking whatever great force had made the sound.

A crack appeared in the tiles to my left and traveled down the corridor, splitting open like a fissure. The split ended just above Tempest. He gazed at it as though he'd never seen such a thing. I started to shout something—tell him to move his ass—when the ceiling opened up and dropped a cloud of debris on top of him. A maelstrom of plaster, metal, stone, and dust rained down until the air was filled with gray and I couldn't see him anymore.

Eighteen

Medical Ward III

Agent Rita McNally knocked before she entered the small scrub room. I tilted my head in her general direction, aware of her, even though my attention was fixed on the glass partition between this room and the next. She was a distraction. She could wait.

Ethan Swift lay on an operating table, surrounded by the best surgical team in the city, his chest wide open and a machine pumping blood for his heart. It had taken ten minutes to get him out of the rubble that had buried him alive, and for a moment, I'd thought him dead. I'd screamed when I saw the blood mixing with cold water—it looked like more than a body could stand to lose. His surviving this long seemed like a miracle; surviving surgery would be a blessing from whoever looked over us.

"How are the others?" McNally asked.

"Alive," I said, cringing as one of the doctors dropped a blood-soaked towel into a wastebasket. Couldn't she have found someone else to ask for a damned status report? "Ga— Cipher is sore and headachy. Onyx has frostbite on his cheeks and arms and three broken fingers. She froze them and then snapped them."

McNally shuddered. "I can't imagine what you're feeling right now—"

"That sounds really condescending, so maybe let's not?"

"Fair enough. I did want to say how proud I am of the way you handled the press earlier. I wish you'd waited for me like I asked, but you answered the right questions and deflected what you didn't need to answer. You did well today, Trance."

I was so not in the mood for a pep talk. Maybe I'd done the damned interview right, but when it came to a real battle, I'd let my team down. Gotten three Rangers injured and one of them dead. Yeah, I'd done *really* well today. "You think so?"

"Of course," she said, missing (or ignoring) the sarcasm in my voice. "You saved the lives of four men, and in the process, gave the press a very positive image of the new Ranger Corps."

"I also killed a fellow Ranger."

"From what I hear, that couldn't be helped."

"Maybe." It didn't matter what could or couldn't be helped, only what had happened. Janel was dead, and I'd killed her.

"The minute Specter possessed her, she was dead, no matter what you did."

"I could have tried something else."

McNally moved to stand by my side. I wouldn't look at her. "Don't second-guess your decisions, Trance. Not decisions made in the heat of battle. Doing so won't change what you did, and it won't change what happened to the others. It will only make you crazy, and cause you to second-guess your decisions the next time you're in the field. That can't happen. Leaders make choices, and they can't wonder if they're making the correct ones. They have to know it."

"What if I don't know it?" I whirled on her, confusion and grief tightening my chest. Through the pale purple haze in my vision, she seemed younger, less impressive—a good target for my anger. "I never asked to lead this team. I never led anyone or anything in my life, and now I have people's lives in my hands. Frost is dead. Cipher and Onyx are hurt. Tempest still could die, and all of that is my fault."

"You didn't drop the ceiling on Tempest. How is it your fault?"

I balled my hands into fists, resisting the very real urge to shatter something. Maybe I hadn't dropped the ceiling, but my actions were directly linked to the fire that had destroyed parts of the sixth floor, and the fight with Janel that left two hallways on the fifth floor with serious water damage. All power had been diverted to maintaining the hospital and emergency center here on the fourth floor. More damage, my fault.

"I'm responsible for his safety," I said. "If I can't protect him, I might as well quit now."

"So quit."

I took a step backward, stung. Quitting was something cowards did. My dad had never run from a fight or backed down from a foe. Rangers faced things head-on. I'd hidden from things my entire adult life, instead of confronting them. "I can't do that, and you know it."

"You also can't guarantee their safety, and you know it."

"I . . ." What? She was right. My anger deflated like a leaky balloon, leaving me stretched and tired. "How did things get so mixed up so fast?"

"I really don't know, Trance." McNally inhaled deeply, then blew out through her nose. "Just remember that you did what you had to do to stop Specter from killing anyone else. For a while he'll be too weak to come after you. Heal up, plan it out, and then go get him."

I snorted. "It's not really that simple."

"I know, but it's something to believe in when hope seems far away. You need to believe that no matter what happens, good will come out on top."

I studied her age-lined face and the determined glint in her eyes. "Were you like this for our elders, too?"

"You mean optimistic and full of charming wisdom?"

I wouldn't exactly put it in those words. "Yeah."

"No, but loss can change a person, Trance. Many of your elders were my friends, and I grieved their deaths. It took many years to forgive myself for . . . not doing more. All I could do was mourn them and remember them."

She touched the glass that separated us from the operating room. "Blame won't bring Tempest back, if it's his time. It will only hurt you and the people who love you. You have to take it as it comes and stay the course."

Stay the course.

The mystery woman's words from my dream. Was I really seeing someone, or was she simply my subconscious mind telling me to shape up? Could I listen to that inner voice and do what needed to be done?

"It must have been hard for you," I said.

"What's that?"

"The end of the War. Losing your job."

McNally smiled, weariness settling into her sharp features. "I was more concerned for you children. We all were. Separating you was not an easy choice, Trance, but we believed it was best. The country needed a fresh start. You kids needed a fresh start."

"It was a good theory, but I think the execution was a little lacking."

"I won't dispute that." She leaned against the partition, hands clasped loosely in front of her. "It was all done so secretly. Only a tiny handful of people in the entire ATF Bureau knew where each of you was sent. Those of us from the MHC who knew you were forbidden from making contact. We never thought we'd see you again."

I was beginning to understand her just a bit. "It wasn't your fault, or anyone else's at the MHC. Something happened, you went back to your life, and then that something unhappened. We all play the hand we're dealt, right?"

She worried her lower lip with her teeth. "Yes, we do."

"Do you think we can beat Specter's hand?"

"I think . . ." She stopped and pursed her lips. Several seconds passed. "I think Specter is as arrogant as he ever was. He keeps attacking sideways when he should come at you head-on. It's a tactical error. That's why you'll beat him. He's bluffing."

I nodded, silently mulling her words. Bluffing wasn't the word I would choose to describe Specter's actions. Deliberating, maybe. Testing when he should just strike a death blow—unless he got off on batting us around like a tabby with a catnip toy.

"I'll stay here," McNally said after I didn't respond. "You should go check on the others. Let them know what's going on."

The only person I wanted to see was Gage. Throw myself into his arms and sob until the hurt and fear went away. I wouldn't, of course, but sitting next to his bed would help.

"Thank you," I said. "Call me—"

"If anything changes, I will. Promise."

I nodded, and slipped out.

Ten paces from Gage's room, Alexander Grayson stepped into the corridor with his back to me. I froze. I didn't want another conversation. I eyed the door to my immediate left. Broom closet. It would be easy enough to duck inside and let him pass.

I exhaled sharply through my nose. The sound came out too loudly, like an indignant snort. Had I really been reduced to hiding in closets from short, balding ATF agents? Never. Maybe he would just keep walking and turn down the next corridor.

He pivoted in my direction. Thin eyebrows arched. Fatigue bracketed his wide-set eyes and drew his mouth into a narrow line. "Trance, how are you?"

"Ask me again on a day when I haven't just killed someone." I regretted the snap the moment I uttered it.

"I apologize. It was a moronic question."

"The gesture was nice, though." Nice and appreciated, no matter the source. But this little man stood between me and Gage and a few minutes of rest.

"I was just coming by to check on Tempest," he said.

"He's still in surgery. We won't know anything for a few hours."

His head bobbed. "I am sorry about Frost. She never really had a chance to come into her power, and that's a shame."

It was an odd expression of sympathy, but I offered a gracious smile. "Thanks, Agent Grayson."

"You're welcome."

Silence. I scuffed the toe of my boot against the linoleum floor. He cleared his throat. I looked at the door to Gage's room. He got the point.

"Is Agent McNally near the operating room?" he asked.

"Yes, she's there."

"Thank you, Trance."

He walked past me, and I let him go. Maybe he wasn't so bad. For a government stooge. A stooge who was nowhere to be found during our fight a few hours ago. Neither he nor Agent McNally had been in the Medical Center when Specter attacked.

"Agent Grayson?"

He stopped at the opposite end of the corridor and looked over his shoulder. "Yes, Trance?"

"Where were you today?"

His head tilted to the left. He smiled. "ATF satellite office in Burbank, checking in with our bosses. But thanks for asking." He turned the corner and was gone.

Pondering that odd little exchange, I slipped into Gage's room. He was watching the door, expecting me, since he could hear me coming halfway across the complex. The moment was an interesting reversal: him in bed, wearing a simple cotton gown and me standing by the bed with a look of concern. He smiled when our gazes locked.

"Hey," he said.

"Hey, yourself." I reached out and ran my fingertip down the side of his face, trying to ignore the fact that he was shaded like a lilac bush. Touching him again warmed a part of me that had remained cold since Janel's death.

"How's Ethan?"

"Still in surgery. They're saying it's fifty-fifty."

Just speaking those words to someone else made them real. My hands trembled. Gage enveloped them in his and squeezed. I drew strength from his presence—the only constant thing in my life for the last five days. Five days that felt like a lifetime of hurt, fear and confusion.

"How are you?" I asked.

"On painkillers. It kind of makes my senses fuzzy, and I don't like it."

"I think you'd dislike the pain more."

"Maybe."

I glanced at his chest and could not imagine the bruise hidden beneath the gown. Black, blue, and green swirling together like watercolors over smashed muscles and tender bone. He was lucky the ice block hadn't fractured his sternum or broken any ribs.

"How are you, Teresa?"

"I'm fine."

"Liar."

I blinked. "I'm fine, Gage."

He pursed his lips.

I studied the thin white blanket that covered his legs. I didn't want to lie to him, not when he'd always been honest with me—when he bothered giving me straight answers, anyway. I didn't have to pretend for him. "I'm seeing purple again."

"What?" He tugged my arm. "Teresa?"

I looked at him, and the concern in his gaze nearly toppled me. "It started again after I killed Janel. It's like before, where I'm looking through lavender sunglasses."

"You need to tell Dr. Seward."

"So he can run tests?"

"Yes. They need to know what's doing this so they can treat it."

"What if they can't treat it, Gage?" I pulled away and stalked to the other side of the room, my insides quaking. Annoyance and fear were playing kickball with my stomach, and I had the very real urge to vomit. "Dr. Seward already told me it will kill me, so what's the point of documenting my symptoms? Want to know why it started? It's because I used my powers today, that's why it's happening, and I can't very well not use them."

"No one's saying to not use them, Teresa. You saved lives today, both times. Seward admitted they don't know why you're getting these symptoms, so maybe tracking and documenting them is a way to figure it out. Maybe you don't have to just let them kill you."

I glared, my fists clenching and unclenching in time with my ragged breaths. "Let them? You think I want to die?"

"Do you?"

I expected anger to drive me out of the room and into a mad fit of screaming. Instead, I deflated. Every ounce of available energy fled, leaving my muscles limp and my mind muddled. I shuffled back to the bed and perched on the foot, keeping some distance between us.

"No, Gage, I don't want to die. I thought being a Ranger again would make everything all right, make me feel necessary. I don't want to go back to pouring shots for drunks and slinging fried chicken, but I don't think I want *this*." I held a deep breath, trying to quell the tumultuous emotions swirling through me, all clawing toward the surface. A long exhale followed, but I wasn't much calmer for it. I was no longer the frightened child who hid with the wounded while others fought, but— "I don't know this person I've become. She's a woman who erects energy shields and tosses power balls at bad guys and leads her friends into battle. She kills, Gage, and she scares me."

"Fear is allowed, you know."

"No, it's not."

"Teresa, you have to stop this. Stop taking everything onto your shoulders and making it all your responsibility to carry. You're one person."

I snorted. "The person you all keep looking at to lead, Gage. You took responsibility for us all once, and I've been chosen to take responsibility now."

"I seem to remember a terrified little girl giving me the

courage to lead. I would have fallen apart that day without you."

His confession startled me. I'd forgotten about that—Trancing the fear out of him. All I really remembered about Central Park was my own terror and inability to stand and face the Banes.

"Good leaders know when to accept that something isn't their fault," he said. "Sometimes the universe pisses in your shoes, and that's just the way it is."

He was right. Instead of admitting it, I said, "I should call Renee. Let her know what's going on and ask her and William to come home. With the three of you down, I can't fight Specter alone."

"I'm not down any longer than overnight. I've got a bruise, nothing life-threatening. And I don't see frostbite keeping Marco down for long."

"He can't shift with broken fingers."

"He's not useless just because he can't use his power."

"I'm not saying he is, Gage. I'd just feel better if the team was together, instead of split up across the continent. Specter has shown he can get at us anywhere, at any time. I don't want us apart anymore."

"Okay."

I studied his face; he gave away nothing. "Was that 'okay, I agree,' or 'okay, I'm done arguing'?"

"Okay, I agree. And I'm not challenging your decisions, I just want to understand them." He shifted over in the bed. "Come here and sit for a minute. You look like you're ready to collapse."

My gaze flickered to the empty spot next to him, still lingering with his body heat. I stood and walked over, the soles of my shoes softly squeaking against the linoleum tile. He lifted his arm. I slid up against his side, crossed my legs at the ankle, and rested my head on his shoulder. He didn't react, even though I had to reek.

"Do you ever get the feeling Specter is playing with us?" I asked.

"What do you mean?"

"Think about it, Gage, about today. Once he had Frost under his control, he could have devastated us. Dr. Seward was helpless, but Specter didn't kill him. Specter could have killed Marco immediately, frozen his lungs or something. He tortured him instead. Frost's powers could have destroyed the entire building within minutes."

"Maybe Specter isn't as strong as we think."

"Or he's testing us." More and more, that felt like the logical explanation. If Specter truly wanted us dead, Gage and I would not have been alive to discuss it. "He's testing the limits of our powers."

"To what end, though?"

"Therein lies the mystery." And the challenge. Unless Specter didn't destroy the building because he was inside it, on the grounds somewhere—no. It was an impossible scenario. Someone, Seward at the very least, should have recognized him if he was lurking around.

We didn't talk for several minutes, content in each other's company. For a little while, at any rate. Long silences made me nervous and left too much time for thinking.

I twined my fingers around his left hand and squeezed. "Tell me something about Portland."

He tilted his head, seeming to ponder the question. "The Portland Art Museum is one of the five largest in the country."

"Not the city, Gage, about you." I stopped myself before I elbowed him in the stomach—an instinctual reaction that would have caused him no small amount of pain.

"You asked about Portland, not me."

I rolled my eyes. "Tell me something about when you lived in Portland. Why'd you leave St. Louis and move there?"

His silence worried me, even though his posture never changed. More than once, I started to twist around and get a look at his face. Some indication of what he was thinking. I stayed put, convinced he'd eventually ask me to leave. I'd crossed some invisible line into a part of his personal life he didn't want to share. Not that he'd shared much.

"I grew up as lost as you did," Gage said, allaying my fears of dismissal. "My instinct to help people was still there, but not the means to do so. I missed Jasper, and I didn't have a lot of friends, so I was really protective of the ones I did. One of the guys I knew from St. Louis ended up in Portland. He got into some trouble, so he called me one day and begged for help."

"You moved halfway across the country to help a friend?"

"Wouldn't you?"

I wanted to say yes. I had been friendly with some of my foster families, friendly with kids in school, friendly with coworkers. None of them were people I'd consider friends.

The best friends I'd ever known were the five Metas who'd come screaming back into my life last week. I'd do anything for them.

"I like to think I would," I said.

"You would." He stroked my hair with a featherlight touch. "You've overtaken me, Teresa. How'd you do that?"

"Pheromones?"

He didn't laugh at my intended humor—again. I needed to work on my jokes. Tension rippled through him, and I felt it easily beneath his thin hospital gown. "Do you think so?"

I sat up enough to meet his gaze and saw uncertainty there, shadowed by crushing sadness. He clearly didn't want his reaction to me—and likewise mine to him—to be merely chemical, or a reaction of his hypersenses. It was in his eyes and in the firm set of his mouth, and in every action he'd taken toward me since we met at that truck stop. People were attracted to each other all the time for purely physical reasons. It certainly explained why my guard fell whenever I was around him.

"I don't know," I finally said. Truthful. "We're both attractive people, and with your sense of smell it makes sense, right?"

He looked sad, almost frustrated. "Pheromones, huh?"

"It's a theory." Albeit one I didn't want to be true.

"So let's test your theory."

I parted my lips to ask for clarification and his mouth covered mine. I recovered from the surprise of it and slanted my head, allowing him in. He hesitated a moment, then his tongue was stroking mine. He shifted and I fell back against the pillow, allowing his body to press against me. I knew it was wrong—wrong time, wrong place, really wrong circumstances—but it felt right. My hands tangled in his short hair. His kisses left my mouth and traveled across my jaw to my throat. He nipped at my pulse point; I moaned.

No, this was more than pheromones.

He stopped and hovered above me, dilated eyes boring into me. Wanting more. "We should stop," he said, breathless.

"Definitely." I was filthy, he was wounded, and every part of me felt guilty for making out with him. Even if it would be a great distraction from the pain of Specter's latest guerilla attack.

"You should make that phone call," he said.

"I should. And then I have to let Dr. Seward know about my vision."

He hugged me tight, his arms so strong and warm around my waist and shoulders. I didn't want to leave his side, not even to do those two important things. I wanted to stay there and be selfish and not be alone if I exploded again.

I couldn't stay. I was their leader. Not by any rational election process. I'd fallen into it. I had to think of my team first, which meant getting off my ass.

"I'll be back in a few minutes," I said. "If that's okay."

"I'd like that."

"Good, because I'm getting used to spending the night with you."

He held me tighter and kissed the top of my head. I sat a moment longer, then drifted to sleep knowing I should be doing something else.

Nineteen

Regroup

Whoa, sorry!"

Renee's voice roused me from the fog of sleep. She stood in the doorway, hands on her hips, her entire image colored a strange shade of fuchsia—quite a sight, since her skin was already blue. Behind me, Gage stirred.

Reality caught up to my brain, and I had the sense to ask, "When the hell did you get back?"

"Twenty minutes ago," she said. "Dr. Seward called, told us what happened, so we had the ATF jet bring us back right away. Marco is up and about, and we're having a late dinner–slash–early breakfast in a few minutes. Thought you'd like to come down and, ah, discuss stuff."

"Thanks, we'll be down shortly."

She seemed poised to go, then surprised me by coming to the bed with long-legged strides and hugging me fiercely. "Sorry about Janel," she whispered. "That sucks ass in the worst way."

I returned the awkward embrace. "Thanks." She retreated to the door and continued to linger. "Anything else?"

"Yeah, how is he?"

Gage groaned.

I wanted to throw a pillow at her, but having none at hand, settled for a terse, "Get out."

She winked and pulled the door shut.

"She does realize," Gage said, "that we're both fully clothed and in a small hospital bed, right?"

"Well, I'm fully clothed," I said, picking at his gown. "I can't believe I did that."

"Fell asleep?"

"Yeah."

"You're human, Teresa, I'm sure you needed the rest."

"MetaHuman, technically."

"Whatever." He turned my head so I was looking into his eyes; I tried to smile. "How's your vision?"

"Still purple." I sighed. "Good news is, I didn't go nova like last time. And no cramps, either. Maybe it will clear up without a crazy lights display."

He nodded, unconvinced. Something indecipherable played in his speckled eyes. "Can I buy a lady dinner?"

I grinned. "Aren't you supposed to do that before you sleep with me?"

"I'm a nonconformist."

"Think Dr. Seward will let you out of bed?"

"He will if I don't tell him."

"Then, let's do dinner."

Marco, Renee, and William were halfway through their meals by the time we arrived. I'd had trouble finding clean clothes for Gage, so I ran back to his room for something less revealing than his open-backed gown. I also took a few minutes to brush my hair, my teeth, wash my face, and change my clothes. A long, hot shower was definitely in my near future.

I sat down while Gage fetched twin plates from the room's food counter. It looked like sandwiches and hot soup. Strange meal until I looked at the clock on the wall and realized it was almost midnight. I'd slept longer than I thought.

Marco picked at the crusts of his sandwich, his glowing green eyes dulled. Pain, maybe, or painkillers. Red blisters left an angry trail down the left side of his face; both hands were still wrapped in white gauze, and three fingers on his left hand were taped together and splinted. Some leader I was, napping away while he and Ethan were in Medical.

Gage deposited my plate and sat down beside me. I stirred my soup. Guilt had stolen my appetite.

"Any news on Ethan?" I asked.

"Sedated, but stronger," William said. "I checked on him as soon as we got back. He's tough for a skinny Irishman."

Renee dipped a crust of bread into her tomato soup. "We also took a look at the battle site." Her wan smile reiterated her earlier sentiment—it sucked ass. "Your powers acting up again?"

"They're fine."

Gage fisted his fork; he knew I was lying. Oh well. I was not elaborating on the problem—not when we were one man down and unsure when or where Specter might strike next.

"How about you guys?" I asked. "Any luck figuring out

how the wrong person was kept imprisoned for fifteen years, while Specter was running loose?"

William shook his head. "According to the guards, they don't do sight checks unless one of the collars malfunctions. After Specter's collar was checked in that first day, he became persona incognita. His collar never malfunctioned, so no one thought a thing of it. About forty of the prisoners weren't seen until recently, when they did spot checks on everyone."

"Spot checks weren't done regularly?" Gage asked, incredulity arching his eyebrows and some measure of accusation in his tone. Accusation toward whom, I didn't know. Certainly couldn't be William.

"Manhattan Island is huge," Renee replied before William could. "As long as they stayed quietly among themselves, the guards didn't want to bother with them."

Gage grunted, unmollified by the response. "And the guy impersonating Specter? What's his story?" he asked, directing the question at William.

"He doesn't have one," William said. "Someone cut his tongue out years ago. They kept him fed, only he's mentally not together. He doesn't know his own name, so I don't think he'd pick anyone out as the person or persons who kept him."

"That's damned convenient."

It was, but that was hardly William's fault, as Gage seemed hell bent on assigning blame in that direction. What was the cliché? Don't shoot the messenger. "So someone else on the island knew Specter was out," I said. "And they deliberately kept up the ruse that he was there."

"There's another possibility, you know," William said. "It's possible someone from the MHC knows he was never arrested. And I don't just mean the dead guy who collared him."

"You mean someone with influence." The possibility hadn't directly crossed my mind until now, and I felt stupid for not entertaining it sooner. I looked at William. "You don't trust McNally or Grayson, do you?"

"Right this minute?" He shook his head. "Except for Ethan, I don't trust any person not sitting at this table."

Renee reached out and squeezed his hand. Their eyes met. A moment passed between them, something spoken with silence and a look. They'd bonded during their trip east. Maybe more if Renee's playful nature had shined through. I glanced at Gage, who was staring at them with a queer expression— something warring between amusement and . . . jealousy?

He caught me looking and cleared his throat. "So what would the ATF, or anyone else for that matter, have to gain by keeping Specter out of jail?" Gage asked.

I pointed my spoon at him. "Precisely."

"Does anyone even know his real name?" Renee asked. "Anything at all about him other than he's a damned coward who attacks through others, instead of showing his own face?"

I shook my head. "No, that just about covers it, Renee."

"And Specter's real name is not on record," William said. "At least nothing I could find. Even the Banes they questioned in Manhattan didn't know who he was."

"Or wouldn't admit it," Renee said.

"Knowing he's still out there is a good incentive to keep your mouth shut."

"Good points," I said. "Nothing Specter has done so far is random. He's had a long time to plan this. He knew enough to find most of us, and kill some of us before we could even assemble. It's like he's feeling us out, getting an idea of our threat level. Hell, I wouldn't be surprised if Specter knew something about why we all got our powers back."

Four sets of eyes stared at me. "What?" I asked. "It's not so big a leap."

"No, it's not," William said. He pushed his plate away and folded his meaty hands on top of the table. "Look, I didn't get shipped across the country like you guys. They fostered me to a big family out in Long Beach, so I've been around the city my whole life. Watching it change and shrink and die, get minutely better and infinitely worse. I've watched everything around this HQ go to shit, while it never changed. Doesn't it bother you guys how good a shape this entire facility was still in when we got here?"

The question drove home things that had niggled at the back of my mind since our arrival. Sure, some of the hallways were dusty and the rooms not up to code, but the medical equipment was first rate, the food healthy, and the sheets clean. Two days after reactivation, and the HQ ran better than it should have for an organization left to rot for fifteen years.

"I am sure they had a caretaker or two, no?" Marco asked.

"Or twenty," Gage said. "It certainly makes you wonder if they knew that our power loss was temporary. That we'd need the HQ again some day, so they kept it in good shape, made sure protocols existed in case what happened last week happened. There's a hell of a lot about our own pasts that we really don't know."

"We could just ask, you know," Renee said. The high-pitched voice of reason. "It's not like Dr. Seward has lied to any of us."

"Seward isn't the one running things," I said. "The Bureau funds us, remember? If we want answers, we need to ask Agent McNally."

Gage tilted his head and gave me a small smile. "I thought you believed she was on our side."

"I do, Gage, which is why I think she'll answer our questions. She was more straightforward than Grayson, that's for sure. I don't think she would lie to us outright."

"Maybe not, but she still has her own agenda. Her answers were controlled, Teresa."

"I know that, but obfuscation isn't the same as lying." I blew out an exasperated breath. "She was up there, while Ethan was in surgery. She does care what happens to us, and given our state of near-crisis, I think she'll talk."

"Now's your chance to ask," Gage said.

Our heads swiveled toward the door in perfect unison, and two beats later, McNally walked into the cafeteria. She paused, her piercing gaze sweeping around the table.

"Good evening," she said. "I hope you don't mind if I join you."

"Of course not," I replied.

She took her time filling a coffee mug, carefully stirring in two packets of sugar and a bit of milk. Each movement made with precision. She sat down in the only empty chair at the table, between Gage and Renee. "I'd heard you were back, and I don't think we've been properly introduced," she said to the blue woman on her left.

After the prerequisite introductions, McNally sipped her coffee and got right to the point. "This morning's rescue is getting a lot of airtime," she said. "As is the impromptu interview Trance gave. Every pollster we've ever worked with is scrambling to put together new information for us, and the early results have been far more positive than I expected."

"How positive is more positive?" I asked.

"Thirty percent of respondents, when asked if the new Rangers will be a positive influence on the world today, said yes."

"Which means seventy percent think we'll destroy the world?"

"Actually, fifty percent replied they were undecided. But again, these are preliminary numbers, from average citizens. On the other side of things, the news media is clamoring for more information and more interviews."

"We're not a sideshow, Agent McNally," Gage said. "And in case you've forgotten, one of our friends is dead and another is critically injured. Posing for publicity photos isn't high on our priority list."

"I'm certainly not saying it should be, but you do need public support, which you are starting to get. You also need to control your public image, or you'll lose what little support you already have. One or two anchors are saying some rather negative things about Trance simply from the way she ended the interview. If we don't correct them, the damage may be irreversible."

I twirled my spoon between my fingers. "Do you really think I care what the public thinks of me?"

She nodded. "I know you do, Trance. You care about this team, and you don't want to worry about Joe Citizen taking potshots at you while you're trying to mount a rescue."

The spoon fell from my fingers, and I glared. She had to know how my mom died. Using that against me was cruel. And brilliant, because she was right. Specter was about all we could handle in terms of enemies right now.

"The instant celebrity status can be beneficial to you," she continued, "but if you don't control the flow of information, it could devastate your public support. Do you remember the negative publicity your elders received during the final year of the War?"

Adults whispering behind closed doors, hiding the daily newspapers. My father set the television stations to news-free networks only, and didn't let the other grown-ups talk about it when I was around. I knew things were going badly, but he shielded me from most of it. Something I now regretted.

"I do," Marco said. He said something in Spanish and, judging by Gage's raised eyebrows, it was laced with profanity. "What is the phrase? From hero to zero in one headline. My mentor was criticized in an article, because an apartment building burned down while he was battling two Banes. *No importa*—never mind he saved the lives of everyone who lived there. The press called him an arsonist."

"That's exactly my point, Onyx," McNally said. "You don't have to do profiles and cover spreads. That's not what I want. Just a short interview on one morning show, to speak your peace, answer a few questions, and make sure everyone knows we will do everything we can to keep things from escalating again."

"In theory it's a good idea," I said. "But I don't want to put all of us in one room, on live television, and give Specter the perfect target."

McNally drummed her fingers against the side of her mug. "Then, we do it pretaped. We give the studio one hour advance notice, go in quietly, tape the interview, and then leave. Simple, sweet, and a much smaller audience."

"Can we preapprove the questions?" I asked.

"I'll see what I can do."

"It's a deal-breaker."

"Then, I'll make certain of it. Anything else?"

I took a moment to study my team. Gauge their reactions. William and Marco listened attentively, giving no nonverbal cues as to their thoughts. Gage kept picking at his sandwich with a half-frown on his face; I wanted to reassure him this was a good idea—as soon as I convinced myself.

Renee alone showed keen interest in the interview. She watched McNally with what I could only describe as fascination. Maybe a little bit of awe, as if she couldn't believe someone would go to these lengths for us. Perhaps she was simply contemplating her fifteen minutes of fame.

"I want the girl from the site," I said. If she refused, we'd be off the hook. "The blonde from the newspaper. Dahlia something?"

"Why her?" McNally asked.

"Because she was intimidated by us. She won't be tempted

to go off on a tangent, or manipulate the questions. If we're boosting our own credibility, might as well boost someone else while we're at it."

"So, ten minutes, pretaped, you write the questions, and she asks them. That's the deal?"

A round of nods from the others sealed my answer: "Yes."

"Then, I'll see what I can put together." McNally's chair scraped as she stood up. "I'll let you know as soon as we've made arrangements."

"I can't wait." Beneath the table, Gage's foot kicked mine. "What? That wasn't all sarcasm."

McNally chuckled and left with her coffee.

"Well, that was quite rude," Renee said. The annoyance in her voice caught my attention, but amusement danced in her eyes. "Can she just take our coffee mugs like that?"

William wadded up his napkin and threw it at her head. He chuckled, Renee giggled, and I sighed with relief. I bit into the turkey sandwich, and my appetite ignited like a spark to gas. I polished it off quickly, along with my soup and some crackers Renee didn't want. I was about to go get a second helping when Marco stood up—leaving.

The food could wait.

"Can I walk you out?" I asked, standing too quickly and knocking my chair over. Gage caught it with one hand and set it upright.

Marco nodded. I followed him to the disposal, and we dropped our plates. Awkward silence accompanied us into the corridor. He turned toward the elevator bank. I zipped past to cut him off before he could press the button.

"How are you?" I asked, and fixed the wounded shape-shifter with my sternest stare. "Really, Marco, how are you doing?"

He studied me a moment, the glow of his lime-green eyes rising and falling like waves in an ocean. Did the color react to his emotions? "If I say I am fine, Catalepsia, you will call me a liar."

"Not if you're really fine."

"I am fine."

"Liar."

"What do you wish me to say?"

"Tell me the truth, Marco," I said, practically begging. Hedging bothered me beyond words. Straight talk or nothing. "Tell me that you're pissed as hell at me for sending you up there to get hurt. Tell me you hate that I got out of it without a scrape, while everyone else I care about was injured. Tell me I'm not my father, and I'm a terrible field leader, and Gage should be in charge like before. I don't care, just be honest with me."

Deep lines creased his forehead, darkening the camouflage coloration of his skin. A cloud of sadness settled over him like a thunderhead, and I found myself both repelled and intrigued. We'd traded more words in the last few days than in the two years I'd known him prior to losing our powers. He'd been held captive and abused before coming to the Rangers, and hadn't talked much to me or anyone else, preferring to spend the majority of his time as a panther. I couldn't begin to imagine what losing his shifting abilities had done to him, or the difficulties he faced because of his fur-mottled skin.

"I am not angry at you," he said. "I am only angry with myself."

I blinked hard, startled by his answer. "Why?"

"Because I charged into a situation without first assessing it, and that is why I was caught and injured. I was careless."

"I told you to go ahead of us."

"I should have been more cautious. Now Janel is dead, Ethan is fighting to live, and perhaps I could have prevented it. I could have done something differently. Better."

"We all could have done something differently." I gently grasped his wrist. Better to avoid his hands for now. "I could have killed Janel sooner. Ethan could have taken two steps to the left. Gage could have not stepped into that doorway. Regardless, we did all of those things. Second-guessing battle decisions won't help us do better the next time. Examining them will."

McNally's voice rang through my head. Damn her, she was right.

"What is the difference?" Marco asked.

"The difference is we accept the choices we make and learn from the mistakes. Besides, if anyone on this team is going to second-guess, it will be me. It's the leader's prerogative. Just like it's my prerogative to cheer you up."

"Find a healer who can fix my hand." He gave no sign that anything I just said made a bit of difference. "I cannot shift until the bones heal, so I am useless to you and this team."

I had no comeback for that one, and an overwhelming sadness struck me. I'd been around these people for days and, except for Gage, had taken no time to get to know them or understand their history during our separation. I hadn't taken the time to be his friend.

"I'm sorry, Marco."

He tilted his head to one side. "For what?"

"For the things that hurt you that no one was there to stop."

A sad smile pulled at the corners of his mouth. "Anything that happened prior to a week ago was never your fault. You cannot be sorry for it."

"Yes, I can, and I am. None of us really talk about those years we were apart, because most of us had pretty awful times of it. I know I didn't have the best years of my life, and I'm glad to have left it all behind. Good or bad, I'm sorry because I'm your friend."

He turned, and I let go of his wrist. I couldn't stop him from walking away and not accepting my words. He surprised me by pivoting back around and sweeping his strong arms around my waist. I tossed my own arms around his shoulders and hugged him back. The superfine hair covering his skin tickled my cheek, soft as velvet. We held each other for a few moments, drawing strength, creating unity.

"I am sorry to be such a gloomy pain in the ass," he said, his breath puffing against my ear.

I laughed. "I'm not so easy to get along with myself. We can start a Pains-in-the-Ass Club, if you like. Definitely invite Dr. Seward to join."

Marco chuckled. His grip loosened, and I stepped back. "Thank you, Catalepsia," he said. "Perhaps one day we will tell our sad stories over a bottle of tequila."

"Something tells me we'll need two bottles."

He smiled, and the sight warmed my heart. I swatted him on the shoulder, then pressed the elevator's call button. It chimed right away, and the doors slid open.

"I'll see you later," I said.

He nodded and stepped into the elevator.

As the doors slid shut, I thought of my promise to Gage. I didn't want to search for Dr. Seward and explain about my sight. Lab Rat was not a title I needed attached to my name, thank you very much. But I said I'd go, and I didn't want to start lying to Gage. Maybe Dr. Seward would be busy; I could say I tried. Or maybe he wasn't even on base, since it was the middle of the night.

And I wanted to see Ethan.

The exterior of the Medical Center looked like it had been scalped, a monument to how badly our safety had been violated—and how horribly I'd screwed up. Carpenters and technicians created a steady stream in and out, even during this late hour. The top floor was missing windows and a roof. The copter wouldn't be making any emergency landings up there for a while; it would have to stick to the helipad on the roof of the Base.

I found Dr. Seward's temporary fourth-floor office empty. He had kept the bulk of his medical files in the central computer network, saving him the work of going through mountains of water-damaged paper files.

Since Seward could be anywhere on the property, I

counted my blessings, skipped past the lab-turned-office, and headed for ICU. None of my most recent trips to Medical had landed me there, only one of my teammates. Another teammate that I didn't know very well. I wanted to know him. I wanted to know all of them again.

No one was monitoring the outer station. I spotted a white-coated shoulder in the office behind it, barely visible behind a white- and red-checked curtain. Either Julie Dent, one of our two on-call nurses, or Dr. Adam Morgan himself, the trauma surgeon they'd borrowed from Cedars-Sinai specifically for Ethan. I slipped past, toward the closed door. The latch unlocked, and I pushed as quietly as I could.

My entrance garnered no attention from the person in the office (or break room, it was hard to tell). On the other side of the door was a short corridor and four divided cubicles. Gentle whirs and beeps came from the slot immediately to my left, and I gravitated toward it.

Ethan lay flat on his back, a thick cloud of white bandages obscuring his chest. Some blood had seeped through straight up the middle, as if a child had dragged a red paintbrush across it. Bruises and cuts covered his arms and face. His hair stood out starkly against his pallor, visible even to my lavender-hued eyes.

He wasn't on a ventilator. An oxygen mask covered his mouth and nose, and a pulse monitor created a steady staccato beep. A variety of tubes and wires crisscrossed his body, and I couldn't hope to know what each of them did or what medicine they provided.

I picked up the chart hanging from the foot of the bed.

I couldn't make heads or tails of the handwriting scrawled across the page. Medical doctors either wrote in another language, or this was done up by a drunk spider after walking across an inkpad. The little cubicle had no chairs; nothing that said it welcomed visitors. Even if a nurse complained, I doubted she would try to force me out.

"Well," I said, "the good news is that you're going to live. Getting squashed under a collapsed ceiling is usually something that happens during the fight, not after, but I guess you're not one for rules. Gage and Marco are okay, too. You came out of it with the biggest scratches."

Nothing. Not like I expected a response, but sometimes . . . "If I start to nag you about waking up, will you sit up and argue with me?"

Guess not.

"William and Renee are home, and now McNally is insisting we do a news show. I think it will be a painful exercise in futility, but she seems to think good press is better than no press. Since Rangers have had no press for this long, I suppose I should agree with her."

I picked at a lint pill on the edge of the blanket. "You know, I think I miss the dull responsibility of making my rent every month, working three jobs to eat, and carrying the burden of being an ex-con stuck in the same state for two more years. Did you know that about me? I know Gage does, and it doesn't seem to bother him, and I can assume McNally and Grayson do, too.

"Yeah, your heroic leader is a criminal. How's that for ironic? I got two years on an accessory charge and served twelve months, courtesy of the lying asshole I thought I was in love with at the time."

After the unfortunate incident with my virginity, I'd barely dated for the rest of high school. Or after the foster care system booted me out at the age of eighteen to face life on my own two (unbalanced) feet. But I couldn't protect my heart forever. I was twenty when I met Kirk. He'd been a regular at one of the two places I waitressed at. He'd chat me up while ordering and leave big tips, and he always had a sweet compliment about my hair or my smile. Somehow he made it seem like I asked him out, when I'm sure it was the other way around. He made it seem like sex was my idea, too. It was great, really great, for almost a year. I was too stupid in love to wonder where he got his money when he never seemed to work.

Three days before my twenty-first birthday, he asked me for a favor. I agreed without hesitation. I still agreed to do it after I found out he wanted me to drive a getaway car, in exchange for a share of the stuff he stole. He said the score would be enough to get us both out of Portland, down to somewhere warm and sunny. I fell for it.

The sound of my prison cell door slamming closed for the first time was the second most terrifying moment of my life. I didn't cry the first night, like they say most people do. My incarceration didn't sink in until the second day, when I had to take a lukewarm, five-minute shower with nine strange women, watched over by two CO's. I'd never felt more naked, more vulnerable or ashamed of myself for ending up there. For the first time, I'd felt like I had completely disappointed my father and pissed on everything he'd taught me—everything he'd raised me to be. That second night, I cried until I threw up, then I cried some more. My cellmate thanked me in the morning by punching me in the eye.

Yep, that was the woman currently in charge of the last of the Rangers.

"I don't want to do the interview," I said, shaking out of my macabre memories. "If we have to do it, though, it's on my terms. I don't want some nosy reporter matching me up to my mug shot and asking about it."

I laughed without amusement and studied the monitors without interest. "It would be almost worth it just to see what sort of lather McNally gets into. She's got this hard-on for controlling our public image. I guess she lived through the brunt of our negative publicity during the War, and she wants to prevent that now.

"But what kind of publicity can you get for a group whose ex-con leader kills one of their own?" I said, thinking of Janel.

"Bad kind."

I turned, heart pounding. The muffled voice hadn't come from behind me. Ethan's eyes had opened a fraction, twin slits of dull color. Looking at me. He licked his lips beneath the mask.

"Hey." I reached for his hand and held it as tight as I dared. His skin was cool, too cool. "Eavesdrop much?"

"Talking to me. Only heard some."

"I was just babbling, trying to make myself feel better. Should I call the doctor? Are you in pain?"

"No."

"No to which question?"

"First."

"So no doctor, but you're in pain?"

His eyes closed, and then opened a bit wider. He breathed hard, creating a cloud of vapor inside of the mask. I pulled it down to his chin, freeing his mouth.

"Thanks," he said. "Others okay?"

"Yeah, a little banged up, but they're fine. We were all worried about you. Renee was pretty jealous about how you flew us down to that construction site, and I think she wants a ride of her own when you're better."

The left side of his mouth turned up, not quite a complete smile. "See what . . . can do."

Now that I had a captive audience, the words wouldn't come as easily. I dragged the toe of my sneaker across the glossy floor. "Is there anything you need?"

"Coffee?"

I grinned; he didn't. In fact, his smile melted away completely, overtaken by stubbornness.

"Coffee," he said again.

"Ethan, I don't think the doctors will allow you to have coffee three hours after major surgery. Besides, you need to sleep, not stay awake."

He shook his head, fear creeping into his eyes. "Stay awake."

"You need to rest, you almost died up there."

"Specter."

I scrubbed my hands over my face. Specter would not come after us again, not for at least a day. He had to recharge his psychokinetic batteries. I could figure out a way to have guards posted in the ICU if it made Ethan feel safer. Anything to help him get some rest, to relax and . . . oh, no.

"You don't want to sleep," I said, picking my words carefully, "because you don't want Specter to use you like he used Janel. Is that it?"

A tilt of his head confirmed my suspicion. He looked away, finding the blanket more interesting to stare at. My heart broke for him. A grown man who looked like a boy and had no one to protect him, except friends just as lost. I perched on the edge of the bed and braced my hands on either side of his arms. He ignored me a moment, and then looked up.

"Specter can't come after us right now, Ethan. It's only been half a day. He doesn't have the strength. Sleep for a few more hours and get your own strength back. Then, if you're still afraid, we'll discuss other options. Just don't let fear make you hurt yourself, okay?"

He nodded, short jerks of his chin to indicate yes. "You're . . . good leader, Trance. Smart."

"Nah, I just can't afford to lose any more men." He chuckled, so I added, "Especially the cute ones. Get some rest. Please?"

"What're you gonna do?"

A good question I hadn't given serious consideration to. Waiting for Specter to attack again was stupid, but we had no way to locate him. Not until he wanted to be found or came at us again. Knowing he could enter the mind of any of us if we dozed off and use our powers against the others frightened me more than I would ever admit.

We had no safeguards against a psychokinetic attack.

The HQ had all kinds of modern surveillance methods that worked best against active powers and physical intruders. Sensors could not detect one mind entering another. The technology didn't exist, and none of us possessed that particular ability.

Gage had made an astute observation an hour ago—so much of our past was still hidden from us, and we had no living mentors from whom to learn. Corps archives were tucked away in the basement of the Medical Center—the official storage place of Corps history. Team photographs, plaques dedicated to those lost in the line of duty, commemorative items for battles fought and won—all once proudly displayed in the Base and the Housing Unit—were now packed away in boxes and bins. Covered in bubble wrap and old newspaper, remnants of a glorious past laid to rest. Records and personnel files, old medical histories, mission reports, diaries, any number of documents were down there as well.

I didn't fear the past, but I'd spent years running from my own, fraught with failures and mistakes. I didn't need to see the failures of our predecessors neatly encased in glass shadowboxes, testaments to everything we'd lost. No, the past was best avoided for now.

I had to focus on the present, because until we discovered something to help us defeat Specter, we were sitting ducks. I said, "I'm honestly not sure. You don't worry about it, Ethan. Just get better."

I leaned down and kissed his forehead. His eyelids fluttered, then closed. I sat a while longer, listening to his breathing even out and deepen, and wished him into a good dream.

We could all use a good dream or two.

Twenty

Filter

*S*he sleeps in the pale blue glow, deaf to the whir of machines sustaining her life; unaware of her companion, who is a shape I cannot discern. He sleeps, too. The room is stark, undecorated, sterile. It feels like a hospital but different. They are forgotten here, in this room they have shared for many long years, as they have shared their lives. They only wish to help. It is all they have ever wished.

Help whom?

She sleeps on without reply.

I watch her as before and realize after a time that she is sweating. It dampens her forehead and cheeks. The room is warmer. Hot. Too hot, but I see nothing amiss. I smell something awful, dangerous.

Her companion makes terrible sounds, and then I see. His bed is engulfed in flames. She knows he is dying. He understands why, and he silently curses their killer. Their minds are linked, as they have always been.

Her eyelids fly open. The fire approaches her own bed. Her luminescent eyes stare in hatred and accusation. Not at me. Through me.

Through the cacophony of voices and colors and lights—

I woke from the nightmare with a shout and fell right out of bed, managing to land hard on my left elbow. I lay there, dazed and panting. Damn it, I hadn't meant to fall asleep. I certainly hadn't meant to dream of that woman again. My subconscious was really starting to piss me off.

I worked my neck to get the kinks out, then sat up and checked the clock—close to 2:00 a.m. I hauled myself up using the corner of my bed. I'd come back to my room meaning to take a shower. Now all I wanted was more sleep.

My bedroom door banged open, startling the crap out of me, and a distraught Renee stalked inside. She was wringing her elongated fingers in an exaggerated manner, twisting them around into unimaginably gross knots and pretzels. Kicking the door shut with her boot and a bang, she flopped onto the foot of my bed and stretched her long legs out.

"I need sex, T," she wailed at the ceiling. Her electric blue eyes shimmered with unshed tears. "Really, really need it, so why do I keep saying no? What is wrong with me?"

"I— What?" I just stared at her, willing her words to make some semblance of sense. "Um, Renee, I think you started mid-conversation here. Want to rewind and try again?"

Her head listed toward me, lips pressed tight. Since I remet her, Renee Duvall had struck me as the most carefree, roll-with-the-punches person imaginable, not unlike how she'd been as a child. Ready with a smile and a saucy quip, I didn't expect the sadness I saw in her now. Or the utter frustration.

"I really like him," she said. "Really, really like him, T. I mean, have you seen his ass? And his abs and his pecs, not to mention his yummy brown eyes? And holy shit, he's a great kisser."

"We're talking about William, right?"

"No, Dr. Seward." She shot me a look. "Yes, William. I mean, we were friends when we were kids, right? And ever since we met again, it's like . . . I dunno, saying 'sparks' sounds stupid. There's something there, T, and I don't usually go all weak-kneed over a guy, but he's not just a guy, right?"

Faced with a friend and her romantic problems, I came to an abrupt understanding of my own limited love life—I had no real advice to offer her, no previous girlfriend conversations on which to draw for reference. I'd dated casually, sure; however, my usual MO was to keep men at arm's length. Letting them in—literally and metaphorically—hadn't been an option for years. Not after being sold out by Kirk. He was why I resisted so hard when Gage made me go all gooey inside.

Renee's admission that she wanted to sleep with William and hadn't also made me smile inwardly. I guessed Gage's veiled annoyance over their burgeoning relationship was a little premature.

I sat near my pillow, drew one leg up, and kept the other foot flat on the floor. Renee just stared at me, silently begging for advice I didn't have. I didn't really know her. And it was a problem—maybe the only one on my plate right now—I could rectify with just a few direct queries.

"You're attracted to William?" I asked.

"Oh yeah, in a big way."

"And he's attracted to you?"

"In an even bigger way." To emphasize her point, she curled her fingers toward her thumb, creating an O that she gradually expanded to an impressive diameter. Her perfectly plucked eyebrows arched suggestively.

"So what's the problem?" What's the problem? Pot, meet kettle.

"Me!" Another plaintive wail sliced through the room. She sat up and bounced fully onto the bed, facing me with her legs folded beneath her. "I could be screwing him silly right now, but I left. I can't believe I left! Why did I do that?"

Deciding that the question was rhetorical and not something I could even pretend to answer, I reached over and patted her knee. I wasn't good at this. My sex talk consisted of jokes and innuendoes shouted between my fellow waitresses, at any of my various jobs, about the men they were sleeping with—size and positions and endurance. Those conversations never got serious.

Renee had come to me for advice, and I'd be damned if I sent her away without saying . . . well, something. "Renee, sweetheart, why did you leave?"

She looked so lost in that moment, so much like the little girl I remembered. "Because I don't want William to be just another lay. I did the slut thing, T, and it got me into a lot of trouble years ago. Everyone wanted to bang the blue girl. I want this to be different. I want him to be different, you know, and not just screwing me because I'm blond and sexy and have big tits."

"Do you really think William likes you because of your breasts? Because when I see you two together, he's looking at your face, not your boobs."

A proud sort of smile cleansed some of the angst from her expression. "I just want this to be different. I mean, we're heroes now, not just people."

"Becoming heroes again doesn't mean we completely stop being the people we were a week ago. No one switches personalities like that. We don't stop being basket cases just because we have code names and uniforms and superpowers."

If only a personality switch was so easy—then I'd have no trouble accepting my leadership role. I wouldn't be terrified of letting everyone down because I was still a ten-year-old hiding from the bad guys. I'd be able to throw caution to the wind and just be with Gage—history be damned—without fearing what he'd think of me later. None of us would walk around with the invisible chains of our pasts weighing us down.

We each had pasts affecting our nows, and I was only just seeing it clearly.

Some leader that made me.

"Have you slept with Gage?"

Her point-blank question started me. My heart beat a little faster. "No, I haven't."

"Do you want to?"

"I think so."

"Why haven't you?" No accusation in her question, just an earnest sincerity—as if my answer would illuminate the reasons behind her own hesitation.

Instead of some convoluted reply, I surprised myself by letting the truth tumble right out of my mouth. "Because I have a hard time trusting men, and the last guy I slept with sold me out to the cops on burglary charges and got me twelve months in jail."

She blinked. "Really?"

"Yep."

"Were you guilty?"

"Mostly of being stupid, hence my self-imposed vow of celibacy. Dancing and drinking with a guy doesn't carry the same emotional weight as sleeping with him."

"I don't know, T." Her mouth twisted into a grimace. "I think I'd rather be a slut than a cock tease."

I bristled, a flush heating my cheeks. "Dancing for a few hours and buying me a drink doesn't give any man carte blanche to fuck me afterward, Renee. You were a stripper. Did you sleep with everyone you danced for?"

She blushed this time, coloring to an odd shade of purple. "That's not the same thing."

"No?"

"No, and I've seen Gage looking at you when you don't see him. Do you seriously think that he's capable of screwing you, and then screwing you over?"

My head jerked as if I'd been slapped, nudging me closer

to the limits of my temper. Renee saw in Gage the same things I saw in William. So why did William actively pursue what he wanted, while Gage played this strange dodge-and-dance with me? I hadn't a clue.

And Renee was waiting.

"Do you think William will do the same to you?" I asked. "Screw you, and then screw you over?

We were coming at identical dilemmas from opposing sides, protecting our bodies and our hearts from the exact same thing—being hurt. For children who'd watched our loved ones die, who'd been ripped from the only lives we'd ever known, and who'd struggled to survive in a harsh, un-forgiving environment, the reaction seemed shockingly normal. Those things were our pasts, though, not our present. We were all together again, doing what we were born to do, and it felt right. Renee and I—and indeed, the four handsome men in our lives—had to stop using the past as an excuse. The past was gone, slipping away.

If only actions were as easy as words.

"You're right, T," Renee said.

She shocked me by stretching out her torso and flinging her arms around my shoulders. I hugged her back—a little unnerved that she was still sitting four feet away and her spine looked like pulled taffy—grateful for the embrace. We'd have to answer the question by ourselves, and she seemed to have come to a happy conclusion. What it meant for William in the immediate future, I didn't know; I just hoped he enjoyed himself.

As for Gage . . . I cared about him, more than I wanted

to admit. His kisses made the weight of the world fall off my shoulders and everything seemed easier. We'd be on the verge of something wonderful, and then he'd put up an emotional wall I couldn't breach and only show me the parts of him he wanted me to see. He was hiding something about his past, which frustrated the hell out of me. He knew I was a convicted felon—my absolute worst secret.

What could be so awful that he wouldn't tell me?

My imagination could certainly fill in the details, but I didn't want to do that. I didn't want to have to pry the answers out of him, either. He trusted me insofar as the job went. He just didn't seem to trust me with his heart and the painful secrets he kept deep inside.

Frustrating didn't even begin to cover it.

I did know one thing for certain, and it was an answer to Renee's question. It hit me while she untangled herself and bounced to her feet, giggling at something in her head as she strolled to the door. After she'd gone, I let the answer bubble to the surface and my certainty in its truthfulness made me smile—Gage would never screw me over.

He might not be as open as I wanted, and I thought I could accept that for now—we'd known each other less than a week, after all. We had time to work out the kinks. And boy, we'd work them out sooner or later. I'd found a man I was very attracted to and who'd earned my trust by saving my life. I wouldn't give up on him.

I had no particular destination in mind when I left my room, and my wanderings took me out under the night sky. In the middle of the property was a small park—although *park* was a kind word. It was a strip of grass among cement sidewalks, with a small sapling and an iron bench. I gravitated toward it for no real reason and sat down on the rusty metal. Wind whispered through the small leaves of the sapling like white noise. Perfect for sitting and trying to think.

I used to avoid thinking, which landed me in too many bars on too many binges—once this was preferable to pondering my miserable existence and trying to piece together the mess I'd made of my life.

No need to puzzle out my present life. It had been laid out in front of me in big letters that spelled out R-A-N-G-E-R C-O-R-P-S. My life and my future, without a doubt.

The mess lay now in how to protect my friends against an enemy we couldn't see and couldn't fight, and to find meaning in it all at the end of the day. Every time we claimed victory over one of Specter's attacks, an innocent died. It wasn't the way we wanted things; it was just how they happened. Specter needed a weakened mind. He could not inhabit a dead body, and when a body died around him, it weakened *him*. Created a need for a long rest. It gave us time—cold comfort for his victims. Our victims.

"Teresa?

My attention shifted to the sound of Gage's voice. He walked toward me, a purple apparition (a color I was truly starting to hate) under the light cast by nearby lamps. Fatigue slumped his shoulders, but he walked with purpose, arms crossed loosely over his chest. My heart sped up at the sight of him, the conversation with Renee still ringing in my ears.

"What are you doing up?" I asked.

"Looking for you. What are you doing out here?"

"Avoiding sleep, I guess."

He sat next to me. For an instant he faded out of sight, blotted by a dark smudge of purple. I blinked hard; he reappeared. Just my imagination coupling with fatigue.

"What's the matter?"

"Just thinking," I lied.

"About what?"

"William, actually." Gage flinched—interesting. I tilted my head, ignoring the strange, swirling sensation in my guts. "What? Jealous I wasn't thinking about you?"

"No, it's just that I saw him a few minutes ago heading toward the gym. He seemed . . . frustrated."

I snorted laughter. "I bet. Doubt he'll stay that way once Renee finds him. We just had a very strange conversation about sex and relationships, and I think she made a good self-discovery."

"About?"

"What she wants."

"And you? What do you want, Teresa?"

"I don't know anymore if I have a choice in what I want."

He frowned. "What do you mean?"

"We can do so much more than what our parents did, Gage. Their lives became about policing the Banes and protecting innocent bystanders more than actually using their powers to benefit the world. Ethan can summon the winds. He could bring rain to deserts, warm winds to a freezing crop. The Rangers have always been about saving, not about helping."

"Saving has its place. We saved those men at the construction site. Saved their lives."

"You're right." Being a Ranger meant being a rescuer, being on call to save lives and protect from attack. But our lives had to amount to more than that, had to be part of something bigger than the next Bane strike. It was what I'd been searching for my entire life—a purpose to fill the void that even Gage's friendship couldn't touch. "There's got to be more. I have these powers for a reason, and it wasn't to pull men out of rubble. There has to be something bigger."

"You know," he said, tilting his head to one side, "you're beautiful when you're being idealistic."

I grinned. "Soak it up, because I tend to err on the side of cynicism."

He studied me with his flecked eyes—eyes I desperately wanted to see in their full silver detail, instead of tinged lavender—taking in details without passing judgment. Only I wanted him to judge me, damn it. I wanted his opinion. Wanted to know what he was thinking.

"Gage, for the first time in my life, I'm part of something. You know what it's like to be an outsider, we all do." A tingling sensation began in my stomach, and it wasn't from the conversation. Crap. Familiar symptoms in a new problem, rearing their ugly heads. Concentrate. "These powers of mine have a purpose and an intent, and I can't ignore it. Even if what I'm here to do is die saving the rest of you."

"You're not doing to d— Teresa, you're trembling."

I was. When had that happened? I tried to stop and couldn't. No cramps this time; just an overwhelming chill sending tremors through my arms and legs, across my torso and up to my scalp. A million ants crawled over my skin, dancing senseless patterns that tickled and scratched. Why now? Why the hell now?

"Teresa?"

He grabbed my hand; I barely felt it. I blinked hard and rubbed my eyes. The purple had settled. I saw only a vague outline of his head in the murky color veiling my vision.

"Gage?" My own voice sounded strange, fearful and choked.

"What is it?"

I turned my head, seeking some other shape or building, and saw nothing. Even the vague outline of Gage's head—if I'd even seen it the first time—was gone. No spots of light or dark, just a deep violet shield. My heart thudded hard.

"What, Teresa, what's—?" He inhaled sharply. "Your eyes."

I groped blindly for him, and his other hand squeezed my shoulder. "What about them?"

"I don't—they're completely purple. No iris, no sclera, nothing, just purple. Teresa, can you—?"

"I can't see. I can't see a damned thing."

There is nothing quite as frustrating as going temporarily blind when your top priority is locating and stopping a killer. I don't do helpless easily or well, and sitting on an exam table while people talked around me raised my frustration level to a dangerous high.

"Her body is building up an excess of energy again," Dr. Seward said. He stood somewhere to my immediate right.

"But that doesn't make sense." Gage, on my left and holding my hand. "She expended a lot of power yesterday, both at the rescue site and upstairs. How can it be building?"

"I don't know, Cipher, I really don't."

"I mean, we can't just sit up on the roof and hope she goes nova again without killing herself."

"No, we can't do that, especially with news copters flying in and out of our airspace now. She will have to release the pent-up energy eventually, and it will have to go somewhere. My fear is that the stress to her body will cause a seizure, or worse."

"Like a heart attack?" I asked.

"Possibly. Seizure, heart attack, aneurysm. We spoke about this yesterday, remember?"

I rolled my eyes. "Kind of hard to forget. What was I supposed to do? Not save those people at the construction site?" Fabric rustled, and I wondered if Seward was shaking his head.

"Not helping someone in need isn't an option for most Rangers. I should know that by now, and it's pointless to ask you to go against your nature. But as a physician, I can't simply stand by and watch you kill yourself."

"Do you have a better alternative?"

"I have a colleague at Johns Hopkins who's had moderate success with cryogenic stasis—"

"Forget it."

"Trance—"

"Never in a million years, Doctor," I snapped. "I will not be put into a tube and frozen on the off chance you can even defrost me in a year and fix what's wrong. I was not given these abilities so I could be put in cold storage. I have them for a reason."

"You really believe that?"

"Yes." *Stay the course.* "Stasis is not an option."

"It's okay," Gage said. His arm slipped around my shoulders, and I leaned against him. "We'll figure out something else, Teresa."

"We need some time to study your test results," Dr. Seward said. "We have more information to work with this time than we did before. If there's an answer in all of this, we'll find it."

"What do I do in the meantime?" I asked. "I can't find Specter like this. I can't even find the toilet like this."

"The others will be awake again in a few hours," Gage said. "We'll talk about it then, okay? We'll figure something out as a team."

Team. "Is Ethan resting better? He was worried before, about getting taken over."

"He seems to be resting comfortably now," Seward said. "He's very strong, Trance, and there's a great chance that with enough time, he'll fully recover."

I snorted. "Time is something we seem to be in short supply of lately." But relief tempered my annoyance.

"He's alive, Teresa," Gage said. "That's what matters."

I wanted to take comfort in the simple thought. We were still alive and able to fight another day. Nevertheless, what good did that do when you couldn't anticipate the next battle in an undeclared war? Hours were ticking away. If Specter attacked before my eyesight returned, I'd be useless. Helpless, just like when I was a kid. We didn't know where Specter was or who he would possess next. The others couldn't confront him alone.

The door hinge squeaked. Footsteps whispered over the linoleum. Papers rustled, and then the door closed again. No one spoke.

"Who was that?" I asked.

"One of my assistants with a test result I asked for," Dr. Seward said. "And I think I have moderately good news for you."

"Moderately?"

"The test confirms something about your powers I had suspected from the start, and I think it may help us figure out a way to stop these overloads."

"What is that, exactly?"

"Have you ever changed an air filter?"

I blinked, frowned. "Yeah, a few times. The maintenance staff for the hole I used to live in was nonexistent, so I had to do a lot on my own. Why?"

"Your powers don't come from nowhere, Trance. When you create the orbs, as you call them, you draw energy from around you and sometimes from yourself."

That explained the warmth and sudden appetite after power bursts. So far, I was following his logic. Still didn't know what air filters had to do with it.

"Your body draws in the energy and converts it," Seward

continued. "It takes what it needs, just like an air conditioner sucking in air through its filter. It blows the cool air back out, just as you manipulate the orbs. An air filter traps dirt and pollen, and over time, it builds up."

His analogy hit with perfect clarity. "My body can't filter out everything it draws in. It builds up like gunk in a lint trap, disrupts my vision, and affects my bodily functions. Right?"

"Yes. The disrupted vision is simply a symptom of a building problem, just like the cramps you experienced the day before yesterday."

Gage cleared his throat. "So what was that thing she did outside? When she exploded and collapsed?"

"Her body figured out a way to expel the buildup on its own. However, it was an extremely traumatic, violent eruption, and it could have killed her. If we can't help you dispel the buildup from yesterday morning's activities in some other manner, it could happen again, a worse eruption, that could have any number of side effects, including heart attack, stroke—"

I held up one hand, palm out. "Okay, I got the list the first two times. Your people figured this much out. How hard can a cure be?"

No answer. Great.

"Can I go back to my room now?" I asked.

"You really should stay here," Seward said. "But I can't stop you from leaving."

"Thank you."

"If your symptoms change, you'll come back." It wasn't phrased as a question, so I nodded an affirmation.

Gage kept his arm around my waist as I stood up. I wobbled; his grip tightened. The trembling spell was over, but my legs felt like gelatin. With Gage's support, we left.

"I guess this is my body's subtle way of saying 'Get some damned sleep,' huh?" I asked.

"Something like that."

"You have any pet dander allergies?

The muscles in his arm rippled. I could only imagine the look on his face. "No, why?"

I smiled in his general direction. "Because if these spells keep up, I may need to invest in a Seeing Eye dog."

He didn't reply.

It seemed funnier in my head. As usual.

Twenty-one

Exploration

G age never let me go, and on the elevator ride up to our floor, I noticed something: I reeked. Really reeked. I hadn't showered in . . . well, days. Between the grime and stagnant water from the construction site and the battle sweat of the previous evening, I needed a shower badly. Fresh clothes couldn't hurt, either. Keeping me so close to his side when I had to look like hell and smell like crap warmed my heart. I would have pushed me away a long time ago.

The elevator stopped. The doors swished open, and Gage led me out. Instead of hanging a left as I expected, we immediately turned right. I recognized the tangy scent of the bathroom—soap and hard water and tile cleaner.

"You read my mind," I said.

"I thought you could use a shower."

My heart tripped, and I couldn't stop from asking, "Together?"

He stopped walking, his hold on my hand loosening. "No. I figured I'd get you there and help you get started. I can find Renee if you'd be more comfortable."

Having no sight gave my ears a little extra oomph, but I detected no hidden inflections, no disappointment draped over his matter-of-fact statement. I desperately wanted to see his face. Conversation with Renee aside, I couldn't deny my attraction to Gage, but sex complicated everything, and it would really complicate us. Married Rangers hadn't been allowed in the same units. Burgeoning relationships were split up quickly so as not to complicate unit dynamics.

"I think Renee is too occupied right now to bother bathing me," I said.

"Yeah." More silence. "I didn't bring you here to seduce you, Teresa."

"I know, Gage." I just wanted him near me while I couldn't see. Protecting me. "Are you angry with William about something?" The words slipped out, voicing something that had been bothering me all night. The timing seemed both awful and perfect—Gage would never walk away and leave me stranded in the bathroom. Would he?

"I'm not angry with William," he said, his voice firm. Almost amused. "I was frustrated with myself, and I misdirected. I'm sorry."

"Frustrated how?"

The hand holding mine tensed, but he didn't let go. He cleared his throat—I imagined his face shuttering, ready to stop a conversation he didn't want to have, and I wanted to scream. "Would you like me to leave, Teresa?"

"Stay." I squeezed his hand firmly. "Can't have me slipping and banging my head on the shower faucet, can we?"

"No, we can't." He placed my hand on the tiled wall. "Hang here for a minute, while I get some towels and soap."

"Okay."

The warmth of his arm left. His footsteps receded. The instinct to flee warred with the unfamiliar nugget of attraction that I'd been nursing since Bakersfield, the desire I felt each time he touched me or kissed me. Standing in the bathroom, blinded by my mysterious powers, and unsure if we'd even survive against Specter, I decided I didn't want to think about the consequences of where this could take us. I wasn't a leader. I didn't choose to be. I was a scared, lonely young woman who wanted more than anything to feel alive. Really alive.

I needed this, but when Gage returned, who did I want him to be? The friend I adored would offer a platonic shower, help me get dressed, and shuttle me off to bed. The man I'd crushed on as a child and whose gentle, teasing and passionate kisses lit flames in my belly would offer something more—something that scared me as much as it thrilled me.

I unlaced my sneakers and shed them both without losing my balance. The material was tacky, gritty. They needed to be washed as badly as I did. I shrugged out of a light jacket and let it fall to the floor, and my belt quickly joined it. Barefoot in my jeans and T-shirt, I used the wall for guidance and found a sink.

My fingers traced over the smooth porcelain basin, around the stainless steel faucet and knobs, everything so cool to the touch. The world seemed so much larger as I explored it blindly, linked solely through the tips of my fingers and the scents in my nose. Every flaw in the finish, every layer of soap scum brushed against my skin, as detailed as if I were looking at it.

Cool air whispered across my arms as the bathroom door opened, and then closed. A lock turned with a gentle snap. Footsteps walked toward me. Then the rustle of fabric and the thump of plastic bottles.

"It's me," Gage said.

I waited silently, listening to him move around the room. Behind the row of sinks was a line of toilet stalls, just like any public restroom. Somewhere to my right was a curtained door, and behind it, more curtained changing rooms. Through one more entrance were the showers. Twelve heads, six on each side, with a waist-high tiled wall between each one and down the center for moderate privacy.

The curtains rustled a few times before Gage returned to my side. He took my hand and drew me forward. I took small steps, the tiny square tiles cool and dry under my bare feet. Through the curtain and then to the left. I judged our stopping point in front of one of the changing stalls.

"Your hair is tangled," he said. "May I brush it for you?"

My knees wobbled, and not from fatigue. No man had ever offered to do such a thing. Men rarely noticed my hair at all, except to comment on its length. One rather rude club drunkard had whispered in my ear about how he'd like to wrap it around his hand and yank on it while he fucked me. He got my drink in his face and an elbow in his stomach. I got kicked out of the joint. But that jerk and those grubby bars were a lifetime ago, and I knew as long as I had the Rangers, I would never go back.

"Yes, you may," I said. "Did you bring one?"

He laughed, and the sound rumbled through the room like spring thunder. "Of course."

Fabric swished, and I felt him move from in front of me to behind. He started at the bottom, gently holding the ends and working out the tangles before proceeding higher. I never once felt an awkward or painful tug. The brush whispered, plastic-coated tines massaging my scalp with each pass. Fingers and brush worked their magic until my head tingled and my hair felt light, airy.

The brush disappeared. One hand swept hair away from the right side of my neck, and his fingers skimmed my throat. A tremor danced up my spine. His left hand curled around my waist and splayed across my stomach. I turned my head, craning up.

The kiss sent me spinning. I twisted around to face him, my arms going around his neck and shoulders. His tongue thrust gently into my mouth and slid across my teeth. I pressed my hips against him and felt his growing arousal against my belly. I wanted him—this possessive man who'd diligently protected me, been by my side almost every minute since Bakersfield. If I couldn't see, then I damned well wanted to feel.

He broke the kiss, but kept his head close. Hot breath puffed across my moist lips. "Teresa, I didn't plan—"

"I know." I amazed myself by successfully placing my fingertips across his lips to shush him. "I need this, Gage. Please."

Our world was standing still only for this moment. I couldn't waste it knowing it might never come again.

His breath hitched, and then his hands slipped down my back and under the hem of my tee. He pulled it up and off, freeing my breasts, and then found my mouth again. I took the silent cue and tugged at the button on his jeans, but I couldn't work the belt buckle.

Gage separated us. I heard the clink of metal and rustle of fabric, the soft snick of a zipper, the gentle whisper of clothing falling to the floor. His fingertips tickled my waist, hooked around the band of my jeans, and carefully tugged down. Hot breath caressed my thighs as he stooped to help me step out of my clothing. He didn't stand right away, and I imagined the way he might be looking at me. A surge of heat coiled in my abdomen.

A whisper of air told me that he stood up. "Your purple is spreading, I think."

My chin quivered. "Show me."

Fingers danced featherlight down my left arm and gently urged it to rise. I relaxed, letting him lift my arm, and was surprised when he kissed my elbow. "There's a small spot here." He repeated the motion with my right arm. The second kiss sent butterflies spinning through my stomach. "And here."

He was behind me, both hands massaging my shoulders and drifting down my spine. They stopped on the uppermost curve of my buttocks, and then his lips planted a quiet kiss in the small of my back. Warmth flooded my sex; my muscles clenched. The eroticism of those kisses, across skin that hadn't been washed in days, said so many things he hadn't put into words.

"Here." His warm breath sent more shivers up my spine.

Down he went, planting more sensual kisses on the backs of my knees. He shifted around to the front. I held my breath, waiting to feel where he touched first. He kissed my right knee. I giggled—my one ticklish spot. The left knee earned the same reaction.

"Note to self," he said.

"Don't you dare."

His hot mouth circled my belly button. My stomach tightened. He made no indication of purple skin on my belly, and I wondered if the exploration was over. Then he brushed his lips across the valley between my breasts. My nipples pearled. Another kiss in the hollow between my throat and sternum. Chin, both cheeks, forehead, everywhere except my mouth. No other part of him touched me, even though his body radiated heat. Need.

I tried to control my breathing, to relax, but I didn't know where his cunning lips would land next. His sweet breath caressed my face. He made no further move to touch. Frustration building, I reached out, only to have his hands grasp mine.

"No touching yet."

"Cruel."

"Yep."

My skin was so sensitized that sudden heat or cold would probably make me jump a yard. My heart thundered in my ears as I waited. Anticipated.

He released my hands. A cool breeze signaled that he'd moved away, beyond my reach. Metal squealed. The swoosh of running water startled me. I smelled the light odor of chlorine. More squeaks, then the hushed change of water pressure as Gage adjusted the temperature. A cloud of moist air tickled my ankles. Footsteps squished against the tiled floor. He took my hand and tugged me forward.

"I won't let you fall," he said.

The tiles beneath my feet changed, became warmer and smaller, and soon very wet. Hot water pooled around my toes. I splashed into it moments before the hot spray hit my bare skin. The shock took my breath away. Gage released my hand. I moved closer to the spray, allowing the needles of water to massage away the day's stress. I turned. It coursed through my hair, soaking it to the scalp. I ignored my audience and reveled in the heat and steam; I couldn't remember the last time a shower felt so wonderful.

"What is it? You made a face."

I looked toward the sound of his voice, a little disoriented. It bounced off the walls and mixed with the hiss of the water. "I was just thinking I haven't done this in a while."

"Which part?"

"The shower." But now that he mentioned it . . . "Any of this. It's been a few—a while."

He touched my shoulder, and I jumped. He pulled back, and all I knew was the rush of water streaming to the floor.

"Gage?"

"We don't have to, if you're not ready, Teresa."

He was still giving me an out. Did I want him to stop after

we'd come so far? No. Not even a little bit. I wanted him here with me.

"Did you bring shampoo?" I asked by way of answer.

"Of course."

A bottle found its way into my hand. I tested its size and shape and decided it was mine. "Conditioner?"

"What?"

"The matching bottle that should have been next to this one."

A short pause and then, "I'm sorry, I just brought the shampoo."

"I don't care." I reached out. He clasped my hand. "Help me do this?"

He took the bottle and spun me so I faced the spray. It hammered against my breasts and misted up into my face, creating more delicious sensations. I closed my blind eyes against the assault.

The familiar snap of the bottle cap preceded his hands in my hair. Fingers massaged my scalp, working the cool gel, down to the roots. From the top, across the sides to my temples, around to the middle and down to my neck. Over and over, a mesmerizing swirl of touch and scent as citrus permeated the air.

His hand touched my shoulder and directed me to turn. Hot water pounded against my scalp. It tingled; I throbbed. Who knew hair washing could be so damned erotic? He carefully rinsed the shampoo out and finger-combed the long strands. Never once did he pull or tug or hurt. The hairdresser at Sally's Scissors was never as gentle.

"One step forward," he said.

The new position angled the water toward the middle of my back. Squelching sounds and another bottle snap—he was lathering something up. The scent of jasmine and vanilla joined the citrus.

"Turn around."

I faced the spray, the water once again hitting my breasts and doing an excellent job of heightening my excitement. A washcloth pressed against my back. Gage rubbed the soapy terry rag in slow, circular patterns across my shoulders; lifted my hair to reach the back of my neck and trailed the rag down my right arm. I extended it without thought, allowing him to soap my elbow and hand. He took care to stroke each finger, my thumb and palm, and across the underside of my wrist.

The smooth cloth never broke contact with my skin as it whispered back across my shoulders and repeated the gentle ministrations on my left arm. I panted, unable to take a proper breath, overwhelmed by desire and his massaging touch. Steam billowed into my face. The rag snaked across my back, and then up and down, soapy terry cloth caressing each rib and vertebrae. He gently swept across the small of my back, and then the cloth disappeared. My body ached for his touch. Lost without the grounding influence, I thought I would fall off the edge of the earth.

"More soap," he said.

I waited, my washed skin tingling and the unwashed left wanting. Tiny tremors stole through my abdomen. I clenched my fists and shifted from foot to foot. I wanted—

needed—to touch him. Or myself. Something. No touching, he had said. It was torture of the most exquisite kind, and I trusted Gage implicitly. I just needed some sort of release before I combusted.

He started again with my left ankle, soaping each toe, tickling the sole, up and down my calf. I bit the inside of my cheek to keep from giggling when he washed my knee. With precise movements, he stroked my thigh, his hand rising so close, but never to the right place. My hips jerked, daring him to touch the one spot he studiously avoided. He laughed; I loved that sound.

His hand brushed the crease where my butt met my leg, and I trembled. Ached for him. He switched to my right leg, repeating the careful, torturous motions, from toes to thigh. The sweet ache inside me coiled tighter with every brush of cloth on skin, until I thought I might burst. My lungs hitched. I felt ready to fly to pieces.

One deliberate stroke of the rag scorched down my buttocks, top to bottom. I clenched my inner muscles as tremor after tremor of pleasure surged through me, so fast and sharp that my upper body jerked. I cried out at the sudden, unexpected release. Tipping forward, I pressed my palms against the wall. It passed quickly, but left me breathless, my body trembling for more.

"Teresa?"

I inhaled deeply, my mind reeling. "That was incredible."

"Did you just—?"

"Yep." I straightened and turned toward the sound of his voice, expressing what I hoped was an appropriate amount of awe. I couldn't seem to command my muscles properly. "I have never orgasmed without . . . you know, touching."

"I'd say there was plenty of touching involved." I could hear the smile in his voice, pride in his accomplishment.

"Yeah, but for the most part it was appropriate touching. Don't you want to see how inappropriate we can get?"

"We haven't even finished your shower."

"Don't care."

His hands brushed my cheeks and I pressed into his touch, desperate to see what was in his eyes. Etched on his face. "You're sure?"

Half of me hated that our first time was about to be standing up, in a shower, probably somewhat awkward with me blinded by my own powers. The other half didn't care—craved it, in fact. It had been too long since I'd let myself go, too many years spent bottled up and closed off. I needed the connection, and I wanted it to be with him.

I said, "As I've ever been about anything, Gage," and deliberately drew my tongue across my lips.

The bait worked. His arms were around my waist, and then my back was pressed against the cool tile wall. He captured my mouth in a dizzying kiss, and I returned his eagerness, falling into the heady taste of him. My senses were sharper than I'd ever known. Keener, taking in every detail of smell and sound, memorizing by touch what I couldn't have by sight. His left hand traveled down my right hip and lifted my leg. I reached between us, and he hissed when I touched him. Stroked him. Helped him ease inside.

I gasped as sensation after delicious sensation poured

through me, stroking already hypersensitized nerves. I tried imagining his face, mouth open and panting. Silver-flecked eyes looking into mine, cheeks red from exertion. Water trickling down the line of his chiseled jaw, across his throat, and dripping down onto his heaving chest—so clear in my mind.

Blazing heat spread throughout my body, and we kissed again, our dueling tongues matching his powerful strokes. Nothing existed except our gasping lungs and pounding hearts—creating a spellbinding rhythm that drowned out every other sound. Colorful spots interrupted the veil of purple across my vision and blended into a painter's palette. Joy bubbled up, frothed with bliss and, at last, shattered on the surface.

I cried out as tremors blasted through my body, from my stomach to my breasts, the top of my head to the tips of my toes. My trembling legs slipped. Gage withdrew. Groaned. Warmth hit my belly and was washed away by the shower's stream. Strong arms looped around my waist. I gratefully collapsed against his chest, resting my head on his shoulder. His fingertips tickled my lower back, tracing strange patterns. After a moment, I giggled; I must have had tile marks on my skin.

"Are you okay?" he asked.

"Yeah. That was . . . great. Besides, tile tattoos on the ass are sexy."

He laughed and swept me into another sensual kiss. I couldn't imagine ever tiring of the taste of him on me and the scent of him around me.

"Come on," he said, kissing my nose and mouth, and pulling me back toward the shower spray. "Let's finish before we both prune."

The evening (morning?) ended in my room, both of us clean, in our pajamas—well, boxers for him and a long T-shirt for me—and well satisfied. We had stretched out on my bed, his chest pressed to my back and our legs twined. Gage pushed my damp hair out of the way and planted gentle kisses on the nape of my neck. My insides trembled, my legs were jelly, and I never wanted to move.

"I just realized something," he said as I was about to doze off, his breath hot on my ear.

I blinked sleepily, wondering vaguely if the purple veil was more translucent than a few minutes ago. "What's that?"

"We'll have to do this all over again when you get your sight back."

"I don't know, Gage, maybe next time you should blindfold yourself to make it fair."

"Getting kinky already?"

"Maybe."

He chuckled, tightening his arms around my waist. I closed my eyes and focused on the beat of his heart against my back.

"The others will be awake in a few hours," I murmured, knowing I should do something about that. Have a plan ready, or get dressed. Something.

"We've got time, Teresa. Get some rest."

"'Kay." And I did.

Twenty-two

Epiphany

I watch her sleep as before. She and her faceless companion. She is sweating, and I know why. The room is hot. Too hot. I smell something awful, dangerous, and I cannot warn her.

Her companion is engulfed in flames. She knows he is dying, cursing someone for it, though he cannot speak. Their minds are linked, as they have always been.

Who did this?

They don't answer.

Her eyelids fly open. Luminescent eyes stare in hatred and accusation. Not at me. Through me.

Someone is killing them. Two dead by fire.

Murdered.

Flames surround me now, as well. Flames of color and light, of a thousand voices singing, of power beyond measure.

I burn.

This time I didn't fly out of bed when I woke up. The memory of burning heat still lingered as I stared at the ceiling. The light was off and only a sliver of morning sunlight peeked in through the pulled window shade. Gage still slept behind me, arms around my waist.

I blinked hard. Morning sunlight. I sat up, the nightmare forgotten. Gage grunted; I ignored him.

It was gone. Not even a tinge of violet remained in my vision—only the golden shaft of light drawn across the floor like a beacon of hope.

"Teresa?"

He touched my shoulder. With a gleeful laugh, I twisted around and tackled him to the mattress. I straddled him and gazed into his gorgeous eyes. Eyes I'd missed.

"I see you," I said.

Gage brushed a curtain of purple-streaked hair away from my face and drew me down. I hovered above him, grinning like a fool as he studied my eyes.

"Wow," he said.

"Yeah, wow. Dr. Seward won't believe this when we tell him."

"What do we tell him?"

"Easy." I leaned forward, hair brushing my cheeks. "We tell him you figured out how to clean my filter."

I dissolved into giggles, overcome by the euphoria of having my sight back. Gage hooked his arms behind my knees, sat up fast, and effectively completed a maneuver that landed me flat on my back. He loomed above, laughing along with me, and I got my first real look at the damage done yesterday afternoon. From his throat to his belly button and across both pectorals, a pool of bruising marred his skin. Shades of black, blue, and purple ran like a chalk drawing left in the rain.

"Christ, Gage," I said.

"It's fine."

"Does it hurt?"

"A little. The painkillers wore off a few hours ago." He took my hand and pressed it lightly above his heart. "It's okay, Teresa."

"It's not." The joy of my returned eyesight diminished with the clarity it brought. Half of our team had been seriously hurt yesterday, and they were looking at me to lead. I couldn't keep distracting myself with Gage. My feelings for him were as mixed up as his for me. He wouldn't open up about his past, and yet he'd eagerly engaged in our affair.

Unfortunately, a deeper examination of "us" had to wait until we'd removed Specter as a threat. I had to focus on that and nothing else.

"I should go see Dr. Seward," I said. "Then talk to the others."

"About anything in particular?"

I hadn't told anyone about my dreams, but tonight's had unnerved me. More than just the recurring events and new hints each night, I thought I could connect the dream to a newspaper headline I'd glanced at in Bakersfield last week, one of those things I saw without truly comprehending it. Two dead in a fire, cause unknown. The timing could not be a coincidence.

"Teresa, what is it?"

"Can you do some research for me this morning?"

"Yeah, I suppose. On what?"

I told him, and he listened without interrupting—without expression, too, which worried me. If he was angry that I'd kept this from him, I couldn't tell. "I'll get anything I can on the facility and investigation," he said after a blank-faced silence.

"Thank you."

"Now or after breakfast?"

"We'll talk to the others after breakfast, but if I don't see Dr. Seward now, I probably won't go."

"Why not?"

"Because whenever we talk about my powers, I feel like a specimen under a microscope."

Gage squeezed my thigh. "He's trying to help, Teresa. He really does care."

"I know he does, which is why I'll endure his litany of questions and personal poking." I grinned. "You want to come? You helped cure me, after all."

"Pass."

"Chicken."

"I prefer the term *wuss*."

We laughed. One more kiss, and I hopped out of bed. Time to make medical history with Dr. Seward: "Blindness Cured by Hot Monkey Sex." The title alone would make that paper a bestseller.

I ran into Dr. Seward around the corner from the ICU. Really. We collided with enough force to send me flailing backward onto my ass. I hit the floor with a thud. A sharp jolt sailed up my spine and made my stomach seize. The stack of X rays in his hands went flying and scattered across the linoleum with a sound like splashing water.

"You do sneak about, don't you?" Dr. Seward said. He bent over me and hovered directly in my line of sight. "Are you all right? Can you stand?"

"I've had worse spills. Don't you ever sleep?"

"Not a full night in thirty years."

"Must be hell on your REM patterns."

He offered his good hand—the other was wrapped up in an Ace bandage, something I hadn't been clued in to last night during my blind spell—and hauled me to my feet. He had a firm grip for someone his age, which I could only guess at, somewhere between fifty and sixty. Seemed impolite to ask. I helped him gather up his X rays.

"What are you doing running around like that, Trance? I—" He stopped and seemed to really see me. "Is your vision back? What happened?"

"Actually, that's what I was coming to talk to you about."

"Oh?"

I picked up a film that looked like someone's elbow and handed it over. He shuffled them around, trying to create some semblance of order and hide his curious glances. I felt them, and I heard a hundred unasked questions. The scientist in him was showing remarkable restraint.

"Can we talk about this in private, instead of the hall?"

"Certainly."

He stood, still organizing his X rays, and walked in the

direction I had been heading before our collision, his temporary office. He'd installed himself in one of the labs. It had counter-height tables instead of a desk, and storage boxes were scattered over most of them. He offered me the room's only seat—a backless swivel stool. I declined and perched on the edge of a lab table.

"Did you have another episode this morning?" he asked as he placed his stack of X rays on top of a box. "An expulsion of power?"

"Not exactly. Well, maybe in a way, yes, but . . ." God, this was embarrassing. "Hell, Gage and I had sex."

If it was truly possible for a man's eyes to bug out of his head, that's what Dr. Seward's did. He stared at me like a frightened animal, caught between fight or flight. I didn't blink, sure that I would blush to the roots of my hair if I reacted to his shock, and I couldn't help a small amount of pride in shutting him up like that.

"Did you, ah, come here for a gynecological exam, because that's not really—?"

"No!" Laughter bubbled up, and I waved my hands in the air. "No, that's not—no offense, Doc, but you wouldn't have been my first choice, even if it's why I was here. I'm here because we figured it out, or at least, we figured out one way of doing it."

"Doing what?" He asked the question as if dreading the answer.

"Cleaning my filter."

He blanched and went a little green.

"Hey, you came up with the air filter analogy. Fact is, I was completely blind six hours ago, and I can see perfectly this morning. No color fade, no vision loss, just normal. I thought you'd be interested."

"I—" It came out high-pitched, so he cleared his throat and started again. "I am interested, Trance, just surprised. I didn't expect this particular conversation."

"Neither did I, trust me. But I was thinking about what you said, about how my body uses what it needs and stores the rest. Maybe I just need to burn up that excess energy. If I redirect it into some sort of strenuous physical exertion, I can avoid those nova eruptions and potentially killing myself. I'd really prefer to not die, if it can be avoided."

"It's a good theory, Trance. One we can't test right away. However, you may be correct, and I highly doubt your recovery has anything to do with the presence of seminal fluids." His deadpan delivery made me laugh. "Change in vision seems to be your primary symptom, and we know that prolonged use of your powers causes it to occur."

I bobbed my head, proud of being able to follow along. Prouder, in fact, that he had validated my theory. It was still a far cry from finding and stopping Specter, but I'd found a way to work around my powers, and it wasn't a small thing. Maybe, just maybe, I could do this.

I latched onto my sprouting confidence, a little excited, and said, "So we just have to wait to test it again. I don't know, maybe an hour on a treadmill could even help prevent the purple vision completely. It may not always be feasible to work in a quickie."

"Sexual attraction is a powerful thing." He smiled warmly,

almost fatherly. "Don't discount its ability to heal, rather than hinder."

"You sound like a self-help guru."

He shook his head. "I'm just a man who's seen too much. I honestly never thought I'd see the day when someone told me sex healed blindness."

"You just aren't having the right kind of sex, Doc." Ew, okay, not going there. That time I did blush. As a teen, I'd missed out on the awkward parental sex talk but I bet it would've felt something like this.

"My wife and I do just fine."

Wife? That was news. And I really didn't need to start conjuring up any mental images of their sex life. "Anyway," I said, "since I've got you, I wanted to ask you something."

"Anything, as long as it has nothing to do with sex."

"It doesn't. I was curious about the HQ." He nodded, and I took it as my cue to continue. "Why was it maintained all these years? No one knew why we lost our powers, so no one could have predicted they would come back."

He sank deeper into his chair and pressed the tips of his fingers together into a steeple. "Hope, I suppose. As far as I'm aware, the ATF had no reason to think you would ever be repowered. It's one of the reasons MHC was disbanded and their agents reassigned. Some folks in the Department of Justice wanted to bulldoze this entire complex, to tear out that particular page of history and file it, but they objected vigorously and won."

"Who's they?"

"Rita McNally, Alexander Grayson, and a handful wealthy

supporters within the government. They raised quite the stink and the budget committee relented, allowing ATF to fund a considerably slashed budget for upkeep and maintenance. We'd hoped the Rangers would return to full strength one day, but none of us hoped to see it again in our lifetimes."

"Agent Grayson? He fought for us?"

"He did."

I didn't like the idea of owing Grayson anything, especially the existence of our home base. He was a jackass who desperately needed advice in buying suits, but it looked like he was also one of our champions. "Does this mean I should thank him next time I see him?"

"I wouldn't. The man's head is big enough as it is."

"Good point."

Dr. Seward exhibited an admirable amount of spunk not seen during our previous engagements. He reminded me of an eccentric relative who makes fun of everyone after too many belts of whiskey.

"Trance, may I ask you a serious question?"

As if our conversation so far hadn't been serious? "Sure."

He seemed to struggle a moment, then said, "Do you think your relationship with Cipher will hinder your ability to function as this team's leader?"

I hadn't expected that to be his question, even though I'd asked it of myself quite a few times on the walk over—and not just about Gage. My other team members, too. As I grew closer to them, my ability to sacrifice their lives in the way I'd sacrificed Janel was slipping away.

"I can't honestly say it won't affect me," I replied. "I know it will, and I want to believe I'll still be able to make the tough calls."

"You can only believe it until you're faced with it, and then you'll know for certain. I hope you're right."

So did I. "Thanks, Doc."

"Where are you headed now?"

"I'm going to call a meeting."

"Oh?"

"Yeah, the whole team, plus you and the agents. Everyone at the same time."

His thick eyebrows furrowed as he failed to hide his curiosity. "Some sort of announcement?"

"Something like that."

I left before he could ask me to elaborate. I had to meet Gage in the conference room and see what he'd dug up. Until I verified my suspicions, I'd keep my accusations to myself.

To Dr. Morgan's great consternation, we held the meeting in Ethan's room. Gage felt as strongly as I did about doing this in front of everyone, which crammed eight adults into a small ICU cubicle. Grayson and McNally seemed twitchy, and for good reason, according to our research. I bit back my flaring temper and focused on Gage while everyone settled in. More silver had crept into his light brown hair, collecting above his temples and in his eyebrows—more than had been there yesterday. It gave him an air of physical maturity that better matched the sum of his experiences.

"What's this all about, Trance?" McNally asked.

"The truth about our powers," I said.

She blinked. Grayson tensed. Ha!

"What do you mean, Catalepsia?" Marco asked.

I started with my first vision in the rest stop bathroom and continued into the most recent nightmare. McNally listened with more intensity than anyone else in our audience. She stood by the wall, hands folded over her stomach, eyes drilling holes into me. I couldn't decide if she was finding fault in my words, or planning her rebuttal. Ethan listened through a haze of pain medication, with an occasional tap from Renee to keep him focused. William and Seward seemed equally curious, while Marco sat in a chair with a wholly blank expression. Grayson continued to fidget, not as good at body language control as McNally.

I ended with the dream-woman's accusing stare. "She knew the fire wasn't an accident. They were murdered."

Everyone, with the notable exception of the pair of federal agents, was stuck between confused and mystified.

"You're having visions?" Seward asked, perplexed.

"Apparently so, yes."

"Have you ever had them before?"

"Never. Not even when I was a kid."

"Utterly fascinating," McNally said.

"Fascinating, huh?" I said. "So MHC had no knowledge of these two people who burned to death in a fire last Thursday at one fifteen in the morning? Two people who, for the last fifteen years, have been living in Fairview Center, a chronic care facility in Santa Barbara? A facility that also happens to receive a healthy, monthly government stipend?"

Grayson's skin went the color of paste. He looked petrified, while McNally hadn't lost her cool or her posture. Neither of them spoke. They didn't even look at each other. I thought back to my earlier conversation with Seward. These were supposedly people who'd fought for us? Bull. Shit.

"T, what's going on?" Renee asked.

I ignored her. Gage handed me printouts of newspaper articles and financial reports. I waved them at the agents. "You want to see the hard copies so you know I'm not bluffing?" A lump of emotion—anger, confusion, betrayal, and fear all rolled up into something impossible to swallow—clogged my throat. "Were you ever going to tell us the truth?"

Grayson's head snapped toward McNally. She held my gaze a moment longer, then met his. Her resignation collided with his trepidation, and a silent argument was held. When she once again met my accusing stare, her steely eyes were rimmed with . . . regret?

"Does knowing the truth change those years we stole from you?" she asked.

The tension level in the room quadrupled as my fellow Metas clued in to the enormity of our conversation. Tears stung my eyes as the last hope I'd had of being wrong about this shattered. "You took our powers away," I said.

"Not directly, but we were responsible for hiding the truth from the world," she replied with a hitch in her voice. "You have to understand, Trance, what was happening back then. The country was falling apart around us. People were terrified of Metas, and the Rangers were losing the War. Dying one after another in horrible ways. The fighting had localized to the Northeastern states. The president's advisors were urging him to consider extreme measures, including blanket bombings of New York and New Jersey, and when some of us at the MHC heard that—" She swallowed. "It would have been genocide. The casualties were unthinkable."

"Bombing two states," Seward said. He seemed on the verge of vomiting.

McNally nodded. "Yes."

"Who were those people?" I asked. "The man and woman who died?"

"Your investigative reporting didn't give you their names?" Grayson asked. His first contribution to the conversation and it was sarcasm. Nice.

I lifted one shoulder in a half-shrug. "Your people weren't a hundred percent incompetent. We couldn't find any records, other than John and Jane Doe. Very original."

"Because they don't exist," McNally said.

"On paper?"

"Technically, at all. No identification, no fingerprints. They were both Metas of a power level we'd never seen before. Their minds had been joined together by a machine designed by scientists who'd spent years studying them. Together they created what was called an energy sink. They were able to collect MetaHuman abilities and store them away."

"Where the hell do you find people who can do something like that?" William asked, his deep voice barely above a low growl. "Who studied them?"

McNally took a few breaths, gearing up for some sort of

confession. Her façade of cool collectedness was cracking, and a tiny part of me wished I hadn't done this so publicly. The majority of me enjoyed her discomfort. "About a week before that day in Central Park," she said, "a man came to the MHC office in Burbank. He gave us the name O'Bannen and claimed to work for a specialized research and development firm based in Virginia. They had a branch in Los Angeles, and he told us about a project he'd been developing for his firm involving a pair of Metas whose extreme psychic abilities ran toward the telekinetic end of the spectrum. He'd helped them develop a machine they called a Warden—a way to harness their abilities and remove them from other Metas. O'Bannen offered them as a solution to the War."

"And you took them," I said, disgusted by the idea of bartering with human life.

"Not right away. To do so enslaved them both, you understand, even though O'Bannen assured me they were willing. The cost benefit was difficult to justify."

"Cost benefit?" William said. His hands were clenched tight. "Did you ever talk to them? To the Metas? To see that what you were doing was strapping two people to a machine and letting them rot?"

McNally flinched. "Yes, we met with them. And whether or not you believe me, the truth is they wanted this. They believed, and made us believe, that this energy sink was the only way to stop the Banes and end the War. No one knew how long it would last, only that it was a temporary solution. It was the only one we had. We debated it for days. It wasn't until they sent you children to New York that we accepted the offer. O'Bannen assured us it would only affect the Banes, but he was wrong. The Wardens were unable to differentiate between the adult Banes and you children. Even then, I didn't honestly believe it would work, but it did."

She glanced at Grayson. He continued staring at his feet, an expression on his face I could only describe as constipated.

"As per our agreement with O'Bannen," McNally continued, "we took over the Warden's care. We transferred their equipment to Fairview. I did a little private digging afterward with my partner, Agent Anders, but O'Bannen was, as expected, an alias. No R&D firm in the country would claim him, especially not the two with branches here in Los Angeles. For a long time, I waited for him to show up and demand recompense for his generosity. He never has."

For several minutes, the steady beep of Ethan's pulse monitor was the only sound in the room. It was almost too much to process. The answers I'd wanted for more than half my life had just been handed to me, and I couldn't seem to collect my thoughts.

"Why did you hide it from us?" William asked.

"As I said before, we thought it was the best way to protect you children." McNally seemed on the verge of bursting into tears. Or punching Grayson in the eye for staying so silent. "We thought your powers would be left intact, but they weren't. I can't say I would change the decision given the chance, because I'm not certain we were wrong. But for what little it's worth, I am sorry."

Renee snorted.

"What about the fire?" Gage asked. "Did Specter kill the Wardens to release our powers?"

"It's a possibility," McNally said. "However, their existence was a closely guarded secret. Seven people in the world, including the former president and his chairman of the Joint Chiefs, knew about the Warden and the Metas who powered it. Only three of us in the MHC knew its location in Fairview."

"Who are the three?" I asked.

"Myself, Alexander, and Agent Anders. He died almost three years ago."

"From?"

She narrowed her eyes. "Agent Anders was my partner for nine years, Trance. He had cancer, and he was two years retired from the ATF when he passed away. And now you know the truth. I'm sorry you had to find out like this."

"Like this or at all?" Renee snapped. Her cherry-red lips were pursed so tightly they almost disappeared, and deep frown lines marred her smooth blue forehead. Strangely, she seemed the angriest person in the room.

"Like this. Our investigation into the fire points to arson, but there are no witnesses, and the security cameras were compromised."

"Convenient."

"More likely on purpose. If I knew anything else I would tell you."

"Such as why I'm dreaming about this Warden?" I asked. "And why I got back some bastardized version of my grandmother's powers?"

"Yes."

"What if I asked you to give me a theory?"

She considered the question. "Then, my theory would be linked to your visions. You say the female Warden understood they were being murdered. Without knowing just how her energy-sinking ability worked, I'd postulate she sent the strongest telekinetic power she had out to the body most able to host it. This new power is very similar to your grandmother's, Trance, and powers often run in families. The Warden sent the signal and you received it. In theory."

Damn her, the theory made sense. A lot of sense, especially the family angle. My dad's father had had powers almost identical to my original Trance ability. Janel's mother had also been an ice manipulator. And the whole thing worked with Seward's theory about my body's inability to properly channel the energy.

Another uncomfortable silence filled the ICU as we each sat with our thoughts. Good intentions didn't excuse what the MHC had done to us. And it certainly didn't save us from what was happening now.

"O'Bannen knew about the Warden," Gage said. "Even if he didn't know about Fairview, it's a fair bet he had some way of tracking down the machine he helped build. No one's that generous without an ulterior motive."

"You're right," McNally said. "However unlikely a scenario, it's unwise at this point to disregard anyone as a potential suspect."

"Including yourself?" I asked.

She looked startled for a moment, then nodded. "Myself included. As difficult as it is for all of you to hear, the only person any of you can possibly know for certain is innocent is you yourself."

Once again, I found myself hating her for being right. I knew I hadn't set the fire, but I couldn't know for absolutely certain that Gage hadn't done it—Santa Barbara and Bakersfield were only a couple of hours apart.

No. Timing aside, I knew in my gut that Gage hadn't done this. No matter the secrets he had bottled up inside, being a killer and conspiring to give all our powers back just wasn't in him.

It wasn't.

I batted away the tiny niggle of doubt that McNally had suddenly planted, frustrated I'd even let myself go there. We needed to get back on track.

"What's your plan, Trance?" Seward asked, as though he could read my mind.

"Nothing's really changed," I said, even though a lot of things had, indeed, changed dramatically in the last ten minutes. "We'll still do the interview, and we're still going to find Specter. Any new thoughts on locating him?"

Ethan raised his hand. "Bait," he said.

"What kind of bait?"

"Me."

Twenty-three

Missteps

You want to be bait?" I asked.

"Yes."

"Forget it." I held up my hand before Ethan could argue. "Even if you could bait him, we have no way of trapping him once he's inside you."

"Maybe we do," William said. He stood just behind Renee and kept curling the ends of her long hair around one finger—a gesture both nervous and possessive. "His powers are telekinetic in nature, and what's that except electric brain signals? Could your force field keep his mind trapped here and leave his body vulnerable?"

It was certainly an out-of-the-box suggestion. We were all starting to look at the limits of each others' powers and consider how to best use them to our advantage. "I don't know, William," I said. "I've never tried it before, and I don't know how long I can maintain a force field. It might not be long enough to find his body, and who knows what he'd do to Ethan in the meantime? It's too big a risk."

"So's doing nothing," Ethan said.

"You are six hours out of major surgery, buster, you are in no shape to act as bait. Given your physical condition, Specter might not even come for you. He wouldn't be able to get you out of bed."

"He got Janel up."

"True, but still, no."

"You got a better idea, T?" Renee asked.

"At present? No, but I am not putting Ethan or anyone else in a position to die, because that's what will happen. Everyone Specter has inhabited and we've fought has died. It isn't brave, it's suicide."

"I don't think he'll attack you here again," Seward said. "He has to know you'll be planning for it. He may wait until you're off-site. He's got time on his side, as well as the element of surprise. He can wait while we sit and squirm."

"What if you're wrong?" Renee asked.

Seward shrugged. "Then, I'm wrong. This isn't an exact science, Flex. We can't predict the future."

"I agree with Dr. Seward," Gage said. "Specter knows he hurt us and must realize we've kicked up security measures. He'll wait."

"Agreed," I said. "And it's another good reason to keep this interview location and time as guarded as possible. A studio full of innocent people is no place for a brawl."

"I have a short list of locations," McNally said. She sounded startled, as if she hadn't expected me to still do the interview. "Six networks on standby until tomorrow evening. No one knows what's going on until half an hour before we show up with you and Ms. Perkins."

"Good." I gave her a cold look. "Until then, any suggestions on tracking Specter will be greatly appreciated. As long as they don't involve self-sacrifice."

Ethan ignored me. No one had suggestions.

The meeting adjourned.

At lunch, we learned that the interview was planned for early the next morning. Five o'clock was torture, but secrecy came with minor sacrifices, and sleep was one of them. Gage and William volunteered to go with me. Renee mumbled something about beauty sleep, so I let her off the hook. I just wanted it over.

Gage had suggested he drive up to Fairview and do some sniffing around. It seemed like a good idea, until McNally informed him that the site of the fire had already been cleaned out, post–police investigation. Nothing was left. So the day passed uneventfully. No more shocking revelations. No attacks. No great epiphanies about Specter, either. We were in a frustrating holding pattern.

With nothing else to do, Renee, William and I decided to spend the early evening in the gym. Keeping fit wasn't difficult, given the vast array of exercise equipment available in the Base.

I decided to start simple and set myself up on a stationary bike. Working three jobs and eating when I could afford it meant I looked good in tight leather, but it didn't mean much for proper muscle tone and endurance.

Renee and William attacked a bizarre-looking resistance

machine called a Flexmaster 5000. It had rows of bowed metal rods that looked like mechanical tentacles, and it took them a while to figure out how they attached to the weight bars. I observed from my bike as they joked and teased with the ease of a couple who'd known each other for years, instead of days, picking up a fifteen-year-old flirtation as if no time had passed. Just like me, Renee had faced her fear, and I was glad for them. After thirty minutes, I switched to a stair climber, and they moved to the free weights.

Marco and Gage wandered in a while later. In sweatpants and a loose shirt, Gage was obviously there for a workout, and my irritation level soared. He'd been slammed in the chest with a block of ice the day before and he had a bruise the size of a small child to prove it.

"Hey, guys!" Renee said, waving.

Marco waved back, then stepped to the side. He leaned against the wall to watch—which I appreciated, since his arm was still in a sling and three fingers still broken. Apparently Gage had less sense, because he headed straight for one of the weight benches.

"What the hell are you doing?" I asked, stepping off the stair climber.

Gage froze mid-stride, every muscle going rigid. Okay, maybe I could have phrased my question more diplomatically and used a gentler tone. He turned his head and gave me a funny look I couldn't decipher.

"Working out with everyone else," he said as if it was the most obvious thing in the world.

Which it was, and that was the problem. "No, you're not."

"I'm not?"

"You're injured, Gage, and you should be taking it easy."

His indecipherable expression shifted squarely into anger. "I don't see you taking it easy."

"I didn't get knocked unconscious by a chunk of ice."

"Teresa—"

"No, Gage, you are not working out with us."

And there it was—the shuttered, cut-off Gage I was so good at producing. He squared his shoulders, pivoted neatly on one foot, and marched out of the gym.

I watched the door swing shut and heard the bang. I didn't chase him, though I wanted to. I wanted to grab him and apologize for doing that in front of the others. I'd just embarrassed the hell out of him, and I wasn't even sure why. Hello, overreaction.

Renee and William quickly returned to their work on the free weights. Marco shuffled his feet and fixed his attention on the floor. I ignored them all, flabbergasted and furious. Flabbergasted at his walking out on me, and furious for thinking a few hours of sex could bridge the emotional wall he'd kept carefully between us since we met. Even more furious for not trusting Gage to know his own limits when it came to injury and personal training. For letting my worry and my feelings for him affect my judgment so badly.

Dr. Seward was right.

Shit.

If Gage were ever under Specter's influence, I couldn't deliver the killing shot. I knew I couldn't when Seward asked me, and I knew it again in the gymnasium. I would rather let

Gage/Specter kill me than watch him, or my other friends, die at my hands. It created a liability on the team: me. A bad position for a leader to be in.

"Teresa?" Marco had wandered away from the wall, concern furrowing his brow.

"I'm fine," I said, shrugging it off and hoping I managed a nonchalant smile. "I'm going to get out of here. You guys enjoy your workout."

I scooted before they had a chance to argue. I needed space.

Hoping a shower would clear my head, I returned to the Housing Unit. It felt odd being in the bathrooms alone and able to see. The memories of my shower with Gage were still so fresh, I thought I could feel him standing behind me. Watching me intently, memorizing my curves and flaws.

No. I refocused my attention on Specter. He could attack at any moment, through anyone in the complex whose mind was weak enough to exploit. His victims so far, from the greasy blonde to a near-comatose Janel, had been compromised, whether from drugs and liquor or from injury. We were vulnerable to him, and I hated it. I also didn't know what the hell to do about it.

I turned and let the water cascade through my hair.

The door squeaked. Gage appeared in the shower archway moments later, a towel cinched around his waist. The bruise on his chest still stood out like a splash of blue and black paint; it didn't seen to bother him. Those haunted shadows were back beneath his eyes.

"Hey," he said, surprised.

"Hey." I wiped water from my eyes. "By the way you ran out of the gym, I thought you'd be halfway to Long Beach by now."

"I'm sorry I acted like that."

I blinked. I was the one who was supposed to be doing the apologizing. "I had no right, Gage."

"You were just doing your job."

I planted both hands on my hips, almost wishing he was angry with me. It would be easier if he was angry. Angry Gage was less likely to shut down than Quiet Contemplative Gage. "You drive me batshit, you do realize this."

He smiled. "My sinister plan is working, then."

"That wasn't a compliment." His smile stayed, though its intensity faded. I continued, falling headfirst into my frustration. "You get angry with me for good reason, then apologize for it. You seem to want to be with me, but you won't talk to me. You're standing there in a towel, and all I want to do is rip it off and rerun last night with my eyes wide open, but what happens after? We go back to being Cipher and Trance and forget the rest?"

Utter bewilderment telegraphed across his face. My words stayed in the air, an invisible barrier between us. Many long seconds passed, marked by the constant spray of water against my back. Bewilderment slowly faded to resignation. He padded toward me.

No. Past me. Crap.

One of the scars on his abdomen stood out, contrasting sharply with the bruised skin. It definitely wasn't an appendix scar. He'd never mentioned how he got them; I never thought he'd tell me if I asked, and now I wanted to know more than almost anything. I was desperate to know *him*. To prove that last night hadn't been a huge mistake.

"Tell me something truthful, Gage."

He stopped in front of my stall. "Like what?"

"I don't care. Something I don't know about you, as long as it's honest."

"You don't think I've been honest with you?"

"I think you tell me only as much as makes you comfortable, and you know what? Relationships are uncomfortable. They're hard, and they only work when two people are open with each other. And given what we're up against right now and the sheer odds against us winning . . ."

"What, Teresa? Say it."

"I can't invest in a casual relationship with you when I know it's going to affect my judgment. It will, because it has already, and it should stop right here where it began."

He narrowed his eyes. "This started before last night. For me it started the moment I saw you in Bakersfield."

I shivered under the powerful emotion in his voice. He continued to stand in front of my stall. Indecision played across his face, until something finally won. "I didn't move to Portland to help a friend. I moved there to try and save my brother."

His . . . brother? "Jasper died in the War."

"My foster brother, Nathan. He was two years younger than me, already with the family I was first fostered with." A sad smile tugged at the corners of his mouth. "Nate was a good guy who made a lot of bad choices over the years.

He got mixed up with the wrong people in Portland. Disappeared. I went to look for him. He turned up in a Dumpster two months later." Anger and grief flashed briefly across his face—a look with which I was all too familiar. "I was too late to save him."

Gage stepped into the next stall and turned on the faucet. He adjusted the temperature of the spray, testing it with his fingers. I watched his slow, deliberate movements. I wanted to go to him, hold him, console him. I didn't. If he'd wanted that, he wouldn't have put a six-inch-thick, four-foot-tall tile barrier between us.

"But you stayed anyway," I said, hoping to keep the conversation going, break a few bricks out of his wall now that it was showing some cracks.

"St. Louis was never my home, so I had no reason to go back," he said to the water. "I met a guy who lived across the hall from the apartment I was renting. He ran a teen work release facility, and he got me in touch with some people." He flexed his shoulders, as though buying time before saying the rest. "I joined a corrections officer training program."

I stared, not sure I'd heard him right over the roar of the showerheads. Corrections officer. That explained some things.

"It fit," he said. "I never would have thought of it on my own, and yet being a CO worked. It was damned hard, don't get me wrong, even working with juveniles. But if one kid got out and stayed out, we considered it worthwhile."

The irony that he'd been a corrections officer was not lost on me. Nor was the weight of his story—the familiar search for a job that meant something, and finding one that gave him a sense of purpose. He'd found something in corrections I'd never managed to find as a waitress.

My gaze dropped to the pale lines cutting across his back and abdomen. "Is that how you got those scars?"

Gage closed his eyes and put his face directly under the spray. He stayed there for almost a full minute, until I decided he wasn't going to answer. Then he pulled back, blinked water from his eyes, and turned to face me.

"A couple of years ago, some kids on my block thought I ratted them out to another CO. After they got out of solitary, they cornered me in the gym. I was always a good fighter, but it was four to one." Even though he recounted the event without details or emotion, I saw it clearly in my mind. Felt the accompanying fear and rage, and wanted to smash those four teenage offenders into pulp for hurting Gage.

He continued: "I spent a week in the hospital and was back to work a month later. I kept my guard up for a long, long time. I didn't want to be distracted ever again, to be cornered like that because I wasn't paying attention to my job." He paused. "It's one reason I've held back from you. The way you spin me around scares me."

I was struck dumb by the confession, and since all I could do was stare at him, he returned to his shower. I watched him soap up a washcloth and get to work, while his words tumbled around in my head. "One reason?"

He quirked an eyebrow. "What?"

"I was a distraction, one reason you held back. What was the other?"

"Doesn't matter now."

"No?"

"No, because you're not a distraction, Teresa. None of that old shit should matter anymore."

He was right. Our personal neuroses would never be far from reach—they were too much a part of ourselves. We didn't have to let them control us, though. We could be more than the sum of our parts, by accepting what we were and how we felt, instead of denying it. Use it to our advantage.

"What are you thinking so hard about?" he asked.

"Our next move."

"Which is?"

"Specter, as always." I reached for my own washcloth. "I keep trying to puzzle out ways to capture him or locate his physical body, and I always come back to Ethan's suggestion."

"Using bait?"

"Yes. Not Ethan, though, he's too weak. I doubt Specter would go for him even if Ethan let his guard down long enough. That isn't even the big problem."

"What is the big problem?"

"Holding onto Specter's mind once we've got it." I squeezed the washcloth, watching suds form. I liked this— talking out the problem with Gage and getting his input. "Even if I could make a force field to hold his consciousness, I couldn't keep it up long enough to make a difference. We need a more permanent solution, some way to get both Specter and his host into stasis or something."

"Stasis?"

"Or something. We just need to keep him in one place, away from his physical body while we search for it."

Gage rinsed soap off his face. "What if we're preempting ourselves here? We've had Specter's description out to every law enforcement agency for the last four days. He can't look that different after fifteen years. Someone matching the few early photos we have is bound to turn up."

"Maybe," I said, unconvinced. "But Specter doesn't stay anonymous for thirty years just to get picked up on a speeding ticket and booked into the system. My gut tells me the cops won't find him before we do."

"So even if we figure out a way to bait him, we still need a trap to spring."

"Precisely."

And how do you keep a mind separated from its body? Especially a mind as strong as Specter's?

I hung the hair dryer on its hook and shook out my hair. The purple smudges on my hairline and throat were now as natural to my eyes as plain pink skin had been two weeks ago. I adjusted the short jacket of my uniform, pleased with the fit. Someone had picked it out for me and left it in my room. Renee ranked at the top of my suspects list. I wasn't a fashion plate and didn't care what I wore, as long as it was both comfortable and functional.

The ensemble consisted of a tank top the same silver as a pair of knee boots with wedge heels, a gunmetal-gray three-quarters jacket, and matching low-slung pants. The effect was professional enough for a television interview, with a dash of my own personality to give it some sparkle. I checked my appearance once more before leaving my room.

Gage's door opened just as I closed mine. He stepped out, dolled up in a body-hugging uniform: black slacks tucked into a pair of cobalt-blue boots, topped with a blue-and-black patterned shirt. The colors didn't swirl, exactly, just coexisted in the material so it looked blue from some angles and black from others.

He wasn't paying attention and nearly slammed into me.

"What's your hurry?" I asked. "We're not late."

His eyes blazed. "The trap."

"What trap?"

"Specter's trap. If we can lure him, I know how to trap him."

Speechless, I let him grab my hand and pull me toward the elevator, listening as he rattled off his idea.

Marco and Agent McNally were easy to find. We had to rustle Renee and William out of bed in order to get their feedback. William took the time to throw on his uniform; Renee trudged into the conference room in rumpled pajamas. She yawned as she sat, extending her jaw to comical proportions.

"Please don't tell me, T," she said, "that you dragged us down here to tell you how stunning you look for your television debut."

"You can go back to bed in ten minutes," I said. "Gage has an idea."

Renee held up her hand and made a spinning motion with one finger. I rolled my eyes.

"I still don't have anything in the way of bait," Gage said, when attention turned to him. "But I know how to trap him away from his physical body long enough to find it."

McNally straightened up in her chair, as fresh and awake as I'd ever seen her during the day. "What do you have in mind, Cipher?" she asked.

"Psystorm."

"Si-what?" Renee asked.

"Psystorm. He's a Bane, one of those imprisoned right now on Manhattan Island. I remember him because my mentor Delphi fought him a few times. She also mentioned one day having to train Trance to fight him, because they had similar powers. Back then, anyway."

"The name is familiar," Marco said. "What is his power?"

"With line-of-sight contact, he can seize control of your conscious mind. He can affect your thoughts and the signals your brain sends to the rest of your body. Freeze you up. It'd be a risk to the host, but Psystorm could keep Specter inside one of us."

Renee smacked her hand palm-down on the tabletop. "Wait a second, you just said Psystorm is a Bane. Why the hell would he help us capture one of his own kind?"

Gage leaned forward. "Specter avoided prison all these years and never made an attempt to free the people he led during the War. Sounds like a reasonable excuse for some payback."

"What would he have to lose?" I asked. "We were raised to believe all Banes were bad, but maybe they aren't. We should study Psystorm's background file and figure out a way to make a deal. Not for free, obviously, but we don't know his price until we ask."

"And what about after?" Renee asked. "What the hell's to stop Psystorm from turning on us when it's all over?"

"Nothing, but I think it's a chance worth taking. The alternative is sitting here twiddling our thumbs and hoping for the best next time Specter decides to take potshots at us."

Marco flinched, but I got my point across. I wanted their support—no, needed it—for this decision. If I didn't get it I would damned well do it without them. Psystorm was a Bane, but I had to believe he could change and be someone other than who he'd been fifteen years ago.

"I think it's a good idea, Trance," McNally said. "I'll have my office send over the file on Psystorm, so we can work on your approach. We can't offer him the world, but I'm sure there's something he wants."

"Besides freedom?" Renee asked.

"If that's what it takes," I said. My petulant side didn't want any more help from the MHC, only I couldn't afford to be picky. "Has there ever been an effort made toward rehabilitating the imprisoned Banes? Or did the AFT just concentrate on keeping them locked away from the public?"

"I honestly don't know, Trance," McNally replied. "It was never my area of expertise, nor was it my postwar assignment. However, I'm fairly certain the answer is no. The viewpoint in Washington is that the Banes are simply a menace to be dealt with, not a problem to fix."

"Nice," Gage said with a snort.

"What about now?" I asked. "What if there are Banes who

just want to get out of prison and try to lead a normal life? Or at least a quiet and somewhat productive life. Shouldn't we try to offer them the chance?"

"How do you figure out the difference, T?" Renee asked. "How do you know they're sincere and not just playing you?"

"We probably won't."

"No, you won't, and the wrong ones will go free, and we'll be both blamed and responsible for picking them back up. Isn't it smarter to just leave them all where they are?"

I bristled. "Maybe, but I say we take a chance on Psystorm and see what happens. The rest of it we'll deal with as it comes." Crossing the bridge and all that.

"Fine." She sank into her chair, frustration playing out on her smoky blue face.

McNally stood up and said, "We can go about contacting Psystorm after the interview is over. Right now, let's focus on getting that off our plate."

"Agreed," Gage said.

Renee didn't look at me when I walked past her. She stood and spoke quietly with William. They hugged, kissed. Feeling like an intruder, I ducked into the corridor to wait with Gage and McNally. William joined us a moment later.

"You were pretty quiet in there," I said to him.

"That's because I'm worried about it, same as Renee," William replied. "I think you're right, though. We don't have a choice. It's what's got to be done, and if you believe it, I believe it."

I did believe it. I just hoped the others would be able to forgive me if I was wrong.

Twenty-four

Channel Nine

McNally had picked a small studio, host to several public digicast shows, including a morning and evening news hour. The studio was built inside an old warehouse in West Hollywood and had minimal security. Our window-tinted utility vehicle drove around to a rear entrance. The place didn't even have a security gate. Definitely an obscure location.

An elderly gentleman in a faux-expensive suit waited for us in front of a pair of double-glass doors. He shook McNally's hand, regarding us with open curiosity.

"Miles Lanthrop, segment producer," he said. "I'm so pleased you chose our little studio for this interview, Miss Trance."

I grinned; he was endearing off the bat. "It's just Trance, Mr. Lanthrop. These are my associates, Cipher and Caliber."

Lanthrop shook Gage's hand firmly. He winced a bit when William took hold. He led us through the double doors and down a short, dark-paneled hallway. We passed a series of closed doors. Past the sixth, the hall turned sharply left. Directly ahead was a set of swinging double doors, and through their windows was the studio. To the left was a sound booth and to the right another plain door.

We entered the studio, which was surprisingly active. Three cameras stood at attention, and two operators were fiddling with buttons and switches. A pair of young women with headsets scurried back and forth on the stage, shifting chairs and fluffing fake plants. They'd created an informal living room set—a nice touch.

One face was missing.

"Where's Dahlia?" I asked.

"Probably chewing her fingernails to a nub," McNally said. "The poor thing sounded terrified on the phone. She's had a copy of your questions to go over, so she should be fine."

"If she ever comes out of the dressing room," Lanthrop said. "If you three don't mind having a seat, I'll have my makeup girl—"

"No makeup," I said. "I don't want this to look staged. You get us and all of our pores."

Lanthrop gave McNally a pleading look; she just smiled. I might still be angry with her, but I did like having her on our side.

"All right, then," he said. "The sofa there, stage right, is for you. The chair stage left is for Miss Perkins. We'll be running all three cameras at once and editing it from tape. If you feel the need to address the camera for any reason, try to speak to the camera on your left. It will be in close-up."

"I'm certain," I said, "that Agent McNally has already discussed approval of the final cut? Just to make sure you don't edit anything improperly."

"I understand your suspicions, Trance, but please be assured I have no intention of snowballing you or your friends. I simply want to bring this news to the world, and you are allowing me the chance. Don't worry."

"It's my job to worry."

Gage cleared his throat, put his palm on the small of my back, and steered me toward the stage. I went willingly and sat with Gage on my right. William stood next to us. He'd come as a lookout, not a participant.

One of the headset girls—a PA, I assumed—clipped lapel microphones to our uniforms. She managed to find places that didn't show, and we went through a sound check with a man in the glass booth. They brought up blinding lights and held black boxes in front of us. The other PA patted some powder on my nose before I could protest.

"This is a bit surreal," Gage whispered, hand covering his mike.

McNally and Lanthrop stood by the middle camera, deep in conversation. Two operators had taken position on small stools attached to the hulking equipment, while the third camera remained unmanned.

On our left the first PA opened a door and held it. She beckoned someone forward. A few seconds passed. Dahlia Perkins finally emerged, thin hands clutching a yellow clipboard. She spotted us and stopped. Took a few steps, stopped again. I bit my lip, trying hard not to laugh.

"It'll be easier to ask the questions from over here," I said, waving her forward.

Some of her fear seemed to evaporate. Dahlia strode

toward us with an air of purpose, if not intent, and carefully perched on the edge of her chair. She wore a simple black skirt and jacket, blond hair pulled back into a tasteful ponytail. She looked the part, even if she acted like a frightened teenager.

"It's good to see you again," I said, and introduced her to William. "Are you okay with the list of questions?"

"Yes," Dahlia said. "I still don't understand why you chose me, though. I'm not experienced with live interviews. I'm a writer."

"Because you're not experienced, that's why. I didn't want someone coming into this with a preset notion of how it will run. I didn't want someone to try and toss in a few unregulated questions. This isn't a fluff piece, and it's not a free-for-all."

She nodded.

"And if it goes well, it will look great in your portfolio."

That earned a smile.

"Chad!"

Dahlia jumped. Behind the glare of lights, Lanthrop stormed around, seeking someone. A sleepy-eyed man emerged from a side door, yawned, and shambled toward the vacant camera. Lanthrop muttered something, and Gage laughed.

"What did he say?" I asked.

"Just some colorful curse words," he whispered back. "I guess Chad's been given final warning a few times for being late."

"You heard that?" Dahlia asked. She blushed. "Oh, right, of course."

Lanthrop stepped up to the edge of the stage. "Are we ready to make history? Ms. Perkins, you okay? Need any more antacids before we start?"

"No, I'm fine." She fanned herself with the clipboard, and the blush started to fade.

William took that as his cue to leave the stage. He stood on our right with a good view of the studio, greenroom doors, and the sound booth. Knowing he was there helped me relax.

Please let Specter stay away for a while.

"The intro and questions are up on the prompter," Lanthrop continued. "Just remember to smile, breathe, and you'll do fine."

"And try not to belch on camera," I added.

Gage covered his mouth with his hand. Lanthrop glared. Dahlia paled, finally matching the color of her foundation. Perfect.

"Just remember," Lanthrop said, ignoring me, "this is tape. If we need to stop, we can stop. Let's just aim to not do that very often, shall we? The morning crew will need the studio in three hours."

Gage leaned forward. "If this takes three hours, I'm going to sweat through this sofa. These lights are damned hot."

"Someone crank up the air-conditioning," Lanthrop bellowed as he turned around. He disappeared behind the lights.

"And let the fun begin," I said.

Dahlia licked her lips and tried to smile.

"Rolling in three, two, one . . ."

The smile turned on full wattage. "Hello, and thank you for tuning in for this historic broadcast occasion. I'm Dahlia Perkins, and today I have with me two members of the re-vitalized and re-formed Ranger Corps. The history of the Rangers dates back over one hundred years. . . ."

Ninety minutes later, we wrapped with a joke and laughter. Even though the questions and answers had been staged, we established a friendly rapport that lent itself to spontaneity and jest. Dahlia relaxed completely ten minutes into the interview. We had provided thirty minutes worth of Q&A, but Gage's asides kept cracking us up.

By the time he yelled, "Wrap!" Lanthrop seemed to be teetering on the edge of a stress-induced implosion. William kept shifting his weight from foot to foot. Of our three observers, only McNally was as relaxed as those of us onstage. A bell clanged, announcing the end of filming, and Chad the sleepy cameraman bolted for the greenroom. Lanthrop muttered something uncomplimentary.

"Looks like someone's getting fired tomorrow," Gage said.

"That was amazing," Dahlia said. Bright-eyed and rosy-cheeked, she looked like a seasoned journalist as she unclipped her lapel mike. "Thank you again, so much, for choosing me."

I plucked off my mike and deposited it on the cushion. "You're very welcome, Dahlia. It was a good opportunity for both of us."

"Do you—?" She stopped, pursed her lips, then continued her question. "Do you mind if I ask you something completely off the record?"

"You can ask anything, but I reserve the right not to answer."

She nodded. "Back when I asked one of the questions, the one about whether or not you knew why everyone lost their powers, you said no. You didn't know."

My stomach knotted. "That's right."

"Is that true?"

Had I given that away? I suppose I had hesitated a split second too long, actually thrown by the question. "It was true when I wrote it."

Dahlia considered my response, then smiled. "Okay."

A shadow fell across us as William stepped up onto the stage, blessedly blocking some of those horrid lights. I started to shout for someone to have mercy, but they began to dim on their own. Spooky.

"There a men's room around here?" he asked.

"Back in the greenroom," Dahlia said. "I'm heading that way, I can show you."

"Thanks."

Dahlia shook our hands and expressed half a dozen more thank-yous in the space of thirty seconds, before leading William toward the stage left door. I stood up and stretched, my skin ten degrees cooler with the lights dimmed.

"I wonder when we'll be leaving," Gage said

"Whenever you like," McNally said. I turned and found myself face-to-face with the older woman. She smiled congenially as her curious gaze flickered between us. "They need to start dressing the stage for the eight a.m. digicast. Mr. Lanthrop is thrilled with your work today, by the way. I think you'll like the rough cut, improvisations and all."

One of the PAs bolted through and picked up the discarded lapel mikes, there and gone before I could blink. They moved fast, because they had to. In L.A.'s waning production industry, there was always another intern or wannabe waiting in the wings to get experience at a lower pay rate than the current employee. I could rest soundly knowing no one would ever clamor for my job.

"Guess that's our cue," Gage said as he stood. I tucked my arm around his, and we followed McNally toward the studio doors.

"Did Caliber get lost or something?" I asked.

"Maybe Dahlia tricked him into answering more off-the-record questions," Gage said. "I don't—" He stiffened. His eyes narrowed, nostrils flaring.

"What is it?"

"Do you smell that?" He shook his head. "No, of course you don't."

He turned around, spotted his target, and strode toward Mr. Lanthrop. The elderly man was conversing with a pair of matronly women who could have been news anchors as easily as wrestling champs. I scurried behind, alarmed.

"Mr. Lanthrop?" Gage asked. "I'm sorry to interrupt."

"It's all right, Cipher." Annoyance filtered through his smile. I doubted Gage missed it, he just pointedly ignored it.

"Does this warehouse have a gas lead pipe?"

Lanthrop blinked owlishly. "Um, yes, I believe it does. We

have a gas oven in the break room, if that's what you mean. Why?"

Gage's nostrils flared again as he blew out hard through his nose. "Evacuate this building right n—"

The explosion rattled the ground and blew the stage left door off its hinges. It struck the floor, careened sideways, and whacked the sofa for a loop. Wave after wave of superheated air slammed across the studio, knocking us to our knees. A fire alarm wailed somewhere deep inside of the warehouse's old interior.

"William!" I screamed.

Gage reached for my hand. I shook him loose. He started shouting for everyone to get out and head for the exits, even as I ran the opposite way, toward the explosion and the source of the raging heat.

The PA who'd powdered my nose tumbled out of the open doorway, her face streaked with gray. She fell to her knees, coughed, and tried to run, only to stumble again. I caught her around the waist. She yelped, and I saw the blistered burns on her bare midsection.

"In the . . . break room," she sputtered.

I gave the girl a less than gentle shove toward the studio exit, then dashed through the door. The short corridor was stifling, the ceiling clouded with smoke. Orange flames licked the walls ten feet ahead where another door lay in shattered, charred ruins in the center of the hall. More smoke billowed out.

"We have to get out of here fast," Gage said.

I jumped, heart in my throat. "You scared the hell out of me."

"If the fire gets into the main gas line, this entire place will go up."

Flames shot through the destroyed doorway and into the hall, like a puff of dragon's breath. Just as quickly, it retracted, and a rush of air pulled toward the door, as though playing the entire explosion in reverse. I let it tow me forward, and I grabbed the burnt edge of the doorframe before the drag sucked me inside.

The interior walls of the break room were streaked with black soot and bubbling paint. A table and chairs lay askew in the corner, broken and blistered. The stove was a gutted ruin of twisted metal and exposed wire. William sat upright against the far wall, uniform in tatters, weeping burns on his face and hands. In the center of the room stood Dahlia Perkins, her clothes streaked with ash and not a mark on her exposed skin.

I blinked hard and pinched myself to make sure my eyes weren't affected by the smoke. She was drawing the heat and remaining licks of fire toward herself, into her body. She stood like a statue, fingers splayed by her sides, saucer-eyed, clearly as shocked as we were, if not more.

"Oh my God, oh my God, oh my God," streamed from her mouth.

"Dahlia," I said, hesitant to leave the safety of the doorway. "Sweetie, what happened?"

"We were just talking." She moved her lips as little as possible, as though afraid to disturb the air. "Then I smelled gas. I saw a smoldering cigarette on the floor by the stove, and then it just exploded. I thought I was dead, but I'm not and this is really weird. How do I make it stop?"

"Try pushing," Gage said, standing behind me. "Push the heat away."

She closed her eyes. A heat wave blasted forward, knocking me backward into Gage and sending both of us careening into the wall. I hit the floor on my left elbow and shrieked when Gage landed on top of me and jammed it even harder.

"Sorry!" Dahlia said.

"Think about ice, dammit," I yelled, my elbow throbbing. "Something cold, don't think about the fire." She had drawn most of the heat away—a topic for further discussion once we were out of that blasted hallway—but the crackling of the fire could still be heard behind the walls. The drawback of constructing a studio inside of a pre-existing structure was the unused, insulated space, and the inferno inside of it waiting to get out.

The ice suggestion seemed to work. The rush of air ceased, as did the unearthly glow of her skin. A heavy sheen of perspiration replaced it, soaking quickly through her blouse.

"I don't want to do that again," she said, panting. "Caliber?"

"I'm okay." William hauled himself up, somehow not wincing as he flexed his muscles. Just looking at the blisters and char marks made the skin on my thighs crawl. "Is everyone else out?"

"We think so," I said. "We were all out front."

Gage led the way back down the short hall to the studio. Red lights flashed in the rafters, and everything reeked of burnt wood. We reached the center of the studio, and Gage slammed to a jarring halt.

"Everyone get down!" he shouted.

The order was punctuated by a second explosion as the internal fires reached the main gas line. The ceiling above us combusted in a shower of fire, metal, and glass. Light fixtures groaned, broke, and fell. Walls collapsed, consumed by flame. Intense heat roiled around us.

I hit the floor and rolled onto my back in time to see a steel rod dotted with six light cans plummeting toward my head.

Twenty-five

Inferno

I erected the force field almost without thought, creating a violet canopy over the group. Gage lay next to me, curled onto his right side. Something had struck his face and left a deep gash on his left cheek. William and Dahlia were on my other side; he was protecting her from the debris now bouncing harmlessly off my shield. I could block the physical objects, but not the overwhelming heat or encroaching flames.

The ceiling stopped collapsing, and after the others were on their feet, I let the shield drop. What little heat it kept at bay struck like a hammer, knocking the last bits of clean air from my lungs. I coughed, overwhelmed by the acrid odor and bitter taste. Gage looked green, and I could only imagine how fried his senses were. Dahlia clenched her fists and seemed to concentrate on something—probably snowmen or penguins.

Two thick rafter beams had fallen across the exit doors like a giant metal X. William tested the upper beam. Even with his strength, it didn't budge. He tried the lower beam and managed a few inches.

"Get back," I said. "I'll try to blast it."

They took cover behind the only camera still standing upright. I drew up two orbs roughly the size of grapefruits and lobbed them at the center of the X. The metal dented. Didn't break. I squawked. Tried again. This time it fused the beams together where they crossed.

I gaped at it, eyes watering. "So much for plan B."

"Tell me someone has a plan C?" Dahlia said.

William crouched in front of the fused X and scooted until his lower back was firmly planted beneath the cross brace. "I don't know how long I can hold this up," he said, his voice hoarse and dry. "So when I do, you three go between my legs."

"I'm not leaving you behind," I said.

He winked. "You won't. I promised Renee I'd take her to the beach when this is over, and I hate lying to a pretty lady."

"Just so we're clear." I knelt in front of him, orbs glowing, ready to clear a path. "Now!"

The metal groaned; he didn't. It gave; he didn't. Inch by agonizing inch, William Hill lifted the beams high enough to create a crawl space. I propelled orb after orb, drilling a hole through the wood and plaster to freedom. When the tunnel was open and cool air tickled my cheeks, I reached back and yanked on Dahlia's wrist.

"Go," I said, shoving her into the hole. She disappeared. "Gage, go."

"You go first," Gage said.

"Don't argue with me."

William hissed. "Will one of you jackasses get going? I'm a strongman, not a robot."

Gage plunged into the hole. I looked up at William, able to see every straining muscle, every bulge in his neck and abs and biceps. "When are you coming?" I asked.

"As soon as I can. I've got a date to keep, remember?"

With his promise ringing in my ears, I crawled forward. It was a tight fit, and I was impressed that Gage had managed to squeeze through the narrow passage. How would William manage?

Gage reached for me as I emerged in the dimly lit outer corridor.

"Hey, over here!" William shouted.

I twisted around, still flat on my belly. Someone else was on the other side with him. Legs stumbled into my line of sight, and I recognized the baggy jeans and soiled sneakers. Chad the sleepy cameraman. He was dragging something, and as he stumbled over a bit of debris, a packet of cigarettes fell by his feet.

My stomach clenched. I reached forward, drawing up an orb. The shoes moved out of sight, followed by the silver and red curve of a fire ax. "William!"

"Hey, man," William said. "What the hell—?" His scream pierced the roar of the fire in the same instant the red-coated ax blade passed across the front of the hole. Blood splattered. The beams fell.

"No!" I plunged into the hole. Strong arms secured my waist and held me down. Panic crept into my heart. Bile stung my throat. "Let me go!"

"Trance, come on," Gage said. "The ceiling's coming down on this side, we have to go." He yelped, and the pained sound diverted my attention. A slim shard of wood had impaled his shoulder, just above the armpit.

Dahlia crabbed farther down the corridor on her hands and feet, tears streaking her sooty cheeks. She was coughing and retching. I couldn't leave a man behind, but I had to get them out of there. Dahlia was a civilian. She was my priority.

With a frustrated scream, I lurched to my feet and grabbed Gage by his good shoulder. Together, we hauled Dahlia up and ran. Bits of the ceiling rained down as we raced toward sunlight. Sirens screamed outside, beckoning us forward.

Fresh air filled my lungs, forcing out the smoke in heaving, painful coughs that doubled me over. Tears stung my eyes, and I let them fall. Moisture was good. I had to go back for William. I'd need all the moisture I could get. I turned blindly toward the entrance again, only to find myself tackled to the ground. A third, eardrum-shattering explosion rocked the world. People screamed, and I screamed with them.

Tall, leaping flames consumed the warehouse and belched from every window and door. Yellow, red, orange, and every shade in between danced and sang their terrible song, rending and destroying.

I lunged again. "William!" My voice didn't carry far. A solid body anchored me to the ground. I pushed and pulled. I screamed again, and a choked cry came out instead. My chest hurt. I couldn't draw a breath.

"No, no, no," over and over until my words became sobs, and the pleas became bitter tears.

We stayed until late afternoon, waiting for the fire department to seize control of the blaze and give William back to us. I wouldn't leave without him. I sat for hours in the back of an ambulance, long after they dressed the few burns on my back and stomach. Long after they tended to Gage's shoulder and Dahlia's scrapes. Sat and waited and didn't speak.

Gage left and returned once. He offered a nod that told me he'd placed the call. Renee and the others knew, and I was ashamed that I hadn't been the one to tell her. I couldn't do anything except sit and stare and mourn.

Dahlia remained by my side, a shell-shocked shadow. Had I inadvertently sensed something when I picked her out of the paparazzi crowd? I didn't know. At the moment, I didn't care. She tried to offer a few more teary apologies. I ignored her into silence. She was a mystery I hadn't the faculties to ponder. We didn't discuss her fire absorption, or if she could be out there helping the firemen rein in the inferno. She couldn't control it. I couldn't ask her to try. Not like this.

Police corralled a slew of reporters behind wooden barricades. The throng was more frenzied than they'd been at the building collapse. I could imagine the headlines: "Heroes Torch Studio After Welcome Back Interview."

Lanthrop wandered by once, wondering if I would be pleased to know that he had a copy of the interview. My response was to flip him off. He left us alone after that.

A little after four in the afternoon, a fire lieutenant came over to the ambulance and spoke with Gage. From their body language, I knew what was happening. They had found William.

It was time to take him home.

I spent the short ride back avoiding eye contact with the sheet-covered form at our feet. I hadn't let the EMTs put William into one of their black bags. He startled easily and didn't like enclosed spaces.

Five people hovered on the Base's roof below, waiting for the copter to land. Marco stood behind Renee, one hand on her shoulder. She had her own arms wrapped around her torso several times, as if trying to find comfort in the embrace. They watched us approach, solemn and unmoving.

Dr. Seward and Agent Grayson huddled to one side, along with an orderly who appeared to be in charge of a gurney. The sight of it squeezed my chest.

The copter landed and the green safety light blinked on. McNally turned the lock and pushed the door open. A rush of air from the rotating blades erupted into the cabin, caught the edge of the sheet, and blew an unsecured corner. Gage snagged it and tucked it back under—too late to prevent a glimpse of William's severed leg. Chopped through meat and bone just below the knee by one swing of an ax, and secured only by two inches of muscle and skin.

Renee screamed, arms going back to normal length like a retracting coil. McNally climbed out and steered her away, words lost to the roar of the slowing motor. Gage and

I waited inside while Dr. Seward and the orderly pulled out the backboard and secured their burden to the gurney. Marco appeared in the door, his glowing eyes red-rimmed and bloodshot. He gazed past us, to the passenger trying to disappear into the vinyl bench seat.

"Why did you bring the reporter?" Marco asked.

"Because she's one of us," Gage replied.

Marco furrowed his eyebrows. "Us?"

"I absorb fire," Dahlia said.

Gage grunted. "She's safer here, so we brought her along."

Marco looked at me, and I nodded my agreement. He offered his good hand to Dahlia. She smiled, took it, and climbed out. Gage followed, and then turned around to wait for me. I stared at the floor with zero desire to leave. He waited silently for a while, then followed the others inside.

The pilot locked down the copter controls, making no move to evict me. The others were gone, probably waiting for me to appear and decide what to do next, and all I could do was hide in a stationary helicopter. Hiding was not something I did often, but the idea of facing my friends—the people whose lives I was responsible for—terrified me on a basic level. I had failed; someone died. Again.

I always lost.

Specter found us at the studio, but how? Fewer than fifteen people knew about the location. Most of them found out an hour before we started. Specter knew to look for us at the HQ, not at a tiny public broadcasting studio in West Hollywood. Outside the team, only Seward, McNally and Grayson knew about the interview, and they were all on our side.

Maybe.

McNally and Grayson had lied to us about how we lost our powers. They had known about Fairview and the Warden. They were certainly both smart enough to commit arson and get away with it. Hadn't Seward said Specter was likely to strike at us off-site? But why would any of them help Specter kill us? Why not simply shoot us all and be done with it?

Chad the cameraman had been the perfect target for Specter. The boy was tired, overworked, with a weak mind sensitive to suggestion, stuck in that perfect place between sleep and awake, where Specter liked to strike. Only someone possessed could start a fire with the intent to hurt so many. Only Specter-possessed could a sleepy-eyed teenager take an ax and chop through someone's leg, slice through muscle, splinter bone, spurt blood.

My stomach twisted. I lurched out of the copter, scurried across the landing pad, and vomited into the gravel. Bitter acid scorched my throat and tongue, and I continued to retch long after my stomach had emptied. Angry tears spilled down my cheeks, somehow finding expendable moisture in my exhausted, dehydrated body. I spat a wad of phlegm and wiped my mouth, my entire body trembling.

Cool wind pushed a lock of sooty hair into my eyes, shading me from the setting sun. It dipped low on the horizon, its bottom edge just touching the Pacific Ocean. Beams of gold and red sparkled against the winter sky and slivers of visible water, setting the entire world on fire.

"Stay the course," I said, frustrated with the meaningless words. I glared at the sunset. My strength gave out, and I sat down hard. The odor of charred wood was ever-present, grafted to my skin. Seeped into my uniform. I knew I should change, but I preferred the grit. In the past I had gone weeks without clean clothes. I'd soaked shirts and bras in hot water and glycerin soap in lieu of proper laundering. It had seemed more important to spend my money on food and heat than detergent.

Had living here softened me so much? Provided a false sense of security by the notion of a job I couldn't get fired from?

Not true. I could get fired. I could very easily fire myself for incompetence, only I knew I'd never leave this place. The Corps was all I had. I'd sooner die than disappoint them—if I hadn't already.

Footsteps swished across the landing pad. I ignored the pilot. I was out of his copter. He couldn't make me leave the roof. The steps stopped behind me.

"Any symptoms?" Dr. Seward asked.

I tilted my head. He looked so sincere, thin mouth puckered into a little ball, that I swallowed a sarcastic retort. "No. Nothing that isn't the direct result of smoke inhalation and long bouts of crying."

"I can give you something for the headache."

"How about the heartache, Doc? Got anything for that?"

He looked up, toward the sunset. Red light reflected in his eyes and off the rims of his glasses. "Time heals all wounds, right? Except for the ones we keep ripping open anew." He crouched, hands dangling between his knees. "I am so sorry about William."

"Me too."

"Your father used to come up here to watch the sun set. Not as often that final year, but for a long time before. Your mother was deathly afraid of heights."

I hadn't known that about her. "I'm not afraid of heights, just of everything else." Had I really just admitted that to Dr. Seward? I had all the insecurities of twenty people my age, and no one to talk to about them. I had to be brave for the team, brave for my friends. I couldn't afford to be weak, hence my hiding on the roof instead of facing them with my grief. Facing their grief.

"What are you afraid of, Trance?"

"Losing it all." I flicked a stone and it skittered across the cement. "My whole life, everything I value has been taken away from me. Friends, jobs, money. Freedom. My mom and dad, my powers, my memories. William. Control over any aspect of my life, all taken away. And I can't stop it."

"Few of us ever maintain the control over our lives we would like to have, but we do what we are called to do, Trance. When your powers returned and Rita McNally called me, I left behind a wife, two grown daughters, and a life in San Diego to come here."

"I didn't know that." I was dumbfounded, having never considered his personal life. Hell, it took hard thought to re-call his first name. What did that say about me?

"My wife, Annabelle, is furious at me right now. Fifteen years ago, after we secured you children new lives, I handed in my notice and walked. It was supposed to be my retire-ment from twenty years of service."

"Why'd you come back? Why didn't you stay with your family?"

He smiled, a warm gesture that crinkled the corners of his eyes. "My mother worked for MHC and the Corps, as did my grandfather. It's always been a part of my life, and I've sacrificed a lot for it."

"Has it been worth it?"

"Most of the time, in moments like this. People forget that Rangers are human beings with feelings and fears and love and pain. It hurt your predecessors to think the people they were fighting for no longer gave a damn."

"But you give a damn."

"Yes. You have a gift, Trance, to make people listen and follow. You can rebuild the Rangers and repair the indignities of the past."

"Be the leader my father was?"

Dr. Seward shook his head and put his hand on my arm. "No, be the leader only you can be. Don't compare yourself with the past, because it's gone. Blaze your own path."

Stay the course.

I wanted—no, needed—to do right by my friends. Stopping was only part of my course, bite-size and easy enough to work with; a chunk of the larger picture of rebuilding the Corps and, just maybe, reuniting the Metas without the dividing lines of the past.

The golden sun melted deeper into the ocean. I squinted into the glare, watching red and deepening purple spread across the sky. The sun would rise and set every day. The world would continue, lives would be lived, babies born, as inevitable as breathing. Those things lay outside of my control.

Everything else lay within me. The desire to change, to do right by my fellow Metas, and to stop the century-old rivalry between Rangers and Banes. To destroy whatever misunderstandings and supposed differences had put us on opposing sides of a battle that no one could ever hope to win. Maybe I would fail and that was okay. Failure and success were out of my hands; the power to try was not.

Grief had to wait a while longer. I had work to do.

"Did the pilot go inside?" I asked.

"I think so. Why?"

"Can you find him and tell him we're leaving in half an hour?" I stood up and dusted off the seat of my pants. "I'm going to Manhattan. There's someone I need to talk to."

Twenty-six

Psystorm

Twenty minutes after the ATF's private jet took off from the Burbank airfield, my Vox beeped. I ignored it as long as I could stand it, and then accepted the signal.

<Trance, this is Cipher. Where the hell are you?>

Across the cabin, Agent McNally cleared her throat. She'd secured permission to use the jet and made arrangements to get us from the airport in Newark to Manhattan Island Prison. I'd asked her to come along in case I needed her clout to get access to Psystorm. His powers put him among our most dangerous enemies, and access to him was likely restricted. McNally had argued against not telling the others, and against not taking anyone else along for backup. I listened to her advice and then promptly ignored it.

I held up my Vox. "Cipher, Trance here. I'm almost over Nevada, why? Where are you?"

<Nevada? What the hell are you doing in Nevada?>

"I'm not in Nevada, I'm flying over it. Or rather, I'm in a jet that's flying over it."

He didn't seem to appreciate my attempts at levity,

because venom coated his next words. <What the hell are you doing, Trance?>

"Taking the next step in ending this. You were right. Psystorm is our best chance at stopping Specter."

<You're going to New York alone? That's stup—>

"Stupid, irresponsible, and foolhardy, yeah, I got the list." I cut my eyes at McNally. "You know what's more foolish? Taking every able-bodied Ranger I have left to an island full of people who hate us. One wrong move, and it would be Ethan and Dahlia against the world. Do you want that?"

Silence.

"Gage?"

<I hate that you're right.>

"I know."

<Do I have to say be careful?>

"No, but I like hearing it."

<Be careful.>

"I promise."

<Let me know when you get there.> His cold tone left no room for negotiation.

"You'll be kept informed, Gage, now go get some sleep. Out."

I put the Vox away before he could respond. McNally was staring at me, a peculiar expression on her face—a mix of amusement and commiseration.

"You're lucky to have him," she said.

"I know."

She settled back into her seat. I closed my eyes and dozed

for much of the trip. Only a few hours of sleep in the last couple of days was starting to wear me out.

McNally shook me awake a while later. I rubbed my eyes, oddly refreshed from the nap. I half expected to find my vision clouded by violet, but it wasn't. Not even a hint of side effects, yet, from my earlier power use.

We'd arrived on the East Coast. We transferred from the jet to a copter that had seen better days. Ten minutes later, we set down on top of the observation tower on Ellis Island— one of the many security checkpoints surrounding Manhattan Island Prison.

High walls of electrified fence ran the entire perimeter of the twenty-thousand-acre island. Dozens of sections were reinforced with stone and mortar, completely blocking access to the Hudson, East, or Harlem rivers. Underwater tunnels like Lincoln and Midtown had been destroyed, sunk beneath their respective bodies of water. Every bridge except the Henry Hudson was half gone. Guard posts stood on the fractured ends of those bridges, overlooking the island.

We exited the copter and were greeted by four men armed with rifles and tasers. They led us across a grassy area to the steel and concrete tower.

After speaking briefly with one of the guards, McNally flashed her ID and we were taken into an interrogation room. Apparently she had called ahead; we were expected. Good, it made my job a little easier. We waited on one side of a glass floor-to-ceiling barrier separating one side of the room from the other. A chair was bolted to the floor on the opposite side. The table and chairs on our side were loose. McNally sat down, while I perched on the edge of the table.

Minutes later, the door to the other room opened. Two armed guards entered backward, rifles trained on the door. A man shuffled in, jeans and sweatshirt sagging on his thin frame. His brown hair was thinning on top, making his hollow cheeks seem sharper, more pronounced. The security collar around his neck looked like a freakish punk accessory. Metal bands secured his arms to his chest, wrists to each other, and loose ankle shackles gave him little room to walk. It was a waddle-dance to get him to his chair. Four more armed guards entered behind him.

The prisoner looked more like an exhausted auto mechanic than a supervillain.

Guards secured him to the chair. He submitted to their handling. Either he didn't care or he was drugged. His eyes might have been glassy from the bright lights shining down from the ceiling. He answered my unasked question by lifting his head and looking right into my eyes. A gentle nudge tickled the corner of my mind, and I felt his curiosity. Pain, fatigue, and restlessness warred just behind it, but his interest in the interview's purpose won out.

Who are you? His words rang in my head, a voice as frail as his neglected, forty-something body.

"My name is Trance," I said, unsure at first if he could hear me through the glass wall. He nodded, so I continued. "You were once known as Psystorm."

"Yes," he replied out loud. "Still am, I guess. I don't remember you."

"Probably because I was ten the last time you might have seen me."

He studied me through the glass, his expression unreadable. He nudged again, gently. I imagined a violet wall between us, strong enough to block his attempts to peek into my mind, and he jerked backward in his chair. The movement startled his guards. They all raised their weapons. Psystorm ignored them.

"You've got some power there, kiddo," he said. "Trance, is it?"

"Yes."

"What do you want?"

First step in negotiating with bad guys: Offer them something they want and make it sound like a favor. "To get you out of here. Off the island, out of prison."

No reaction, not even a glimmer of hope. "Working vacation, I take it? And then right back here when you have no more use for me?"

I shook my head and took a step toward the partition. "No, for good. Your help in exchange for a full pardon of all past crimes. Stay clean, and you won't end up back here for future crimes."

"Who do I have to kill?"

"It's not that kind of job."

"I'm listening."

Another step. I kept the mental shield in place. Without knowing the exact limits of his powers, I didn't want any chance of manipulation on his part. My part was another story entirely.

"What do you know about Specter?" I asked.

His head listed to the left, a gesture that came off as bored rather than thoughtful. "You'll have to be more specific, kiddo. Specter led us during those final years, and you very well know it. We both know how his powers work, and we both know he's a bloodthirsty, power-hungry son of a bitch. So why don't you ask me about something you don't know."

Second step in negotiating with bad guys: Establish rapport.

"Fair enough. Tell me, then, did you know Specter wasn't on the island these past fifteen years?"

"No, but you start to hear things, especially when you're living with the same seventy-two people for so long."

The number gave me pause. Sixty-five Banes had been imprisoned on the island, not seventy-two. He continued before I could ask him to clarify.

"Some guys liked to brag," he said. "A few years ago, I started hearing rumors about Specter. He wasn't on the island. Someone had bribed two guards into collaring the wrong guy, and those guards doled out extra food and goodies to the guys who kept the doppelganger fed. Kept the ruse up."

"Do you know names?"

"Yep."

"Any you'd care to share?"

"Absolutely not. In a place like this, you learn how the pecking order works. Some of the names are lot more powerful than me, and pardon or not, I have no intention of landing on their shit lists. No help to you there. If they want to sing about the old bastard, they can come forward by themselves."

Self-preservation seemed to win out time and again. "So tell me, Psystorm, if you hate Specter so much, why did you follow him?"

"Because he was the strongest." An implicit "duh" in his statement. "The weak follow the strong. You should know that well. You are the lead Ranger, are you not?"

"I am."

"Good. There's nothing more insulting than negotiating with a lackey." I didn't respond, so he continued, "Specter wanted power. We wanted to survive. It was a pretty simple choice to make."

"Murdering Rangers was a simple choice?"

His eyes blazed, the first real sign of emotion since our interview began. His anger poked at my mental barrier. "I hate to sound elementary school about this, kiddo, but you started it. Your parents and your teachers, they killed first. We were playing by their rules."

"That's a lie," I said before I could reconsider.

Surprise replaced anger, and Psystorm smiled. "Revisionist history, I should have known. Your old man ever tell you about the first battle? The one that kicked off the War?"

"Trenton, New Jersey. Six jewelry heists in one hour, three million dollars worth of jewels and cash stolen and four people killed, including a Ranger."

"Wrong."

He said it with such utter conviction that I believed him. I didn't want to, but I did. My head swiveled toward McNally. She stood with her arms folded, back straight, and eyes on the floor. Her stance and silence only served to confirm that Psystorm was telling the truth. Revisionist history, my ass. It sounded like good, old-fashioned lying. More lying by MHC. And what about my father? Had he known the truth, or had he somehow been duped, as well? Had he lied to me?

A cold rage churned deep inside me. "Then, what's right?" I asked, giving him back my full attention.

"Ocean City, Maryland," he said. "Twelve days before Trenton. Three of us were down there, laying low. You remember the names Acid and Somnus?"

I tried to recall them, to give us something else to connect over, and failed. They were not only unfamiliar names, I had no conscious memory of hearing them in reference to a Bane, living or dead. "No, I'm sorry, I don't."

"I'm first to admit we weren't saints. The three of us made a lot of money robbing private residences. All I had to do was knock on the door and hold the home owner in my thrall while my partners emptied the place. We were criminals, yes, but we avoided violence whenever possible. When things started getting hot, we went down to Maryland to hide. We had no intention of starting trouble, just getting our shit together, so we holed up in a rented house and kept to ourselves."

"The fire." I remembered the newspapers strewn across our apartment, headlines about half a mile of the Ocean City boardwalk burning to the ground. Arson was mentioned—nothing about Bane interference, no mention of a battle as the cause of the blaze. Just my dad talking about a Corps Unit being dispatched and trying to save as many lives as possible.

"The fire," Psystorm said. "I bet your old man never told you that we were down there trying to help save lives. Pulling kids out of burning hotels, keeping folks calm until your precious Corps Unit showed up. Only they didn't stop to ask questions when they arrived. They saw us, recognized us, and assumed we were responsible."

I inhaled, held it, until he said what I hoped he wouldn't.

"Your people killed Acid and Somnus for trying to help," he continued. "That's all we were doing was trying to help. No one reported our presence, because it would make you people look bad. They shot first, never asked questions, then covered it up. That started it for me, kiddo. After your old mentors killed Somnus, my wife, it didn't take much for Specter to convince me."

Grief for two people I hadn't known, two innocent lives lost, struck me hard. Senseless, all of it, the whole damned War. Could the death and destruction have been avoided completely? The notion made me want to vomit.

"I'm sorry."

He blinked, eyebrows raising. "Too bad your precious predecessors weren't sorry. I followed Specter out of a keen desire for revenge. Not against you kids, though. Those last few weeks when he wanted to exterminate children . . . a lot of us started to speak up, only it was too late. When we lost our powers, the feds tossed every one of us onto this forsaken island and locked it down."

His attention shifted to McNally. She continued to stare at the floor, and I wondered now if she regretted staying in the room. She must have known Psystorm would air all sorts of dirty laundry implicating MHC in even more not-so-nice things. She just stood there, listening, and didn't react. Didn't try to find fault in any of his statements. Didn't try to excuse herself this time.

I kind of admired her for it. I also wanted to blast her through the wall.

He was watching me again. "What exactly do you want from me, Trance? Loyalty?"

"No, just a promise. In exchange for this pardon, you help us find and contain Specter. Once he has been permanently neutralized, you're free to go."

"Neutralized?" He spat the word, as though it was a curse on his name. "You want me to help you kill him?"

"Contain him. I should want the bastard dead for the things he's done to us this past week. He's been responsible for the deaths of seven Rangers, my friends, but I'm tired of killing. I just want him stopped." Besides, if we killed him I'd never know who was helping him. I'd never sniff out the traitor who had spilled about Fairview, the interview, everything.

I moved forward again, until my breath puffed vapor circles on the glass partition. "Don't misunderstand me, Psy-storm. I don't want to restart the cycle of killing that brought us to this moment, but if it comes down to his life versus the life of anyone else, he can die."

He puckered his lips, eyebrows slanting. The expression held for the space of several breaths, then his face softened. He looked almost peaceful. "I'll help you."

"Thank you." I stumbled over the words. As much as we

needed him, a tiny part of me hadn't expected his acquiescence. An earlier portion of our conversation came back. "Just one thing, though. You mentioned you lived with seventy-two people on the island? How's that possible?"

His damned eerie smile returned, and he said, "We were powerless, Trance, not neutered. Men and women, prisoners or not, still have sex. Babies are born, which brings me around to one condition affecting my acceptance of this deal you're offering."

"Which is?"

"My son. I want him to come with us. He goes where I go, so if he stays on the island, then so do I."

Surprise washed over me. In war, they teach soldiers to dehumanize the enemy, to make killing easier. I'd been raised to believe the Banes were monsters, less than human, so it had never occurred to me that the imprisoned Banes had constructed real lives for themselves. Once powerless, the country had essentially forgotten about them. News reports never mentioned the population increase inside the prison. No one wanted to remind the world that the Banes were still people, too.

"Where's your son?" McNally asked. "We'll send someone to get him."

Psystorm closed his eyes briefly, and then reopened them. "He's on his way to the main gate. They'll find him there."

"I'll go." McNally turned to me. "We'll meet you at the helipad."

———————

Caleb was younger than I expected, and he walked with the slumped shoulders of a boy who'd seen too much for only five short years on earth. His mop of black hair and almond eyes were not from his father. The only resemblance to Psystorm was in his sharp nose and thin frame. The boy ran to his father the moment they saw each other. Psystorm swept him up in his arms, holding him close. Unlike his father, Caleb wasn't fitted with a security collar.

McNally shuffled us toward the waiting copter. I allowed father and son to climb inside first. She grabbed my elbow, pulled me back, and then slipped something into my hand. A black box, smaller than my Vox, with a plastic cover and switch.

"For the collar," she whispered. "Just in case. One push will render him unconscious. Two will kill him."

I pocketed the device, sick at having it offered in the first place. She didn't trust Psystorm. Having it was the responsible thing. I would risk my life at his hands, but not the lives of my remaining teammates.

We climbed inside, and I sat across from our guests. Caleb gazed around the interior, wide-eyed and trembling. He had never been outside of the prison gates. The upcoming jet ride across the country was an experience he would never forget. He sat nearly in his father's lap, hands bunched in Psystorm's shirt.

"Are we gonna fly, Daddy?" he asked. "Fly like birds?"

"Yes, we are, Caleb," Psystorm said, voice soft and reassuring. A doting father. "We'll fly up with the birds, and in a few hours, we'll see a brand-new ocean. A pretty one, much bluer than the river. Do you want to see that?"

Caleb nodded, his longish hair flopping into his eyes. "Can Mommy come and see it, too?"

"Mommy's too sick to come this time." He looked at me over his son's head. I forgot the block and was barraged with an overwhelming sense of sadness. "Maybe next trip, okay?"

"Okay."

It was odd that Psystorm hadn't negotiated for the release of Caleb's mother. Or mentioned her in any way, other than just being too sick to travel. It could have been true. It could have been an angry ex's way of getting his son away from the woman who birthed him, or a doting father's method of telling his son they were leaving Mommy behind. I didn't much care, as long as Psystorm did what he promised.

We lifted into the air and turned toward Newark. Caleb pressed his nose against the glass and watched. It was the middle of the night, close to dawn. The sun would chase us home. We'd arrive on the West Coast before it rose there. It would rise, though, and finally end the longest day of my life. The death of a friend, the discovery of a new Ranger, and the freeing of a Bane who wanted a better life for himself and his child. It was too much. All I wanted right now was to crawl into Gage's arms and sleep. Barring that, a big, steaming mug of coffee would suffice.

My stomach grumbled.

"What are you thinking about, Trance?" Psystorm asked.

I looked up and smiled. "You can't read my mind?"

"I could, but I won't without your permission. Trust has to start somewhere, right?"

"You're right."

"So?"

"I was trying to imagine the looks on peoples' faces if we tried to hit a drive-thru in this thing. I don't know about you, but I'm starving."

"You're starving? You should see what we had to get by on. It's been fifteen years since I had a simple cheeseburger, much less a filling meal."

Caleb ignored our conversation about food, too intent on the colorful lights streaking by below. Could those thin arms and bony knees be a result of his father's narrow build, or was the child truly malnourished? I had a hard time believing our government would knowingly allow children to suffer. Logic told me the imprisoned Banes would have done anything to hide the existence of those kids from the guards. They ran the risk of having their children taken away.

Had keeping Caleb a secret been selfish on Psystorm's part, or simply the blind act of a loving father? Looking at them together, I was inclined to believe the latter.

"Has Caleb ever had a doughnut?" I asked.

"No," Psystorm said. The boy didn't seem to notice he'd been mentioned.

I picked up a pair of headphones and put them on. "Pilot?"

<Go ahead.>

"If you see a bakery on the way back to Newark, I want you to land. We're stopping for breakfast before we head home."

<Copy that, Trance.>

I gave Psystorm a withering stare. "Don't make me regret it."

He shook his head and pursed his lips, chin trembling. I felt his gratitude and didn't shield myself from it. For the first time in my life, I felt kinship with a Bane.

My dad was probably rolling in his grave.

Twenty-seven

Medical Ward IV

No one was waiting on the Base helipad—a welcomed change from last night's arrival. Caleb seemed nervous to exit the copter. He clutched a box of bakery doughnuts to his chest as his dad carried him off. We had capped his sugar limit to two doughnuts every four hours. The boy was content enough to just have the sweet treats close. On the other hand, I had downed a twenty-four-ounce black coffee (which had little effect on my energy levels) and desperately needed to pee.

McNally led the way across the roof to the stairwell door, Psystorm and son between us. It was still mostly dark. Slivers of light danced on the eastern horizon. If Specter stayed par for the course, we had a good six hours or so before he was strong enough to come after us again.

It wasn't enough time.

Halfway down, footsteps thundered up the stairwell. One set, moving fast. On the third-floor landing, we stopped and waited. Gage appeared moments later, red-faced and a little out of breath. He ignored McNally, spared a contemptuous glance at Psystorm, then stalked over to me.

"We need to talk," he said without preamble.

"It's good to see you, too." I was too tired to properly field his indignation. "Mind if I pee first?"

The question caught him off-guard, and he stumbled over his response. "Fine."

"Agent McNally, can you take Psystorm and Caleb over to Medical and have them checked out? I have a feeling Caleb's never visited a regular doctor."

Psystorm shook his head, confirming my suspicion, and the trio continued down. I descended to level two and left the stairwell. Gage followed silently as I sought out the bathroom facilities. He waited by the sinks while I dashed into a stall and disposed of that morning's caffeine distribution system.

He waited until I was washing my hands to speak. "What the hell were you thinking, Teresa? Going out there alone was stupid."

"Going out there alone was the smartest thing I've done since I took this damned job."

"You could have been killed."

"I wasn't."

Nothing I said was calming him down; in fact, he was only getting angrier. His cheeks had flushed and his hands trembled. "How the hell am I supposed to protect you when you rush off and leave me behind?"

"Protect me?" I stared at him, flabbergasted. "Gage, you're not my bodyguard. I made a leadership decision. Period."

So many things seemed to perch on the tip of his tongue, only to be beaten back. My irritation level was approaching critical. I needed sleep, a shower, a decent meal, and time to regroup—not Gage and his merry-go-round of emotional bottlenecks. Not now, not again. I couldn't take it anymore.

I stomped my foot. "Goddammit, will you just say whatever it is you're thinking?"

He flared his nostrils, jaw clenched, eyes narrowed. "The second reason," he ground out.

"The what now?"

"The reasons I've held you at arm's length, Teresa."

Our conversation from the night before came thundering back. Reasons he'd kept me at an emotional distance, despite the way everything felt right when we were together. "You told me they didn't matter anymore."

"I lied, okay? I'm a big fat, fucking liar. Don't you get it? My entire life I've lost every person I care about. My parents, my brother, my mentor, my foster brother. My buddy who got me into corrections died four months ago on the job, killed by the same kids who almost killed me. Hell, two of those kids died in a yard fight last month. I couldn't save *any* of them."

Moisture pooled in his silver-flecked eyes. I wanted to reach out and comfort him; his body language shouted at me to stay away. My trip to New York had scared him on some level I didn't understand, because I didn't know this part of him. But emotional barricades were finally coming down—hopefully for good—and I had to let them crumble.

"Do you know what I was doing the night we repowered, Teresa?"

I had no idea what he'd been doing and couldn't recall ever entertaining the question. He'd mentioned the painful repowering in passing, but not his whereabouts immediately before. Poised on the edge of telling me, I almost told him not to. The tone of his voice as he barked his rhetorical question said I wasn't going to like the answer.

He swallowed hard and continued. "I'd given up my apartment, given away my possessions. I was down to the things in my suitcase, and I was sitting in my car with a handgun I'd bought off a street dealer the night before. It had one bullet."

My stomach soured. I definitely didn't want to hear this—barely could over the dull roar in my ears. My heart slammed against my ribs. Hot tears stung my eyes.

"I was done," he said in a hollow voice. "Sick of being hurt, sick of burying people, sick of never feeling complete. Just . . . finished. The last straw had come the week before. I was helping my landlord clean out an abandoned apartment and found a pile of old newspapers. One of them had your mug shot right on the front page, below the fold. I hadn't seen you in half a lifetime, but I knew you."

Heat flamed in my cheeks. "You knew I'd been in jail."

He nodded. "You saved me that day in Central Park, when you Tranced me. I was so scared and you made me brave. Then we lost our powers, and I let everyone be separated. We all suffered, and to find out you'd been so close for so long . . . that I could have done something to help you . . . I failed you like I failed everyone else."

Emotion clogged my throat. I couldn't seem to breathe.

He swallowed hard, eyes focused on the floor. "So I was sitting there with the hammer back and ready to do it, debating between my mouth or temple. I looked up and dared God to stop me. Told Him I needed to know I still had something out there to live for, because I was sick of death and misery. I asked for the chance to protect and save one person, just one life to prove it wasn't all pointless.

"Know what happened next?"

I shook my head, not trusting my voice, my heart aching for him.

"Nothing. So I put the gun in my mouth and pulled the trigger."

My insides quaked as the weight of the admission sank in. His pain had driven him to fire with intent. He'd wanted to die. The tears spilled over, blazing down my cheeks.

Gage snorted, the choked sound almost a sob. "It didn't fire. The goddamn gun jammed. I was so furious I decided to try St. John's Bridge, instead. Halfway there is when it happened. I didn't really understand that my powers were coming back until the streetlights blinded me and a horn deafened me.

"When I got it under control, I skipped the bridge and started driving. I chose south. Then my Vox beeped, and it felt like I was going the right way for once. I stopped at a motel outside of Bakersfield, and on my way to grab dinner at a truck stop diner, I heard voices. Then my Vox beeped again and there you were." His voice softened with a hint of awe. "You, Teresa, of all the people it could have been. It made me so ashamed of what I'd done."

Breaking to pieces in front of me, he finally lifted his head to meet my gaze. Twin tears tracked down his cheeks, into the collar of his shirt. "It sounds corny, I know, but you were my sign, Teresa. My one last save. I just meant to be your friend and protect you, and then I started feeling things. . . ." He blanched, the words gone.

I didn't know what to say, or how to process so much stark truth. All of the pain that had driven him to such a desperate place, to try and take his own life—no, not try. He'd meant to succeed; only dumb luck had saved him.

"Gage, you got what you asked for," I said, throat clogged with something I couldn't simply swallow away. "You did save me, just by being with me. If you hadn't found me in Bakersfield, we each would have been alone when Specter attacked, just like the others. We'd probably both be dead, along with Renee and Ethan and Marco, and now Specter would be laughing through his victory."

I took his hand and squeezed. I hated being his reason for doing anything, especially living. It was too much responsibility. He'd gotten his wish; it had to be enough. "You saved me, Gage. You fulfilled your end. You can stop trying to save me now and just be with me while we have time."

His expression closed off for a moment, leaving no clues as to his thoughts. I knew that look too well.

"Stop shutting me out," I said. "Not now, when you're finally letting me in. Do I really have to tell you that everything you told me stays here? I'm not judging you."

Surprise finally demolished the wall, and I saw a depth of emotion in his eyes I'd never seen before. Calm settled over him. His tears had dried. He seemed to have reached a silent bargain with himself and his wrenching confession. "I'm sorry I yelled," he said.

"And I'm sorry you were so worried, truly sorry, but I don't regret going. Psystorm would have been freaked out by a whole squad of us showing up to retrieve him. He actually seems to respect me more for going alone. He's on our side."

"How can you be sure?"

"Because of his son, Gage. We talked about a lot of things during the ride back, and one thing I trust is his love for Caleb. He'll do anything to provide a good life for his son, including helping us. He has no standing loyalty to Specter or anyone else on the island."

"What about the kid's mom?"

"All he would say about her is that she's ill. Figuring out who she is shouldn't be too hard. Only twenty-one of the Banes were female, and Caleb is obviously of Asian descent."

I filled Gage in on everything Psystorm said about Specter, the fires in Maryland, and his involvement in those final battles. Even though the information would be hashed and rehashed later, I needed Gage to support me when we talked to Renee, Marco, and Ethan. He had to understand that this was our only option.

"You have a fail-safe for his collar?" he asked. Figured of all the things I'd said, he focused on that.

"Yes, Gage, I have a fail-safe." I patted the pocket next to my Vox. "But I truly don't think I'll need to use it."

He stepped closer and took my other hand. "I know you

don't, and that's why you need it. If Specter somehow takes over Psystorm, we'll need the fail-safe to put them down."

"I just hope we can keep Psystorm a secret from Specter. Not like I've got a clue how to do it." And if we truly had a mole among us, he probably knew already. Damn it. "How's Renee doing?"

"She's quiet, mostly. I think she's projecting her anger onto Dahlia. She's been pretty rude, even for Renee."

"She's grieving. She'll come around." I leaned my hip against the sink, wishing I had something to do with my hands. Damned uniform needed pockets. "How about Dahlia?"

"Adjusting. Dr. Seward had her over here for a few hours, testing out her abilities. She can absorb an awesome amount of heat. He thinks she can learn to push the heat back out, use it kind of like an expulsion of force."

"Did she say anything about being able to do this before?"

"No, but she would have been five years old back then. I doubt the powers had manifested yet." He took a few steps forward. His hand lifted, as though to touch me, then fell back to his side. Concern shone in his expression. "How are you doing?"

"No side effects, or purple vision."

"Good to know, but that's not what I meant."

Of course it wasn't. "I'm angry. I keep telling myself I can't let anger get in the way of good judgment. I'm tired, but I don't feel like I have time to rest. I'm so sick of being afraid that I want to crawl under a rock and forget all of this exists. More than anything, I'm . . ." Something blocked the words. They seemed selfish.

"What?"

I didn't respond. The words wouldn't come. He dipped his head and a hundred emotions—all usually so blocked off from me—seared through his kiss. Things spoken and kept silent, secrets revealed and past pains let loose. I responded gently, not allowing it to deepen. His admission still rang in my head—it would take a lot longer than five minutes to absorb. And we still had people counting on us. On me.

He sensed my hesitation and pulled back, hands loosely framing my cheeks. "What is it?"

"I'm scared, Gage. Scared of failing again and getting the rest of you killed."

His eyebrows knotted. "You didn't fail William."

"Didn't I? I let him stay in there and die."

"He chose to stay behind. William understood the risks, and he knew it was the only way to get the rest of us out safely."

"I should have tried something else." My fists ached. I unclenched them, then stepped back. Away from Gage. The tears were back, and I tried to force them away. "I should have saved him for her." I was crying anyway, damn it.

I couldn't do this, and damn the Wardens anyway for putting me in this position. For giving me powers I didn't want and making me responsible for lives I couldn't save. For proving I'd never live up to the legacy my father left behind. A sob choked me, and I gave in to the grief. "He promised Renee a date and now he'll never take her, and I should have brought him home, like I brought you home. I failed. I'll always fail."

"You've succeeded more than you've failed," he said quietly.

The last thing I wanted was for him to make me feel better—to make this failure smaller than it was. "Don't patronize me, Gage. Not ever."

"I'm not. But you can't save everyone, Teresa."

The sincerity in his words enraged me in a way I couldn't control. I wanted my grief, damn it. I wanted to be allowed to wallow in this misery for two goddamn minutes. Alone. My hands clenched into tight fists.

"I can't save everyone?" Falling back on old habits, I said the one thing I knew would push him away: "Look who's talking."

He backed off. Anger flickered in his eyes briefly, followed by hurt, then was gone. Switched off and put away and I felt like shit for having said it. "Don't you ever fucking throw that in my face," he growled, then spun on his heel and stormed out of the bathroom.

The bang of the door shutting echoed for a long time as I sat alone and cried.

The fight left my nerves frayed and my stomach queasy, and I needed to get my mind off it. To calm down so I could figure out how to apologize. I needed to do something, so I headed to the fourth floor of Medical. The majority of activity seemed to be happening there, so it was my best source for a distraction.

Familiar voices from one of the patient rooms slowed my pace.

"Is this really a good idea?"

"You will not know unless you try."

"That sounded way more ominous than I bet you intended."

"One attempt, *por favor*?"

I slipped up to the door and peeked inside. It was empty of equipment, furnished only by two metal folding chairs. Marco sat in one, awkwardly holding a box of matches between his chest and sling with one unlit match in his good hand. Dahlia stood a few feet from him, hands clenched by her sides, dressed in a set of extra-baggy sweats. She'd cleaned up since the fire and seemed less flighty, more in control.

Neither noticed me lurking in the doorway. Marco struck the match; the red tip flared and ignited. Dahlia's face pinched. The flame went out with a tiny tail of smoke.

"Crap," she said.

Marco took another match from the small pile on his lap. "Try again." He struck it.

The flame burned. Flickered. Extinguished. Four more matches met the same end. I started to break my silence and ask what they were trying to accomplish.

"Are you only drawing the heat to you, or are you attempting to connect to it first?" Marco asked. "To truly feel the energy?"

"I'm not sure," she replied. "How do I do that?"

"I am uncertain. My powers are quite different."

I stepped full into the room. "When you feel the heat of the flame, imagine it as an extension of yourself," I said, startling them both. "Make it part of you, like another limb you can control."

Dahlia's startled expression quickly melted into determination. "I can do that."

"It's how I work with my orbs."

Marco struck a match. This time, Dahlia raised her right hand and extended it toward the flame. Concentrated. It flickered. Shrank. It seemed to go out, then flared back to life. Shrank again. Flared again. She repeated the activity until the fire crept too close to Marco's fingers. Then she extinguished the flame completely.

"I did it." The absolute joy on her face made me smile back. "I didn't just absorb the heat, I actually controlled it."

"Excellent," Marco said.

"How long have you guys been working on this?" I asked.

"About seven matches," Dahlia said.

"You're a fast learner."

"How long did it take you to learn to control your powers?"

I thought back to Cliff and the parking lot in Bakersfield. "I kind of learned on the job. In some ways, I'm still learning to control it, so don't rush yourself. One match is a lot different than a four-alarm fire."

My reality check dimmed some of her excitement, but she recovered her poise quickly. "You're right, and I will definitely keep practicing. Thanks for the tip."

"You're welcome."

"Are you all right, Catalepsia?"

I hesitated. I might have shared my Gage-related stupidity with Marco if Dahlia hadn't been in the room, but it was too personal to talk about in front of a semi-stranger. "I'm just tired," I said. "Keep at it, Dahlia. I'll see you guys later."

As I walked back out, I heard the unmistakable hiss of another match igniting.

I found Renee in one of the waiting rooms playing a board game with Caleb. They sat on the floor, surrounded by chair cushions, intent on something involving colorful plastic pieces and a pair of dice. I watched from an observation window. They were alone together, an odd pairing, and he seemed unbothered by her smoky blue skin. Her mouth was pinched, her eyes puffy. The cloud of effervescent energy that followed her everywhere was gone, and I ached for her pain.

I could only assume Psystorm was still being examined by Dr. Seward, hence the impromptu babysitter. They continued to play for several minutes, oblivious to my presence.

Caleb rolled the dice and squealed, delighted by the spaces he could advance his green playing piece. He grinned toothily at Renee, and then spotted me over her shoulder. He waved. Renee turned. She narrowed her eyes, and I braced for a verbal onslaught.

"You look awful," she said.

Not quite what I was expecting. I slipped in through the half-open door and crouched between them. "I thought the dark circles under my eyes would complement the lavender hue of my forehead."

She cocked her head, and I saw unexpected forgiveness. Grief, too, that would take much longer to erase. She had opened up to William, despite her fears. I hoped the loss didn't shut her down again. She deserved happiness. We all did. Even those of us who couldn't stop pushing happiness away.

"Hi, Caleb," I said, sitting next to the boy. "I see you met my friend Flex."

"She's teaching me to play a game," he said proudly. "I never played this one before, but she said it was fun."

"Is it fun?"

"It's easy. Flex said she liked it when she was my age, so I said we could play. She's sad, and games make me happy when I'm sad."

I blinked. "Yes, she is sad, Caleb. How did you know?"

"I can tell." He rolled the dice, moved his piece forward, and looked up at me with solemn eyes. He spoke so matter-of-factly I was almost frightened. No five-year-old talked like that. "Daddy says I'm special like him. I know when people are sad."

"Could your mommy do that, too?"

He shook his head. "She used to turn into a cat. Now she's sick, and she can't do it anymore."

Interesting. A Bane shapeshifter. I touched the boy's hand. He stopped fiddling with the dice and looked up at me. "Do you know why your mommy is sick?"

He shrugged a thin shoulder.

"Were a lot of people sick?"

"Mostly grown-ups. Not everyone, though, because Daddy never got sick. Me, either."

Something to add to my list of questions for the ATF. I hadn't seen Grayson since yesterday. He was probably busy spinning our publicity from yesterday's fire and our first, aborted attempt at being proactive in addressing the public. Or ratting us out to Specter.

Ugh, I needed to get my rampant paranoia under control until I had proof stronger than a hunch. I asked Caleb, "How long has your mom been sick?"

"I don't know." He puckered his lips and blew air between them. A frustrated raspberry—the questioning would have to end soon, or he'd simply clam up. He reminded me of my own therapy sessions just after the War ended. I didn't want to talk about it, and no one could make me.

"Two years, give or take," Psystorm said.

Renee and I turned together, our collective attention snapping toward the door. He stood just inside the waiting room, Dr. Seward a few steps behind. Caleb leapt to his feet and bolted into his father's arms. Only apart for a few minutes, yet they embraced as if it had been days.

"I think they started putting something in the drinking water," Psystorm said as he shifted Caleb's weight to his hip. How that skinny man kept the child—small or not—in his arms remained a mystery. "It started to taste odd, so I stopped drinking it for a while. Made Caleb stop, too. We had some bottled water stored away. A lot of people who didn't have it bottled up started getting sick."

"Sick how?" I asked.

"Stomach cramps and vomiting, mostly. No one died from it. Most of them got really lethargic, disinterested. Like they were drugged, and then when we got our powers back, they didn't seem to care. Didn't try to use them or practice, or even discuss a, uh, breakout."

"Did you?" I asked, standing quickly. "Discuss a break-out?"

He stared, seeming quite surprised. "Wouldn't you? None of us wanted to be there, Trance. We just hadn't possessed the means to escape."

"It's been a week, Psystorm, why hasn't anyone tried?"

"Lack of motivation, I suppose. We'd all be on the run, criminals worse than before, when all we are now is unwanted and forgotten. As much as I hated the island, I couldn't drag Caleb into that kind of life and make him a fugitive."

"Let's hope the others share your reasoning skills."

"They won't lay down for you forever, Trance. Sooner or later, someone will try to get out. It only takes a tiny fissure to create a chasm."

"I've considered that, believe me. I just can't think about it right now. Not until Specter is neutralized. Once that's done, I'd like to hear more from you about life on the island. Others you think have . . . not changed sides, exactly. Have stopped wanting to fight."

He snickered. "Looking for new recruits?"

"No, just fewer enemies." I gave him a pointed look. "I think you'll agree we can all use fewer of those."

"Indeed."

Dr. Seward hung back by the door, trying to melt into the wall and out of the conversation. He had a chart in his hands.

"So what's the verdict, Doctor?" I asked.

He cleared his throat. "Aside from needing a good dose of vitamin supplements, father and son are both relatively healthy," he replied. "Caleb is within the ninetieth percentile in growth for his age group. I recommend a visit to a dentist in the near future, but all in all, he's doing very well."

"Hear that, kiddo?" Psystorm said. "Fit as a fiddle."

"Strong as a horse," Caleb said with a toothy grin.

"Do we have a room for them over in Housing?" Renee asked, standing next to me. The shadow of sadness that had enveloped her on the helipad lingered. Only time and patience—and maybe a distraction like Caleb—would chase it away.

"Not yet," Dr. Seward said. "I'm certain we can appropriate one shortly. I think we've all had quite the active night and could use some rest." The last phrase and a very pointed look were shot in my general direction.

"What time is it, anyway?" I asked. One useful thing my uniform did not hold was a watch.

Dr. Seward checked his wristwatch. "It's quarter to eight."

"In the morning?"

"Yes, Trance, it's still morning."

Apparently the short nap on the copter wasn't quite enough to recharge my drained batteries. I focused on the time, but it took several tries to make proper sense of it. "Okay, then, two p.m., conference room. Until then, let's get some rest."

"Sounds like a plan," Renee said. "I think—"

An alarm, similar to the ring of an old-fashioned telephone, chimed outside in the corridor. One long pull, one short, one long, over and over. Caleb slapped the palms of his hands over his ears and pressed his face into Psystorm's chest.

"Is that a fire alarm?" Psystorm asked.

"No," Seward said, eyes widening. "It's the alarm in ICU."

"Ethan," I said, already running past Seward and toward the emergency stairwell.

I reached the ICU doors first. Two nurses stood outside, clutching each other and whispering. Ignoring them, I barreled through and nearly tripped over someone sitting in the middle of the short corridor between the station and the entrance to Ethan's room.

"Marco?"

He blinked up, a weeping gash on his forehead. He clutched his bandaged left hand close to his chest and didn't seem to see me at first. A cool breeze ruffled his unkempt hair. Fresh air.

"What happened?" I asked, squatting down.

Marco looked past me, toward the ICU cubicle. The swinging doors I'd entered through slammed open. Renee, Seward, and Gage skidded to a collective stop an instant before mowing us both down. Renee scooted around and looked inside.

"Where'd he go?" she asked.

"Tempest is gone?" Dr. Seward said.

"I came to check on him," Marco said. He reached for me and squeezed my hand. "He was sleeping and began to thrash, as if in a nightmare. I shook him. *Dios*, he was terrified when he woke. He kept asking if his eyes were yellow, was Specter here, were we safe?"

He went silent. I rubbed the back of his hand, urging him to continue.

"I told him we were fine, no one was here. He did not

believe me and tried to get up. I held him down. He said we were not safe with him around, and then blasted me through the door. He was so sure Specter was coming after him next, Catalepsia."

"How did Ethan get out?" Gage asked.

Renee jacked her thumb toward the ICU unit. "Drilled his way out with a wind driver, looks like. There's a big-ass hole in the wall, folks."

I stood and nearly fell in my haste. Sure enough, the wall just behind the bed was gone. Blasted as efficiently as a deep-core driller's best work, cleanly through plaster, brick, and mortar to blue sky. Air rippled through my hair as I shivered.

"That's impossible," Seward said. "The man was twenty-four hours out of major surgery. He can't even walk, let alone escape."

"He doesn't need to walk," I said. "Just fly. Son of a bitch."

"We shouldn't have told him about William," Renee said. "He was already scared of Specter and what he might do."

"We couldn't not tell him." I slipped my arm around Renee's waist, and her head lolled against my shoulder. "Ethan didn't want to be here, so he found a way to leave."

"He could kill himself out there," Gage said. Any anger he'd withheld from me had been redirected into concern for his friend. "He isn't strong enough to keep up his power for long, and if he can't find a safe place to hide . . ."

No need to finish the thought. We all understood.

"We must find him," Marco said.

"We will," I said. "Right now."

So much for a few hours of rest.

Twenty-eight

The Blue Tower

An odd silence had fallen over the HQ grounds as Gage, Renee, and I stepped out to begin searching for Ethan. We managed to cover six feet of sidewalk past the Medical Center's doors before my Vox squealed, startling everyone. I pulled it off my belt.

<Ah, hello?> Dahlia's voice over the Vox.

"Dahlia, it's Trance," I replied. "What is it?"

<We have a tip. A man just called the police switchboard, and they, um, transferred the information to the ATF satellite office and then to Agent Grayson. It's really neat, though, that the police can—>

"Dahlia, information."

Renee snorted. Dahlia was young, terrified, and very green, but she was trying to be helpful.

<Oh, right,> she said. <Apartment complex over on Stanley Avenue, the Blue Tower. The landlord called and said he had a tenant who kind of matches the police photos of Specter that we sent out.>

Gage's head snapped toward me. I met his gaze and saw surprise there. "Kind of matches?" he asked.

<He said the tenant's name is Marcus Spence. He's lived there for eleven years. The landlord only spoke to the tenant the day he signed the rental agreement, and hasn't seen him coming or going in three years.>

"So this Spence guy could be a rotting corpse, and the landlord wouldn't know it," I said.

<Gross. Somebody would have smelled him.>

"I was making a point, Dal. What's this landlord's name?"

<Andrew Milton.>

"All right, thanks. Trance out." I put the Vox away and turned toward the Base. "Field trip. And I want Psystorm on this."

"What about Ethan?" Gage asked.

I flinched. I hated putting Ethan off. He was my friend, he was injured, and he was out there alone. Alone by choice. "Specter's still our top priority," I said, meeting everyone's gaze in turn. They seemed to accept my statement. Foe over friend.

No matter how much it hurt.

The Blue Tower was a few miles away in old West Hollywood, overlooking a strip of sidewalk sporting names of celebrities past. The entire area had once been a glamorous place to live and work. Then too many earthquakes and quite a few Bane attacks had changed the landscape.

Since the War, drinking had become a favorite pastime in

many cities, and the most successful chains were, like Whiskey Jack's, the ones that threw sex legally into the mix. We passed at least a dozen such places on the first four blocks of Hollywood Boulevard. Gage maneuvered the tinted-window Sport down the crowded early-morning streets, past a few crumbling theaters and boarded-up tourist shops.

Six blocks down from the last open bar, we found the Blue Tower, just off Stanley Avenue. A square building painted sky blue, it lived up to half of its name. It resembled a penitentiary more than a housing complex, with scattered windows and no balconies. I couldn't imagine what it had been before it became low-rent housing for the city's forgotten.

Gage pulled into an underground parking garage, casting the dim vehicle into darker shadows. I leaned against the dash, watching every corner and cranny, expecting a trap. None sprung. If this was bait, Specter didn't seem to know we'd taken it.

As we walked, Psystorm's eyes never stopped moving, as if he expected an attack at any moment. On some level, I understood—he'd been imprisoned for a long time, and now he was back in a world with no walls around it, about to betray a former ally. Not conducive to a sense of personal safety.

We found the landlord's office—a white door next to the first floor elevator with a MANAGER sign and separate opening at the top. Gage pressed the buzzer, and it screeched angrily on the other side of the wall. Footsteps shuffled.

"If it's rent," a voice shouted, "just slip it under the door."

"Mr. Milton?" I said.

"Who is it?"

"We're following up on the tip you gave to the police this morning."

A latch turned. The upper half of the door swung out, almost clipping Renee's forehead. Andrew Milton stepped into the half frame, a tall and overweight man with the lingering build of a retired linebacker. His bald head and lack of beard did nothing to hide sagging jowls and liver spots.

He stared at Renee first, either shocked by her blue skin or admiring her black leather uniform, and then at me. He dismissed Gage and Psystorm with a flicker of his eyes, and went back to staring at Renee.

"Hey, over here," I said, snapping my fingers to get his attention. "You have a tenant named Marcus Spence, correct?"

"Yeah, up on the fifth floor," Milton said. "Why?"

"You tell me, Mr. Milton. When you called the police, you seemed to think Mr. Spence fit a particular profile. Why?"

Milton shrugged, less interested in the conversation than in the cleft between my breasts. "He looks like the guy, is all. I've been here twenty years, you know, I know my tenants. This guy Spence hasn't left the building in three years."

"What about rent?" Gage asked.

No acknowledgment, still talking to my cleavage. "Pays in cash every time. I never see him, but someone slips the envelope under the door. Utilities are included in rent. He's got no phone lines or Web connections up there, so I don't know who he talks to. None of the neighbors complain, though, so I leave him be as long as he keeps paying on time."

"Does he ever have visitors?" I asked.

"None I ever saw, but I don't watch the front door all the time."

"So he could have left without you knowing."

"Yeah, I guess."

"Did you run a credit check on him?"

Milton snorted. "In this neighborhood? People don't have credit. He gave me three months' rent up front, lady, so I was inclined to give him the apartment. Wish all my tenants were so good to me."

Gage produced a folded photograph from his uniform pocket and held it up. "Are you sure this is the man who's been renting from you?"

"Yep, that's him, only older and in a wheelchair."

My hand jerked. "Wheelchair?"

"Yeah, sucker can't walk. Said it was a stroke or something. Apartment wasn't good for handicaps, but he didn't seem to care. Just wanted someplace quiet, he said."

He's telling the truth, Psystorm said in my head. I looked at Gage. He nodded; his senses said the same.

"What room?" I asked.

"Five E," Milton said. "Fifth floor, end of the hall. Look, you people aren't going to start up trouble, are you?"

I let the "you people" comment slide. "We'll do our best to question Mr. Spence quietly."

"Good, 'cuz I don't know if my insurance on this place would consider you an act of God. I don't have insurance for superpower destruction, you know. After the War, everyone dropped that from their premiums."

"They may want to think about adding the clause again," Renee said.

Milton blanched.

"Look," I said, "contrary to recent events, I have no intention of burning your building down, so relax." Still, it didn't hurt be prepared. "How many people live here?"

"Eighty or so. Six floors, five apartments on each floor."

"Are most of them at work?"

"In this neighborhood? A lot of them work out of their homes, if you get my meaning."

"Loud and clear, but we're not the police and not here for them. I just want an idea of who might or might not be home right now."

Milton hung his head and groaned. "You're going to burn the place down, I know it."

I rolled my eyes. "Mr. Milton—"

Bells clanged, thundering so loudly I couldn't concentrate, and the sprinkler system spat tepid water from the ceiling. Gage must have been extending his hearing to get an idea of the number of people in the building, because he cried out and dropped to his knees, palms over his ears. He could control the level at which his senses operated, but getting caught like that had to hurt like hell.

"You see!" Milton shouted. "I knew it, I knew it. Act of God, I tell you, it was an act of God."

He yanked open the bottom half of the door and stormed past us, his feet squishing on the rapidly soaking carpet. He raced down the hallway, toward the front door, still cursing and complaining about insurance.

"I do not believe this," I said.

"Could someone have set off the alarm by accident?" Renee asked. Water rolled down her face and plastered her hair to her back and shoulders.

"No," Psystorm said. "No, he knows we're here. It's a distraction."

Gage dropped his hands and looked up. Pain was etched across his face, but he seemed to have his senses under control. "Do you smell the fire?" I asked as I helped him stand. He stepped away as soon as he was on his feet.

"It's above us," he said. "Second floor, I think, and getting bigger by the minute. If the sprinklers don't stop it, we're going to have an inferno on our hands." The sprinkler system slowed from a spray to a trickle, and finally stopped altogether.

"Hell," I said.

"Give it time," Psystorm said.

Far away, someone screamed, audible even over the blare of the alarm bell.

"We split up," I said. "Psystorm and I will head for Spence's apartment. You two make sure people are getting out of this building, and then call Dahlia. Maybe she can get down here and do something with the fire."

"She's still green, T," Renee said.

"She's strong and we need her."

I turned. Someone caught my wrist and pulled me back. Gage's mouth opened—no words tumbled out. We really needed to talk when this was over. "I'll be careful," I said.

After he and Renee disappeared down an adjacent corridor, I turned to Psystorm. He was hard to read, showing no outward signs of fear or concern, just a weary sense of duty.

"Let's find the stairs," I said.

Twenty-nine

Marcus Spence

By the fourth-floor landing, I realized what was bothering me: no one else was in the stairwell. Even with the alarm ringing on every floor we passed, I hadn't seen a single person evacuate the building. Milton could be wrong about so many folks working from home, but I doubted it, and it made me wonder how many times a week someone pulled a false alarm.

I pushed the exit door open.

"This isn't the fifth floor," Psystorm said.

"I know, but I don't think people realize this is a real fire." I pounded my fist against the first door I saw. "Hey! Get your ass moving, this isn't a drill, there's a fire downstairs!"

The door whipped open with a rush of cold air. A teenage girl stood there in too-tight clothes, a toddler balanced on one hip. She had a bruise on her jaw, another on her bare ankle, and aimed a revolver at me with her left hand.

"Who the hell are you?" she asked.

I twisted the gun away from her with ease. Safety was off—great. "Get anyone else who's with you outside right now. The second floor is on fire."

Her round eyes widened. She put the toddler down with a terse "Stay here," and bolted back inside. Psystorm went to the next apartment door. The girl returned with an infant in her arms and a bag slung over her shoulder. She grabbed the toddler's hand and yanked the child toward the stairwell.

We didn't stop until we'd banged on all five doors. Only three opened; the others remained silent. Ten people raced into the stairwell. Psystorm and I followed them in. The air had heated a few degrees; the fire was moving quickly. Up we went, to the fifth floor, banging on doors as we moved down the hall. Two opened, two didn't, and we found ourselves in front of 5E.

Psystorm put a hand out to stay me and closed his eyes. The alarm seemed impossibly loud here. I'd be hearing it in my sleep for days. He dropped his hand and looked at me.

"Something's wrong," he said. "It feels like Specter, but also not. His power is missing."

My stomach fluttered. I didn't like the sound of that. "Could his conscious power be elsewhere?"

He shook his head. "Even if it was, I'd still get a sense of it inside of his physical body, something linking the conscious power to his bodily form, like a tether. All Metas have it."

"And now there's no tether."

"Right."

"Shit."

"Right again."

My Vox beeped, and then, <Trance, Cipher.> I grabbed it. "Cipher, Trance, go ahead."

<Dahlia is on her way. The fire is pretty well contained on

the second floor. Looks like most of the residents are out and the fire department's on the way.>

"Copy. We're about to go inside."

<One more thing. We talked to the tenant whose apartment is the source of the fire. He said he was just starting to wake up, pretty groggy from a bad hangover. Then he remembers standing over the kitchen stove with a bottle of vegetable oil and the wall on fire. He didn't remember lighting the burner or squirting the oil.>

"Sounds like he had help," Psystorm said. "He might still be in one of the tenants, Cipher, so watch your backs down there."

<Copy. Cipher out.>

Once the Vox was tucked safely away, I turned to Psystorm. "So? Do we knock?"

He looked at my hands, and then quirked an eyebrow. The gesture was cute, sort of cocky, and it made him look ten years younger. "How about I let you knock?"

"You're sure this is Specter?"

"Positive."

I grinned. "Okay, I'll knock."

We backed up a few paces, and with Psystorm behind me, I pushed two apple-size orbs at the doorknob. They hit above and below the hardware and shattered the cheap particle board with a sound like snapping celery. A few chunks flew our way.

We surged through the door and into the worst odor I'd ever experienced. Rot and human waste, bottled up together for weeks, if not longer. I stumbled backward, into Psystorm, gagging on the fetid air in my lungs. He coughed, hands on my waist, holding me upright. In the dim light of a half-open window, I saw my archenemy in the flesh for the first time since I was ten years old.

His wheelchair sat across the small living room, next to a dusty sofa. Huddled under a stained cotton blanket, the fragile old man didn't move or acknowledge our presence. Red spots, likely sores of some sort, lined his lips and chin. Liquid leaked from his rheumy eyes and half-open mouth. His hair was pure white, face lined with age and abuse. Frail hands clutched the edge of the blanket, skin marred with liver spots, bones gnarled from arthritis. An oxygen tank was hooked to the back of the wheelchair, and a yellowed nasal cannula wrapped around his head. The urine bag attached to his chair had overflowed, leaving a dark puddle on the frayed carpet.

Tears stung my own eyes—from the smell or the sight of this neglected old man, I wasn't certain. Crying over Specter. What would William have thought?

"Is he even alive?" I asked, surprised at the quiver in my voice.

Psystorm slipped around me and took a few steps forward. "He's alive, but no one's home. Just like I felt in the hallway, the tether is gone. He's powerless and if he's in there somewhere, he's down deep."

"Can you reach him? Get Marcus Spence to come out and talk to us?"

"I'll try." He crouched in front of the old man, allowing an arm's reach of distance, and closed his eyes.

I did a quick sweep of the apartment. The bed was neatly made, not slept in for a long time. Thick coats of dust covered most of the furniture, including the kitchen counters. The toilet had backed up, which accounted for some of the smell. I located a can of room freshener, sprayed liberally, and closed the door tight. All the food in the fridge was spoiled or a day from it, and a small family of roaches scurried out from under the garbage can when I kicked it.

Someone had kept an ailing old man prisoner in this apartment for an unknown length of time, living in his own filth, with no food or filtered water. In spite of myself, and in spite of the horrors he'd done fifteen years ago, I felt sorry for him. Specter was a shell, barely alive by all rights. He couldn't have been the one responsible for the hell we'd lived through this week.

I returned to the living room. Psystorm sat on the floor in front of Specter, hands folded in his lap. A single tear rolled down one cheek, and it told me everything I needed to know. I stopped, afraid to intrude.

Psystorm turned his head. Grieving eyes met mine. "I've never felt anything like this. Such despair. Eagerness to simply die and let it be over with."

"Did he tell you anything?"

"I could glean a few things, mostly images. He didn't surrender with the others on Manhattan. Someone else was collared in his place. He escaped west, hid out. Had a stroke a few months after the War ended and has been wheelchair bound ever since. He had a second stroke four months ago. A hospice nurse used to come twice a month to check on him. He's had other visitors, but I can't see them clearly." He blanched. "The catatonia is recent, very recent. Days, maybe a week."

The timetable fit with the recovery of our powers.

"It's incredible, Trance. It's like someone ripped out his soul and left a wailing animal in its place. He just wants to die."

I shivered, despite the stifling air. "What can do this to a person?"

"An extremely talented telepath."

"Could a telepath actually take someone's powers?" As soon as I said it, I had my answer. The Wardens had done exactly that to us—stripped us of our powers. But they hadn't taken them to use as their own; they stored them away. Whoever took Spence's powers did so with another intent.

"How could that work?" I asked. "Dr. Seward told me once that as MetaHumans, our bodies adapt to accommodate our powers. I've had firsthand experience in adapting to new things, and it's not pretty."

"Things have changed, Trance. You know that better than anyone."

My hands clenched. We were now facing an unknown enemy with a stolen ability, hell-bent on destroying every living Ranger (and probably Psystorm, now that he was helping us). No name, no leads, no way to ferret this person out.

"We'll take him with us," I said. "Let's get out of here before the fire gets worse. We can try to get into his mind again back at HQ."

Psystorm stood up and stepped behind the wheelchair. I bent and unlocked the wheels. As I straightened, a shadow moved in the apartment's shattered doorway, a familiar shape loomed, and the equally familiar snap-clack of a shotgun slide broke the room's silence.

Andrew Milton stepped into the foyer, shotgun against his shoulder, eyes glowing yellow-orange, and fired at Psystorm. I threw up a shield too fast to brace myself, and the impact of the buckshot against the shield tossed me sideways. The report thundered in my ears, and the shock of my tailbone cracking on the hard floor sent bolts of pain up my spine.

Milton loaded again, another snap-clack. Psystorm shouted. I sat up, despite my body's angry protests, and lobbed a cherry-size orb at the landlord. It hit center mass like a bullet and sprayed blood as it entered his chest. He screamed and squeezed, shooting off one more blast that hit the ceiling and took out a fluorescent light fixture in a cloud of sparks and glass.

"Psystorm!" I shouted over the fire alarm still wailing in the hallway.

"Got him!"

He stood stiff and straight behind the wheelchair, eyes fixed on the figure in the doorway. His entire body seemed to ripple with energy. Both eyebrows dug in and knotted. Beads of perspiration broke out across his forehead and upper lip. His breathing sped up.

"He's strong," Psystorm hissed. "Too strong."

"Hold on to him."

"Trying."

I scrambled to my feet, ignoring my bruised butt. My head spun. The stale air didn't help. I crouched next to Milton's body. Felt for a pulse. Nothing. The light was gone from his open eyes. The power of Specter was somewhere in the room now, caught by Psystorm.

Into my Vox, I shouted, "Cipher, it's Trance, we need backup here."

<Trance, are you on the fifth floor?>

"Yeah, apartment five E. We'll need emergency extraction. Can the copter meet us on the roof?"

<It just dropped off Dahlia, so yeah, I think it can be back in less than two minutes. Fire's almost under control.>

"Good. Two minutes. Out."

I heard the concern in Gage's voice, and all of the unasked questions. I was proud of him for keeping it as short and professional as possible. If Psystorm could keep Specter's doppelganger under control, perhaps we could get them both back to HQ and figure out our next step. The force controlling Specter's power was stronger than we'd anticipated. Psystorm had paled considerably, and sweat dribbled down his cheeks in thin rivers. He'd bitten through his lower lip and blood flowed freely.

"Damn you," Psystorm muttered. "I'm losing him, Trance. He's trying to take me."

"What can I do?"

He hissed through his teeth, buckling under the strain of his mental battle. "Collar."

"What?"

"Use the collar."

Outside, sirens created a disturbing symphony of background music that punctuated his agonized statement. Pain radiated from his pores; desperation clung to every word. Specter's power was tearing him apart from the inside out. Knocking out Psystorm would either trap the power, or set it free. Set it free so it could make me kill again.

No, dammit.

"What will happen to him?" I asked.

"I'll hold on to him."

I pulled the fail-safe device out of my belt pocket and used my thumbnail to flick open the plastic cover. Spence's body jerked; his weeping eyes closed. Psystorm screamed, doubling over like he'd been stabbed in the gut. The air in the room crackled like a static-filled sweater. I had to stop this, had to push the button. Dread squeezed my heart, and for one brief moment, time stopped.

My hesitation cost us.

Psystorm and Spence raised their heads in perfect unison and fixed matching sets of glowing yellow eyes on me. My thumb twitched. Psystorm lashed out with an uppercut that caught the bottom of my jaw. My head snapped back. Pain blossomed, coloring my vision red. I hit the floor. The fail-safe dropped. Skittered away. I rolled toward it; didn't see the boot until it connected with the side of my head.

Consciousness ebbed and flowed in colorful rivers of pain. I grasped for something, anything to ground me. Footsteps shuffled across the laminate floor. Wheels squeaked. Someone rifled through cabinets and drawers. Then a smell, sickly sweet and eye-watering, overpowered the room's existing stench.

My Vox squawked. I opened my eyes. The room reeled, spun, and finally settled. The unused fail-safe lay on the edge of a tattered rug, just a few inches away. My right hand crawled toward it, inch by inch. Focus, focus. I ignored the throbbing in my jaw and temple. Focused on the black box.

The boot—Psystorm's—came down on my hand. Bones snapped and blood vessels exploded. Agony screeched up my wrist and arm. I screamed and kept screaming as he ground down. My senses numbed. I pulled my left hand around and summoned whatever power I could. Lobbed the orb at his leg. My shrieks became his as the point-blank blast shattered his ankle. He fell, releasing my hand.

I surged forward and grabbed the fail-safe. Finally pressed the trigger. Psystorm's prone body jerked, then fell silent.

One down.

Wheels squealed again. I rolled, drawing my broken hand to my chest. Spence gazed at me from the kitchen—how the blue hell had he gotten over there?—the yellow haze in his eyes fluctuating rapidly. He wasn't contained; Psystorm hadn't been able to hold on to him. If he had, then Spence's eyes should be normal, uncontrolled.

God, no.

I coughed, overwhelmed by the sickening odor. Nauseated by pain. Spence raised one palsied hand and grabbed a dial on the stove. His expression was as weary as his eyes were mad.

Gas. "Shit," I said.

Spence sneered.

I launched myself at Psystorm and landed across his legs, mustering every ounce of strength I still possessed. The stove burner snicked once, twice. A blue flame appeared. I tossed up a force field, closed my eyes, and held on as an inferno swept through the apartment and consumed us.

Thirty

Retreat

I f I lost consciousness, it was only for a moment. The force field dissipated seconds after the initial maelstrom; I had no strength to maintain it. Heat raged in the apartment. Flames clung to the furniture, drapes, and bookcase. Another odor ravaged my battered senses. I didn't look. I didn't have to. I could imagine the burning body, probably still upright in his wheelchair.

My lungs seized. I coughed until my chest hurt. With my undamaged left hand, I checked Psystorm for a pulse and was relieved to find one. I'd never forgive myself if I made little Caleb fatherless. Of course, that ultimately remained to be seen. We were surrounded by crackling, leaping fire. It licked the walls, bubbling paint and scorching the ceiling, where gray smoke swirled.

I used one hand for leverage and stood up. Everything tilted. My broken hand throbbed, my head pounded, and my jaw probably sported a pretty welt. Certainly felt swollen. I grabbed Psystorm's wrist and pulled. He slid forward an inch. I pulled again, the muscles in my biceps straining. A few more inches. At this rate, we'd be out of the apartment by next week.

I let go and turned in a circle, desperate for something to use. Anything to get him out of here and back to his son. A bit of cool air wafted through the raging heat, drawing my attention to the window. The blast had shattered it and burning curtains rustled in the wind. I dashed over and knocked the curtain rod off and away.

A fire escape presented itself, a rusty structure that overlooked the city street. A crowd had gathered below. Someone saw me and screamed. I didn't see the familiar faces I wanted.

I grabbed my Vox from my belt. "Cipher, I need you guys up here now," I said without preamble. "Anyone there? Hello?"

<Trance?> I'd never heard anything as sweet as Renee's voice. <We saw the explosion. What happened?>

"Long story, no time. I'm at the fire escape on the fifth floor, street side. Psystorm is out cold, and I can't move him myself. Is the copter still nearby?"

<Yep. What do you need?>

"Get on it, and get up here, now. This fire is getting hot."

I put the Vox away, uninterested in a reply. Just results. I inhaled the fresh air, getting what I could, and then plunged back inside. The fire's intensity had increased considerably in only a few minutes. Heat pressed in, squashing me from all sides, shrinking the room. Orange and red flames licked the carpet, edging closer to Psystorm. I squatted by his head.

"You are so going to make this up to me."

Nothing could prepare me for the agony I felt as I looped

both hands beneath Psystorm's armpits and lifted. My right hand shrieked and pulsed. I swore over and over—words I'd forgotten, or didn't realize I knew. Tears streaked my cheeks. I concentrated on my feet, on each careful step backward. Toward the window. Breathing as shallowly as possible.

Air whirled around us, pushing the fire away. The roar of the copter's motor mixed with the rumble of the blaze and created a cacophony of noise that stabbed into my brain. My hip hit the window sill. I sobbed, relieved. One leg over the edge, ignoring the broken glass. I pulled him through. Balanced, then the other leg. His lower half was still inside. Another burst of strength tugged him out, and we both fell over onto the metal grillwork of the fire escape. It rattled, strained. Held.

"Trance!"

I opened my eyes. Renee's head loomed over the rail of the escape, her stretched-out neck disappearing from sight. I tried to speak and coughed instead. Her hand appeared, holding a rope and straps.

"Here's a harness," she said.

"Can't. Hand's broke."

She looked over her shoulder, back at the hovering copter. I turned my head and saw its location, once again amazed at how far Renee could stretch her body. Gage was in the cab, holding her around the waist. She seemed confident that he'd secured her and brought her other hand out.

I helped when I could, and we managed to get the harness around Psystorm and locked into place. Renee retracted to the copter's interior, and it began to ascend. The rope grew taut, slowing drawing Psystorm into a standing position. Once there, the copter paused. I wrapped my arms around his shoulders, cinched my legs around his waist, closed my eyes, and held on as we rose into the sky.

The pain medication started kicking in around the time I finished my story, told in fits and starts from the back of a parked ambulance. The paramedic kept shoving an oxygen mask over my mouth and nose. I kept pulling it back because the others couldn't understand me. He finally gave up and let me talk. I'd inhaled smoke before and lived; I wasn't going to worry about it now. I did, however, thank him for wrapping my hand and giving me that lovely shot.

Gage sat by my side, listening intently. I caught him staring at my chin several times. A blood knot had swelled there and must have looked awful. I was grateful Psystorm hadn't knocked any teeth loose.

"So we don't know if Psystorm has Specter caged or not," Renee said. She stood outside the ambulance with Dahlia, the day's resident hero. Her power had kept both the first and second fires from incinerating the entire building. The only two lives lost were Andrew Milton and Marcus "Specter" Spence.

"No," I said. "I don't think he is, because this Specter-wannabe was still controlling the old man after I knocked out Psystorm."

"Well, shit."

That about summed it up.

"So the new theory is, someone else has been manipulating Specter's powers this whole time," Gage said. "It had to be someone who knew the original Specter wasn't on the island, someone who wanted to use his notoriety."

"But you can't just steal and use someone's powers, right?" Dahlia asked.

Gage shook his head. "We can't, and I've never heard of anyone who could, but nothing is like it used to be. People are getting powers who didn't have them before. You're proof of that."

"Can't be a power thief," I said. "If it's even possible, why not take the powers of everyone he's killed so far? Janel and William and Angela and all the others. He'd be collecting the powers, not just killing us off."

"It's pretty obvious Marcus Spence never got his powers back last week," Gage said. "Maybe someone else did, and they wanted us to hunt for Spence. Keep us distracted and away from whoever is really doing this. This person could have helped keep him out of prison."

"But why stop taking care of him? He suffered up there for a long time."

"He was a murderer, T," Renee said. "Who cares?"

The drugs made my indignation difficult to find, so I settled on a grunt. She hadn't seen the rotting shell Marcus Spence had become.

Renee came up with the obvious observation: "Someone had to have been paying his rent for him these last couple of months, since the final stroke. Can't we trace that?"

"Not when it was paid in cash," Gage said. "And he's dead, so it's not like we can just ask. Who could possibly benefit from wiping us out?"

Renee shrugged. "The Banes?"

"I doubt it," I said. "Psystorm was pretty adamant about most of Specter's followers during the War disliking him, hating him even. They were led by the strongest among them. I doubt this has been some sort of elaborate plot they've been cooking up since the War ended."

"Guys?" Dahlia said. Her voice quivered, and she looked at us with the trepidation of someone who feared immediate pain if we disagreed. "What about someone in the MHC? I mean, they knew about the Warden and Fairview, and Spence couldn't possibly have, right?"

Silence. One day on the job and she was voicing concerns I'd had and never shared out loud.

Dahlia continued: "The feds designed and maintained the prison, right? Someone in the ATF had access to the prisoners and guards, in order to fake Spence's lock-up. Only three people there supposedly knew about the Warden. It makes sense, right?"

I thought of Rita McNally, a woman who'd been with us through all of this, who stood by the side of our parents and mentors fifteen years ago. She seemed weary, yet steadfast. Could I have been wrong in trusting her? Had Grayson, with his cheap suits and bad attitude, sold us out so he could play supervillain for a while? Was this other agent, McNally's partner Garth Anders, even really dead? Hadn't she said three years ago?

"It's within the scope of probability," Gage said. "It would help to have access to the old MHC records."

"What would the ATF agents do if we knocked on their front door and demanded answers and records and personnel files?" Renee asked. "All the stuff you ask for when you're investigating something."

"Not a whole hell of a lot they could do, except throw us out or have us arrested for trespassing," I said.

"I'm serious."

"So am I, Renee. The Corps isn't the only operation overseen by the ATF. We're a branch to them, and a defunct one, at that."

"Well, we're not their employees."

"No, to them we are potential problems," Gage said. "Why do you think McNally and Grayson hang around all the time? Support is one thing, but they're here to watch us and report back."

Something else was bothering me, and I couldn't put my finger on it. Something to do with Psystorm. "All we've got are theories," I groused.

"Agent McNally has been helpful, yes," Renee said, "but what has the ATF really done for us?"

"Money," Gage replied. "They pay for everything we have at the HQ. Our uniforms, our equipment, the copter and cars. It's not like we could afford going freelance."

"Still," I said, "it's about time we demanded answers and soon. I'm sick of being taunted by this psycho-in-Specter's clothing and suspecting everyone who's supposed to be on my side. I want to find him. I want this done."

Gage draped his arm around my shoulders; I leaned gratefully against his chest and inhaled the clean scent of him. I had to be stinking up the back of the ambulance. Par for the course lately.

"What about Psystorm? Will he be okay?" Dahlia asked.

"I hope so," I said. "He may be able to tell us something more, but I used his collar. He could be out for hours, and I'm not sure breaking his ankle helped much."

Renee flinched. "He broke your hand, T."

"He was being controlled."

"Are you sure?"

"Yes, Renee, I'm sure." I pinched the bridge of my nose, amazed at how numb my face felt. Nice drugs. "Look, guys, today sucked. It really did, but we can't blame everyone who's trying to help us without more proof."

"'Sucked' does not encompass today," Renee said.

"If you want poetry, hire a poet. And I'm all out of sub-tlety, too, so I apologize in advance if I offend anyone now or in the near future."

"I think you're also a little high," Gage said.

"Probably so, my teeth feel kind of numb." I beamed a smile at him. "The good news is, no purple vision. Not even a fleck of violet."

"Best thing I've heard today."

My drugged brain couldn't properly catalogue the con-versation of the last ten minutes. It felt as though I'd listened to someone else have it, instead of actually participating. I'd have to rely on the others to refresh my memory. Pain or not, I couldn't have this haze over my brain for the rest of the day.

We could be attacked again, or not—it didn't matter. We had to be ready, and I couldn't lead if I was high. I had to lead.

"So, the way I see it," I said slowly, measuring my words, "one of two things is going on. One, we're going to start our search over tomorrow from scratch, because whoever is so hell-bent on killing us is still out there and gunning. Or two, with the original Specter dead, he or she assumes we think it's over and leaves us the hell alone."

Renee snorted sharply through her nose. "Do you really believe in option two?"

"No, but it sounds nice."

Instead of a sneer, Renee produced a smile. She stretched her entire torso far enough to throw her arms around my neck. Her shoulder pressed into my swollen chin; I winced, but still returned her hug.

"It does sound nice," she whispered.

"That looks so gross," Dahlia said. "Do you have to do it?"

Renee laughed as she let go and retracted back to her regular size. "It's my power, darling, get used to it."

"Come on, let's get Teresa home," Gage said. To which Renee added, "We need to get her and Marco matching slings."

I stuck my tongue out at her—a move that seemed quite serious at the time and not as childish as it would have without the use of narcotics—and said, "For that, you don't get to sign my cast."

"Good, I would have put dirty limericks on it anyway."

The comment struck me as quite hilarious; I started giggling and couldn't stop. I looked at Gage. His face seemed contorted, stretched thin, very funny. "Know what really sucks, though?" I asked between intakes of breath. "I may never play the guitar again."

Someone was snapping their fingers, trying to get my attention. I turned and found Renee in my face asking, "Could you play before?"

"No."

She looked over my shoulder, presumably at Gage. I refused to look for fear of another giggle fit. Instead, I let them talk about transportation home and settled into a drug-induced euphoria for the duration.

Thirty-one

Regroup II

The novelty of waking up in a hospital bed ended completely after the fourth occurrence in a week. Throbbing pain drew me from the thick darkness around my mind, from which I had ventured out once. Someone setting a broken bone in your hand will rouse you from anything short of a coma. I remembered muttering about no more meds, and then drifting until my wish came true and the morphine worked its way out of my system.

Same drab walls. Still no clock. Between the drugs and jet lag, I had more trouble than usual orienting myself. Everything felt thick, murky. I managed to turn my head slowly in both directions. I was alone. The room's door stood open.

My right hand reached up and a bolt of pain stabbed through it. Note to self: learn to be left-handed for a while. I tilted my chin and spotted the fresh white cast from elbow to knuckles. Only the tips of my fingers were exposed, little pink sausages, slightly swollen.

The raging headache was down to a dull roar, pressing gently behind my eyes and across my chin. Great plan I had.

Follow a tip, find Specter 1, get beat up. The only plus side to the fire at the Blue Tower was our discovery of Specter 2. Unfortunately, all plus sides come with downsides, and ours was a doozy: the doppelganger had access. Access to the ATF was the only way to keep Specter out of prison and get rid of the records. Access to and knowledge of the Warden in order to kill the Metas attached to it and release our powers—more that still made no sense. How had the doppelganger managed to secure the Specter powers in the first place?

Could the Wardens have sensed Marcus Spence was incapable of handling his powers anymore and gifted them to someone else? If so, why? Or had the powers bounced around like dandelion fluff until attracted to a capable body? Was the new user experiencing side effects like me?

All the questions and speculation were making me crazy.

With my left hand I felt around on the side of the bed until my fingers found the button to raise it. Gage appeared in the doorway before I could press anything. Bless him, he was probably listening and heard the sheets rustle. His smile swelled my heart and set butterflies loose in my stomach. I knew of nothing better to wake up to in the morning (or evening, afternoon, whatever).

"Hey, beautiful." He reached out and took my left hand, holding it loosely like he thought he would break it.

"Liar."

"Never. You're still beautiful, just a little more colorful now."

"Oh, right, black and blue on top of the purple."

"It goes well with your uniform."

I finally managed my own smile. He looked so tired. Dark smudges had appeared beneath his eyes, and his skin was ghostly.

"Have you slept?" I asked. "You look like hell."

"I slept for a while this afternoon. It's evening now, so you've only been resting for about six hours."

Six hours—too much and yet not enough. I really wanted to curl up and sleep until my body stopped hurting completely. Maybe next week. "Did I miss anything? Ethan?"

His expression clouded. "Still nothing. Marco is going out of his mind. I think he feels responsible for letting Ethan get away, and I can't snap him out of it. Dahlia's with him right now, though, so he's not alone. She has a peculiar knack for charming people."

"Does she?" I hadn't interacted with her as much as I'd have liked, and I regretted it. She was still learning the ropes; I needed to be available to her, to teach her.

"Yeah, she dragged him down to the housing basement to pick out a uniform for herself. She even picked out a code name. Ember."

I turned it over in my mind. She didn't create fire, just manipulated the source of it, absorbed its heat. Like the glowing center of a coal. It fit.

With the team accounted for, I grasped for something else to say. Anything impersonal—I wasn't quite awake enough to follow the usual pattern of our more intimate conversations. I surprised myself by blurting out, "I'm sorry about this morning."

His hand tightened around mine. "I know you are."

"You told me something very private, and I was a bitch for throwing it back in your face." Even through the fading haze of painkillers and everything that had happened in between, shame crashed over me. Utter shame at how I'd behaved—a petulant child misdirecting her anger. Not a trait becoming to the leader I was trying to be.

"I know you were hurting when you said it."

"It's no excuse."

"No, but it's an explanation." He sucked his lower lip into his mouth. "I didn't tell you those things for sympathy or pity. I know I run hot and cold, and I didn't want you to think it was you. It's not."

If he'd forgiven me, he didn't say it. I didn't want it, even if I had thought I deserved it. I needed to learn patience. He needed to stop seeing me as his cause. We'd both be happier for those things.

"No, it's not me," I said. "It's both of us, Gage. We both have things to figure out before we can really make this work. But I want to try. Do you?"

"Yes," he replied without hesitation.

"Good." As much as I wanted to linger on that promise, I had to drag our conversation back to current things. "So, Dahlia. Is she engaging Marco because she's really into this superhero gig, or to humor him?"

Gage lifted one shoulder in a noncommittal shrug. "More the latter, I think. She's still pretty skittish, especially around Renee. And for some reason, she's terrified of Agent McNally."

"Probably because she's convinced herself that the feds

are our enemy." I frowned, then rethought the expression when my chin and lips twinged. Even scrunching my nose increased the intensity of my headache.

She may have been listening for quite some time, but Agent McNally chose that moment to scare the pee out of me by saying, "I hope you don't think so, too, Trance."

Gage jumped a mile and squeezed my hand hard enough to elicit a yelp. I was down to one good hand. If he broke it out of fright, I'd be very screwed. I didn't know if it was possible to create an orb with both hands bandaged. One day I would have to experiment while wearing mittens.

"I'm sorry," she said, stepping into the room. "I didn't intend to startle you, and I apologize for eavesdropping."

"How much did you hear?" I asked. Bit by bit, my racing heartbeat slowed to a normal rhythm. New headline: "Hero Felled by Fear-Induced Myocardial Infarction."

"After Ember's choice of code name. It's good." She smiled, defusing any sense of annoyance she should rightfully feel. We had been talking about her behind her back, after all.

I cocked my head to the side. It wasn't as intimidating as my hand-on-hip stance, but you work with what you've got. "Can we trust the ATF?"

McNally's eyebrows arched slightly. "You get right to the point, don't you?"

"Someone's still trying to kill me, and he or she got damned close this morning. We are now fresh out of leads and shit out of luck. I need straight answers, and even though you lied to us once, I'm probably as likely to get them from you as from anyone else in the federal government."

The complacent smile never wavered. "I admire your candor, Trance, and in the interest of honesty, I don't know. I can't speak for every agent in the ATF. As for myself, yes, you can trust me. I had no idea Marcus Spence was living here in Los Angeles. I don't know who started the fire at Fairview, or who is manipulating the Specter powers now. Please believe me when I say that I'm on your side, and if I had information to share with you, I would."

A glance at Gage and his subtle nod confirmed her words. I loved having a human lie detector by my side to validate my own judgment. "You lied about our powers," I said.

"And I admitted to my mistake in doing so. I can't change that I lied to you. All I can do is try to make amends now." She smoothed one hand over her perfectly coiffed hair. The style was immaculate, every hair exactly in place. My mane of random tangles and waves shifted if I breathed too hard.

"Okay. Hey," I said, the thought striking without warning. "How's Psystorm? Is he awake?"

"Last I checked he was showing signs of waking and his vitals are strong. Dr. Seward had to remove the collar completely in order to treat the burns it created. While I believe we'd all be safer if he remained in deep sedation until this is finished—"

"He doesn't have Specter contained."

"I believe you. And he may have valuable information hiding in his head. But the staff is prepared for any eventuality."

Translation: We're taking no chances. "How about Caleb?"

"He knows his father is sick and that he's getting better. I believe he's in the waiting room, coloring in a picture book."

Waking soon meant I could talk to Psystorm and get a better idea of what had gone on inside of the heads of Milton and Spence during their struggles. I couldn't begin to imagine how telepaths used their powers, or how their inner sight worked. If Lady Luck decided to smile on me, she would let Psystorm remember something. Anything that hinted at who was controlling the Specter powers.

Gage shifted, looking for a comfortable way to stand facing both of us. He seemed to give up the fantasy and aimed his body at me while twisting his head every few moments to acknowledge McNally. His indecision amused me.

"So what do your bosses think of today's events?" Gage asked.

"I don't know. I haven't reported it yet."

His lips parted in surprise. "Really?"

"You aren't the only one to call a few loyalties into question. Until we figure out who this doppelganger is, I'm keeping what you tell me between us. If my boss doesn't like it, that's not my problem. My loyalty is to you both and to your teammates. It always has been."

"Good luck putting that across on Grayson."

She shrugged. "The Bureau of Alcohol, Tobacco, Firearms and Explosives may have a hand in your funding, but I don't answer to Grayson, and neither should you. We've done nothing except bring hardship on you, and you're intelligent enough to do this alone."

"You have no idea how much I love hearing you say that,"

I said, and I meant it. More and more I felt the stranglehold of authority closing its grip around my throat. We were not meant to operate like this—run by committee and second-guessed by people with no powers experience. Ranger or Bane, it no longer mattered. Few could understand us; fewer tried. It was easier to compartmentalize us and order us around.

No longer, not if I had anything to say about it.

Right after we neutralized the doppelganger.

"Agent McNally, why did our parents lie to us?"

"About what, Trance?"

"About what really started the War?"

She was silent for a long time. "Because they were the good guys. Or they were supposed to be."

The answer was so simple, and it made perfect sense. "So Psystorm is in a coma, Ethan is MIA, and Marco can't morph. Dahlia is slowly getting the hang of things. I am once again in a hospital bed, and somehow Renee has still managed to be the only person not wounded."

"Physically, at any rate," Gage said.

A reply died on my lips. He was right, and I felt like an ass for forgetting. It was barely thirty-six hours since William had died, soon to be one week exactly since we regained our powers and the world spun on its head. Something told me our Specter impersonator never intended his hunt-and-slaughter to last this long. He or she could get desperate. Slip up. It was our only real chance at catching him.

I reached for Gage and squeezed his hand. "I'm sorry, I'm just ranting a little and waiting for my vision to inevitably turn purple." The threat of going nova again was the absolute last complication I needed on my plate.

"Any excuse for a filter cleaning." The corners of his eyes crinkled in an adorably boyish way that made me wish Mc-Nally was elsewhere. I could get lost in his eyes and in the way they looked right through me. Saw every part of me.

Wait.

"Eyes." I craned my neck to see past Gage and look at McNally. "Do we have a file on Marcus Spence?"

"A slim one, why?" she said.

"I was just thinking something. We know Specter's eyes glow yellow when he's using his powers on others."

"You're correct, Trance, but what—?"

"Do his eyes glow when he's not using his power?" Her expression slackened; it hadn't occurred to her either. "Would we even know it if we passed Specter Two on the street?" Or had been working close to them all this time?

"I don't honestly know. I never engaged Specter personally, and no one I've spoken to has mentioned it."

"Psystorm would know," Gage said. "He knew Specter for months, if not years, before the end of the War. Specter had to power down once in a while. Of course, I'd prefer if his eyes glowed all the time. It makes finding him a little bit easier."

"Nothing about this has been easy," I said. "Why should this be any different?"

"Hey, guys!" Dahlia's panting, overeager voice boomed though the quiet room, almost as startling as McNally's earlier entrance. She skidded to a stop just inside, half-hidden behind Gage. He scooted to the side, and I blinked.

She had certainly chosen a uniform. Shimmering yellow fabric clung to her short, thin legs, ending with stirrups that hooked under the two-inch heels of her black boots. The top of the unitard looked like a shelf-lift corset, outlined with black and orange piping. She wore a short, elbow-length black jacket over it, giving her shoulders some modesty. Her long blond hair had taken on an orange hue—either a color job, or her powers were changing her body, kind of like Gage's hair had changed from blond-brown to sandy-salted. Even McNally seemed stunned by the wardrobe choice.

"What is it?" Gage asked.

"One sec." She waved at someone in the hallway. Seconds later, Marco appeared by her side.

He was also out of breath, red-cheeked, intent on something. The haze of self-pity surrounding him since Sunday had finally lifted—a very good sign. "You look terrible, Catalepsia."

"So I've been told," I said. "What's going on, you two?"

They shared a look and a smile, and I found myself daring to hope for good news. It had to be good news. They kept nodding back and forth, each prodding the other to relay their information. Cute, if annoying. I cleared my throat. It got their attention.

"I believe I know where to find Ethan," Marco said.

Next to "I know where to find Specter Two," those were the best words I could have heard.

Thirty-two

Alicia Monroe

No amount of personal pain or pleading from Dr. Seward could keep me from accompanying Marco and Gage on their quest for Ethan. Renee and Dahlia agreed to stay behind and hold down the fort, and after a few heated words with a sleep-deprived Seward about my condition, we set out in another tinted-windowed vehicle. Gage drove; Marco rode shotgun to give directions. I sat in the back, biting the inside of my mouth to suppress yelps of pain each time we hit a bump or pothole.

After the end of the War, Ethan Swift had been fostered to a family in Kingman, Arizona. I was first to admit that the MHC could have vetted our foster families a little better before handing over twelve traumatized teenagers. Ethan's placement, though, astonished me. Marco and Dahlia found the records on the HQ's computer system and it read like a bad television movie.

Roger and Camille Bacon, according to all neighborly witness reports, seemed like the perfect couple. He worked an IT job and brought home a good living. She stayed home to raise their two children and had been a foster mom for seven years before Ethan came to live there. The children they fostered always complained when they had to leave. Local Family Services praised the couple up and down for straightening out a dozen children.

The pretty façade didn't hint at the volatile underbelly. I couldn't judge the Bacons by a file, so I didn't know if they were ill prepared to handle Ethan's particular condition, or if the other children simply adjusted and never told about the Bacons' methods of "straightening them out." Police reports said Ethan first ran away six months after arriving at the Bacon household. He was found two days later, living beneath an overpass, and sent back. He ran away again the following year. He made a complaint—later lost from his file—about his treatment by the Bacons. An investigation turned up nothing and the matter was dropped.

He asked to be given to someone else. The Bacons fought to keep him. For four years he lived under their roof, until he turned eighteen. He filed criminal charges of negligence and abuse, which were later dropped by the DA for lack of evidence. No medical reports, no broken bones, no bruises, no corroborating complaints. Just two upstanding adults who tried their best to raise a troubled boy with authority issues.

The file ended there. Marco had dug a little deeper and—with Dr. Seward's help—discovered the names of two other children fostered with him during that time. One of them, a boy named Charles Abbott, lived in New Hampshire and worked for a car dealership. The second, a girl named Alicia Monroe, had a California driver's license and a current address in Burbank. Quick phone calls turned up two more tidbits—she managed a restaurant called Totino's, and she had left work early yesterday and taken sick time for the rest of the week.

Gage exited the 405. We circled around and passed an apartment complex on the right, down past an abandoned movie studio lot, and further into Burbank. As one of the few remaining "nice" neighborhoods in Los Angeles, the cleanliness was striking. Paved streets, living palms, painted buildings. The battle scars worn by the rest of the city had been expertly covered up.

Renee beeped my Vox while we were still a few blocks away. "Go ahead."

<We got a little more on Alicia Monroe,> she said. <She was taken from an alcoholic mom when she was eight and put into the foster care system. She was twelve when the Bacons took her in, about three months before Ethan left. She stayed there for less than a year before moving on, and was eventually adopted by her next family, the Monroes. She took their name, went to college, got a management degree, moved around for a while before settling here in L.A. Never married, no kids.>

My mind spun with the influx of data. I tried to pick out the pertinent information and store the rest. She sounded like a decent girl, the kind of person you could count on when in trouble, and the only person from Ethan's past currently on the West Coast. He may have gone to her for help. It was our best hope, and our one shot at finding him.

Gage located the apartment building easily enough,

tucked away on a quiet side street near old downtown Burbank. Five stories, stucco roof and adobe walls, it screamed of a style no longer popular, yet still timeless. Outdoor staircases ascended to the upper floors, and long walkways connected the separate bungalows, probably six or eight to each level.

We parked in a private lot across the street. Didn't get out right away. Gage closed his eyes and concentrated. I scooted forward between the front seats, watching his face as he listened to the apartment life. His eyes scrunched. The corners of his mouth drooped. Minutes passed.

"I think I found the apartment," he said, eyes flying open. "No voices, but I heard two distinct heartbeats and a television program."

"If they're home, then they are likely distracted by the television," Marco said. "They should not see us sneaking up."

"Let's hope," I said.

We exited the van and crossed the street. A teenage girl walking a dog abruptly changed sides when she saw us. Otherwise, we went undisturbed. Everything felt different in this part of town. Quieter, more relaxed. Far away from the hustle and boom of the ravaged, more industrial parts of the city.

Ethan knew how to pick a hideout.

Alicia lived on the third floor, number 5, nestled in a corner that would have made me jumpy, wondering who was lurking in the shadows by my front door. Two windows were shuttered on the inside. A straw welcome mat lay on the stoop, decorated with daisies and faded grass. Homey and girlish, rolled into one.

Gage turned one ear toward the door, listening. "Still

watching television, I think," he said softly. "The heartbeats are at rest, close together. About twenty feet from the front door, in another room. The bedroom, maybe."

Made sense for someone still recovering from surgery to be in bed. This Alicia must be a special person to take off work at the drop of a hat for someone she'd known as a child, unless they'd maintained contact over the years, which was entirely possible. It only reminded me of how little I still knew about Ethan.

"Should we knock?" Marco asked.

"Well, I hadn't intended to break the door down," I said.

Marco quirked an eyebrow. He was on the verge of retorting when my Vox beeped. I grabbed it.

<Trance, it's Flex. Good news. Psystorm is awake and he was asking for you. His brains aren't scrambled too badly, and he keeps babbling and apologizing for your hand, which is sort of sweet.>

"That's great, Renee, but we're kind of busy here."

<You'll want to hear this, T. I asked Psy about Specter's eyes, because McNally mentioned it a few minutes ago and it was fresh. Anyway, he said that Specter's own eyes don't glow unless he wants them to, for effect, you know? It's only when he's possessing someone, that's when the host's eyes go Day-Glo.>

"Shit." Helpful and also terrifying on some basic level.

<Yeah, and there's more. He keeps insisting he talk to you as soon as possible. Something about a face he saw in Spence's memories, and he won't tell anyone but you. Says you're the only one he—>

Static interfered with the rest of her statement. I tapped the side of the Vox. "Flex? Can you hear me? Flex?"

Marco pulled out his Vox and tried. "Flex, it is Onyx, come in. Flex, Onyx. Hello?" Same static. "Strange."

More than strange. Downright unsettling. Psystorm saw a face, someone he knew I would recognize. Was it the same face the female Warden had seen before she died? We had to keep this visit short.

"Someone's moving in the front room," Gage said. "A woman just asked if he wanted anything to drink." His entire face lit up when he smiled. "Ethan just said he wanted some apple juice. He's here."

I fisted my good hand to stop from throwing my arms around Gage and settled for a face-aching grin. Relief settled over me, calming some of my queasiness. Only a small niggle of worry remained, slanted toward the loss of Vox communication with HQ.

Ethan was here, and he was safe, and that was what was important. I pressed the doorbell. Gage winced. Damn, I should have warned him to dial back his hearing before I rang. I caught his eye and mouthed *I'm sorry.*

He shrugged it off, centered himself. "She's coming. At the door. Walking away. She's telling him who's here."

"What's he saying?"

"Nothing yet." He grinned. "He asked if a guy with silver eyes was outside, and she said yes. He said no use in pretending we aren't home, they know." A pause. "Here she comes."

The front door swung open. Alicia Monroe moved into the doorway, arms folded across her ample chest. She was a stocky woman, big-boned without being overweight, with close-cropped black hair and piercing blue eyes. Tattoos covered her neck and peeked out from the sleeves of her T-shirt. If I hadn't known she was a restaurant manager, I would have pegged her for a bouncer.

"I know who you are," Alicia said. A gentle lilt remained in her voice, softening it and creating a mismatch with her tough appearance. "Come on inside."

She stepped back and allowed us entry. The apartment was small, clean. Tan walls, checked navy curtains, a collection of matching catalogue furniture that completed a very country style. It smelled like apples and patchouli—two more things defying me to categorize her.

"How is he?" I asked.

"I'm not a nurse, but I think he's good. I don't have anything stronger than ibuprofen for the pain he's in. He won't complain, though. He's keeping down fluids, and he had some tomato soup last night."

My eyes flickered toward the bedroom door, half open to reveal a slab of sunlight on the chocolate-brown carpeting. The quiet murmur of a television set trickled out.

"Thank you for taking care of him, Ms. Monroe," Gage said.

"It's Alicia, please. I wanted to call you guys when he showed up. He made me promise not to. I kind of owed him, so I didn't."

I shook my head. "It's okay, Alicia. He was with someone who could take care of him, and that's all that matters."

A bell dinged in the other room. Alicia smiled, showing

rows of perfect teeth. The first left incisor had a jewel embedded in it. "He's calling for you. I'll wait out here."

Gage and Marco remained still, and it took a moment to realize they were staring at me; deferring to their leader the task of talking to Ethan. I squared my shoulders, nerves twisting my stomach into knots for no good reason. It was only Ethan, for crying out loud.

I stuck my head in through the door. The bed was angled away, toward the room's single window. A tall, narrow chest occupied the space between the suede-covered headboard and the door. I pushed, allowing myself room to enter. A longer dresser that matched the chest stood against the opposite wall, covered with bottles and compacts and jewelry boxes overflowing with baubles. Skeins of red fabric draped the walls and gave the room a calm, meditative quality. No drapes covered the open window, allowing a perfect view of Mt. Wilson.

The television was mounted on the wall, its volume now muted. A bedside table—an obvious match to the rest of the room's stuff—held an array of cups, bowls, pill bottles, and a damp washrag. I tore my eyes away from the details, finally giving Ethan my full attention. He lay in the middle of the bed, surrounded by pillows and a rich-looking satin coverlet. All of the red in the room made his hair look more orange than usual, contrasting sharply to the pallor of his face. Pale or not, he looked ten times better than the last time I'd seen him. Stronger, more capable.

He blinked rapidly, like an animal expecting to be hit at any moment. I anticipated defiance, to be on the receiving end of a defensive rant, or even to get a snarled demand to go away and leave him alone. Instead, I saw a pool of shame in his eyes.

The nervous swirling in my stomach faded quickly. My shoulders relaxed. A dozen different thoughts raced through my mind, a dozen questions and demands. He didn't give me a chance to speak first.

"Geez, Teresa, you look like shit on toast."

A *so do you* response died on my lips. I surprised myself (and probably him, too) by replying with, "Do you know how much it's going to cost to fix the hole you put in the Medical Center wall?"

Ethan's lips parted. His brow furrowed. He didn't seem to know if I was joking or serious, and for a brief moment, neither did I. "Are you going to bill me for it?" he asked, hesitation in his voice.

I pursed my lips and pretended to mull it over. "I suppose I could just have it taken out of your paycheck for the next couple of months."

He stared.

"Or . . ." I drew out the alternative for effect. His face was priceless. "Or, you could come home, get better, and promise to never run away like this again. That kind of repayment appeals to me more."

The corner of his mouth twitched. I didn't speak, didn't even blink until the twitch became a complete smile.

"I was a coward for running away. I'm sorry, Teresa. But I kept thinking about Janel and William, and I just couldn't stand the idea of Specter hurting anyone through me. I panicked."

I climbed onto the bed, stretched out next to him, and slipped my arm through his, mindful of the still-fresh wounds on his chest.

"Careful. If Gage sees us, he might get jealous."

"We all feel that way, you know," I said, ignoring his tease. To which he responded, "What? Jealous?"

"Dork." I pinched his arm lightly. "You never want to hurt people you care about, Ethan, and it's worse when you can't even make the choice; when someone takes that control away. I can't promise it won't happen, and I can't promise a happy ending to all of this."

He snickered, resting his head against my shoulder. "You really need to work on your pep talks, if you're trying to sell me on coming back."

"If you want pep, get a pill."

"There's the Teresa I know and love."

"Hah. So, Alicia seems nice, in an I'll-beat-you-up-if-you-hurt-my-friend kind of way."

"She's great, really great. How did you find her, anyway?"

"Are you questioning my detective skills, Wind Master?"

"No, just your present deductive reasoning skills. That hand looks sore, and it wasn't broken two days ago, which means you've been sidelined by both injury and pain pills recently."

"Good call. Marco found her, with a little help from Dahlia."

He twisted his neck and stared blankly. "The reporter?"

"Yes." So Renee told him about William's death, but not our newest club member? It shouldn't have surprised me, given Renee's dislike of Dahlia, but it did.

"Just part of a very long story, which includes a few more fires and a Specter impersonator who's the real person bent on killing us all in a violent manner. How about we start the story on the way home, where there are nice, happy drugs waiting for you in Medical."

"Yeah, okay." He smiled. "Let's go home."

Getting Ethan downstairs without jostling his wounds too much took some gentle maneuvering from Gage and Alicia. The backseat of the SUV wasn't the most comfortable, but it was all we had for transportation. We stepped away to give Ethan and Alicia a few private moments.

Marco slipped over to me, eyebrows knotted, tense. "I have been unable to contact Flex," he said softly. "I receive only static on my Vox."

"Did you try Dr. Seward?"

"Yes, but I cannot get through to anyone."

"I'll try mine," Gage said, then wandered a few feet down the sidewalk.

The Vox issue still worried me. It could easily be a communication systems failure, considering that a lot of the equipment hadn't been updated in at least fifteen years. Another, more dire, scenario wanted to present itself, but I was tired of assuming the worst in everything. No more jumping to conclusions.

Alicia and Ethan finished their good-byes, and after a round of thanks on both sides, we got in. I slid into the backseat with Ethan and offered my lap as a pillow. He seemed both sad and determined; Alicia was a special person to him, and I was a little sorry to separate them.

As Gage climbed into the driver's seat, he shook his head at me—nothing on his Vox, either. Anxiety settled cold and heavy in my gut, and our Voxes remained silent the entire drive back to HQ.

Thirty-three

Vanished

A throng of reporters surrounded the main gate, in the same positions they had occupied for the last two days. Cameras and recording devices were thrust at the van. Questions were shouted that we couldn't hear and had no intention of acknowledging anyway.

Gage pulled up to the security box and entered our pass code. The gate swung open, its sensors allowing just enough space for the van to squeak through, and closed again before the reporters could attempt a break-in. Part of me expected some sign of danger, a reason for the Vox malfunctions. The grounds, however, were silent.

Utterly deserted.

We drove around to the front of the Medical Center and parked. Gage tilted his head and listened. We waited. His preexisting frown of concentration deepened into something else.

"There's no one in there," he said. "Medical is empty."

"What?" Marco asked.

I slid forward on the seat. "How's that possible? Half a

dozen people work there." Not to mention it was where we had left Psystorm and Caleb.

"I don't know. I can't hear anyone. No heartbeats, no voices. A telephone's off the hook and someone's computer is playing music, so it's not my ears. No one is in there."

"What about the other buildings?"

"I'd have to get closer."

I hated splitting up, even though it was our best course of action. We had people missing; we had to figure this out and fast. Remaining together only doubled our timetable. "Ethan, stay in the car," I said. "Gage, go check out the other buildings. Do not go inside, just find out if anyone is in them. Marco and I are going to take a peek in here."

They nodded, offering no arguments. The less they questioned my decisions, the scarier this whole leadership thing became. Ethan propped himself up into a sitting position so he could hit the horn in case of emergency. He shouldn't be here. I should have assumed the worst-case scenario and left him with Alicia. Too damned late to fix it now.

I squeezed his shoulder, trying to offer some silent support, and then climbed out.

Gage paused to sniff the air. "There's smoke somewhere. Just a hint of it, not a huge fire. I can't tell from what direction."

"It's okay," I said. "Just please, be careful and do not engage. I doubt our Voxes will work any better here than they did across town, so be prepared to scream if you need help."

His eyes narrowed, not quite a flinch—some look of extreme concentration. Its intensity did nothing to calm my nerves. Adrenaline surged through my veins and set my fingertips shaking.

He looked over my shoulder at Marco. "Hey, Walking Wounded, take care of each other, okay?"

"We will," Marco said. *"Promeso."*

Gage darted away, sticking close to the shrubs and saplings that lined the sidewalk. I watched him a moment, trying to dispel the sense that I'd just sent him off to be killed. It was an irrational fear, nonetheless present and overwhelming. Specter was here; I knew it in my heart. I also knew that despite my fear and hesitation, this would all end tonight.

"Trance?"

I nodded to Marco. "I know, let's go."

We started on the first floor and discovered nothing, and more of nothing on the second. A few computers were still on, screensavers in full swing. Whatever made everyone abandon the building happened within the last hour. We saw no outward signs of a struggle—no dropped files or scattered instrument trays. Desk chairs were pushed in neatly. They'd just vanished.

Dr. Seward's temporary office was vacant of personnel, same as the other rooms. I nudged his computer mouse and an open file appeared. He had been reading up on Dahlia Perkins. Half a dozen articles she'd written for her paper were displayed in as many windows. Fluff pieces, mostly.

On a whim, I picked up Seward's phone. No dial tone. I studied the lab tables, the floor, the stool, looking for any sign of a struggle. A spot of blood, a piece of broken glass. Some clue as to what had happened here.

"This is insane," Marco said. "Ten people do not simply vanish."

"No, they don't. Something forced them to leave." Neatly.

"And go where?"

"I have no idea." Another building, I hoped. I couldn't stand to entertain the thought that Gage hadn't picked up any heartbeats because they were all dead.

The private room where Psystorm should have been was empty, and there we found the first real sign of wrongdoing. The sheets were twisted, dangling to the floor. All the monitors were off, and the connecting wires lay tangled together. A spot of blood colored the sheet where his IV had been pulled out and dropped.

"He was moved in a hurry," I said.

Fabric rustled behind me. I turned to see Marco standing in his underwear, pulling at the surgical tape binding his fingers. Dumbfounded at the sight, I didn't react until the bandages fluttered to the floor. "What are you doing, Marco?"

"I can track whoever was here, but not like this."

"I thought you couldn't morph with your fingers broken."

"I can, but it will hurt. My fingers will still be broken." He grimaced. "My paw will be broken. We have no choice."

"Marco—"

He turned, dropping his underwear. His body shrank. Skin darkened and black hair grew into a shining coat. He groaned, and the pained cry turned into a feral hiss. He hunched over, his back legs changing shape and adding roped muscle. I watched the transformation, as awed by it as the first time. The grown panther turned to face me, favoring his left front paw. He blinked greenish eyes, and then got to work sniffing things.

I peered out the window, hoping for a glimpse of Gage somewhere on the grounds, and got a view of the city. Not helpful. Panther-Marco growled. I turned. He loped out of the room, intent on whatever he smelled. I followed at a distance, letting him do his thing. His three-legged limping ended in the waiting room down the hall. He stopped in the doorway and growled.

My stomach heaved. Julie Dent, the on-call nurse who always seemed to be around, lay in the middle of the room, surrounded by overturned games and coloring books and broken crayons. Her neck was twisted at a strange angle, wide-open eyes dull and lifeless.

"My God." I didn't have to touch Julie to know she was dead. I did anyway. Her skin was warm; she hadn't died long ago.

Marco growled, sniffed her hair. He sneezed, growled again, and began another fast three-legged limp down the corridor. I trotted after him.

Back to the stairs and down. On each landing he paused. I opened the floor exits. He sniffed. We continued. He left the stairwell on the second floor, speeding up from a gentle lope to a full-on run. Faster than I was, even on a broken paw, he turned a corner before I was halfway there. I found him scratching and snarling at a utility closet door.

I twisted the knob with my left hand. Locked. A dime-size orb into the keyhole shattered the lock. The door swung in. I found a switch and turned on the light.

Two rows of industrial shelving held dozens of boxes of supplies. Cleaning solution, bleach, mop heads, sponges, a couple of brooms and dust pans. Marco went inside. He nosed a box on a bottom shelf, *Scouring Pads* handwritten on the side. I pulled it off the shelf and placed it gently on the floor. The tape was cut, flaps folded in.

I looked into his feline eyes and swore I saw fear. He wanted me to see what he smelled. I pulled out the flaps. My entire body went cold, and I had the very real urge to piss myself. I saw the colorful wires, the connections and screws and chips. The thing that scorched itself into my brain was the timer, and the little red numbers ticking down from :32 . . . 31 . . . 30 . . .

"Move!"

Back down the hall, I ran faster than I'd ever run in my life. I smashed through the stairwell door, Marco on my heels, whining with each step on his broken paw. Once through the door, he bolted down the stairs. I took them two at a time, skipping as many as three in my haste, and somehow never fell.

I hadn't thought to count, to try to measure the remaining time. Blind panic took over. My heart thundered. As long as Marco remained ahead of me, I simply ran. We hit the bottom of the stairwell and burst through the exit, raced across the lobby and pristine floors that had seen the steps of hundreds of Rangers, through the sliding glass doors my ancestors had passed between, the building I'd been born in.

"Keep going!" I shouted at Marco, and he did, galloping toward the Base.

I yanked open the driver's door of the van, ignoring Ethan's questions. I cranked the engine, reached across the wheel to shift with my left hand, and slammed my foot against the gas pedal. The van surged forward. In that instant, the Medical Center exploded. A maelstrom of sound, fire, and flying debris shot toward the van.

Before I could drive ten feet, the first shock wave struck. We spun out of control, and the counterclockwise rotation slammed my left shoulder into the door. My head cracked off the window. Colorful lights danced in my vision and the constant spinning nauseated me. I tried to gain control of the wheel and turn into the spin. Through the windshield and hail of debris, I saw a familiar blue-clad shape. Looked right into his silver-flecked eyes.

"Gage!" I screamed.

The fender of the van clipped him, knocking him sideways and out of sight.

Ethan shouted. All motion stopped abruptly as the van hit something else. Metal crunched. I lurched into the passenger seat, landing on my cast-covered hand. Pain blurred my eyesight and threatened to steal consciousness away. Something hissed. Probably the engine. I couldn't move, could barely breathe.

My head and hand throbbed. My stomach lurched, and I vomited onto the floor. Bile seared my throat and tongue. I retched hard, turning myself inside out.

"Teresa?" Ethan's voice, tentative.

I grunted—the only reply I could muster.

"Did we hit him?"

I spat, swallowed. My eyes watered. "Yeah."

"Can you move?"

"Think so." I tested my legs, ankles, hips, found them able. "You?"

"I'd rather not."

With a deep breath and an acute amount of pain, I got my left arm beneath my body and pushed myself back into the driver's seat. The cast had not cracked, but my entire right arm ached like a son of a bitch, and my exposed fingers were swollen. Blood tickled the left side of my face. One more head wound and I'd have no brain cells left.

The van had smashed into an parked car, a good fifty yards from the smoldering, burning ruins of the Medical Center. Didn't know whose car, didn't much care. Ethan was wedged on the floor of the backseat, his head resting against the passenger side door. His lip was split and bleeding, and he was paler than white.

"Are you stuck?"

"No," he said, panting the words. "Think I ripped some stitches, though." Sure enough, scarlet was seeping through his T-shirt in several places. He wasn't that white from blood loss—shock was setting in hard and fast. It was my fault—me and my brilliant decision to take him out of the safety of a friend's house and drag him back home.

My door opened. I shrieked, panic ripping through me.

Marco stood there, completely naked, his mouth twisted in a grimace. Nicks and burns covered his bare torso, and he cradled his swollen left hand close to his chest.

"*Dios*, are you two all right?" he asked.

"We'll live," I said. Relief at seeing Marco on both feet did little to curb my rising fear. "Where's Gage? Did you see him? I think we hit him."

Marco shook his head and darted away.

"Stay here," I said to Ethan.

He grunted. "No problem."

I slid out of the van, amazed I still possessed the coordination to do so. My legs wobbled, but didn't buckle. We'd stopped at the front of the parking lot. Only four cars were there, and we'd hit the nearest. Waves of heat rolled away from the blazing fire. My lungs seized, and I coughed until my chest ached. Should have built up a freaking tolerance to smoke by now.

"Catalepsia, here!"

I ran toward the sound of Marco's voice—behind the van, back toward a hedge that separated the lot from the street. We'd flattened part of it. I saw the top of Marco's head on the other side of the hedge, skirted it, and dropped to my knees next to them.

Gage was curled on his side, face twisted in pain, eyes squeezed shut. His chest rose and fell steadily and that, more than anything else, settled my nerves. A little. I brushed the tips of my fingers over his forehead, through his hair.

"Gage, it's me," I said. "I am so sorry."

He grunted. "Shit, that hurts."

"What hurts?"

"Ribs."

Frustrated tears stung my eyes, their presence made worse by the billowing smoke all around us. Sirens wailed in the distance. The fire trucks didn't have the gate code.

"Marco, get to the gate. Make sure emergency rescue can get inside to put out the fire."

"No," Gage said. Something in his voice sent a chill down my spine.

I gaped at him. "What? Why not?"

Gage sat up faster than I expected. I fell backward onto my ass, too surprised to react when he punched Marco square in the jaw. Marco flew sideways, cracked his head off the curb, and lay still.

I stared, momentarily forgetting to breathe. Gage twisted around, still sitting. My stomach lurched. If I'd had anything left to vomit, I would have.

Specter's yellow-orange aura glowed from Gage's eyes. A wicked smile twisted his mouth. "What's the matter, Trance?" The voice no longer belonged to Gage, but to someone—something—else. "Don't you want to be alone with me for a while?"

Thirty-four

Specter 2

W e stared at each other for what felt like hours. It was likely just seconds. I saw no familiarity in the face that I knew so well and cared for so much. Just the icy glare of someone foreign and evil. A murderer controlling Gage's body. It was my fault, and I found no comfort in the fact that he had no weapons, or that Gage's powers couldn't hurt me.

"Speechless?" he asked.

I swallowed. "Who are you?"

"Who I've always been."

"You're not Specter."

"In a way, I am. Specter was the name given to a man who once wielded the powers I possess."

"Why?"

He clucked his tongue against the roof of his mouth. "Why don't we take a walk? I will better explain things to you."

"No."

His eyes narrowed. He pointed at Marco. "Shall I kill your friend there to prove my point? Or shall we just take a walk?"

"Where?"

He reached for Marco.

"Okay," I said quickly.

He stopped, stood, and then offered me a hand. I ignored him and stood on my own. Dizziness nearly toppled me. I sucked in a deep breath, trying hard to focus.

"Watch your step, Trance. Don't think I can't hurt this boy. I can manipulate his senses until the stress puts him into a coma. Or perhaps open up his sight and look into the sun and blind him."

My insides liquefied. My worst nightmare was standing in front of me. The only no-win situation I feared encountering. Our only proven methods of forcing Specter out of a body were unconsciousness or death. I couldn't entertain those thoughts yet. Killing wasn't an option. Knocking him out might be possible, but I needed to stay with him. At least until I figured out where his corporeal body was and how to trap him.

"I won't fight you," I said.

"Good girl. Now walk toward the Base."

I did as he asked, not looking at the van as we passed side by side. If Ethan was listening, I prayed he kept silent and out of sight. The only way to end this was to play it out. Something about this wolf-in-Specter-clothing seemed familiar . . . the way he talked, the words he chose.

"I knew you'd be the most difficult," he said casually. He could have been discussing a recipe. "I knew the first night, in the motel. Your powers are incredible, Trance, and quite fascinating. I had to know why you, too, had been gifted powers not your own."

I almost stopped walking, but didn't want to give him another excuse to threaten someone. He didn't know why he had his powers, either. Or she? I had to get more information before he just hauled off and killed me.

"You think my powers were a deliberate gift?" I said, refusing to look at him.

"In a way, yes. Your powers were likely, as hypothesized, the last attempt of a dying woman to manipulate powers she'd been hoarding for fifteen years. Similar energy powers run in families, so the match to your grandmother's power made sense. She tried to even the odds by giving you something she thought you could handle."

A tremor ripped down my spine. Only eight people knew about Agent McNally's theory on my powers. Oh God, who was he? Was it McNally herself? The notion he actually was Gage was there and gone instantly. Impossible.

Wasn't it? McNally had warned me that the only person I could truly trust was myself.

No, I knew Gage, dammit. It wasn't him. And it didn't explain how this doppelganger came into possession of the Specter powers. Unless—hell. Unless Marcus Spence had family we didn't know about.

We entered the Base. He pointed toward the elevator. It opened when I pressed the call button, and inside we went. This was too planned, too perfect. My brain roared on information overload. This couldn't be happening.

We rode up silently and stopped on the third floor. He nudged me out and to the left. The gymnasium was this way and, sure enough, he pointed me toward those double doors.

I inhaled sharply and pushed. Stale air greeted me, as did the sharp odor of blood. Three steps in, I stopped, unable to see in the dim light. Gage moved behind me and flipped a switch. Fluorescent light flooded the room.

I backed up, right into his chest, my lips parting.

The room was the size of half a basketball court, with high ceilings and mats rolled across half the hardwood floor. The wall opposite the door was a bank of windows, the wall to our left all mirrors and dance barres. Unused equipment—a trampoline, uneven bars, a vault—were still shoved in the left corner. My attention was drawn to the objects directly ahead and slightly to the right.

No, not objects. People.

In the near-center of the room was a balance beam. Renee was tied to it with colorful jump ropes, her arms and legs stretched and twisted into pretzel-like shapes, knotted around each other in ways even her flexible body was not meant to turn. Her eyes were open and fixed on the ceiling. Sweat dripped down her face and had pooled on the floor beneath the beam. She seemed past pain, past agony, square in the center of shock.

Dahlia lay on the floor below the beam, bound in a practice mat like a jelly roll, with only her head sticking out. Unconscious? Dead? She was too far away for me to tell. Dr. Seward and Agent McNally were likewise tied up with jump ropes—and drugged or concussed—on the floor near a second balance beam. Psystorm was swathed in karate uniforms, the colorful belts cinched around his legs, arms and torso creating a motley straitjacket. He was blindfolded by a black belt, his body carelessly dumped in the far right corner of the room. Only Caleb and the rest of the medical staff were missing from the waking nightmare. No, someone else was missing.

Fuck. Me.

Anger replaced horror, and the anger quickly melted into rage. These were my friends, tied up and tormented by a deranged federal agent who was blackmailing me with Gage's body. As absurd as it sounded, I'd walked willingly into a no-win situation and needed a miracle to get back out again.

It took every ounce of self-control to not charge across the room and release my friends, consequences be damned. Instead, I pivoted and faced the doppelganger.

"So what are you going to tie me up with, Alex?" I asked. "Fuzzy handcuffs?"

Not-Gage blinked. His slow grin gave me the chills. "You think I'm Agent Grayson?"

"Aren't you?"

"Telling you would ruin the surprise. How do you know I haven't been Cipher this whole time?"

"Because I know him."

"Yes, you do, and quite intimately."

I glared, but kept my mouth shut.

"Cipher's trying very hard to wake up, Trance. He's fighting for you. He may even be in love with you."

"Fuck off."

He quirked an eyebrow and crinkled his nose. It created an absurd expression on Gage's face. "I haven't seen this vulgar side of you before. I am certain, however, if I'd gone into anyone else's body, you'd have blasted me by now without regard for that person's life."

Seen that side of you before. He was playing now. I couldn't let him bait me and reel in the line. I would have killed anyone else if I had to in order to save more lives, only I would have cared. I would have cared a lot. Not Gage, though, not when we'd come so far. I couldn't lose him by my own hands. "You're wrong."

"Am I?"

Instead of giving him the satisfaction, I changed the subject. "What the hell are we doing here?"

"Finishing this, Trance. We've been dancing around each other for the better part of a week, and I'm exhausted. You've worn me out."

"So end it already and stop fucking around." My left hand burned, itching to create and unleash an orb. To release the pent-up fury flickering just beneath the surface. I swept my hand out, indicating the room's five prisoners. "You could have killed them all before I got back, and then pounced. Why the show?"

"I need an alibi."

My lips parted. He watched me, curious, studying my reaction. I couldn't seem to move, think. Utter a sound. He had the upper hand completely, and all I had was the very real urge to curl into a ball and scream.

"You're thinking now," doppelganger-Gage said. "Wondering. Who do you think I am, Trance? Still think I'm Agent Grayson? Or is he stuffed in the trunk of the car you crashed into, slowly suffocating to death?"

"You're a bastard."

"Funny you should say that. But I'm also damned. I have been since the moment I was cursed with these powers, " he said with a weary sigh. "I've been in all of their heads, you know. Your friends. A little gas in the vents to loosen them up and make them sleepy. Then a walk down here to tie themselves up. I know what they think of you. Want to know?"

"Have I said 'fuck off' yet?"

He strolled past me, my hostility rolling off him like water off a duck, gazed at his prisoners, hands folded behind his back, pleased with himself. I kept even with him, allowing only a few feet of distance between us, and froze when he stopped halfway to the balance beam.

"Did you know Flex still blames you for Caliber's death?" he said. "She hates that Gage is alive and William is dead. Deep down she thinks you let him die. That you left him behind. Of course, you and I both know the truth—"

I hit him hard with a closed fist, awkward with my left hand. The blow glanced off his chin and did little more than piss him off. He threw a jab I couldn't avoid. It smashed into the blood knot on my chin and splattered crimson all over his shirt. I fell to my knees, blinded by the fiery agony in my face. Blood drizzled down my neck. The world tilted.

"Don't do that," he said. "I don't want to kill you yet, but I will keep you docile."

Docile? I struggled to breathe, to maintain some sense of composure, when all I wanted to do was collapse. Giving up would hurt less. Forcing him to kill me would end this sick game. Tears dribbled down my cheeks, and through them,

I saw clearly—my friends tied up like animals, used as bait, and my lover lording over it all, controlled by a madman. If I gave up, I doomed them all to death, and if hell existed, I would burn for it.

If I gave up, the future of the Rangers died with me.

"Why?" I said, practically spitting the word.

"Why what?"

"Why are you really doing this?" I lifted my head. Another tear squeezed from the corner of my eye and joined the river of liquid already staining my chin and throat. "Why are you killing us off? Why did you kill those Metas and destroy the Warden?"

He sucked in his lower lip, a very Gage-like gesture. He seemed to war between his own desire to gloat and some need to keep it secret. Knowledge made him feel superior, gave him an edge. I needed to turn that edge against his throat and press.

"You weren't a Bane before," I said, pushing a little harder. "You probably aren't a Meta at all, just some nobody who thinks mass murder makes them somebody."

He scowled. "You know less than you think."

I hauled my weary body up, ignoring the throbbing in my face. Intent on him. "Once we're all dead, then what? The Banes get turned loose to wreak havoc on the world? Is that what you want?"

His scowl softened into surprise. "You didn't know about the MHC's fail-safe protocol, did you?"

I shook my head, wary of his tricks.

"Of course you wouldn't. It's something they designed

thirty years ago, Trance. I'm surprised no one ever mentioned it. Especially McNally, since you two seem very chummy. Of course, this isn't the first time she's withheld information under the guise of your best interests. I suppose she didn't want some sort of Ranger riot on her hands when you actively hated the idea."

"What idea?" I snapped, tired of his pontificating.

"Mass murder. Did you know they have been systematically piping a depressant into the island's water supply for the last ten years? And they've recently increased the dosage, making it so strong some people are getting sick. I suspected as much for years, but Psystorm verified it when he spoke to you about Caleb's mother."

Gage hadn't been in the room during the conversation about the prison's water supply. Neither had Grayson, for that matter. I looked at the bodies tied up on the floor. What was out of place?

He continued: "The MHC had something else prepared, Trance, completely unknown to their superiors at the ATF. A fail-safe protocol to eradicate the Banes, to be used only in the event that your powers returned, and all active and capable Rangers were killed in action. It was meant to protect regular human beings from the Bane threat. To destroy the most dangerous weapons in the world in one fell swoop."

Psystorm. The little black box.

"The collars," I said.

He nodded.

Bile surged into my mouth. I swallowed hard. That's what this was about: genocide. Destroying everyone with powers.

"It won't work," I said, unable to keep my voice steady. "You know it won't, don't you? I mean, you could have killed all twelve of us right away, and then what? Look at Ember. The Banes have children on the island who are uncollared and powered."

"I admit, Caleb and Ember were unexpected, but I had to see this through." He looked at me with weary eyes. "Perhaps this time it will be better."

This time. My guts twisted. "So all the old Rangers and Banes die. Rangers at Specter's hand, the Banes at the push of the government's button, and then all is well? What gives you the right?"

"Have you ever been away from home for so long you've lost yourself and everything you know? Of course you have. You lost your powers for fifteen years, and you spent the time wallowing in a life not yours. Trying to fit into a world that didn't want you. So did Cipher. I can feel his disgust with the way things were. Being normal and how it nearly destroyed him. They stole your identity and your life. If given the chance, wouldn't you have done anything to be here today? To be what you were always meant to be?"

"Yes." I said it before I thought better. It was the truth. I despised those feelings of alienation, of knowing I wasn't meant to be a regular girl. I went to extremes in my personal life to find something to fill the aching void in my heart. And now someone decided my life and my pain was on the sacrificial altar? Hell, no. I'd fought too long and hard to carve out the life I had. It was not his to take away. We'd all worked too damned hard.

A frustrated scream lodged in my throat. "So what happens now? You've told me your dastardly plan. You're holding my boyfriend's body hostage, and my friends are all tied up. You're either going to kill me now, or make me watch you kill my friends first. Why keep stalling?"

"I like this body, so young and vibrant, and so in love. I wish you could feel it for yourself."

"Why don't you memorize it?" I said, dripping with sweet sarcasm. "Then go back to your real body and jerk off for a while. Maybe you'll feel a little bit less like a murderous psychopath. Or do you like jumping into the body of a healthy, thirty-year-old because you can't get it up for a woman in real life?"

I saw the blow coming and ducked. His fist sailed over my shoulder, putting him off balance. I brought my knee up into his stomach, hard, right into Gage's existing bruise. He doubled over and hit the floor. I drove my left elbow into the center of his back. He grunted, dropping like a stone. I turned and lobbed a concentrated orb ten feet toward the center of the balance beam holding Flex hostage. It shattered. Ropes broke. She tumbled to the floor, shrieking as her tortured arms and legs retracted to their normal size.

Something caught my ankle and pulled. I couldn't compensate and toppled forward, smashing my cast-covered arm into the floor. White-hot agony killed my screams. I couldn't breathe. I waited for it. The last strike, be it from a gun or a blow to the head.

Nothing.

I rolled onto my back. The shrieking pain reduced itself

to a dull roar and settled behind my temples. Still no killing blow. I sat up with some effort. My head spun in counter-clockwise circles. I closed my eyes until it passed. The room came into focus. My heart pounded. The sight didn't shock me like it should have—just created a sense of utter failure.

Doppelganger-Gage stood by the rear wall a few paces from the exit, out of immediate reach, watching me intently. He held a knife to his throat, just below his left ear. The blade pressed hard into the skin and had already drawn a thin line of blood. His expression warred with itself, wavering between frustration and anger.

"I'll kill him, you know I will. Are you going to settle down?"

"No, I won't."

He blinked. "You won't?"

"No." Rage burned from my very core, tingling every nerve ending, blinding my other emotions. I was sick of being manipulated by this monster, and I was ending this one way or another. I just hoped Gage could forgive me. One day I might forgive myself.

"Not even if I kill one of your friends? Flex, perhaps? Or your new pal Psystorm? I know you'd hate to be responsible for making that sweet little boy of his an orphan."

More fuel to the fire. My hands clenched. I saw purple, and this time, it wasn't filter overload. Just rage. "*You'd* make him an orphan, you unforgivable bastard. You're going to kill them all anyway, so nothing you do in this room is my fault. You made me kill for you three times too many. I killed Frost for you. I won't kill for you again." My left hand came up to shoulder height, and an orb the size of a grapefruit coalesced above my palm. "I won't let you kill anyone else, either."

His eyes narrowed. "I haven't killed, Trance. There is no blood on my hands."

"You set the fire that destroyed the Warden. You manipulated their deaths. You possessed people and put them in harm's way. Their blood is on your hands as surely as if you'd stabbed them in the heart yourself."

"Semantics, Trance, but if it's literal blood on my hands you want . . ." He pulled the knife's blade across Gage's throat, from ear to Adam's apple. Blood spurted. The yellow glow bled from his eyes as the doppelganger released him. Gage hit the floor hard.

Screams filled my ears as I bolted to his side. I pressed my left hand against the wound, trying to stanch the steady flow of blood. I couldn't tell if he'd hit the artery. I didn't want to know. I just held on.

"Dr. Seward," I shouted. "Agent McNally, anyone! Please, wake up!"

Renee stirred. Not helpful. I couldn't move without letting go, couldn't use orbs to free the others without letting go. I just pressed down, Gage's blood so hot against my skin it seemed to burn. I pressed and watched, expecting one of my friends to wake up suddenly, their eyes yellow and their body possessed. Any one of them could be the doppelganger.

"Hello?"

My hand jerked, startled by the voice. I held my breath, wondering if I'd imagined it. A few seconds later, the call repeated itself. I knew his voice—my number one suspect. Fear and hope collided. I had to bank on hope, for Gage's sake.

"In here! Please, I'm here!"

Alexander Grayson burst into the room at a dead run. A short, frumpy man whom I disliked on principle, and here he was, saving my ass with dirt on his rumpled suit, a bruise on his cheekbone, and a distant look in his eyes. Eyes I instinctively studied—no yellow glow. Maybe he really had been stuffed in a trunk. But by whom? My entire list of suspects was tied up, injured or both.

"What the hell's happening, Trance? The Medical Center is—" He surveyed the room. Sweat glistened on his forehead, and his eyes seemed to grow impossibly wider when he saw me. Really saw me. "Holy Mother of—"

"Is the fire department here yet?" I asked.

"I don't think they're inside, no." He took a few steps closer, his attention fixed on the slowly spreading pool of blood beneath Gage. "My God, what happened? I'd just parked my car when—"

"It's Specter, really long story. Please, just put your hand here and hold pressure on Gage's throat. We need to get the others loose and call an ambulance."

Grayson took my place, his hand pressing down hard where mine had been a moment ago. Gage was pale, but breathing steadily. The blood loss horrified me. If God existed and liked me even a little bit—highly debatable—then the doppelganger had missed the artery and just done scary, reparable damage.

I skipped past my bound friends and ran to the wall of

windows, lobbed an orb at the glass, and watched it shatter outward.

The roar of the nearby fire and scream of alarms became louder, and the acrid scent of smoke filtered inside. The open window presented me with a clear view of the decimated Medical Center, burning out of control. An empty scene of destruction. The loss of a hundred years of Meta history. Red lights twirled and spun on the other side of the main gate, which stood closed. Locked. Could I break it down from here? Probably not.

I bolted for the door.

"Trance?" Grayson asked.

"I need to get closer to the gate to let them—"

"Trance!"

"What?" I turned, annoyance turning to shock as a bullet struck Grayson in the center of his forehead. The sound of the shot followed, an echo my brain was too slow to catalogue. Blood, matter and bone sprayed on the wall. Grayson fell to the floor next to Gage, who was still slowly bleeding to death.

Fear rooted me. I didn't dare look. My legs tingled. I had made a deadly tactical error.

"I truly hated that man. No need pretending anymore, Trance. Turn around."

I did so, slowly. Insides twisting. Desperate for my eyes to find fault with what my ears heard. Dr. Angus Seward stood halfway across the room, a still-bound McNally at his feet, a revolver raised and pointed. Plain brown eyes gazed at me with keen interest from beneath bushy white eyebrows. As

I watched him, his eyes began to glow yellow-orange. The glow lasted only a moment, before fading back to brown. A chill clawed its way from the top of my neck to the tips of my toes.

"Not quite what I had in mind," Seward said. "Happy now? We both have the blood of others on our hands."

The hard edge in his voice cut like an invisible blade. Warmth and compassion—two things I had always associated with Angus Seward—were gone. Erased. Replaced by cold calculation and tinged with anguish.

Fury continued to boil just beneath the surface, fueled by betrayal and loss. And foolishness. How had we been so blind? Not seen it? We were the perfect fools, about to die senseless, avoidable deaths. He had the upper hand now, just has he'd had it all week. Playing us like a guitar, knowing every chord to strum and sweet spot to pick.

"I knew it," I said, even though I knew nothing.

He cocked his head. "Knew what, my dear?"

"That whoever was playing as Specter had a dick the size of a walnut."

His warning shot hit the wall inches from my fractured right hand. I didn't jump. Wouldn't give him the satisfaction. It seemed to impress him.

"You know, Trance, I briefly considered trying to make a deal with you."

"Oh?" My gaze flickered toward Gage. Time was not on my side here.

"You and I are unlike any other Metas, Trance. We received powers we were not born with, something never before seen in Meta history. Your transformation fascinated the scientist in me, as did my own. I shouldn't have delayed your deaths, but I had to know more. I had to understand why."

Little things started clicking into place. I felt sick. And used—well and truly used. Bastard. "You set the fire. You destroyed the Warden and released our powers."

"Yes."

"Why? The fail-safe?"

"Yes."

"You did all this just to ensure the Banes were wiped out."

"We've already discussed this."

"No, we haven't. Why do you hate them so much that you'd sacrifice so many lives just to see the Banes dead?"

His hand trembled, altering the aim of the gun. Several times his mouth opened and closed as thoughts started and never finished. He swallowed hard, Adam's apple bobbing. "Fear."

"Fear of what?"

"Of what would happen when the Warden failed and the powers came back. Fear of how twelve angry, mismatched young adults would handle six times their numbers in vengeful enemies. Fear that those lines of division the MHC created between Rangers and Banes would once again consume the world."

While his fears weren't unfounded, the logic wasn't there. "How did you find out about the Warden?"

"That's a long story."

"Summarize it."

He was stuck in that strange place between not wanting to justify his horrible actions, and wanting to finally tell someone and ease a hefty burden. I wasn't there to absolve him of his sins, but I wanted to know why, dammit.

"You were wrong, Trance," he finally said. "I was a Meta before all of this."

I couldn't have heard that right and stared at him, too stunned to say a word.

"Weren't expecting that, I see." His shoulders sagged a bit. "I had no idea. Not until we all lost our powers. Whatever mine were, they were so weak I never knew I had them until they were ripped away. The experience was exactly as you children described it."

"How could no one know?" I managed to ask.

"I don't honestly know the answer to that, and it's possible there are more like me, who never knew they were Metas. It's not as though being Meta is detectable in a blood test."

Good point. But still!

"My mother's family had no history of Meta powers, and I'd never known my own father. So I spent the next few years obsessed with finding him. With the country in so much turmoil, it was difficult to get the records I needed. My marriage suffered tremendously.

"I'd spent twenty years in service to the Rangers and MHC, and just when I thought I could retire and spend the rest of my life with my wife and our girls, I drew further away. And I was too scared to tell her why."

The heartbreak in his words dug deep. I had to fight against their impact, to keep my anger up. I couldn't feel sorry for him. It was a betrayal to my friends, both alive and dead. "Was your father a Meta?"

"Not just a Meta," he said. "He was a Bane."

"Holy shit."

"Indeed. His name was Shade. I'd already worked five years for the MHC when he was killed, and in researching Shade I made a connection no one ever had before—officially, at least. I discovered Shade had a son. I had a half brother."

Only one answer, horrifying as it was, made any kind of sense. "Specter."

"Tragically, yes." Even now, years after discovering the fact, he looked pissed. "My inevitable inquiries at the prison came to the attention of Agent Garth Anders."

"McNally's partner?"

"Correct. Anders knew almost since the end of the War that Marcus Spence wasn't on the Island. The MHC found out too late and didn't want a public panic, or to admit to missing a Bane. Anders was assigned to seek him out—off the record. When he found him, Spence had already had one stroke. Anders never considered a feeble, wheelchair-bound man to be a risk, so he didn't tell anyone he found Spence."

"Why did he tell you?"

"Well, at this point in the story, Anders had just been diagnosed with terminal brain cancer. We'd worked together years before. He may have been clearing his conscience."

"Anders told you about the Warden?"

"Yes. He knew the Warden was a temporary fix. The technology would break down, or one of the Metas powering it would die. If that happened, then the fail-safe collars were the only thing that would protect us. I was inclined to agree. Our country was barely surviving the destruction of one Meta War. We'd never survive another.

"After Anders passed, I went to see Spence. I needed to look my half brother in the eye and see the monster who'd murdered so many. But he wasn't Specter anymore. He was a wasted shell of a man, and part of me understood why Anders couldn't turn him in."

Just as I'd felt sorry for the broken old man I'd found at the Blue Tower. None of us was immune to pity, it seemed. "But why destroy the Warden?" I asked. "Why kill *us*?"

"Destroying the Warden was simply to help along the inevitable. I looked up you twelve, you know. You were all unsettled, disillusioned, unsuccessful in so many ways, and I believed you would never step up and be heroes. But killing you before you repowered would look suspicious and could be traced back to me."

The clinical way he spoke about our intended murders compounded my hatred of the man I'd once considered a friend. "So you . . . what? Asked Spence to do it remotely after he got his Specter powers back?"

"I did. He agreed."

"But he didn't get them back."

"No. The night of the Fairview fire, Spence suffered a third stroke. It left him catatonic, and I received his powers instead. I didn't understand why until McNally postulated her family connection theory."

Disgust bubbled up. It had all been some big improvisation from a man caught between personal vengeance and doing what he thought was best for the world. "So you left your brother to rot in his own filth, while you stuck to your plan to slaughter us?"

"Spence was a murderer a hundred times over."

"Maybe, but no one deserves to die like that. You're just one big, fat fucking fraud, aren't you?"

He wilted just a little. "Yes, I suppose I am."

"Would Annabelle have wanted this?" I asked, my voice quaking. "Would your wife and daughters still love you, knowing what you've done?" His daughters, who were potentially Meta, too—damn.

"I don't know," he said. "Annabelle divorced me four years ago and took the girls to Europe. It's all for the best. I'm sorry, child."

He took aim at my head and squeezed the trigger.

Thirty-five

Rescue

I threw up a shield, caught the backlash as the bullet ricocheted, and stumbled backward into the window's frame. Broken glass cut my lower back and I cried out. The shield dropped. He fired again. I waited for the inevitable pain—for the bullet to tear through flesh and muscle and bone.

Nothing.

The fired bullet hovered in front of my eyes, six inches from striking distance. Just spun there like a freeze frame. I stared. Seward stared. A shadow moved by the door. I looked first.

Caleb stretched his little arm out and up, palm forward, like a child raising his hand in class. Wherever he'd been left, he had obviously gotten out. Dust and grime coated his face and clothes. His lips were puckered into a tiny hole, almond eyes wide and angry. I had never seen such intense fury on the face of a child.

"You hurt my daddy," Caleb said. His voice was heartbreaking, even as the vengeful glint in his eyes froze my blood. He ignored me, even when I pulled away from the window and screeched in pain. He only had eyes for Seward.

Seward's eyebrows furrowed, then flattened. He looked at his hand—at the gun he held and could no longer manipulate. Confusion twisted his mouth into a grimace. Every muscle in his face went slack. A power struggle played out in the fifteen feet separating the two.

"Caleb," I said, taking a step forward, my torn and bleeding back on fire.

"He hurt you, too," the boy said. The gun in Seward's hand began to turn, twisting back on the man holding it. My heart pounded in my ears. I couldn't let the little boy kill. Seward wasn't allowed off that easily, and no way did a child deserve to carry such an awful thing around for the rest of his life.

"Caleb, make him drop the gun. Please."

Seward's hand stopped moving. Caleb looked at me. Tactical error. With Caleb's attention diverted, Seward gained the upper hand. His eyes sparked. Caleb winced, whimpered. He closed his eyes, his child's mind caught up in a nightmare of Specter's making. A silent war waged between the two telepaths, one with fifty years of life experience and one with five. A child versus a man, and I had no doubt Caleb would lose.

I just didn't expect him to lose so fast. The air in the room became crisp, keen, like lightning about to strike. Twin sets of yellow-orange eyes glared at me, one child-size and one adult. I lobbed an orb at Seward—how could I bring myself to fire on a child?—and Caleb blocked it. He sent the orb pinging into the wall near McNally's supine form. The orb struck and blasted a hole the size of a soccer ball through concrete and plaster.

Specter-Caleb spread his palm in my direction and then clenched his fingers. An invisible hand closed around my throat and squeezed tight. My lungs seized, desperate to draw in air. Black spots danced across my vision.

Was this how I died? Choked to death by a possessed five-year-old?

I was on my knees, but didn't remember falling. I tried to concentrate on summoning an orb. Purple sparked, unable to coalesce. Gage's voice was in my head, telling me over and over that he cared for me. That it was okay. I tried to say it back and couldn't. I was dying. If life after death existed, I hoped he would know me there.

Roaring filled my ears. A tiny pin of lavender pricked the periphery of my mind. I latched on with all I had left, balled it up, and pushed. Power surged forward, along with the last of my strength.

The roar in my ears became a man's scream. The pressure on my throat ceased. Air rushed into my starving lungs, and I collapsed on the floor. A few seconds passed before I mustered enough energy to push up with my left arm. I gasped, every joint aching. Caleb was huddled in the corner of the room nearest the mirror wall, arms around his knees, weeping. A big, black shape hulked over Seward's body. It took a moment to process the sight: Marco's panther form had Seward by the throat.

Time ticked by, each moment filled with my attempts to breathe and the quiet sound of Caleb's sobs, and then the cat released his prey. Blood dripped from his long teeth, matting the fur around his mouth. He looked at me, feline eyes reflecting the utter sorrow no real animal could ever hope to understand. He stood on three legs, limped sideways, and finally collapsed.

By the time I crawled to him, he had transformed back to Marco, lying on his side, broken fingers swollen to the size of D batteries, blood coating his mouth. He had a black eye, bruised jaw, and half a dozen minor scrapes. But he was alive and staring at me.

"Almost did not make it," he panted. "*Lo siento*. So sorry."

I wanted to laugh. It turned into a choked sob. Tears filled my eyes, burning my sore and damaged throat. "You made it in perfect time, pal, now don't move."

I crawled onward. Seward blinked at the ceiling. A burn the size of a half-dollar smoked just above his heart. Blood oozed from four wide puncture wounds in his neck. He made no attempts to stop the bleeding, and neither did I. More blood dripped from the corner of his mouth, joining the puddle on the floor beneath his head. I didn't want to cry for him; the tears came anyway. Hot and sharp, they stung the corners of my eyes.

I touched his cheek. I had no words. There was nothing left to say.

Seward blinked once, and then the light faded from his eyes. His chest rose once more and stilled. No exhalation, no choking gasp. Angus Seward died quietly and unforgiven for so many sins.

I lurched away, crawling on one hand toward Gage. Openly crying. The skin on his wrist was cool. I sobbed harder when I found a pulse. Tears streamed down my cheeks. I pressed against the wound on his neck, but the blood flow had slowed on its own.

"Caleb," I said. "Please, sweetie, come here."

He did, finding some sort of strength in himself to ignore his fear.

"Can you do me a favor? I know you're scared, but it will help your daddy."

He nodded, solemn and teary-eyed.

"I need you to run outside as fast as you can, okay? Run toward the big copper gate. You'll see lots of people and fire trucks. There are good people in those fire trucks. You know that, right?"

He nodded again, though I doubted he did. He'd probably never seen an active fire truck while living on the island. It didn't matter. I explained about the emergency entry—a big red button, to him—and how to use it. He repeated back what I'd said, and then took off at a dead run to let the cavalry inside.

Across the room, McNally stirred. I held onto Gage and cried. We hadn't come this far to lose anyone else. Not with our enemy, at last, defeated.

It was finally over.

And also just beginning.

Thirty-six

Recovery

I t sounds so crazy that it has to be true," Agent McNally said, keeping her voice low so the bustling staff at Cedars-Sinai Medical Center didn't overhear.

I'd spent the last few hours alternately telling her Seward's story and receiving status reports on my people. I didn't much care that I was bleeding from a dozen places, had nearly been choked to death, and had probably rebroken my hand. My body was completely numb, pain receptors blown, and I wasn't allowing myself to be treated until everyone else had their turn.

Cedars-Sinai hadn't quite known what to do with the lot of us when four screaming ambulances tore into their emergency lane, but McNally had used her impressive vocabulary to bully the staff into clearing out a section of the ward for us, allowing us the privacy we needed.

Psystorm (whose real name, I learned, was Simon Hewitt) and Caleb were physically uninjured from the experience. The boy spent every waking moment in the ward crying in his father's arms. He'd watched his father be tied up and drugged, and then he was locked in a storage closet. Caleb's escape was a blessing. His nightmares would end one day, but for now they were very real.

Dahlia was up and moving. She'd been injected with drugs to keep her unconscious, and she only vaguely remembered having Specter poking around inside of her brain. Conversely, the doctors had shot Renee up with muscle relaxants. Her body had been stretched and twisted and left in impossible positions for too long, resulting in multiple muscle tears. They were too small to repair surgically; they required time and staying still, which Renee did not do naturally.

Marco spent two hours in surgery. Morphing and running on broken fingers had shattered several tiny bones that needed to be repaired before they could heal. His own concussion was minor, and the handful of burns he received during the Medical Center explosion would heal.

By the time I got the news on Marco, word had spread of our invasion of the hospital, spurring a secondary invasion of reporters and cameras. The security guards had their hands full corralling them all into the ambulance bay. They had a long wait; no one was talking to the press until I knew my people were okay.

As expected, Ethan had pulled some of his old stitches. Once they decided his insides were all in the correct places, they fixed his external wounds and put him to bed. He'd remained stuck between the seats until rescue workers pulled him out. He came through the final fight without—as he'd feared—hurting any of his friends.

I watched the waiting room doors swing shut behind

Ethan's surgeon. "So how much of this do we release to the public?" I asked McNally, rubbing my eyes. The only person still in the woods was Gage, but I didn't know how much longer I could keep myself upright.

"We can decide that later," she said. "For now, they only need to know that there was an accident, and that your team is recovering. The rest can wait."

"Good."

Another hazy hour passed before Gage's surgeon finally came out, and I might have tackled him if I'd had the energy. I was impressed I managed to stand up.

"He was lucky," the doctor said. "The knife nicked his carotid artery without severing it. The wound was repaired, and he's received two transfusions to replace his blood loss. He also has three fractured ribs that will take several weeks to mend."

"So he's—will he be okay?" I asked.

"He's shown an impressive will to live. I do believe he'll make a full recovery."

My anxiety fled when the surgeon said that, and with my anxiety went every last ounce of energy. I passed out in his arms.

Twelve hours later, I had a new cast on my right hand, eighteen stitches in my back, a bandage on my chin, and a raging sore throat. Except for Renee, Gage, and Ethan, everyone else had been officially released, but they remained in the ward anyway. Although two buildings of HQ still stood, we hesitated to return. It felt haunted, incomplete. Stained. I'd wanted change, but not on this level. And not so quickly.

I spent my time in an uncomfortable chair next to Gage's bed. He had remained unconscious after the surgery for no physical reason his doctor could find. It could have been because of Specter's possession. I didn't know; I just wanted him to wake up. They say coma patients can hear you, so I talked as much as my sore throat would allow and sucked on ice chips in between.

During one of those breaks, Dahlia wandered over. She slipped through the curtain surrounding the bed and stopped at the foot. I looked up and smiled. She stayed quiet.

"I know I look horrible, but you don't have to stare," I said hoarsely.

"I'm sorry," she said, eyes widening. "I didn't mean to stare. I just wanted to ask you something." I nodded, giving her silent permission to continue. "Well, it's about the MHC and what you said before."

The things I'd said before had been not long after our arrival, in a fit of blind anger and panic. I'd repeated what the doppelganger (I still couldn't reconcile the killer with the Angus Seward I'd known and trusted) said about the fail-safe; killing the last surviving Banes as a safety measure. Ranted on my own feelings of betrayal for not being told about the collars or the Wardens.

"I was pissed. Shouldn't have."

"You wouldn't have said it if you didn't mean it, Trance." Good point.

She stepped around the bed, moving closer. "Well, what

if we didn't have to work for the Bureau anymore? Instead of being employees for an agency that foots the bills, we go out on our own. Freelance heroes, rather than corporate ones."

A nice notion, only she'd forgotten one small problem. "We don't have the money, or the resources."

"What if we did?"

Something in the way she asked warned me it wasn't just a rhetorical question. Freelancing was an option I'd considered seriously for the last couple of days. I no longer trusted ATF, even if MHC ceased to exist on any official level. We weren't what they'd created with the Rangers a century ago, and we could never fit back into their mold. I didn't want to, not now that I knew the truth about the Warden and MHC's fail-safe. The truth about Agent Anders and Dr. Seward. So many lies.

The Ranger Corps was finished. It physically ceased to exist fifteen years ago, and the last of its recorded history had burned down with the Medical Center. Something new started last week, and we'd failed to see it until today. I'd failed to see it. Now my vision was clear.

No going back.

"What did you have in mind, Ember?" I asked, using her code name on purpose.

She smiled. "I have access to some money. A lot of money, actually, and I think this would be a very good use for it."

"How much money are we talking about?"

"Three million."

"Dollars?" If I hadn't been sitting down, I'd have fallen over. I couldn't wrap my head around that kind of number.

"I know it's not a lot," she said, and I blanched at the comment, "and it will probably spend fast. I mean, we need a place to live and security measures and transportation—"

"Whose money is it?"

"Mine. It's been in trust for a while, and I never wanted it until now." Something burned in her eyes—determination, intent, and a little bit of excitement. "I just wanted to make sure you were on board with going freelance before I did anything."

I was more than on board with the idea. It was something we needed to do and, while part of me wanted to interrogate Dahlia about the source of this trust fund, most of me didn't want to jinx her insanely generous offer.

We would have a purpose again—of that I had no doubt. Joy bubbled up inside me like a fountain, frothing out in a gale of giggles. It hurt to laugh, so I sobered quickly. The euphoria, however, remained close to the surface.

"I take it you like the idea," Dahlia said.

"Sweetheart, I love the idea, and if this works out, then, I think I love you."

A grunt—not from me, and not from her. I looked at the bed. Gage had peeled one eye open, and was staring at me through the slit. The eye blinked, and the corner of his mouth quirked up into a smile.

Dahlia made a discreet exit.

Gage worked his other eye open. My heart swelled under the intensity of his silver-flecked gaze—eyes I'd seen closed by the slice of a blade and feared would never look at me again. I slid onto the bed next to him. Tears welled and I didn't fight them.

"Hey," I whispered.

He licked dry lips. I brushed an ice chip over the rough, chapped surface, offering him a small measure of relief.

"You hit me with a car," he said, low and tired.

"That's what you get for standing in the middle of the road."

"I tried to fight. He was so strong."

"It's okay, Gage. We won." I bent my head and brushed my lips across his. The kiss electrified me and sent my heart galloping. Maybe we still had a few personal kinks to work out of our relationship, but I wanted our touches to feel like this always. I slid down next to him and rested my head on his shoulder.

"We're okay?" he asked.

"We're okay. We're all okay."

And who knows? I might even learn to like this whole leadership thing.

Fantasy.
Temptation.
Adventure.

Visit PocketAfterDark.com, an all-new website just for Urban Fantasy and Romance Readers!

- Exclusive access to the hottest urban fantasy and romance titles!

- Read and share reviews on the latest books!

- Live chats with your favorite romance authors!

- Vote in online polls!

 www.PocketAfterDark.com

Kick-butt Urban Fantasy from Pocket Books!